SENSATION OF DEATH

In the kitchen now everything stopped; the air around Marlo was too still.

She was alone and she could feel sensations hissing around her, slithering, coiling tighter, crushing her.

The feel of pure rage burned her, the same thing she had felt just before Ted Royston was murdered. It boiled up from the linoleum floor and curled around her legs like red snakes. Her throat tightened and Marlo placed her hand over it, her heart racing.

Rage had killed Elsie Gerhard here, not an accident.

Marlo closed her eyes and tried not to think about the color red, how it had called to her, how Cherry's crystal had caught her, warned her.

She opened her eyes to find Spence and Cherry's worried expressions. The tea kettle was hissing . . . and Elsie had been killed. Unable to speak, to voice what reality denied, Marlo felt Spence's large, warm hand along her cheek.

"What's wrong, honey?" he asked gently.

Avon Contemporary Romances by
Cait London

HIDDEN SECRETS
WHAT MEMORIES REMAIN
WITH HER LAST BREATH
WHEN NIGHT FALLS
LEAVING LONELY TOWN
IT HAPPENED AT MIDNIGHT
SLEEPLESS IN MONTANA
THREE KISSES

CAIT LONDON

HIDDEN SECRETS

AVON BOOKS
An Imprint of HarperCollins*Publishers*

AVON BOOKS
An Imprint of HarperCollins*Publishers*
10 East 53rd Street
New York, New York 10022-5299

ISBN: 0-06-055589-0
www.avonromance.com

First Avon Books paperback printing: February 2005

Printed in the U.S.A.

10 9 8 7 6 5 4 3 2 1

To Gavin, Tanner, Grace Anne,
and 35mm camera buffs everywhere

Prologue

"GET OFF MY TAIL, BOZO," DIRK FORBES MUTTERED.

The headlights of the big truck behind him, clearly visible in his rearview mirror, pulled closer. Blinded momentarily, Dirk cursed and automatically reached to flip the mirror into a lesser reflective position. Temper burned him. He'd just spent a fortune on his new customized four-door pickup, and no hotshot trucker was ruining it.

On the curving mountainous highway with a deadly plunge into a canyon on one side, safety depended on driving skills, a series of reflective warning signs, and a questionable strip of metal, already scraped and dented. The December night in the Northwest's Cascade Mountain pass was frigid; the danger increased with the mist that threatened to turn to snow.

Snowplows had piled mountains of snow on either side of I-90, but the highway was clear enough for safe travel.

And Dirk's ex-wife hadn't wanted to wait; Traci had been desperate to leave the small town she'd grown up in, desperate in a way that he'd never experienced. She hadn't given reasons, and trying for a reconciliation, Dirk wasn't going to let her down. When Traci had called frantically, he'd dropped everything to come collect her. . . .

He tapped his brakes; the rear lights should warn the driver behind him of following too closely. A patch of unexpected ice could take a vehicle out of the most skilled driver's hands. . . .

At midnight, Traci slept on the passenger side, her head resting against a pillow. In the extended cab behind Dirk, Cody, his three-year-old son, was also asleep in his heavy-duty safety seat, his face pale within his jacket's red hood.

Cody had been asking for his favorite toy, a fire engine with a ladder, siren, and tiny firemen. But in her haste, Traci could only manage her son and his favorite blanket, a few necessities, and teddy bear.

The big truck took Dirk's warning, backing off a bit, and he relaxed slightly. He reached to smooth his ex-wife's dark waving hair. Traci was still pretty—and real sweet. Maybe she still loved him, just a little bit, enough to give him a second chance—he'd ruined the first.

A sense of pride filled him. *She'd needed him. . . . He'd been the one she'd called to take her away from Godfrey in such a hurry.*

He tugged up the coat covering her. At the cusp of a new year and a new start, he was filled with hope. Maybe there was a chance they could be a family again, and this time Dirk wouldn't ruin it. "I'll try. I'll really try."

Why was Traci acting so afraid? Why had she called him, asking him to take her away immediately?

When she wasn't so panicked, they'd settle into a nice motel, and Traci would explain. Then Dirk could fix the problem, and she'd trust him again.

Confident that he could handle any problem Traci had, Dirk smiled. He'd hold his son close and be a good father. He'd find that job Traci always wanted him to have. He was already taking those anger management classes and all the counseling Traci wanted, and everything would be like it was—better, maybe.

The truck behind him pulled closer and to the outside line, preparing to pass. Dirk slowed as the truck pulled alongside.

He glanced at the trucker's cab and recognized the driver immediately.

And then Dirk knew why Traci had been so fearful, so desperate to be taken away from the small mountain town.

The truck driver's face was that of a killer.

Moving over slightly, Dirk concentrated on holding his pickup off the highway shoulder. One tire in the snowbank and—

The violent thrust of the heavy-duty truck knocked the pickup into the guardrail and flipped it into the night.

Dazed and dying, Dirk heard Traci's scream in the distance, then the silence as they seemed to float downward through the pale, eerie night.

His last thought was of how much he loved his wife and son.

One

Two and a half years later

"WHERE ARE YOU, CODY?"

Spence Gerhard's question echoed, unanswered in the forest's misty silence. Alone in the vast and rugged Washington state Cascade Mountains near Snoqualmie Pass, he cautiously stepped over the rocks and gray boulders of the mountain.

He moved down the canyon's steep incline, through the layers of mist, waiting for the answering call of a child—instead, a heavy silence shrouded the mountains. . . .

Above him, on I-90, the sound of passing traffic echoed eerily. That December, two and a half years ago, snow had blanketed the mountains. . . .

And then a pickup had flown over the edge of that high mountain road. The bodies of Spence's sister, Traci, and her ex-husband had been discovered within the crumpled pickup at the bottom of the canyon. A new blanket of snow had gently covered the wreckage, making the recovery of the adults' bodies even more difficult.

But the body of Spence's nephew, Cody, had never been found.

Three-year-old Cody couldn't have survived the wreck. But where was his body?

Spence breathed in the cold mountain air, the early-morning mist chilling the skin above his beard. A small stream, fed by melting snow, gurgled and frothed, and underbrush crackled slightly as animals foraged beneath it.

In muted shades of blue-gray, Douglas fir trees bordered the tumbling stream. Then, soaring in tall points, the forest shot up into the sunlight just coming into the mountain's shadows.

Spence tugged down his knit cap and raised his jacket's denim collar. Dirk's rusted, crushed pickup fender lay on the stream's opposite bank, where workers had salvaged the wrecked vehicle, piling it nearby.

Spence glanced upward to the highway where the guardrail and curve signs had been replaced after the accident. He listened to the sound of an approaching eighteen-wheeler, gearing down in preparation for that dangerous curve.

The flatbed semitruck was piled high with huge logs. From the sound of the gears, the driver was experienced at driving the same deadly, sharp curve, moving slowly around it. Through the years other people had misjudged the banked angle of the curve and died in the same place as Spence's sister. But, familiar with the highways around Godfrey, Dirk would have known how dangerous this particular curve was. He'd have been aware of the death awaiting anyone who misjudged it—

The cost of raising the wrecked vehicles to the top of the steep grade was prohibitive; an eerie pile of colored metal was overgrown by brush and inhabited by small animals. Layered by mist, the mound of wrecked and rusted vehicles seemed to be waiting for a new addition. . . .

The logging truck geared up again, preparing for a run at

the next incline, and Spence watched one of last year's aspen leaves, battered by weather, as it coursed downstream. The force of water, rushing through the wrecked pickup, could have carried Cody away. . . .

On the other hand, the fresh bear sign at the time of the wreck wasn't encouraging. And there were the bobcat and cougars. Cody couldn't have survived, one way or the other. Anything could have happened to Cody, and Spence prayed that the child hadn't suffered.

Spence might find peace—if he could just find some sign of Cody, of his remains, of his clothing. . . .

A red chipmunk raced through the shadows of the pines and over the brambles that had grown through the wreck.

In the first week of June, birds were starting to move in the tall pines that seemed like ghostly sentinels in the mist.

Spence crouched to cup icy water from the tumbling stream into his hand and sipped it quickly. He scanned the rocks beneath the clear water, searching for any sight of Cody's car seat—Traci had been adamant that the boy be safe.

She hadn't taken Cody's toy fire truck; it was still in his room. If she had planned this trip, she would have taken it and other things.

A small herd of mule deer grazed in a tiny sunlit patch of grass, and Spence removed his flannel-lined jacket.

At altitudes of around three thousand feet, June's morning sun was burning off the mist. The high mountains were still snowcapped, the clear water lakes filling with runoff. . . . Spence knew this area well. He'd searched every inch of it, desperate to bring closure for his mother.

He inhaled the crisp bite of Douglas fir, the damp scents of moss and earth, and watched another leaf, drifting down the stream. He rose to follow it. Just maybe it would lead to Cody's tiny remains.

The leaf he'd been watching shot over a tiny ripple; it lodged with others in a rocky bed that Spence had already dug years ago. He'd pried away the rocks, searching for any sign of the boy.

Spence's fist tightened, cracking the small branch he'd been holding, and the grazing mule deer, always alert to hunters, leaped over the brambles and into the woods.

Familiar with the area where his sister had died, Spence jumped onto a fallen tree and walked across it to the other side of the stream. After the wreck, rubbish had been strewn along the stream's bank—fast-food wrappers, coffee cups. When Spence had collected Cody's teddy bear and his favorite blanket from the snow-covered rocks, they still held the boy's scent. *Cody, where are you?*

Spence pushed away the sudden clenching of his heart and the guilt that he hadn't protected his sister from her ex-husband. He needed a clear mind if he was going to find Cody's remains . . . then he began to search meticulously, covering ground that he had before, looking for new animal sign that just might lead to the little boy's remains. . . .

"They're getting stronger, aren't they? The feelings?"

Marlo Malone barely heard her friend's question. Amid the colors on the patchwork throw pillow Marlo had just sewn, the red shade had bound her. She traced the patch of material, a remnant from her sewing shelf.

In her shop, Fresh Takes, neatly arranged with fabrics and decorator books and display photographs of her budget decorating jobs, Marlo focused on the mirror. It caught the light from the window, almost blinding her. That shaft of light hit the red fabric beneath her sewing machine needle. The material seemed as warm and alive, almost as if someone had just worn it. . . . What was it trying to tell her?

She shook her head; she didn't want these sensations; she didn't want the red fabric to tell her anything.

Marlo lifted her sewing machine needle and spread her fingers wide on the material, waiting for—for what?

"You're spooking me out," Cherry Parker whispered. "What are you seeing? What are you feeling?"

The sensations came to Marlo in spurts, always in twos or threes. Then sometimes, they wouldn't come for months. They'd started coming infrequently when she was nineteen, and Marlo didn't want them.

She didn't want to know when people died—not *before* their deaths, not before . . .

She wanted routine and schedules and safety. When she stepped outside those borders, anything could happen. . . .

"Nothing. I'm not seeing anything." Marlo shook her head, fighting off the disturbing sensations quivering within her. She forced herself to look away from the fabric to her friend.

She centered on fighting the sensations, on pushing them away. Marlo knew the routine that would take her back to safety; she mentally repeated the litany: She was thirty-two now and divorced, and in her own life and in her own shop. She concentrated on putting herself into physical surroundings—Marlo's Fresh Takes shop was lined with shelves, threads, paint, fabric samples, and bolts of material. Cherry's long, lithe body was sprawled on Marlo's metal frame display bed.

But the red of the throw pillow she'd been sewing called Marlo back to it again. In an attempt to shake free, Marlo stood up from her sewing machine and walked to stare out of her shop window.

In June's late afternoon, Godfrey, a small town just off I-90, was quiet.

Too quiet. The deathly silence spread across the shadows of the stores crossing the street, tall and short, alternating with strips of sunlight. A pickup glided through the shadows and strips of sunlight—

Marlo could feel the quiet, hollow and waiting inside her, like something was going to happen. But what?

As she had before, Marlo struggled to place herself in reality—safely away from the stirring of her senses. . . .

Godfrey was just the same as when she'd grown up—a tiny town circled by mountains that seemed to hold up the sky. Designed to look like a tiny Swiss village, Godfrey was a little bit bigger and busier now, but the "old-time" families were rooted together, familiar with each other's lives.

Nestled at the base of steep mountains, offset from the usual collection of I-90's busy truck stop, big new chain-owned motel, and gas stations, the small town was just like many others in the Cascade Mountain range. There were a couple of mom-and-pop motels for the travel-weary, plenty of outdoor recreation activities and festivals, a city park and swimming pool, a small school supported by active parents. In winter, storekeepers grumbled about snowplows that threw snow high on the sidewalks; ski resort lifts traveled up and down the slopes.

In early June, a few retired "summer people" were already moving back into their remote cabins and homes in Godfrey. Partiers were also moving in, and the nearby mountain's ski resorts were warming up their outdoor pools and hot tubs. Azaleas and creamy rhododendrons were preparing to bloom.

Ed Miller's roofing truck passed in front of the shop's window, and automatically Marlo returned Ed's friendly wave.

Marlo inhaled sharply. Six years ago, just after her divorce, she'd sensed somehow that Ed's ladder would shift and he'd fall, breaking his leg and putting him out of work for months. It was only an uncertain sense, when she'd seen his wooden ladder, hung on the side of his truck, but one that had come true.

On the other side of the street, an upscale RV that had probably seen Arizona's sand last winter, was parked in the Royston Furniture parking lot.

Across the street, five heavy-duty motorcycles were parked in front of Ben's Cycle Shop. The bikers were tough-looking in road-worn leather and dark bandannas. They kept to themselves, and in summer, lived in a communal back-woods house where their "babes and babies" visited.

Keith Royston stood in his furniture store's parking lot now, talking with the driver of the van that usually followed the bikers into town.

Marlo forced herself to focus on Keith: He was good and safe and exactly what she needed. Routine, comfortable dating had soothed the ripples caused by her divorce. Keith was very careful with her, and life moved quietly with him. In his slacks and dress shirt, rolled up at the sleeves, he was a gentle, sweet man, a good friend.

She smiled slightly at the familiar scene; Keith would be asking the van to move. He'd worked hard to keep his father's furniture store alive by upgrading it to appeal to the wealthy vacation home owners—sitting next to their upscale SUVs and luxury cars, the rusted and battered van wouldn't do. With a movie star or two already settling up on Indian Joe's canyon, Keith's furniture business had shifted into more sophisticated offerings.

Lorraine Ellory, Keith's salesclerk and accountant, came to stand in the shadows of the store's loading dock. Sleek, dressed in a short skirt that showed off her long legs, Lorraine's sultry look seemed lost on Keith.

The van driver leaned his head outside the window and his bandanna was red—

Marlo braced herself against that faint quiver of her senses. Something red was calling her. It came through the glass, always glass, to touch her, to call to her.

She pushed it away, but it came back again in her mind, taunting her. . . .

Cherry stood behind Marlo. "You just went stiff as a board. I wish you'd just stop fighting whatever vibes you're getting. I've seen people with intuitive talent sense things . . . They have the same look, as if everything just went still inside them. You've got real talent, and you're not letting yourself open to it. I've been trying for years to snag some psychic talent, and no matter how much I meditate, it doesn't come. I could help you, though, if you'd let yourself go. I've read enough books on extrasensory perception. I could connect you with someone to develop your skills. I've lived in communes where psychic phenomena were pretty common."

"Well, it's not happening here—not with me."

"Liar," Cherry returned, with the ease of a good friend.

The van moved off Keith's parking lot, and Marlo pushed free of the web that seemed to tangle around her, taking away her breath. She'd held the sensations inside her for years, and she wasn't exploring what she didn't want. "Once you fasten on to something, you just don't let it go, do you, Cherry?"

"No. I've seen you in action, fighting whatever is bothering you, and you don't even know you're doing it. Neither does anyone else, because you're not outing yourself—Do you know how much I want what you have? I've waited and waited, and I've studied enough to know what I'm talking about, if not experiencing it. You know something is happening to you and won't admit it. Will you?" Cherry demanded in a disgusted tone.

But Marlo was staring at the glass window, and when she should have seen her reflection, she saw the image of the three-year-old boy grin up at her. She'd babysat for Cody while his mother had worked—Traci Forbes had been a clerk at the hardware store. Since Traci had had to work on Saturdays, she'd been thrilled with Marlo's Saturday-only day-care center. And working long hours in her budget decorating business, Marlo had needed to fill the corners of her empty life with the laughing children.

But Cody had died over two and a half years ago. Now, he would have been five and a half.

Why was he in her mind now?

She opened her hand on the cool windowpane, attempting to reach through to him. The glass warmed beneath her hand.

What was Cody trying to tell her?

Or was she on the edge of losing her mind?

She refused to believe in the supernatural; she refused to believe that Cody's ghost was trying to contact her. The glass was warmed by the sunlight, that was all. . . .

Spence Gerhard's battered brown Jeep Wrangler pulled in front of the shop, and Marlo jerked her hand away from the window. "Your boyfriend is here, Cherry."

In the open cab with roll bars, Spence was wearing a black sweatshirt with the pocket ripped half-off and punctuated by holes that revealed a white undershirt. His wraparound sunglasses shielded his eyes, a dark strip across a tanned, rugged face. His black hair hung down to his shoulders, and stubble covered his jaw.

As if sensing that Marlo was looking at him, Spence turned and met her stare through the glass. Holding her stare, he removed his glasses, and his deep-set eyes seemed to cut through the glass and into her.

They were cold, empty eyes, rimmed by shadows.

She refused to back away from the window into the shadows, refused to shift her eyes from the lock of his.

The battle was always there within her, the need to comfort him, forgive him.

But his need ran to a bitterness she would not give, punishment he felt he deserved. He'd wanted her hatred since she was nineteen—

Spence swung out of the Jeep and rounded to the passenger side, where he leaned against the vehicle and crossed his arms. A heavy-duty revolver was in the holster at his waist; next to it was a leather pouch containing bear spray and a wicked-looking hunting knife in its sheath. His worn jeans were crusted with dirt and frayed at the knee. The arrogant posture was pure Spence and had enough sexual impact to start most women drooling for a taste of what they could never tame.

Cherry spoke softly, "I know that look. It's all hollow and haunted, and he's angry at himself for not being here when Traci and Cody were taken—or his mother died. He's been hunting his nephew again. The guy needs some closure. You could probably give it to him if you'd go along with a séance and let Cody speak to him from the grave. . . ."

"Cherry, that may be what you're into, but I don't believe in it." Marlo smiled softly; they were an odd pair, the workaday-oriented quiet woman, and her exotic, freethinking friend. Cherry always saw the unexpected facets and best qualities of everyone; she loved unconditionally, and that was why Marlo loved her. Their three-year friendship had always been exciting and enjoyable, adding spice and fun. And she seemed to add stability to Cherry's life, a sense of home that she'd never had.

The crystal hanging from the window suction cup had been a gift from Cherry, and now it caught the sunlight, turning and sending light into the shop. Marlo stared at it, and the colors seemed to shift, as if within the hard surface there were secrets waiting to be unraveled.

Glass. Lately her insights came through glass.

She had to stop. *It* had to stop.

Once again, Cherry's soft, cultured voice drew Marlo back into reality. "You didn't think you'd like sunbathing in the nude, but you do. I had to fight to get you to do it, but you enjoy it, the same as you like pedicures and facials. You need me, kiddo, to keep you from molding. . . . I need you for balance. You're the best friend I've ever had, and you've never once put me down. . . . But I'm not giving up, you know."

An affectionate woman, Cherry moved close to hug and kiss Marlo. "Hugs. Kisses. Got to use your potty. Be just a minute," Cherry said, and hurried back to Marlo's apartment behind the shop.

Spence continued to stare at Marlo through the window as she started to position fabric over her cutting table. She wouldn't cut it now, though. Not with Spence determined to nudge her temper; she could ruin it.

Marlo's hands shook as she smoothed a wrinkle from the stack of blue fabric squares. Spence liked drawing her out, making her crackle with anger, and she refused to be his entertainment—or his punishment.

Cherry came out of the rear apartment. "I'm not done with you. Spence is not my boyfriend, and you know it. We just live together. Sex was nice, though, for a while, but that was because I thought his karma needed comforting. I mean he hasn't gotten over Traci's and Cody's deaths, and then wham bang, his mother slips and falls in April. He's feeling pretty guilty about not being here for them while they were all alive."

Marlo raised an eyebrow. Her friendship ran deep enough that she could question Cherry's motives, and her sexual habits. "You're comforting him? You're so generous. You needed a place to stay before we were good friends. You were his house sitter for six months, until he quit his job and moved back two and a half years ago."

"Spence is a lonely, haunted soul, and I like him. If I could, I'd jerk him out of that guilt trip he's on. Sex didn't last long—I mean *for* very long after Spence moved back. We're more like friends—we've always been friends. I like living with him and helping him with his outfitting and guide trips.

He doesn't ask questions and takes me how I am—except if I use fabric softener that smells like flowers with his clothes. Apparently, that's not good for hunting. He says deer can smell him a mile away in the mountains. I like to cook. My parents liked to get rid of me, so they sometimes enrolled me in cooking schools. Spence likes to eat whatever. He pays the bills, and I like that. It works out. And the guy is having a real bad time about his family. They said his mother was dead the minute she hit the floor."

"My mother misses her. All the Bingo Girls do."

Cherry slung the strap of her bag onto her shoulder. "Well, gotta go. I told Spence to turn up during my shift at Werner's Cafe for a free dinner on me—and to pick up my mountain bike and some supplies for customers we've got in a couple days. They don't want to backpack much—real partiers, more than anything—so we're taking Taco Bill's llama, Spot, on the trail. Oh, and I've got to get some trail mix. I could just live on that stuff."

"You've eaten rattlesnake. You love anything," Marlo teased.

Reformed and now a health food addict, Cherry winked impishly. "Try it. You might like it. When we come off the trip, I might bring you a rattlesnake for dinner. I'll even cook it for you."

When Marlo shuddered, Cherry grinned; she reached to hug Marlo and kiss her cheek. "Just teasing. Bye, hon. Spence is going over to his mother's house for a few hours until he picks me up after my shift. He's got some mail and computer work to do there. I might coast down that mountain in daylight, but I'm sure not pedaling back up it."

Cherry hurried out the door. Spence was already lifting her bike into the back of his Jeep. They spoke briefly, and beside Spence's tall lean six-foot-four body, Cherry's six-foot lithe one looked very feminine. Her blond hair and blue eyes perfectly complemented his dark coloring, male and female . . . perfect, beautiful sexual partners.

Marlo inhaled sharply—she would have preferred her friend to have someone more dependable than Spence, who'd made it perfectly clear he wasn't settling down. Spence's dark hair looked as if it hadn't been cut in months, his eyes were glinting as he looked down at Cherry, who lifted her face for a brief, welcoming kiss. Spence leaned slightly to oblige, then he shook his head.

Cherry's expression was sympathetic as she reached to smooth his cheek. They were clearly lovers—or as Cherry had said, former lovers, wrapped in intimacy, sharing their lives.

Through the window, Marlo studied them. They looked well-matched and, like most inhabitants of Godfrey, dressed in worn jeans and everyday comfortable clothing. Cherry's hair was blond, short, and raggedly cut; her eyes blue and wide, and she hid upper-level intelligence with a dumb bimbo act that Marlo had dismissed long ago. Cherry's red paisley sweater was tight; her crystal necklace caught the dim light.

The crystal turned slightly, and a shaft of blinding light speared through the window to Marlo, holding her.

They remained beside the Jeep, talking quietly, and Marlo could imagine the question; she'd heard it before: "Did you find anything?"

The shake of Spence's head was negative. He grabbed the roll bar and swung into the driver's seat while Cherry settled in the passenger's bucket seat. She draped her arm over the back of his seat. The gesture wasn't possessive; it was true Cherry, meant to comfort.

Alone in the shop, Marlo closed her eyes and gripped the small square of dark red fabric in her scrap basket.

Red. The color kept leaping at her. *Why?*

And why had she seen Cody's little face in the window?

Marlo struggled for a logical explanation: Had Spence's rugged features brought the child's to her mind? Cody's hair was tousled and wavy, only a little lighter than Spence's; but the child's eyes were that same light brown, almost gold in certain sunlight.

Marlo shook her head. Whatever was stirring around her, she wanted it to stop.

"Cody, go to sleep now. It's time to rest," she whispered to her empty shop the same way that years ago she had told Cody that it was time to take his nap,

She could almost smell his baby fragrance. . . . Why after all this time would Cody seem so close to her, almost as if he were trying to reach her?

Marlo wrapped her arms around herself, then briskly rubbed her hands on her face. She didn't want this—whatever it was that told her something would happen—she didn't want it at all.

She busied herself with the material, aligning it to the cutting table's marked squares.

Everyone had uneasiness in their lives, Marlo told herself as she smoothed her hair.

She did not believe in ghosts communicating with the living, she decided as she brushed her bangs away from her eyebrows. She really should make an appointment to get her hair trimmed, and she was definitely not a medium for the supernatural.

Her hands trembled as she reached for a pair of scissors. Why then, the voice inside her asked, did she sense that Spence's mother would fall and die over a month ago?

Why and how did she know of other things that had happened?

Marlo released the breath she had been holding and forced

herself to cut one square of material for the throw pillows. Using a cardboard template, she cut another and another, focusing on the fabric and not on nonsense, provoked by Cherry's insistence on her intuitive ability—her nonexistent ability, Marlo corrected.

Her scissors slipped, ruining the fabric square, and Marlo quickly tossed the pieces in her scrap basket.

She looked around her shop. Everything was neatly organized, just like her life.

On her desk, a large, thick, zippered notebook held her daily schedules, the hours exactly noted and detailed, all neatly organized, just flexible enough to accommodate clients' needs. Meticulous about her time, Marlo always kept the calendar workbook with her.

She moved to the display bed where Cherry had slightly mussed the quilt. Marlo bent and smoothed it until the butterflies were all straight and neat, just as she intended to live her life.

Cherry's birth control pill dispenser had slid from her hobo-style purse and Marlo shook her head, sliding it into her jeans. Cherry was always losing something, and she would eventually call for her pills.

Marlo straightened away from the bed and, placing her hands on her hips, turned to survey her shop. It was all hers; she'd built it by herself, and the apartment in the rear was just for her.

Order and schedules had always been a part of her life. It was only when she stepped out of them that life seemed to tear apart. She'd done that twice, and each time met disaster.

At six o'clock every morning, she rose to dress, stretch, and prepare for running. At times, Keith ran with her. She'd jog down the sidewalk, past Jane's Five and Dime store, past Fat Eddie's discount gas station, past the grocery store and its parking lot, to the Firemen's Park, around it twice, then back up the other side of the street, past an assortment of hardware stores, her mother's thrift store, the bank, and its drive-in window. Then, warmed up, she'd sail up the residential side street, pushing for the burn.

The return trip was slower, allowing her to cool down before she reached the driveway leading to the back door of the shop.

She'd unlock her back door, step into the soothing quiet of her apartment, her retreat, where she wouldn't have to deal with how people looked at her—the woman who had put her husband through college by scrimping and saving every penny, only to have him graduate and dump her.

The scenario of a cheating husband using his wife wasn't that uncommon, but Marlo's pride had been badly damaged. Maybe she was so wrapped up in trying to be a good supportive wife that she simply hadn't been prepared for her marriage to be found so empty and ugly, all dreams stripped away.

Marlo inhaled slowly. All she wanted was to have everything in place, to save a bit and enjoy her life and friendships. She didn't want surprises—at thirty-two she'd had enough of them.

More than anything, she wanted the safety of knowing what came next in her life.

She didn't want the sensations that came to her, more frequently now. Even now, they teeter-tottered around her, seeking control. . . .

Marlo held very still, drawing in the essence of the old store that she had remodeled.

Everything was going to be fine. She was just like everyone else. She'd had some hard times, but she'd pasted herself back together and gotten on with life. She'd keep to her schedule. The seasons would change like always: In the fall, hunters would be flooding the town, trucks lined up at the check station. In winter, Mac's Tow Truck service would be working full-time to tow in damaged cars, pulled from snowdrifts. The state highway department would make an extra, complimentary swing through Godfrey. They helped out the city crews because Marge Sutton, the city clerk, had told her husband, Jake, on the state crew, that if he knew what was good for him, he'd cooperate.

In spring, the deer moved up the mountains, returning to the lush alpine pastures. In late summer, Marlo would pick huckleberries on the mountains, making jelly in neatly labeled jars with her mother. She'd continue to build her business and enjoy life—and everything was going to be just fine.

Marlo studied the bulletin board, the photographs that she had taken tacked to it. People she'd known all her life looked back at her, captured in glossy prints as they went about their lives. A framed crayon drawing from a little boy in Chicago, who had seen her new spot on television, hung next to the bulletin board, sent by his grandmother.

Rhythms, life seasons, work every day, enjoy the safety of the small town she knew so well, and everything would stay the same—

Marlo walked to her desk, a real prize she'd gotten from her mother's thrift shop. In the garage that was now her workshop behind Fresh Takes, she had refinished the piece, and the maple wood gleamed. As she did often, she studied the systematic notes for this day and the rest of the workweek. Her finger ran down the blocks of time she'd set aside for working that morning in the shop, then a noon appointment at the Klikamuk Ski Lodge, an initial walk-around with the owner, who wanted to refurbish the contemporary-styled rooms into a cottage decor.

In exchange for brightening the rooms, Marlo intended to barter for a few pieces of the used contemporary furniture that would be shipped off for auction. After the walk-around, she'd return to the shop, consult her notes, start working on rough ideas for the lodge, make her business calls, then dress for dinner with Keith Royston.

Marlo placed her hand flat on her daily calendar, anchoring herself to it, her safety. She'd keep to her routines, her schedules. If she stepped out of the order she had created, something could happen . . .

She hurried to the neatly kept shelves of fabric and paint samplers, quickly stacking a decorator magazine that had shifted slightly out of the stack.

Everything had an order, and she had to keep it; she had to keep control. She returned to her notebook, skimming the day's neat, well-organized notes. Everything was as it should be—

Her life was in place.

Everything was the same as always.

Or was it?

Two

SPENCE HAD GROWN UP IN THIS HOUSE ON 109 JAMES Street, and it looked the same—small and tidy. But inside, the silence roared, reminding him of his mother's death.

He opened the doors of the small garage at the end of the driveway and once inside, ran his hand across his lifetime love, a lowered 1954 Chevrolet, his first car. When he first saw "Lettie," he had been just fourteen and aching for a sixteen-year-old's driver's license.

Lettie had been down on her tires and her luck, pushed to the back of a car lot and home to more than her share of mice. Spence had taken every job he could to get extra money to pay for her and had lived for the day she was his.

The day he had brought Lettie home seemed like a century ago. He had a girlfriend who sat close to him, and when he shifted, young Spence had edged his arm out just a little to brush her breasts.

A little later on in their dating, he moved his hand from the stick shift to her knee.

And when the nights were dark and sweet, and he was a

high school senior with his needs running high, his hands and lips busy, Lettie's windows were covered with steam.

Spence smiled fondly as he ran his hand over Lettie's smooth fender. His girl had been a sweet little package, who had worn his high school ring and letterman sweater. He'd felt like a superhero when those adoring hazel eyes had looked up at him and she'd snuggled close. . . .

His fingertips traced a path from Lettie's front bumper to her back. After high school graduation ceremonies, there had been a thin scar that ran the length of the car; it had been cut into Lettie's pampered finish. It had taken him hours of hard work to prepare her for painting again, and whoever had committed the crime had never been discovered.

"Ah, Lettie-girl, we've come full circle, you and I. Now we're all we have left." Spence pulled the push mower out onto the driveway and filled it with gas. He liked tending the yard, just as he had done for what seemed like all his life.

As a boy who learned quickly how to take his father's place, Spence had learned the value of paint and caulk and understanding how to fix, rather than buy new.

By the time the town handyman had deserted Elsie Gerhard and a nine-year-old son and a six-year-old daughter, Spence had already been adept at small fix-ups. Since then, when his father was last seen with the lady in her RV, Spence had learned a lot more, earning money to pitch into the family pot.

How could a man who had appeared to be so loving, discard his family as if they meant nothing?

The bitterness still burned, and Spence jerked the cord of the lawn mower. He waited until it finished its sputtering, coughing act, then adjusted the throttle. He began pushing it across the small, neat front yard. He'd tossed his shirt over a trimmed bush and waved at the carload of teenage girls who whistled and woo-wooed, as they passed in the Smiths' station wagon.

His mother's backyard was larger, her garden overgrown. Her rhododendrons would bloom in two weeks. Her azaleas would be vivid in fuchsias and purples. The bushes needed pruning, but he couldn't bear to touch them.

Finished now, Spence put the lawn mower back into the garage with Lettie, collected his shirt, and entered his mother's too-quiet house.

He stood for a moment, half-expecting her to come to hug him, cheerfully ask about his day, and frown at his clothes, then quickly order him to shower and come to the table where he could "eat a real meal."

But Elsie Gerhard's happy voice never came; the house remained still.

She should have never been standing on that step stool. He should have been here, should have changed that lightbulb for her.

But then, he hadn't been here for Cody and Traci either, had he?

And dammit, he should have taken responsibility for the baby he'd created. He should have married that high school sweetheart who gave herself so sweetly to him in Lettie's backseat.

He'd been furious, and she'd cried—they were both just kids, and she'd wanted him to marry her.

Hell, no, young Spence couldn't have that—he had a big scholarship at the university and a future ahead of him. He could see his dreams going down the drain, and at the time, he'd had enough responsibility to last a lifetime—he'd wanted "to live for a while, to do more than get stuck with a family right off the bat. I've already raised one kid, my sister, and I'm not ready to do it again."

Spence could still hear that teenage girl sob painfully, the sound echoing in Lettie's dark interior.

He'd probably hear her cry forever.

Was he any better now?

Older, wiser maybe. Maybe not.

After his shower, Spence changed clothes and listened to the telephone messages for him: One couple, who had scheduled for the backpacking trip, wanted to cancel and requested a total refund. "Too bad," Spence said, "the agreement says if notified within two weeks, you'll get a full refund, and after that, it's prorated. I have to make a living, guys."

The next message was from Cherry, who reminded him to come to Werner's Cafe for the evening special, the cook's lasagna.

Spence flipped through the mail he had delivered to his mother's house: the usual bills, literature, and information on his investments, a few queries for his hiking and camping services, and a flowery thank-you note from one of the Bingo Girls for installing her new drapery rods.

The messages continued, one from a friend whose finances Spence was building, and another from Bingo Girl, Nadine Kozakura, who wanted him to stop by and fix her plugged kitchen sink.

With a sigh that acknowledged some things never change, Spence bypassed his computer setup in the living room, the faxes in the machine, and settled in to watch television. The Bingo Girls had come to clean and do his laundry. Elsie Gerhard had cherished her small neat home, her family, and her friends, just as they had loved her.

Spence returned Nadine's call and listened to her chatter on while he shuffled through the other mail. There were benefits in the home fix-up business, especially when it concerned the Bingo Girls. Fixing Nadine's garbage disposal would probably gift him with "home-cooked food."

His mother's birdcall clock chirped the six o'clock hour and Spence would wait until the cafe's dinner crowd thinned before collecting Cherry's free dinner.

Despite the game show on television, the house seemed too quiet. Too restless to concentrate on his computer and his portfolio, Spence rose to walk through the small, neat rooms. His bedroom was the same, filled with football and track trophies, a picture of his mother and him at his college graduation on his dresser. A toy dump truck stood next to Traci's picture. She was holding Cody on her hip and smiling, a little sadly, at her mother's camera.

But Spence's teenage bed had been changed to one perfect for a three-year-old child. The bedspread's pattern curved like a road map bordered by brightly colored buildings and trees. The blanket and teddy bear that Spence had found at the site of the accident lay on the small bed.

Beneath the window was Cody's big fire engine, the one his father had bought his "big boy." There was plenty of room in Dirk's upscale pickup for anything Traci had wanted to take—like a suitcase of her clothes. Why hadn't Traci taken the toy?

Why hadn't she called Spence if there was a problem with her ex-husband, if he'd been threatening her?

Spence picked up the teddy bear and pressed it to his heart. In a shadowy corner, the eyes of a plastic turtle toy box stared at Spence. A mobile hung near a window, the tiny airplanes motionless now, when once Cody loved to blow into them.

Spence moved close to the tiny planes. The air was so still that his quiet breath stirred them to life. Where was Cody?

Rather, where were his remains?

Spence blew on the mobile's planes again, and they circled slowly. He rubbed the bandage on his forearm, the result of disturbing a bear in its lair. How many times had he raked the rubbish from a bear's cave to find Cody?

This last bear had taken residence beneath the flooring of a deserted house. The small bear's charge had been furious, its grip on Spence's arm enough to wrench the muscles. The bear hadn't liked the spray and had yelped, releasing Spence.

Cody hadn't been beneath the flooring. He wasn't anywhere.

The hallway light slid into Traci's old room, the one she'd returned to after leaving her husband. Dirk hadn't made good his promise to stay away from other women, to stay at his job at the post office and away from amateur wrestling. He'd lived for the crowd, playing up to them—and the women.

Traci had said that Dirk had stopped threatening her—but had he?

Spence walked into the small, feminine room. Traci's clothes were neatly folded on the bed, apparently ready to be sent away, because Elsie couldn't bear other people wearing her daughter's clothing.

Elsie had gone through every pocket of Traci's clothing, looking for some reason that her daughter would abruptly decide to run away with Dirk.

"She still loves him, and he loves her. He just wasn't mature enough when they married and had Cody, that's all," Elsie had said firmly three years ago. "Dirk is in Wenatchee, far enough that they won't see each other every day, giving them both some space. He's working at an automotive store and at an apple orchard in his free time. He's also drug-free and taking anger management classes. He's getting his feet on solid ground now—they've been talking."

Elsie had stared meaningfully at Spence. "Don't you start up with Dirk now, Spence. If Traci is seeing him, with no complaints, then you let nature take its course. You've got a good job in Seattle, and you're dealing with your own life.

Just let Traci and Dirk work it out. You ought to see him with Cody. Dirk is just realizing what a husband and father should be. I know you're worried about your sister, but stay out of this, Spence."

Spence had launched his arguments against Dirk, but his mother had been firm. "You're going to have to give up protecting us both someday, Spence. Maybe you were a man too soon, taking your father's place when he left. But you've got to let Traci make her own decisions. They're trying really hard on this relationship."

When Spence had tried to dissuade Traci from seeing Dirk, he'd met the same resistance, only more adamant. "Yes, he's threatened me—before. But that was when he was on drugs. And I've seen him at his worst, so I'm taking my time. We're working really hard, Spence, and I'm not just your baby sister anymore. I'm a mother, and I have my own job now. This is a step-by-step, day-by-day thing, and I'm holding my own with him now. I'm not going back to Dirk too quickly, especially not now, not with Cody."

Yet Traci had been seen by customers in the grocery store, parking her car next to Dirk's pickup and gathering Cody into her arms—crossing to secure him into the child's car seat Dirk had transferred.

Weary from his guide trip and from pampering the city photographers and from answers that wouldn't come, Spence walked into the kitchen.

A framed photograph on the wall showed his mother, happy among her friends. Fresh from a Bingo Blast at Godfrey's Community Hall, all five retired older women wore their ball caps and their Bingo Girl's T-shirts. Each one carried a decorated canvas bag that held her markers and necessities. They'd each just won money for their joint fund, marked for their "big" trip to Reno, where they could get into real gambling.

Spence rubbed his injured forearm, the bruises showing

now, but the bear's puncture wounds weren't deep and were easily cleaned. Though such an injury could infect easily, emergency rooms and doctors weren't for Spence. His first aid kit was well stocked; he knew how to use it and recognize the warning signs that would send him to a doctor.

He should have changed his mother's kitchen lightbulb, but when a chinook began to melt the mountains' snow, he'd been eager to search for Cody.

His mother shouldn't have been on that step stool—not with her bad hip. Spence should have kept up her small home better—he should have spent more time with her.

A year ago he'd argued with her about seeing Ted Royston.

The only time Elsie had really lit up after Traci and Cody died was when Ted came around. For those six months she'd dated Ted, Elsie had been excited, energized, as if something drove her.

Maybe Spence was jealous, maybe he had been the only man in his mother's life for so long that he couldn't stand another man moving in—that was what old Ted had said, wasn't it?

And just maybe it had been time for Elsie to forget about Wes Gerhard ever returning and step out and enjoy life a bit.

But not with Ted Royston, a man who had a reputation for making the rounds with women.

Spence opened the refrigerator. The bright light within revealed spotlessly bare glass shelves. He reached for the bottled beer he kept stocked for his brooding times.

The light glanced off the kitchen's new linoleum, and Spence remembered how his mother's blood had pooled beneath her head and crept beneath the refrigerator—

If only she'd had some peace about her grandson—but Spence hadn't been able to give her that. . . .

Spence twisted off the bottle's lid and flipped it into the sink, where he intended to put a few more.

He drank deeply and walked back to sit on the oversize chair his mother had arranged to have reupholstered for him. He lifted his legs to the matching footstool and thought of her pride the day he'd come in from a weeklong guide trip to find it.

He rubbed the brown imitation leather arms, then his fingers dug in. His mother knew that something still rode between Marlo and him, and she knew that every time Spence sat in the armchair that Marlo had re-covered, he'd think of her.

She still got to him.

Five-foot-six of curves, light brown hair, and hazel eyes that could turn green as new grass, Marlo had stared back at him through the Fresh Takes window.

Just every once in a while, he had to push her, just to see her reaction—that lush mouth tighten in a stubborn jaw, the color rise on those pale cheeks, hiding the spray of freckles across her nose.

That much hadn't changed through the years—the need to get to Marlo, just to see that cool, efficient perfection slip a bit, and those eyes flash with something few people knew about Ms. Malone.

Few looked beneath that sweet, forgiving nature, that gentle heart. But prodded just right, she was an all-out competitor, and when she got upset, she stepped out of those carefully sculpted borders and was unpredictable. Aroused enough, nettled just right, she'd take any challenge . . . Now that was a neat little secret maybe only Spence knew.

If she'd been any other woman, and he felt the same, Spence would be in bed with her now.

But she wasn't, and there it ended.

"I'd like you here every night. Dinner is almost ready—a nice fat salmon on the grill, stuffed with lemon and parsley. It will be only a few minutes," Keith was saying as he tossed salad in the kitchen of his contemporary rock-and-wood house. The day-by-day routine was very comfortable, and Marlo enjoyed slowing down, dressing up just a little, leaving her shop, and feeling like a woman.

Standing in the hallway, adjusting the pen-and-ink print of a killer whale that was slightly tilted, Marlo was caught by the spacious bedroom that she'd decorated for Keith. Immaculate, cleaned by a maid who worked only for Keith, in his home and at the store, the room looked as perfect as his showroom.

The small homey touches that Marlo had added hadn't warmed the bedroom. With an expert's eye, Marlo gauged the room. Shades of brown, contemporary furniture, burnt orange accents blended nicely and ran into the area rug, the highly varnished hardwood floors. Carved geese almost took flight on the wall, and a rough woodsy tapestry hung above the bed. A magnificent armoire hid a television set, a DVD and sound system; the armoire's walnut style matched the custom-designed bookcase bed.

The tall chest of drawers also matched, and framed photographs of Keith's family ran across the top. The posed family picture with his parents included his sister, Paula. The Royston children were always perfectly groomed and polite, quiet and bookish.

Another picture was that of Paula and Marlo, each wearing high school cheerleader costumes and posing impishly with their pom-poms. Paula hadn't been a cheerleader—her parents hadn't approved of the "waste of time"—and Marlo had arranged to borrow a costume for her. The picture had been taken in Elsie's backyard, and Paula had been thrilled.

Marlo traced Paula's young face, remembering her friend—and how she had started to slip away from reality in their junior year. Six feet tall and awkward, Paula had been painfully thin, with wary, huge blue eyes and a complexion that was punctuated by breakouts. By their senior year, Paula was on medication and in therapy. After a breakdown at nineteen, she had been institutionalized.

Though Mrs. Royston was a registered nurse who worked in various clinics and traveled in the region to fill in as a temporary or a private nurse, she had decided that Paula needed "more care."

Marlo's mother had been disgusted. "Paula needs love, that's all," Wilma had said.

Marlo had tried to give Paula that, love and attention, but she had withdrawn. She hadn't wanted to see Marlo, or return to Godfrey—

Marlo found her face framed in a small mirror. She couldn't move. The shadows seemed to move; something held her and the reddish tint in the orange seemed to liven into hard bright red. . . . *Red.*

Keith came to stand behind Marlo and placed his arms around her. He playfully rocked her body and nuzzled the side of her cheek. "Admiring your handiwork?"

The reddish shade shifted back to dark orange. *Red . . . Why red?* Marlo forced her eyes from the mirror and leaned back against Keith's safety. He gave her comfort and stability when she needed it—like her fear about appearing in front of the television cameras to demonstrate budget decorating tips. "It's . . . the decor does suit you, Keith."

"You're very intuitive about what suits people, aren't you? Well, you suit me." His kiss on her cheek lingered into another one, and Marlo sensed him waiting for her to turn to him. The hesitation was always there, the invitation for her to move forward in their friendship. He was waiting for her to decide that they could be friends and lovers.

"I'm glad you're my friend," she said, placing just that necessary bit of distance between the position of friend and lover and commitment. "I would have never written that newspaper column about budget decorating ideas, or submitted my pictures and article to that magazine."

"Which led to that television spot in Club Renew. The pilot got picked up for a nationwide replay on a home-decorating show. You're a star, Marlo," Keith teased. "I like your hair like this—down. It smells like freshly cut grass, or flowers. I can't decide which."

"There are other decorating hosts on Club Renew TV. I'm just one of several . . . I've been thinking about cutting my hair, updating a bit. Cherry thinks I'd look good in a shorter, spiked cut." She thought of Lorraine Ellory, whose black hair was long and sleek, gleaming sensually around her pale, perfect cheeks. Lorraine was definitely interested in Keith, but he hadn't seemed to notice. Though she was outwardly efficient and pleasant in dealings with Marlo, Lorraine seemed to be like a cat waiting to pounce—and to claw. "Are you certain that you're not interested in Lorraine? She has beautiful hair. She's a beautiful woman."

"Absolutely not. But she's smart and perfect for working the showroom, and a whiz at computers and bookkeeping. She understands there is nothing between us. I like your hair as it is. You always look good, Marlo. If you listened to her, Cherry will have you at the Downtown Tattoo Parlor."

His voice held disdain, and Marlo turned to him, leaning into the safety and comfort he always gave her. Keith's arms tightened around her, but the stillness in his body said he was waiting for her to open that other step between them. "Cherry is my friend, Keith."

He had that grumpy little-boy look that said he wasn't happy, but he wasn't pushing the matter.

For now, she just wanted to fend off the sensations she did not want, and so she diverted the conversation, "You arranged that TV host spot in Club Renew, and I know it. One of your customers is on the board of that television station and carries a lot of weight."

"Now, you know Leon Zalman, too. You did a fine job decorating his lodge."

"It wasn't exactly a budget job. It was just a matter of ordering miles of leather-upholstered furniture, some area rugs, and that chunky walnut furniture. And a few local artisan pottery pieces, some sculpture around deer horns, and there you go."

Keith held her away and brushed her lips with his. He let her answer in a light kiss, then he took her hand and led her into the dining room. "True, I made a little profit from the furniture you chose. But your little touches made it more homey, and that's what he wanted. You impressed him, Marlo. Admit it."

"I was impressed with the offer to do a regular fifteen-minute spot as a host on Club Renew. That is good money for something I do every day. They send a cameraman right to my shop, or we go to where I'm working. If I have a good project at hand, it's taped in advance."

His gaze took in her green sweater and slacks. "Mmm. I like it when you dress up a bit. I like that outfit. The shade deepens your green eyes. While I'm bringing in the salmon and baked potatoes from the patio, choose something nice and quiet on the sound system in the living room, will you?"

His fingers toyed with her hair, and again, Marlo sensed that Keith wanted her. It would be so easy to open the intimate-door to Keith.

But Keith deserved more than a woman who hadn't resolved the bitterness of her divorce—and who feared the restless sensations inside her.

Instinctively, Marlo moved away, into the living room. She

wanted to take that step with Keith, to open herself to him, but somehow she wasn't ready.

For a moment, Keith stood in the dining room, looking across the open space to her. Then from a decanter, he filled two wineglasses and carried them as he walked toward her. He handed one to her. The wine was expensive and Marlo's all-around favorite: a Napa Valley merlot with blackberry flavor. He sipped from his glass and studied Marlo. "I suppose I could blame your ex-husband for your fears. Trust isn't easy for you—when it comes to men, or relationships—is it? That bastard let you work like a slave to put him through college, then he—"

She shook her head and held up her hand, indicating she wanted to hear no more about Ryan Malone. At twenty-one, she'd thought she could settle for less than love, and at twenty-six, she'd known how foolish she'd been.

Marlo moved to the sound system and opened the beautiful, smoothly polished doors. The CDs were neatly alphabetized, and she chose five, placing them into the machine's slots for continuous play.

The easy-listening music spread gently over the living room, which she had also decorated for Keith. Everything was neat and in its place, the colors balanced, harmonizing. Plants softened the cream-and-brown tones, an area rug separated the two dark brown leather couches. The fireplace added to the inviting arrangement, designed for easy conversation and relaxing. At a touch, the framed contemporary painting by a local artist would revolve, and a big-screen television set would replace it.

Everything in the room was sleek and hidden as Keith had wished . . . except the framed photographs on the mantel. In the sleek decor, the ornate metal frames seemed unusual, but Keith had wanted them.

Ted Royston had hated Marlo's taste. After Keith's home was decorated, the elder Royston had stormed into Marlo's shop. "You took advantage of my son wanting you. You overcharged him for that—whatever design he calls his house. I've already told him to ask for his money back. But he won't, because he's got the hots for you."

Marlo sensed Keith watching her and turned to him. She let herself settle into the easy familiarity that she had always felt with him. He'd always been a part of her life, the safe part. "I miss Paula. How is she?"

"The same. My sister is not going to change. I've adjusted to that. Through the years, we've brought her home, but she always wanted to go back. We're on e-mail now, and I visit once a month."

"We were such good friends, but now she doesn't want to see me. Rosewood Village Care Center is not that far, and every once in a while when I go to Seattle, I call to see if she'd like me to drop in. She doesn't seem to want to talk with me. I guess seeing me upsets her."

Keith swirled his wine and studied it. He spoke quietly. "She gets that way. She's terrified of the outside world and feels safe there. She barely wants to see me."

"I'm sorry you're not closer."

He smiled softly at her. "Always sympathetic. Always understanding. There aren't many women like you. Ready for dinner?"

"Starving."

After dinner and the movie, they sat on the sofa and listened to music. "More wine?" Keith asked, but he was already leaning forward to fill their glasses once again.

Marlo accepted the glass and ran her finger around the rim, making it squeak. Keith grinned at the play and settled back beside her. His fingers toyed with her hair. "I love your hair . . . This is nice. You, here with me."

"Yes, it is."

"Come here," he invited, leaning toward her. Marlo returned the easy kiss and allowed Keith's tongue to flick her lips. "You taste good."

"I'm a little woozy, and you know it. I'm not used to more than one glass."

He chuckled softly. "Ah. Now's my chance."

Marlo leaned toward him and lifted her lips. His fitted over hers perfectly, sweet and gentle and yet with enough hunger to tell her that she was a desired woman.

"You're definitely good for the ego and not a shabby cook either."

His smile curved against her cheek. "I could be good for other things. You're so cute when you're soft like this. When you're working on a project, you seem so cool and businesslike, which is good, too."

He eased back against the couch and drew her with him. "Lie here a while against me. You could get to like it, and someday I'm going to get you to take me seriously."

Making love with Keith would be so easy, Marlo thought as she lay against him. Her body said she needed sex, the old needs warming within her. A friend and an easy companion, Keith had always been gentle with her. For six years, Keith had been patiently developing that trust—and in the last two, they'd been moving toward a distinct but easy dating relationship. She rose over him and took his face in her hands. "You're such a nice guy."

"I am, aren't I? And you're a little snockered, aren't you?"

"What would you say if I planted a hot one on you?"

His shy grin had always been charming. "Why, Ms. Malone. I'd be delighted."

"And then I'm going home."

"But maybe you'll find me irresistible and maybe you'll stay. Maybe our Wednesday dinners will be every night.

Maybe you won't want to leave, and you'll let me take care of you every day."

"Now that's confidence."

The kiss was long and sweet and good, and when Keith's body stirred beneath hers, Marlo smiled against his lips. "I occasionally need to feel like a woman."

"Who's complaining?" His hand smoothed her hair, twisting a strand around his finger. "Don't cut it. I like the feel of it against my skin."

She needed this softness, the easiness and warmth between then, the comfort he gave her. But she wasn't ready for more, and Marlo moved away. "I should go home."

Marlo shifted her Ford pickup, a big powerful four-wheel-drive shiny black monster, a neat little reward to herself for years of hard work. She slowed, preparing for the stop sign at the end of the quiet street. The red color seemed to catch her headlights and bounce them back at her, intensified by the windshield.

She shook her head. Whatever was stirring inside her was something she did not want.

She did not want to think about the little boy's face she'd seen in her shop window. It wasn't there. Cody was only in her mind, a sweet little three-year-old boy whose life had ended two and a half years ago.

Marlo sat at the stop sign, gripping her steering wheel, though no other cars were coming. She didn't want to feel this stirring . . . she wanted it to go away . . . "Go to sleep, Cody," she murmured firmly, surprising herself.

Cherry's talk of reaching Cody through a séance had gotten to her, Marlo decided.

The night was too still, holding her there at the stop sign, and Marlo fought to place herself back into reality, away from the call of her senses . . .

At ten o'clock, Godfrey's residential streets were quiet. The houses and yards were neatly kept, the surrounding mountains soaring into the starry night sky.

Lori Talbert's boyfriend had parked his truck in front of her parents' house, and the silhouettes in the cab said they were making out. Bose Johnson, a retired hunting guide, was out walking his miniature poodle. Danny Ferris's Healthy Breads truck was parked by the sidewalk. He and his wife were probably bowling in the summer couples league.

Ted Royston's house was on the opposite side of the street, a corner lot with an empty lot next to it; it had been empty since his murder in January. The two-story house in an early-twentieth-century design contrasted with Keith's modern redwood frame home and its vaulted ceiling and hardwood floors. The Royston yard was unkept, though Marlo knew that Keith had hired a teenage boy to trim the yard in the summer. The windows caught the streetlight in silvery squares.

Somehow Marlo had known that Ted Royston would die violently. She'd felt the violence stirring around him as he passed her shop's window one day.

But then, old Ted had been a ladies' man and angered a few husbands in town. He'd set off a few summer tourists' husbands and lovers, too. Logic said that one day, someone would be seeking revenge.

He hadn't been wise to brag about his coin and gun collection, and both were missing. The investigation of his death was lengthy and focused on the man who had the last public argument with Ted just a day before he died.

Marlo rubbed her forehead; the ache there seemed to be one with the hum of the motor. Spence might have confronted Ted about dating Elsie, but he wouldn't have hurt an old man, battering him violently.

Despite strenuous investigation, the prime suspect in Ted's

homicide-robbery had a perfect alibi—Spence been in his cabin with Cherry and one of her girlfriends, who had stayed the night.

Accustomed to traveling in deep snow, Spence's ability to come off the mountain hadn't been questioned, nor his anger with the old man for dating Elsie. But two witnesses saying that he never left that night was an unshakable alibi—since one of the witnesses was a reputable New York attorney, Janie Mills-Franklin.

Ted's house seemed to hold Marlo, and she forced herself to clutch and brake, easing out onto Godfrey's main street. Up the street, cars, trucks, and motorcycles were lined up in front of the Red Hog Tavern. Mike Preston's city police car was gliding by quietly, and Minnie O'Neil was walking her big malamute. Rocky Morales, who had a remote cabin in the mountains, waved as he drove by. A man and a woman were jogging side by side, coming toward Marlo's pickup.

The town seemed just as it always was, and Marlo wrapped that safety around her as she slid into a dead-end alley. The wide alley was actually the driveway to an old garage that she had converted into a workroom for larger projects. When she pulled into her parking place beside her shop, her headlights picked out the big man seated on her back porch—Spence Gerhard.

Inhaling sharply and bracing herself to talk with Spence, Marlo switched off the motor and turned off the headlights. Spence stood slowly and lifted the beer bottle to his lips. He tossed the empty bottle into her trash can.

He'd changed into a clean black T-shirt with a BITE ME logo and jeans that had seen better days, his hair tied back in a ponytail. Spence looked nothing like the investment banker he'd been two and a half years ago, neatly clipped and well dressed.

But that irritating arrogance was there, nudging her.

Spence Gerhard was the speed bump of her life, the one man who could grate on her nerves. She didn't like anger, especially in herself, and Spence knew how to light it.

When Marlo slammed her pickup door, he crossed his arms and watched her walk toward him. From the tilt of his head and that curve of his mouth, she knew that he was set to torment her.

She hurried past him and up the steps to unlock her back door.

"That's quite the truck."

When she ignored his comment, Spence said, "Cherry sent you Werner's best lasagna. I guess she didn't know you had a date."

Marlo turned to take the carton he held out to her. "She knows I like Werner's lasagna and that I don't have time to cook. Thanks."

"Dinner with good old Keith again?"

Marlo turned back to open her door; she didn't intend to answer any personal questions from Spence. He'd left her life a long time ago. "Good night."

She entered her apartment and closed the door. When the light knock sounded, she shook her head and closed her eyes. Then she opened the door to Spence. "What?"

He grinned down at her. "You're welcome. I've been watching television at Mom's and catching up on stuff there . . . saw your television spot, the way you demonstrated those faux wall finishes, dabbing that sponge on the wall."

Marlo took a deep steadying breath. "Anything else?"

"No," he said easily, watching her. "Just thought I'd mention it."

Spence was up to his usual—baiting her, waiting for her temper to fire at him. She should give him the pills Cherry had forgotten, but she was just too angry to deal with him any more. "You can go now," she said.

"I've got time to talk with you. So how've you been?" He placed his hand against the wall beside her head and leaned in close to her. The angles of his face were too hard, too masculine, the face of a warrior, a taker, a mix of cruelty and something else that could sweep out and catch her unawares. She didn't want to think of it as beauty. She didn't want to think of it as something she wanted to grasp and hold and control, to pit herself against and to triumph.

Whatever lay deep inside Spence triggered something rebellious inside her—enough once to make her forget the good-girls-don't rule and she'd stepped over a forbidden edge. . . .

His fingertip traced her cheek. "You've got that closed-in look like you're trying to take me apart. And you're also looking pink and fuzzy like when you and Cherry are stepping on the wild side and sharing a glass of wine. Ah, I know . . . you had wine tonight, didn't you?"

Marlo narrowed her eyes at him and tried her best to look stern and forbidding.

Spence needed someone to forbid the hell out of him.

"None of your business," she stated very properly.

He was still looking down at her and grinning when she closed the door. She hesitated and considered ignoring his next knock on her door—instead, she jerked it open.

Spence's smile was gone, replaced by a haunted, concerned expression. "You should get married and have those kids you want, Marlo. You keep fooling around and putting it off, and you'll never have the family you want or someone to take care of you when you're old and gray."

He'd dropped that teasing expression. Every few months, he'd have that same look—haunted by guilt.

And every time, she wanted to comfort him. That natural urge just sprang out of her before she could rein it in. Maybe it was because they'd grown up together, and she'd seen how his father's desertion had scarred him. And just maybe it was true that first loves were remembered forever.

"Spence, you can't blame yourself for Traci's death, or your mother's, or Cody's. Whatever happened would have, whether you were here or not. Stop blaming yourself."

"And who are you to know that, exactly? My mother shouldn't have been changing that lightbulb, let alone climbing that step stool. She had a bad hip. I should have paid more attention to her. You don't know what could have been prevented, Marlo." His burst of anger wasn't meant for her; Marlo understood how deeply Spence punished himself.

She tensed and wrapped her arms around herself. She knew that Elsie would be hurt almost ten months before she died. Somehow Marlo knew that day they were having tea and looking at Elsie's favorite albums . . .

But Marlo didn't want to sense anything. She shivered, though the night wasn't cold. Whatever was calling her had to stop.

Spence inhaled slightly and shook his head. "Honey, I lost myself a long time ago. What I should have done, I didn't."

Then Spence turned and walked into the darkened alley and toward the streetlight. His head and the lower part of his torso was in shadow, but just then, a police car passed on Main Street, siren shredding the night. The cycling red light briefly caught on Spence, silhouetting his body . . . the color flowed over him and onto Marlo's pickup windshield. It seemed to hit the glass and pulse at her as if it were alive.

Marlo held her breath. Whatever was going to happen would have something to do with the color red.

She rubbed her forehead, to the headache there, and again pushed away the idea that she had any intuitive powers.

She was tired and she'd had too much wine and Spence Gerhard had always set her on edge—because he meant to, because he wanted to dig her anger out of her, and she wouldn't let him. . . .

Marlo's hand went to cover her heart, as if to still its rapid flutter. She did not need the turmoil that Spence could raise in her.

He'd been furious with her for giving his mother hope that Cody might still be alive. . . .

He'd been furious with his mother for daring to hope—

Yet Spence kept looking for the remains of his nephew.

She should leave well enough alone.

But she couldn't.

Three

"SPENCE, YOU'VE GOT TO LET THIS GO."

Marlo's voice was only a whisper in the night, sliding around Spence to hold him still. In the shadows of the driveway, caught by the sound of her voice, he turned it over in his mind. Soft with compassion, it was just the tone he didn't want to hear from someone he'd wounded so badly.

He stretched out his hand and gripped the shop's brick wall for support in his unsteady emotions. Marlo should hate him; she didn't. Her capacity for love and forgiveness had always been beyond what he could understand.

Spence could deal with bitterness from her, but not sympathy. Then, against his better judgment, because he didn't trust himself tonight, Spence walked slowly back to Marlo.

He needed to rake that fury out of her, to feel the disgust she wouldn't give him.

Marlo didn't back away from his fury. She merely crossed her arms and tilted her head and waited for him to explode as he had before.

Dammit. All five-foot-six curved inches of her, those dark earth green eyes, and silky, gleaming brown hair should be—

Dammit anyway. He wanted to hold her, to let the comfort of just doing that, just feeling her warmth and comfort surround him. Their lives had been intertwined since childhood, and Marlo had always soothed him, just the sight of her—strong and safe. Strange how a woman could be stronger than a man, more complete within herself.

And that irritated. Resilient and tough, Marlo had never asked for anything, or seemed to need anything from him, and yet—

Marlo could give him peace—and he had no right to take it from her.

No right at all. *Not from her*.

The anger he should have directed at himself flew across the night air to Marlo. "You know, if you would have kept your mouth shut about Cody *maybe . . . possibly* still alive—"

His accusations had rapped at her before; he'd been just as furious with her as with his mother. "We've been over this before, Spence. Your mother asked me not what I *knew*, but what I *felt*. I didn't *feel* that Cody had died. 'Do you feel that my grandson is dead?' Elsie had asked. And right then—no, I didn't."

"You started a hell of a lot of trouble. She got so upset—off-balance—that she started dating Ted Royston last year. My mother and Ted Royston, that dirty—"

Marlo was tougher than she looked, settling in to defend herself. "Elsie made her own choices. She knew exactly what Ted was, and even if she didn't, everyone in town had told her enough times, including you. And you blame that on me? You shouldn't have gone after Ted like that, telling him to stay away, and you know it. You had no business interfering with that part of her life. Maybe they found something good together."

"Ted only had one use for a woman."

"Don't go there, Spence," Marlo warned fiercely. "I respected your mother, and so did everyone else. People change. Maybe Ted changed."

Spence's low tone was bitter. "Sure. Tell me another one. While they were dating, everyone knew that sleazeball was making passes at other women. Her friends—the Bingo Girls—told her so."

Before Marlo realized that her hand had moved, it rested on his shoulder. "Spence, don't do this to yourself. It's only natural that you would want to protect your mother from—someone who might take advantage of her."

He glanced down at her hand and before Marlo could draw it back, his fingers locked on her wrist, and his other hand settled on her waist. "I've had enough of your sympathy, Marlo . . . and your forgiveness. Maybe that was a long time ago for you, but it wasn't for me. Someone should have knocked that hotshot college kid around—"

"Spence!"

"I'll always regret that I didn't stand by you, Marlo. You got pregnant the first time. It wasn't supposed to happen. I thought we were 'safe' since you'd never done it before. I should have stood by you. Instead, I saw everything that I thought I wanted slipping away—"

"I don't like going over this, Spence," she stated unevenly. "It's not good for either one of us. I lost my baby because something wasn't right."

She had refused to name the baby's father—her own father had been furious with her and with Spence. *You worthless son of a no-good deserting bastard. How would you know anything about honor? About ruining a young girl's life with your own selfishness?* Fred Kingsley had demanded of young Spence. *I know it was you. You dated her for years and I never liked you—Like father, like son. . . .*

Like father, like son—

"You keep everything inside, don't you?" Spence asked roughly. "First there was me, then another jerk, Ryan Malone. It must have hurt like hell to discover that your husband was using your money not only for college, but for his girlfriend. Every time something bad happens to you, you just smile, let the gossip run its course, and go on. How can you do that? Why don't you fight back?"

Marlo looked up at him, and a strand of her hair slid along her cheek as she tilted her head. In the shadows, it looked like a dark brand against her pale skin, and Spence wanted to stroke it with his fingertip, to ease it behind her ear.

Below her bangs, her eyes were brilliant with pride, her body was rigid. He was getting to her—just a little more and she'd lose it. "And how is good old Keith?"

"Boy, you're really pushing, aren't you? Just aching for a fight? I'm not giving it to you, Spence. Keith lost his mother ten years ago, his sister is in an institution, and his father was the only family he had. It absolutely shattered Keith to find Ted brutalized in the home that Keith had grown up in—and that's none of your business. I like him. And your mother liked him, too. She saw him as often as Ted, cooking for him. Your mother was a good judge of character, and I'm not explaining myself to you."

Spence couldn't keep the bitterness from his tone. "Sure. She was such a good judge of character that she believed Dad would come home for years after he deserted us."

"Your father loved her. He loved you and Traci."

"And then he walked off. Just like that, hopped in an RV with a woman one day and never turned up again. For years, I wanted to find him and beat the living crap out of him for hurting her—for leaving us like that. Maybe, just maybe, if he hadn't been what appeared to be a perfect father, it might have been easier to accept him deserting us."

"If you hadn't loved him so much, too. I know how badly

you hurt back then, Spence. That's why you've never married, isn't it? Because you're afraid you're like him and that you wouldn't be a good father—?"

Spence didn't like the way Marlo could move inside him, feel all the raw, bleeding edges he didn't want touched. "Leave it."

"Okay." She nodded toward the big square bandage on his arm. "That looks nasty."

Why was she always so caring, even for people who should disgust her? "Bears like their privacy."

"You were hunting Cody again, weren't you?"

"Aren't I always?" Suddenly, Spence felt eons older than his thirty-four years.

He wasn't expecting her hand to smooth his cheek, the understanding in her eyes that he didn't deserve. "Get . . . away from me."

But Marlo leaned closer, inspecting his injured arm. Her fingers slid from his cheek, and Spence fought the urge to turn his face into her palm, to kiss it.

Marlo traced the edges of the gauze, lightly skimming the pinkish flesh. "It's got heat. Did you disinfect it? Did you see a doctor? The infection from a bear—"

"I've been taking care of myself for a long time now, honey. I know when I need a doctor's treatment bill and when I don't. You always worry about everyone, don't you? Even me?" His voice had lost its bite, soft and deep in the night.

Spence smiled softly and skimmed his hand over her hair. "You've always worn it this way, maybe with a barrette in it, or a ribbon. . . . Mom liked you."

Marlo moved cautiously away. She preferred his irritating taunting to the soft moods that could make her senses quiver uncertainly. "Elsie and my mother were closer than the rest of the Bingo Girls."

"Cherry says you're the best friend she's ever had. And

she thinks you've got an intuitive gift that you're not giving in to. She thinks some cataclysmic disaster happened to you that triggered your 'intuition' and that you're hiding it. I'd say your getting pregnant—stepping outside the rules to satisfy a jerk kid—and losing your baby would be a pretty big disaster."

"That was a long time ago, Spence. I've moved on, and Cherry has a big imagination. It's probably due to all those New Age books she reads. I have to go in. I have a hard day tomorrow."

"Always neat, always on schedule," Spence mocked softly. "You were always that way, very predictable, very neat about your life. Even when you were a teenager, it was like you feared stepping outside of routine."

"I'm tired. Good night, Spence," Marlo walked from him and back to the safety of her home. She controlled her emotions, but Spence understood too much. Because of that, he was dangerous to her, always pushing for a reaction she didn't want to give. Did she want to scream when she'd discovered her husband of six years had been cheating on her—that she'd been supporting him, working day and night? At the time, she'd felt so noble, working to help Ryan Malone through college, but she'd been a fool.

She refused to act the part of a victim and preferred to sail through gossip with a smile, not letting everyone see how badly she'd been hurt.

Inside, Marlo leaned against the door. Spence had just lost his mother, and Marlo had been a part of Elsie's life—and Spence's. In the small town, their lives would intertwine, and Marlo could deal with their past, putting it behind her. She'd moved through emotional doors, closing them softly behind her to become a woman who accepted her life. "I will not play the victim," she repeated to herself aloud.

But Spence had been right; she kept to the safety of schedules. Tonight he'd appeared unexpectedly, jarring her emotions, taking her inside his guilt.

As she slid into her comfortable bedtime routine and changed into her nightgown, Marlo's mind flew through the images Spence had just evoked—the haunting discussions with Elsie. The conflict between mother and son had been palpable, yet Elsie had defied her son. She had continued to see Ted Royston, a man she once detested. She'd dated him for a full six months prior to his death, and Spence had been angry with her—and with Royston.

Several people had witnessed the men's furious last encounter at Werner's Cafe. Cherry had stepped between the men, easing Spence away while Ted was still cursing and provoking him.

And the next morning, Royston was found violently murdered in his home.

Marlo shivered and willed the earthshaking trauma of that time away from her. Spence always had that ability to derail her safe mode, to make her want to hold him—or shake him.

She took a deep breath and willed the comfort of the old building and her apartment to surround her.

The shop in front had once been a toy store, the owner favoring dolls, and the warm nuances of happy children still hovered in the air. Only now a child's body was missing—

Tell me what you feel—not what you think, Marlo. Do you feel my grandson is alive? Do you feel that he is dead? Elsie had asked as she placed Marlo's fingers over the glass-covered photo of Cody.

Marlo shook her head. She'd sensed that Elsie had been studying her for months, but maybe she had been wrong about the boy being alive. Maybe she didn't want to believe the child was pinned beneath tons of rock, or had been carried off by an animal. But there was no way Cody could have survived that wreck.

"Cody, where are you? Please let Spence find you and find the peace he needs so much," Marlo whispered, her senses shifting, stirring.

As she thought of how her fingers had felt, warm and tingling, upon the glass of Cody's picture, of Elsie's determined, watchful expression, Marlo walked to a closet that contained another photograph of the boy.

The small walk-in closet held her various cameras, supplies, lenses and albums. One day, she hoped to have time to convert the closet into a darkroom. As an amateur photographer, Marlo enjoyed taking the pictures of life in Godfrey. An assortment of good equipment, but outdated by the newer models, gleamed on a shelf.

Cody's photograph hung on the wall; it had been her first real achievement in black-and-white portrait photography, and she'd framed it for inspiration.

A red dusting cloth, neatly folded, lay nearby, and the frame's glass picked up the color. In eerie shades of red, the boy's face caught Marlo, and she placed her fingers over the glossy image. *What is it about red? Why has today been so startling?*

Marlo frowned and studied the boy's image. Perhaps she'd done that too many times, and seeing his face on her shop's glass window was just natural. . . . *Or was it?*

Cherry had been wearing a red blouse and a crystal. Red! Glass and crystal . . . they all came together to stir her. Why?

The answer came back easily: Because Spence had stirred her tonight, pressing her into remembering their past and the way she'd been used by Ryan. Spence's emotions, his bitterness and self-guilt had somehow reached into her . . .

"I don't want this," Marlo stated unevenly to Cody's image. "Go to sleep, Cody."

Covered by glass, the reflection of the red cloth on it, the boy's portrait caused Marlo's senses to leap. . . . Glass and crystal, the color red. Cherry had worn a red paisley blouse earlier, and a crystal necklace. . . . *Cherry!* Would something happen to Cherry?

Marlo shook her head and turned slightly to the other pictures pinned to a corkboard. She skimmed her fingers across the neatly filed boxes and negatives on the shelves.

One lens cover had come away and in the glass lens, Marlo saw her image tinted in red. . . .

With shaking fingers, she replaced the lens cap and turned out the light, leaving the darkroom.

She was sweating, cold and shaking . . . just as she'd been in Ted Royston's house after the funeral, and she was never going back. Impulsively, Marlo dialed Werner's Cafe. Cherry answered, the sound of the cash register ringing in the background. "Cherry?"

"Hi, Marlo. What's up? How was the lasagna?"

"I don't know. I haven't tasted it yet. How are you?"

There was a slight pause, and dishes clattered in the background before Cherry answered, "Why? What's wrong?"

"I . . . I just wondered how you are."

"Great, except for the big trucker who keeps making passes at me. Why?" she asked again, this time more urgent.

"No reason. I just wanted to thank you—"

"Got to go, a whole bunch just came in for burgers and fries. Looks like a minibusful. Bye."

Marlo replaced the telephone. "Good-bye. Keep safe, Cherry."

She rubbed her temples. She'd known Ted Royston would die a violent death. Waves of his anger had hit her—*You ruined my boy's house, and you overcharged him for it, all because he wanted you in the sack.*

Somehow just then, Marlo had known that Ted's anger

would turn back on him, raw and ugly and hurting. . . . His witnessed confrontations with Spence over Elsie had made her son the prime suspect.

Was Spence capable of such violence, such rage?

He'd been with two women, Cherry and her girlfriend. They'd witnessed him staying at the cabin all night. . . .

Marlo rubbed her temples and tried to blame her headache on the wine she'd consumed. She didn't want any of this stirring around her; she wanted her life in neat pockets, undisturbed—

"Go to sleep, Cody," she whispered to the shadows.

After a brief visit with her mother at her thrift shop, and picking over the new load of fabrics Wilma had just purchased, Marlo stood at Spence's cabin door. She just had time to drop off Cherry's pills before consulting with Pearl Henderson, who wanted to change her hen and pig and gingham country kitchen into one like she'd seen in decorating magazines. Then it was on to conference with the Klikamuck Lodge owner.

Marlo knocked on the cabin door and looked around Spence's isolated mountain cabin. He wasn't in sight; the winding dirt road leading from town to his log home was empty. Tall pines soared above the cabin nestled below them; to one side a rough but sturdy building housed his camping equipment, which customers sometimes rented. A hauling trailer stood beside the building. Cherry's mountain bike was on the wooden front porch, and Spence's mud-splattered Jeep was parked in front.

Marlo's mother, an active sixty-year-old, had been wearing her pink Bingo Girls hat and T-shirt when Marlo had arrived earlier at the thrift shop. Wilma always called Marlo to look at anything new that might interest her, and often it was furniture that had been traded in at Royston Furniture. Keith had been very careful to give Wilma first choice. The visit to Wilma's Thrift Shop had been filled with the usual discussion—if Marlo's clients had anything that Wilma could use, or if those same people had anything they wanted to sell. After the chat about fabrics for throw pillows and getting Pearl Henderson's pig and chicken canisters—Pearl was leaving the country duck and gingham motif for Marlo's contemporary decor—Wilma had looked at her daughter critically. "You're not sleeping well. Why?"

Why? Why not? Marlo watched a woodpecker sail by the trees outside the cabin. Everything was shifting inside her—

Marlo took a deep breath and rapped on the front door again. Cherry opened it and blinked against the bright morning sunlight.

"Delivery service," Marlo said as she held the birth control container out to Cherry. "You called and wanted these?"

"Thanks," Cherry said as she took the pills.

Dressed in only an overlarge T-shirt, she held the log cabin's door open, yawned and blinked against the morning sun. "I wasn't up to riding down the mountain this morning. I picked up a few dollars pole dancing at the fire house. The boys were having a private bachelor party for Bud Macy. I would have done it for free—you should have seen Bud blush. I had so much fun."

Marlo knew that Cherry had been raised with too many restrictions, and that her uninhibited lifestyle was pure payback rebellion for those early years. "It's okay. What are friends for, if not to deliver birth control pills? And I appreciate you wearing something now."

"I've got to take advantage before the gravity-sag sets in. Come in and have tea with me?" Cherry invited. "Spence is still sleeping. It always takes him a while to come down after being in the mountains for a few days. He had some calendar photographers this time, then he hunted for Cody. . . . His haunted look can tear the heart right out of you."

"I saw that last night. I wish he could let Cody go."

"I sent him over with the lasagna last night because he looked so awful. You settle people, just talking with you, and I thought it would help him. But you could help him even more if you'd let your 'guides' free. You might be able to contact Cody from the dead. You could give Spence peace."

"Boy, like I haven't heard that before. Almost every other day from you. I have no 'guides,' no special voices talking to me, Cherry."

"I think you do. I think you know more than what you say. Just one séance, Marlo, hmm? Pretty please?"

"You can do it, if you want to. Spence would never agree."

"If you did it, he would," Cherry persisted.

"Lay off. Give me a break."

Cherry gave her I'm-so-innocent look at Marlo. "Mmm. How was the lasagna?"

"Thanks for sending it over, even though you had ulterior motives. I'll have it tonight. I'd better go and see if Pearl Henderson can give up her country look, all those ceramic pigs and ducks, and go for a contemporary look. I have my doubts, but I laid out an idea anyway. And by the way, I know what else you're doing. Don't have Spence play delivery boy again. Stop matchmaking."

"But you'd be so great together," Cherry protested. "He's got a thing for you," she confided. "He's different around you. Always pushing just that bit, edgy, you know? He's not a flirter—except with you. He doesn't have to flirt. Good gosh, I think he has me stay here as protection against the women hunting him. Yep, that's my job, just call me 'yard-dog Cherry.' You know that I'm only staying here because he needs someone to take care of him."

"Cherry, I'd rather not have Spence deliver dinner to my back door. We always get into things that are better forgotten."

"But they're not forgotten. Your 'guides' are telling you to open up, and you're fighting them." With one of her lightning changes of mood, Cherry tugged Marlo into the cabin. "Come on. Dare you. Step on the wild side. Double dare you. Chicken . . . puck, puck, puck."

"Was one of your degrees in animal noises? And if I do, will you skip the malarkey?" Marlo asked, teasing her friend.

Cherry grinned and tossed the birth control pills lightly, catching them. "Got to take one of these. Naughty, naughty, Marlo. Who would know you can get pretty salty, nippy, and daring, when you want? Come in."

"If I do, will you put on some clothes?"

"All these 'ifs.' You're so cautious, Marlo. Don't worry. Spence doesn't bite." Cherry was already drawing on her jeans, and Marlo looked around the living room and kitchen combination that led off to a bedroom. On the opened door, a plastic angel held a sign that read, "Cherry." Spence's discarded clothes were draped over the handrail leading to the upstairs loft.

The cabin was very clean and homey, and maybe, just maybe, Spence was sleeping in Cherry's bed. . . .

Marlo braced herself against that thought: She didn't care where Spence slept, or with whom. "Absolutely none of my business," she murmured to herself. *"Nada."*

A big woodstove sat against one wall. A basket of neatly folded clothes was at the bottom of the roughly hewn board stairs. On another wall was a gun rack with a couple of high-powered rifles. Its wooden shelf was piled high with ammunition, and Spence's revolver holster and sheathed hunting knife hung on the deer antlers beside the guns. At odds with the stripped, gleaming logs, a clothesline of Cherry's lacy bras and panties was strung across a corner of the room. An assortment of New Age books ran across a dresser with an abalone shell filled with crystals. Crystals of all colors seemed to be hanging in front of all the windows—except where a dream catcher of feathers and leather hung. Incense and sage bundles lay in another shell.

A shortwave radio occupied a small table by a window. Near the tiny kitchenette were a wooden table and two chairs; a shabby, sagging sofa and chair stood in the center of the single room.

Cherry indicated the sofa and chair. "I don't suppose you could help me cover those. They've got character."

"I could—at cost. Get them down to my shop. You'll have to help and do more than your share, though. I'm really busy."

"Ah, the television diva speaketh."

"I'm only one of many hosts on Club Renew, but thanks for making me feel special."

"You are special. Very special."

Marlo looked away to the two rolled sleeping bags on the floor, Cherry's red backpack piled on top next to Spence's large practical canvas one. She didn't want to think about how sleeping bags could be zipped together—"I'd better be on my way."

"Wait a minute. What about the fabric for the couch and chair? You're the expert." As Cherry walked toward the bathroom at the foot of the stairs, she said, "I need a teapot. Does your mother have one in the shop?"

The door closed behind her before Marlo could answer. "Gee, I don't know, Cherry. You'll have to look," she murmured to the empty room.

The cabin, despite the guns and camping gear, looked very homey, with flowers in a vase on the table, gingham curtains at the window, and throw pillows on the couch. A variety of throw rugs covered the plank floor. The radio was tuned to the morning weather, and the birds were chirping outside.

The sound of Cherry's shower began, and Marlo moved to study the couch and chair. The wood frames were okay, but the webbing beneath the cushions needed replacement. With a little foam padding in the cushions and new fabric, the furniture would be lovely. After replacing the cushions, Marlo sat to wait for Cherry.

A slight rustle drew her attention to a covered, nearby glass aquarium with its desert decor. Cherry's pet tarantula crawled up on a dried limb. "Hi, Godiva. Feeling sociable, are you?" Marlo asked.

The gray furry spider quickly moved back into the sand-covered can that served as her cave, leaving Marlo alone once more. The red light that served to heat the aquarium reflected on the glass walls.

Marlo found her hand opened on the glass, the red tint flowing through her fingers. Godiva's snack, a cricket, leaped against the glass beneath Marlo's hand. Seeking safety, the cricket hit the glass again and again, the vibration almost like a human pulse. . . .

Marlo jerked her hand away and closed her eyes. A cricket hitting glass, seeking escape, was natural. The red shade that had touched her skin meant nothing. *Nothing*.

Once again, she forced herself back into the reality of her surroundings. The cabin's log walls gleamed, the aroma of coffee filled the room, though Cherry always drank herbal tea.

On the scarred coffee table in front of the sofa, Cherry's crystal necklace lay inside an oyster shell among other shells and barnacles. The crystal caught the filtered light and seemed to collect the opalescent pink inside of the shell.

Marlo shook her head, because the crystal seemed to be saying something—and she didn't want to feel, to sense . . .

Focusing on the album that had been opened, Marlo recognized the pictures taken years ago. Spence at his high school graduation, his diploma in one hand and his scholarship papers in the other . . . Elsie, standing proudly beside Spence. Spence with his arm around Marlo . . .

Marlo shook her head and tried to stop the memories that came flooding back. Spence had always been so much in her life, and now they were lifetimes apart.

Clearly, Spence spent most of his nights in this cabin, not at his mother's.

Marlo understood perfectly. *Spence wouldn't stay at the Gerhard house, because he couldn't bear the memory of Elsie lying dead on her kitchen floor . . . because his sister's and nephew's rooms were empty. . . .*

Footsteps sounded on the loft above her, and Spence, disheveled by sleep, scratching his chest and yawning, appeared. Seemingly unaware of her, Spence came slowly down the wooden steps.

Marlo took one look at his naked body and turned away. Spence was all lean muscle and cords, the filtered light from the window catching the flow of a powerful big male, clearly aroused. The white bandage on his arm contrasted that gleaming dark skin—skin she instantly wanted to touch, to smooth.

Her throat was too tight to speak, or to swallow. "Spence," she managed unevenly.

"Cherry . . . just don't talk. God, it's bright in here. The light is hitting the back of my eyeballs. And turn that radio off." His footsteps sounded, a chair scraped, and Spence cursed darkly. A click sounded, and the radio stopped.

Marlo stood uneasily, determined to face a grumbling naked man without showing any discomfort. She wasn't a girl any longer, and Spence wasn't getting to her. Spence now had on sunglasses and was digging through the clothes basket. He held his forehead and straightened to draw on boxer shorts.

Dressed now, Cherry stood grinning at the bathroom door and lifted her finger to her lips to silence Marlo. Spence walked past Cherry to the kitchenette, where he poured a mug of coffee. He lifted it to inhale and sighed luxuriously.

"Thanks," he said humbly, and carried it toward the small wooden table. With his other hand, he reached down inside his shorts and extracted a sheet of fabric softener. His expression was that of disgust as he balled it into his fist and tossed it to the floor. "I hate smelling like flowers."

His eyes were apparently closed as he sat on the kitchen chair. He gripped the mug as if it were his lifeline to the only spaceship in the galaxy. Then he yelled, "Cherry! You here? Did you check out that first-aid kit?"

"Plenty of anti-itch cream for the customers, boss. Bad night?" Cherry asked as she took a towel from a stack in another basket. She arranged it over Spence's shoulders and picked up a comb and barber's scissors from the table. "Ready?"

Spence's grunt apparently answered all questions. He held up his hand in a cease-and-desist gesture. Cherry waited, scissors and comb in hand while he sipped his coffee. He gave an appreciative sigh, settled back, and lifted his face.

With a grin, Cherry began to run a battery-powered razor over Spence's stubble. "There. Close enough?"

Spence rubbed his jaw, nodded, and stuck out his hand like a surgeon demanding an instrument from a nurse. Cherry placed the razor in it, and he ran it over face.

When he was finished, Cherry began to comb and snip Spence's hair. When he raised his hand to signal that he wanted another drink, she stopped and waited.

Marlo held her breath, her hands itching for her camera. A relaxed male, oblivious to anything but enjoying his morning coffee, would have been a perfect portrait in muted shades, tanned skin over powerful muscles, a six-pack belly, and a soft drape of worn boxer shorts over those powerful thighs, his legs spread out before him.

The filtered light gleamed on one side of his rugged features, while the other side remained in shadow. The sweep of his lashes curled, the light dancing across the thick ends, just there on his eyebrow, a hair left the thick line. A slash of his cheekbone ran into a hard jaw and a muscular throat.

The cabin's muted light ran across his shoulders and the dark shadow of hair on his chest. Light and shadow, Marlo thought, the contrast intriguing to her as a photographer—and who was she kidding?

Spence had a raw masculine appeal that any woman would appreciate.

He yawned and rolled his shoulders and groaned. His hand remained circling his mug. He groaned again when Cherry removed the sunglasses. "We've got company," she said.

Spence blinked at Marlo. Then his eyes closed, and he shook his head.

"Very funny. So what is Marlo doing here?" he asked.

"Cherry forgot something at the shop. I've made the delivery, and I was just leaving," Marlo said. She could feel him awakening, the hum of his body.

"I was just dreaming about you," he said quietly, and the deep lazy tone seemed to seep inside Marlo's body.

"A nightmare?" But Marlo remembered the shocking arousal of Spence's body as he had descended the stairs.

"Sure. That's what it was, a nightmare," he agreed dryly. "So how long have you been here?"

"Long enough."

"See anything you liked?" He was always there, always sensually testing her.

"Not especially."

Cherry clicked her scissors and winked at Marlo while she

placed a tiny pink butterfly clip in Spence's thick hair. "I think Marlo would look cute in a short haircut. What do you think, Spence?"

Spence's light brown eyes shifted, caught the light, and changed to gold, narrowing as he studied Marlo carefully. "I think she doesn't have the nerve. She's had that same hairdo since she was a kid. Marlo doesn't like changes."

He had hunter's eyes, Marlo thought suddenly. Waiting, watching, wanting. . . . He'd been dreaming of her.

Sexually?

In her?

She held her breath, stunned by her thoughts. But then, Spence was experienced at playing women, and he knew exactly how to shock her to take her past her borders, to take her temper higher.

"This style is easy to manage," she said, defending herself.

"You just don't know her. Marlo has just a touch of the wild," Cherry stated. "With that sweet face and those wide eyes, she'd be perfect for a 'boy cut.' It takes a very feminine face to carry that really short hairstyle."

Spence studied Marlo from her feet to the top of her head. Then his gaze locked with hers. "She's too traditional. She'd never go for it."

Marlo had had enough. She inhaled deeply and stood. "My good deed for the day is done. Bye."

"Wait!" Cherry gathered the towel from Spence's shoulders and took it outside to shake it.

Spence's dark eyes never left Marlo. "So how's it going?" he asked quietly.

"Fine. How's it going with you?"

Cherry came back into the house and began sweeping up the hair around Spence's chair. She briskly ran the broom over his bare legs, and Spence didn't move; he continued to look at Marlo.

Link! She felt the warm soft glow inside her that Spence's penetrating stare always brought. "I'd like to see that 'wild' side, Marlo. It's been a few years," he invited softly, deeply.

"She brought my birth control pills," Cherry said. "I can't skip a day. Not that I've had sex for a long, long time, but they keep the cramps from—"

Spence actually winced. "Jeez, Cherry. I don't want to know."

Cherry patted his shoulder and grinned. "My man here hasn't had sex for at least two years. That was me, I guess, before we decided that it wasn't working in bed. I can wear any stud down. He can use all that stored-up energy to help us load this furniture into his trailer and haul it to your shop."

"My couch and chairs? They're just broken in and comfortable. Is nothing sacred?" Spence stared coldly up at Cherry. "I've got two couples coming in. They're using this place after Cherry and I take them for a little hike around the mountain. They'll need somewhere to sit."

She patted his head. "I already talked to Wilma. She's got a rattan set at the thrift shop that she'll let us borrow, so don't fight this, hon. They need upholstering, and working with Marlo, I can get a real deal."

Spence leveled a stare at Marlo. "Women should leave things alone. That couch and chair were here when I bought this place over ten years ago. I spent plenty of nights sleeping on that couch. If you think it needs new covering, put a blanket over it," he said as he rose to his feet. He retreated to the bathroom, clearly disgruntled. The door slammed firmly behind him.

Marlo had to laugh. "You shouldn't have done that."

"He'll go along with it. He just likes to grump," Cherry said with a grin, as the sound of Spence's shower began. "Are you keeping that dream journal I asked you to?"

Four

THE KNOCK WASN'T IN MARLO'S DREAMS. IT SOUNDED AGAIN, and she turned her head to check the time on her bedside clock—two o'clock in the morning.

Keith had called promptly at ten for their usual wind-up-the-day talk. Lying in her bed, talking with him about everyday things, the new organic and traditional furniture designs, had settled her. A few minutes of skimming her notes on basic input from the Klikamuk Lodge owners, Pearl's redecorating project, and listening to the radio's weather report, and she had slid into an uneasy sleep.

Awake now, Marlo rose and walked to the window viewing the driveway; she pulled aside the curtain and opened the miniblinds. Spence stood in a slice of light coming from Main Street; part of his face and body in shadow. A slight rain beaded the glass between them, and Marlo was suddenly struck how much of Spence was unknown to her, despite their early dating years and family closeness.

His grim expression didn't change as he motioned for her to come open the door.

On her way to her private entry by the driveway, Marlo

Marlo had dreamed of Cody in the night, reaching out his arms to her, but she wouldn't give Cherry more fuel for her Marlo-the-intuitive argument. "No. I don't have time for that silliness."

Cherry placed her hands on Marlo's shoulders, and her voice was very quiet as she asked, "Have you gone back to Ted Royston's house? You were really spooked when you were over there after the funeral. I thought with you seeing Keith so much that maybe he'd have you over to help him clear it out."

Keith had asked Marlo many times, but she found excuses not to return to the elder Royston's house. "You're imagining things, Cherry."

"But you aren't. That house said something to you that rattled you. You said you felt something, and that's why I think we should sneak back in without Keith around. Or we could just ask him outright if we can go in and do a séance to see what happened to the old sleazeball."

"No." Marlo never again wanted her skin to crawl like that, to feel the hair at her nape lift, the echoing silence screaming painfully at her.

Cherry shook her head. "You really should give in to your 'guides,' Marlo, and stop fighting whatever is wanting you."

Was it Cody? Why did his photo hold her? Why did the color red seem to catch her?

"No," Marlo repeated firmly. "I'll help you load the furniture, then I've got a full day of work ahead of me."

Cherry's you're-a-chicken taunt would last for hours: "Puck, puck, puck, chickie, chickie. . . ."

hurried to pull her sweatshirt and jeans over her cotton nightgown. She opened the door to find Spence on her small back porch, his hands dug into his jeans pockets. "Cherry needs you. Come on."

"What's wrong?"

"She's been hurt." He looked down at her bare feet. "Get your shoes. She's at Mom's place. Let's go."

He waited while Marlo struggled to absorb his words. Then she shook her head and slid her feet into her loafers.

Marlo barely had time to close the door, and Spence was grabbing her hand, moving into the night. She knew the back alley route well and ran to keep up with his fast stride. "How bad is she? When did it happen? Spence?"

"She's bruised pretty bad, and she had this glazed look, as if she had taken drugs. He came at her from the back, and she doesn't know who he was. He must have been in good shape, because Cherry didn't have a chance against him. She's had enough self-defense classes—the bastard never gave her a chance."

Spence led the way through a small connecting path behind Marlo's workshop and down a side street. "Why are we going this way?" Marlo asked.

"It's quicker, and he dumped her at Mom's. She won't leave the house, not even to come to you. She's sitting in a corner of Mom's bedroom, holding a shotgun. If he's watching, he can see the front of the house. I don't want him to know I came for you."

At his mother's house, Spence picked up a piece of garden gravel and tossed it at a window. Heartbeats later, Cherry came to a window and unlocked it.

"In," Spence ordered, and when Marlo hesitated, he simply lifted her and slid her into the house.

"Oh, Marlo!" Cherry was in Marlo's arms instantly, her body shaking. She sobbed as Marlo held her tightly. Inside the darkened house, Spence locked the window and moved into the kitchen, giving the women privacy.

"I'm all dirty, Marlo—he hit me from behind, and when I was down, he kept hitting me! It was awful, Marlo. I was standing outside the truck stop, just looking up at the sky and feeling the mist on my skin. I was so hot and a little woozy . . . I love the mist. It's so refreshing and I wanted to take off my clothes and—" Cherry began to sob and, hiding her face in her hands, turned suddenly from Marlo.

Marlo came to place her arms around Cherry. "Honey, we've got to call the police."

"No. I'm not going to let anyone know this happened to me. Some people would say I was asking for it, because I'm a nudist and a stripper. This guy likes to humiliate before he can— He's got the oddest voice, like a snake hissing. Not deep, but maybe someone with a throat injury, you know? I think maybe someone came by and interrupted him before he could do anything. I guess I was a little woozy—sort of floating there in the mist—then I wasn't. I knew everything that was happening. He took my crystal necklace."

Link! Marlo remembered how that crystal had drawn her the day before when Spence had collected Cherry.

She pushed away the sense that whatever she had anticipated was tied to Cherry's horrible experience. "Oh, honey."

"I need to take a shower. Come into the bathroom with me. I don't want Spence to see the rest of me—he's furious enough now. I've never seen him so mad."

Marlo looked at Spence who was leaning against the kitchen doorframe, his hands in his pockets. His expression was a mix of fury and frustration. "I put the teakettle on to boil. Chamomile tea always settles her. We have to act now, Cherry. The guy could be getting away now. We should get the police on this and take you to the clinic."

"I don't want that. Not again. I was just sixteen on the Riviera, and my parents didn't believe the guy I was dating—the son of their best friends—would do such a thing. They said I encouraged him—it's all coming back again. . . . Marlo?"

"Spence is right, Cherry, and Mike Preston, our police chief, is a good guy—"

Cherry shook her head, and Marlo sensed that she was struggling for control, fighting hysteria. "No. I'm not going through that again. I'll be fine and I just want you and Spence for now and then I'll go somewhere else for a few days."

"It's that trucker who's been bothering you. I'll find out his route and—" Spence began. "The police can have him after I'm finished."

His anger wouldn't calm Cherry, who had just experienced another man's rage. Marlo spoke quickly to temporarily defuse him. "Spence, let me talk with Cherry alone, please? She wants to take a shower."

Cherry began to laugh wildly. She pointed to Marlo's clothing, the nightgown's rosebud ruffle showing below the hem of her sweatshirt. "Now that's a fashion statement."

Marlo recognized hysteria and moved in to hold Cherry tighter. "Shh . . . everything is going to be all right. I'm here with you now, and so is Spence. We're not going to let anything happen to you."

"It already has," Cherry murmured hollowly. "He said I was a bad girl. Maybe I am—"

"You are not. Don't you ever say that."

Spence waved his hand in a go-for-it motion, but his bitter expression didn't change. "Convince her to report this. Now . . . tonight," he ordered darkly.

"No. I'm not doing it, Spence. You're the safest and best thing in my life, except Marlo. You two are my first real best friends."

Cherry walked to him and Spence's arms closed around her shaking body. "Come here, Marlo. I want to feel us all together, to feel the love we have between us. I need it to replace—what happened before. Please."

Marlo braced herself, but walked to place her arm around Cherry.

"You two are my family, or as close to one as I've ever had. My parents don't have half a heart between them," Cherry whispered unevenly. "I'm not going to the police. Spence doesn't need any more gossip. He went through enough when Ted Royston was killed in January. Then Elsie died in April, and Spence . . . he's hating himself now for enough things, and right now, he's beating himself up for not being at the truck stop."

Cherry turned to Spence and gave him a wobbly smile. "I made my choice of where and what I would be doing, hon. You have no reason to blame yourself for not being at the truck stop. Put your arm around Marlo, Spence . . . tight and safe. She's got forgiveness in her, a world of it. And I want you to feel it—it's important to me. You couldn't have been there . . . you can't watch me all the time. There's too much hate in the world—and you can't go kicking yourself around for things you can't help. Marlo, put your arms around us. Just everyone hold everybody tight."

Spence's expression was frustrated. "I hate this group hug stuff. It doesn't change anything. Cherry, we're wasting time."

Marlo understood instantly. Cherry had experienced violence, and she needed comfort and closeness with her "family." "This is important to her, Spence."

When his arm gathered her close and Cherry's face was next to hers, his look at Marlo was deep and searching. "Always there, aren't you, Marlo? Always caring and putting others first."

She wasn't expecting his soft, searching kiss, as if he'd

needed soothing, too, but it was more—it tasted of hunger and forgotten dreams. . . .

Or was it her own hunger and dreams, skipping over the years?

She could feel the wild creature inside him, rage trimmed by a softness and a feeling of helplessness.

His hand opened on her back, smoothing it, as he continued to look down at her. But his gaze was shielded, wary.

Marlo carefully removed herself from Cherry's and Spence's arms and leaned against the opposite side of the hallway. He continued to hold Cherry and rock her in his arms, but his eyes never left Marlo's.

The hiss of the teakettle sounded, and Marlo used it for an excuse to move into the kitchen. "I'll make tea."

She hadn't been in the house since Elsie Gerhard had fallen to the linoleum floor, fatally injured. In the kitchen everything suddenly stopped; the air around Marlo was too still.

She was alone and she could feel sensations hissing around her, slithering and coiling tighter, crushing her.

The feel of pure rage burned her, just like that she had felt before Ted Royston had been murdered.

It boiled from the linoleum floor and curled around her legs like red snakes.

Her throat tightened, and Marlo placed her hand over it, her heart racing. Rage had killed Elsie, not an accident.

Marlo closed her eyes and tried not to think of how the color red had called to her, how Cherry's crystal had caught her, warning her—

She looked up to find Spence's and Cherry's worried expressions. The teakettle was still hissing . . . and Elsie had been killed. Unable to speak, to voice what reality denied, Marlo felt Spence's large warm hand along her cheek. "What's wrong, honey?" he asked gently.

Cherry's hand locked on Marlo's. "She's so cold. She's feeling something, and it's terrifying her. She senses things, Spence, just like I told you. That's why your mother asked her about Cody. I told you why she reacted that way then, and you didn't believe me. Look at her. Believe it."

Spence frowned harshly, lines deepened around his mouth. "She's just upset about what you've been through. So are you."

Cody's framed picture was still on the wall, the one that she had felt when Elsie asked her if the boy was alive. . . .

Cherry and Spence seemed to be talking in the distance, speaking about someone Marlo knew. She looked at the fresh bruise on Cherry's cheek and the rage that had caused it seemed to link to the sensations in the kitchen. She shook her head, trying to clear it, and Spence stood with his arms across his chest, his expression forbidding. "Leave it, Cherry. Anyone who woke up like Marlo just did, to find her best friend beaten, would need a minute to catch themselves."

"Tell me what you saw, what you felt, Marlo," Cherry persisted eagerly.

Spence's sound of disgust preceded his move to the stove to remove the kettle and make tea. His back was tense; his pain of losing his family was visibly fresh and raw.

"Nothing happened, Cherry. It's just like Spence said, I needed a moment to catch up."

"I don't believe you. But I'm not up to arguing with either one of you tonight. I'm taking my shower, alone. When I come out, I don't want to hear one word about talking to the police. Been there, done that, and it wasn't pleasant."

Cherry moved into the bathroom, and Spence placed the tray with the teapot and his mother's cups on the table. They were the same ones that Elsie had used when she'd asked Marlo to come help her with pictures that day, when she'd asked Marlo to touch Cody's picture, when—"Sit down, Marlo," he said.

Marlo couldn't stay in the kitchen and moved into Elsie's small living room, Spence brought in the tea tray, placing it on the coffee table. He poured the tea. "Drink. You look like you need it."

"You're going after that trucker who had been paying so much attention to her, aren't you?"

He listened to the sound of the shower for a minute before answering. "Just as soon as Cherry feels safe—if she ever does."

In a gesture of frustration, Spence pushed his hand through his hair and shook his head. "She was going to walk here afterward. Walk . . . she knew I was working on the computer . . . I should have been there, waiting for her. . . . He threw her out on the lawn like a piece of garbage. She can't remember anything past—She was in the bar earlier, dancing on a tabletop. She wasn't drunk—"

"I know. She just likes to move to the music. She's still a child in some ways. She doesn't like to believe in evil."

"True. She's unguarded and maybe living in a fantasy world, shoving away the way her parents treated her. She seems to seek love and doesn't have the normal sense of danger. It took me a while to realize that. She's fearless when we're in the mountains. Thank God the guy didn't have time to rape her—I didn't know she'd been raped before. Did you?" he demanded roughly.

"Yes, I did. She didn't go into details though. I know she's had several boyfriends, but she seems on good terms with all of them."

"Including me? I didn't do it, Marlo. But that's what they'll think—a shack-up situation gone wrong, a jealous lover. But I'm not worried about that—I just want the guy caught. . . . The shower has stopped. Go in the bathroom and check on her, will you?"

Marlo understood his concern and his pain. She reached to smooth back the damp strands from his face, then ran her fingertips over the lines on his forehead before she realized that she had touched him. An aching tenderness darkened his eyes, and Marlo jerked her hand away, holding it with shaking fingers. He frowned slightly and looked down at her folded hands. "You shouldn't touch me, Marlo," he stated unevenly, huskily. "Not you."

She fought to find steady ground, to divert him from the tension between them. "Cherry is right about one thing, Spence. You can't protect her all of the time. Just like you couldn't protect Traci and Cody, or your mother."

He stared at her. Then in a sudden movement, Spence reached down and caught her upper arms and lifted her up to him. "What did you mean by that?"

"That's what this is about, isn't it? It's about more than Cherry, though you do care for her. You're furious with yourself because you weren't at the truck stop. You're angry because you weren't here when Dirk picked up Cody and Traci, or when your mother wanted to change that lightbulb. You can't be everywhere, guarding everyone, Spence."

Anger flashed in those gold eyes before they narrowed, pinning her. The air seemed too still, to prickle with tension, then Spence asked softly, carefully, "What's wrong with you, Marlo? Why did you stop in the kitchen a while ago? Are you sick?"

She couldn't tell him—she couldn't tell him how she knew, but she knew that rage had taken Elsie's life, not an accident. . . .

Or maybe she didn't know. Maybe she was just off-balance because of being awakened to the brutalization of her best friend. . . .

Spence's hands framed her face; his thumb was caressing her cheek. "You look scared. Whoever this guy is, he's no sweetheart. That's why Cherry needs to report this. Then maybe they can catch him before he gets another woman and finishes what he started with Cherry. She may have information that could lead to him."

But Marlo was more terrified of herself, of what her senses told her—Elsie's death was because of rage, terrible earth-shaking fury burning out of control. . . .

Cherry stepped out of the bathroom, huddled in a fuzzy chenille robe that had been Elsie's. "I want Godiva," she said unevenly. "I want to know that she's safe. In a different life, she could have been someone's grandmother, you know."

Marlo went to Cherry and placed her arm around her. "Cherry, have some tea."

"Everything is going to be all right," Cherry said. "That's what you're supposed to say—'everything will be all right.' "

Her eye was swollen, almost closed, and there were bruises around her throat. But Marlo forced herself to say the words. She urged Cherry into the living room, covered her with an afghan, and gave her the herbal tea. "Drink. Spence, go get Godiva."

"The hell I am. I'm going after that trucker. He's been hanging around her, trying to catch her attention. He might have decided he had waited long enough."

Marlo placed her hands on her hips and turned to him. "I'm not going to argue about this. She wants her spider, her friend. Just do it, Spence. We'll be fine."

"Kiss him," Cherry murmured with a wobbly grin. "For good luck. Like in the movies where the hero goes off into battle and there's always that one last kiss. I really want my spider, Spence. What if Godiva doesn't get misted, or she gets too cold, or—"

His expression was almost comical as he looked at Marlo,

then at Cherry, then back to Marlo. He seemed to take a deep, steadying breath and spoke as if to a child, "Your spider is going to be just fine, Cherry. If she passed from another life to change into a spider, she's tough, and she's going to be just fine."

Cherry blinked and a big fat tear fell down her cheek. Spence looked helpless, then he turned to Marlo. The narrowing of those dark eyes warned her as they lowered to stare at her lips. "I ought to get something out of arguing with two women at the same time."

"No," Marlo said firmly, and backed slightly away.

With a defeated groan, Spence looped out an arm and brought her close to him. His voice was uneven and husky, as if he were uncertain of her. "If it will help Cherry, you'll just have to sacrifice."

"And you're so noble, of course—"

Then his lips were on hers, not hard and demanding, but warm and magical, as if he was tasting her. Marlo stood very still, her arms at her side. But her very being was centered upon the touch of his lips, just where they brushed hers, the way his chin grated slightly against her skin, the scent of him—soap, the fabric softener he loathed, fresh air, and a combination of darker, more potent scents. "You taste the same—sweet," he said huskily.

Spence's kiss wasn't the same. He'd been too careful, and in the midst of Cherry's ordeal, somehow that grated on Marlo.

Then he stepped back and nodded briefly. He glanced at Cherry, who was huddled beneath the afghan, her eyes huge in the shadows. "There—does that help?" he asked, as if indulging a child.

When Cherry nodded, her voice was childlike, "Everyone in the world should have more kisses and hugs from the ones they love to keep away the bad stuff. You know, sometimes I wake up crying, and Spence comes to tuck me in. He's solid, like you, Marlo. You've both given me a place to fit in."

Spence turned back to Marlo, his eyes dark and dangerous. "Whoever he is knows that Cherry and I live and work together. That's why he dumped her here—to make his point that he could have had her. It could be anyone from the cafe, or the resorts, a customer who had made a pass, or the truck stop—any one of a number of men that had the wrong idea about her and that she turned down. While I'm gone, get her to reconsider filing a report. My rig is going to stay in the driveway, so it looks like I'm here. I'll find a car and be back."

When Spence stepped out of the window, Marlo locked it. Behind her, Cherry said, "I am not going to report this. I will not jeopardize Spence. I know what he went through when old Ted Royston was killed, how he was a suspect because of the argument. I don't want Spence to go through that again. And I know that in a case like this, the first thing the police think about is a lover's quarrel. Now he's like the brother I never had. I thought it might be a go with him, but it wouldn't be right. I gave that up a long time ago, but I love him so much. Everything is all mixed up now, but I just knew it would be right if you kissed him, like friends. Like a mom and dad should kiss."

The wistful tone wasn't lost on Marlo. She came to sit next to Cherry and hold her hand. "He's right about filing a report. It may save another woman from whoever attacked you. This guy might do even worse to her."

"No. No way. Not after what happened when I was raped. They think it's the victim's fault—I felt like I'd been opened up and gutted. Why don't people understand that everyone needs to be loved?" she asked, as her tears began to fall.

Marlo dabbed them away, rocked Cherry in her arms, and told her what she wanted to hear—"Everything is going to be just fine."

"And you're going to tell me what you felt when you went into the kitchen," Cherry finished as she straightened. "I know it was something, Marlo. . . . You saw something, felt something, didn't you, Marlo? You turned white and you shook and Spence saw you do it, too, so it wasn't only me."

Distracted from her own terror, Cherry stood to her feet and pulled Marlo to hers. "Let's go back to the kitchen, and you can tell me everything you felt."

Cherry's face was bruised, dark marks ran around her throat, but the eye that wasn't swollen shut was alight with excitement. When Marlo resisted Cherry's pull toward the kitchen, she decided that anything was better than to have her friend focus on her last few hours. "If I tell you, will you reconsider filing a report?"

"Sure, I'll reconsider. Tell me."

"I think something awful happened in that kitchen. I don't think Elsie died because of an accident."

Cherry sucked in her breath and it came out as an explosion. "I knew it! You *are* psychic. Now we'll just have to have that séance. Let's do it now, while Spence is away. He won't have to know. You can call Elsie's spirit, and we'll know. Come on, Marlo, I'll get a candle, and—"

"No. I don't want any part of it—"

"Okay, if not Elsie, then we've just got to break into old Teddy's house and see what went on there. We know that was violent, and his spirit is probably still there, just needing to unload—you just turned pale again, Marlo. You felt something, didn't you? About old Ted?"

"No," Marlo lied, because she remembered the eerie feel of the Royston house. "Not a thing."

"Come on, Marlo, let yourself go. Let those guides speak to you."

"And you'll file that report?"

Cherry's animated expression closed, and she shook her head. "I said I'd reconsider, and I have. I'm not doing it. I've paid my dues there, and I won't again. I won't have people looking at me and whispering."

"So you're just going on as if nothing happened?"

"I have to, or I'll come apart. The first time I was assaulted, my parents didn't believe me. I was in therapy for years afterward. If they had believed me and didn't think those bruises had been my way of trying to get attention, maybe things would have been different. I'm going to take a little vacation—France or somewhere—and when I look okay, then I'll be back. Meanwhile, you're going to take my place on that backpacking trip. Spence has got some big shots and their girlfriends coming in, and it could mean a real jump in his business. There's no one else that I'd trust, but you, Marlo. You and I went camping last year, and I know that you're good—remember that time we sunbathed nude on top of the mountain, got covered in bites, and burned our buns?"

Marlo stared at her friend. "How can you just jump around from one disaster to the next and ask Spence to kiss me and get me to say things I don't want to say? No, and double no."

Cherry smiled and placed her hand on Marlo's cheek. "Pretty please? For me?"

"We're supposed to be worrying about you, Cherry. Not Spence's business, or how I feel some things—"

"Ah, back to that! Now that it's out, can I tell Spence that you admitted it?"

"Not on your life."

"Then can I cut your hair?"

"Did you lose this?" Spence asked as he lifted Cherry's crystal necklace in front of the big trucker. "You should have hung it somewhere less noticeable than on your windshield mirror."

Outside the truck stop, the eighteen-wheelers stood in parallel rows, the spaces between shadowed from the racks of lights above. Between two rows, Billy Bob stood. The trucker was seven feet of hard muscle, wearing a sweatshirt with the sleeves torn away and tattoos over bulging muscles. His blond hair was spiked and his moustache draped down the side of his mouth to meet his beard. The thin trimmed line of his beard framed his jutting jaw and ended in a chain through his pierced ear. His voice sounded like a bear's low warning growl and echoed off the metal sides of the trucks. "Give me that."

Spence decided against that hard-rock jaw and his kick went for Billy Bob's knees to bring the trucker down those necessary inches. "She's a sweet kid, Billy Bob. And you're going to feel a little bit of how she felt before I turn you in."

The trucker staggered and bent to rub his injured knee. "Boy," he said in a deep Southern accent, "You just earned yourself a heap of trouble. But first, how did she feel? Why are you turning me in? And who are you turning me in to?"

"The girl you took this from was beaten. You shouldn't have hung around."

The trucker blinked owlishly and backed against his rig. He grabbed Spence's shirt and hauled him up close. "Cherry lost that—that girl who lives with you. I found it beside my rig. I don't steal, boy. And I don't hurt women."

"You worked her over pretty good before you dumped her at my place," Spence was having second thoughts about just how soft the trucker's belly was— His one-two punch only brought a frown.

"I don't even know where you live, boy."

By this time, two other truckers were standing between the rigs, sucking on their toothpicks. "I wouldn't pick one with Billy Bob, son," one of them warned. "He's slow to get riled, but you're done for if you get his temper up. I saw him mash a fellow like a bug once, when the guy wouldn't leave a waitress alone. Billy Bob has this Southern gentleman thing going on."

"Let's keep this private, Billy Bob," Spence said, as the big trucker pushed him slightly away. "Either way, I'm here to give you a taste of what you gave her."

Billy Bob tilted his head and looked puzzled. "I don't need their help to take care of you, boy. Are you sure it was Cherry? Did she say it was me? She didn't, because the police would be here. Are you just looking for reasons to pick a fight? Are you just mad because Cherry is starting to like me? You know, it's for a woman to decide the man she likes. If you're suffering over a bleeding heart, this is no way to settle it, son. You ought to have a heart-to-heart talk with the lady and see how the wind blows. That little sweet potato pie won't like you getting all pushy. Then if I have to pop you one, I'll lose all those points I've been making on getting the little lady."

The trucker seemed genuinely puzzled. "Just take it easy, okay, son? She won't like this wild hair of yours."

By this time, Spence was questioning the wisdom of his accusation and the "son" and "boy" labels were starting to grate. "Let's talk privately, shall we?"

Billy Bob followed Spence to the other end of the eighteen-wheeler. Spence explained briefly what had happened to Cherry and why the police weren't involved—yet. The big trucker's expression crumbled. "Now that's just pitiful. Who would want to do that to a sweet girl like her? Sometimes there's some play in the sleeper rigs, but if—where is she now? Maybe I can help. Maybe I can find out who hurt her, then I'll beat the living—I want to see her. You think she would let me see her?"

Spence thought of Cherry's bruises, her swollen eye. If Billy Bob had anything to do with hurting Cherry, her reaction would be telling. "Sure. I think she'd see you."

* * *

"Why did you bring *him* here?" Marlo demanded, when the men stood on the Gerhard front porch.

As the rain continued to fall from the porch roof, Spence held up the yogurt carton that held Godiva. "To help me carry Godiva?"

"She sure is a pretty spider," Billy Bob said as he stood behind Spence and explained, "Cherry brought her to the truck stop one day. Do you think one of the guys Cherry is teaching to strip might have hurt her?"

"No, they're all sweet boys," Cherry said as she came to stand beside Marlo. "Some of them have taken high school French."

"Oh, well. I guess that makes them okay, then." Spence closed his eyes and shook his head. "I told you not to teach them, Cherry."

"She doesn't need that now, Spence," Marlo cautioned. "Someone is going to notice that eighteen-wheeler parked in front of the house. When it pulled up, the whole house shook. Your mother's hanging cut-glass snowflakes on the windows are still quivering."

"I intend for everyone to notice, and he didn't fit into the car I borrowed. I'm going to tear up this goddamn town. Cherry, do you want to see Billy Bob? Is he the one?"

Cherry reached for Godiva and cradled the carton to her body. "Are you kidding? That's the gentlest man I know. Did Spence come after you, Billy Bob? Did he hurt you?"

"Not one eensy itsy bitsy," the trucker said shyly. "Are you going to let me come in and talk with you, Miss Cherry? Just to see for myself that you're okay. This boy didn't hurt you because you're favoring me now, did he, sugar plum? He was mad when he came after me. Not the hot kind, but the cold kind that means business."

Cherry's one good eye and both of Marlo's were narrowed

at Spence. "Why do men always think they can solve everything with a brawl?" Marlo asked.

Billy Bob had fished a mini flashlight from his chest pocket and the beam caught Cherry's bruised face. He paled instantly and turned, his big shoulders hunched. "I think I'm going to be sick."

Cherry shoved Godiva's carton at Spence. "Shame on you. You shouldn't have brought him here."

"I thought you might recognize him."

"I do. He's one of the sweetest guys I've ever known. If I had told you that I thought he was special, you would have started that big brother protector act. You could have scared him off, Spence." Then she went to Billy Bob on the porch, patted his back, and took his hand. "Come inside, Billy Bob. I'll get you something for that upset stomach. It's not so bad, really."

Billy Bob carefully bent his head to enter the house, Cherry at his side. At the doorway, Marlo's arms were crossed, and her foot was tapping as she continued to stare at Spence. He didn't like the steady beat of her foot. Somehow it implied that he'd done something wrong—and he hadn't. He'd done what any man would do, go after a woman-beater, and he'd brought home a trucker to be cuddled and cooed over. Somehow, that left him odd man out in the threesome . . . in his own house, he decided righteously. "Nice shoes," he said to Marlo. "I'll get Godiva's aquarium."

He turned and started down the steps and stopped. He turned around to study Marlo and decided the aquarium could wait as he came back up the steps. Her hair was cut close to her head, creating a perfect frame for those expressive, flashing eyes. "I like the haircut."

"I didn't have much choice. It distracted her."

Spence smiled briefly; Cherry had her own weapons, and she knew how to get her way. "I thought she didn't like

Billy Bob. She said he'd been around, and she's been putting him off."

"She was playing hard to get. A lady never says yes right away, and she wanted him to think well of her. And if you call that big, booming voice a snaky hiss, like someone who has had a throat injury, you need your hearing checked. And by the way," Marlo said quietly, "the other thing I agreed to was helping you on that next guide trip. On top of her own problems, she's worried about your business. Her bruises aren't exactly good ad material, and she's going to be stiff."

"You? On a guide trip with me?" Spence's expression was blank, almost comical.

Cherry, still holding Billy Bob's hand, came back to retrieve Godiva. "Tell him, Marlo. Tell him . . . tell him . . . do it, do it," she prompted Marlo.

"Tell me what? Is she going to file a report?" Spence asked, turning to her. "That really needs to be done, Cherry. And you need to see a doctor, not worry about a guide trip."

"Marlo needs to tell you that—" Cherry stopped in midsentence when she looked at Marlo's stern frown.

"Not another word, Cherry," Marlo warned quietly.

"Pretty little bird," Billy Bob crooned. All three hundred pounds of his solid muscular body seemed to hang near Cherry. Then his fist curled, and the tattooed dragon on his biceps showed its teeth. "A lady shouldn't ever be touched like that. And if I ever find out—"

"Hush, Billy Bob. Violence cannot answer violence. It only creates more. That's a double-no. I'm not going through that again," Cherry said. "I want her to tell you something else, Spence."

"Like what? What could be any more silly than her going on a guide trip with me?"

Marlo shook her head and stared at Cherry. Spence had always noticed that the two women communicated silently. Now, he wasn't certain he wanted to know the silent argument—it reminded him about the time he asked something about women's PMS and had to wade through a discussion that no male should even be near.

"No," Marlo stated firmly. "We made a bargain, Cherry, remember? You cut my hair, and I'm doing this insane guide thing with Spence. I'm going to have to close my shop, cancel appointments, manage smart guy here, plus sleep on rocks and get wet and cold, and don't you dare say anything."

"Pretty please?"

"No."

"Don't I have anything to say about Marlo taking your place, dammit?" Spence demanded.

"No. Marlo got all snarky with me, Spence," Cherry singsonged like a child telling on another. The impish look in her one blue eye ruined the wounded tone. "Lost her temper and everything. She yelled. Here I am, all battered, and she—"

"Boy, you really pull a guilt trip out of the drawer, don't you?" Marlo threw up her hands, shook her head, and walked back into the house. Spence studied the way the ruffle of her nightgown flounced and swayed below the hem of her sweatshirt. If she was still wearing her nightgown, that probably meant she wasn't wearing a bra.

After that thought, Spence's mind went blank.

"She yelled," Cherry whispered in a conspirator's triumphant tone. "If you hadn't turned up, I think I could have gotten her to crack, and I could have gotten my way about that séance."

"Don't you two have anything more useful to do than to talk about me?" Marlo demanded from inside the living room. "Didn't something really awful happen tonight to Cherry that is more important than whatever you two have cooked up about me?"

Spence entered the house and secured the front door. He

turned to see Marlo seated on the couch, her arms and legs crossed. Her stare sizzled through the shadows to him.

At that moment spending time with Marlo, setting her off, had tremendous appeal to Spence.

Billy Bob tested the opposite end of the couch and settled where Cherry had indicated that he sit.

"I don't want to talk to you," Marlo stated, as Spence came to sit down beside her and drape his arm over the back of the couch. He'd perfected that move long ago, brushing his arm against her breast to see how soft—it was very soft, a sign that she truly wasn't wearing a bra. He almost felt guilty, because Cherry's trauma was more important than his need to check out Marlo. But somehow, his body had thrown him a curve. He wondered if she had slept without briefs and had just drawn her jeans up under her nightgown.

While he stared at her, debating the mind-blowing mystery of her underwear, Marlo wiggled her bottom away from his. That was difficult to do because Billy Bob's bulk had them all wedged pretty tightly on the sofa.

Cherry cradled the yogurt carton, sat in an opposite chair, and held an ice pack to her face. She looked at the three of them on the sofa, and stated cheerfully, "I'm feeling much better."

"You should be reporting this." Marlo had that sulky look, all hunched into herself. "It's almost morning, and no one seems to be tired. What do we do now?"

Spence ran his finger down her nape, just to test her sizzle, and said, "I like the haircut. Without the bangs, I can see what you're thinking. Maybe spending time on that trip with you isn't such a bad idea after all."

"Leave me alone. Stop crowding me."

Cherry stood suddenly, stretched her arms high, and yawned. "I'm tired."

She eased onto Spence's lap, leaned back to place her head

against the other sofa arm near Marlo, and stretched her legs and feet across Billy Bob. "Cover me with the afghan, will you, guys? I've just got to take a nap."

In seconds, Cherry seemed deeply asleep. Marlo smoothed her forehead and frowned at the bruises. "She does that when she can't take any more stress—just goes into an instant sleep wherever she feels comfortable."

Billy Bob stretched his arms across Cherry's legs and held his hands upright, so as not to touch her, a sign of his reverence. "Poor little honey-bird," he crooned.

Spence noted Billy Bob's big hands, then looked at Marlo. The slight shake of his head signified that he didn't think the trucker would have hurt Cherry. "I don't want to leave her. That trip can wait. I'll cancel it. Listen, this is business that has to be taken care of—we've got to find this guy. He needs to pay. What's more, what if that happens to another woman—what if it's you?"

His hushed frustration and anger shook the room, reminding Marlo of the way her senses had jumped in the kitchen. If Spence had any glimpse that his mother's death was a murder, he'd—

And what could she say? *Gee, I think—but for no reason or fact—that your mother was killed. I just feel that happened, and I just could be going nuts.*

Spence had suffered enough with the death of his sister and nephew. He'd driven himself past human limits to find Cody's body. Marlo couldn't drag out anything worse, any suspicion that Elsie might have been killed—after all, there was nothing factual to indicate that.

She stroked a damp strand of hair from Cherry's cheek. "She couldn't bear for you to cancel this trip because she knows it has big potential. You advertised that you'd have a female guide with you, and I'm elected. Every time I suggested someone else, she started crying again, worrying about you. She loves you, Spence. She's the most unselfish, giving person I know. I'm doing this for her, to help her get through this."

Spence straightened the afghan over Cherry. "She just looks so—like a kid."

"You love her, don't you?" Marlo asked softly.

"Yes, I do," Spence and Billy Bob answered in unison.

"I know," Cherry murmured sleepily. "I love you, too. Marlo loves me, too. That's why I'm staying in Godfrey. Because you guys are my family."

She lifted slightly and moved across Marlo and Spence, who tensed and grimaced painfully, to sit in Billy Bob's lap. "Hold me."

With Cherry on his lap, the big trucker looked panicked. "She needs that sometimes. Just do it," Spence said as he rubbed his injured arm. "And you better not be the one who hurt her."

Billy Bob glared at Spence. "You'd better get out of my face, boy."

" 'Boy'?" Spence's tone warned.

Marlo was already on her feet; the night couldn't get much longer, and Cherry didn't need two clashing males. "Come on, Spence. Let's see to that arm. You're favoring it. The bandage probably needs changing. Your mother's medicine cabinet probably has something we can use."

His eyes narrowed up at her with a look that labeled her as a meddler in an argument he intended to finish. "Okay, hon. Whatever you say. I'd just love that," he said too smoothly, in a tone she didn't trust.

"I taught that girl, Cherry, a lesson she won't soon forget. We don't need her kind in Godfrey. . . . She's a bad influence on Marlo and she's changing the shape of how things should be—how they've always been. . . ."

The biker rode through the mountains' mist. A borrowed car had served to hold the girl, until she'd tumbled onto Spence's front yard, but now the motorcycle engine roared, and a feeling of power surged through the biker's body. "I always feel high after my anger fades—powerful—and I had been very angry at the girl showing off her body like that, swaying to the jukebox music, laughing with the men. Cheap tramp-girl. Bad girl."

The biker smiled coldly beneath the ultratech helmet. "I looked like any other biker on I-90, sitting at the truck stop, eating and watching that girl dance. She was a very bad girl, and she needed punishing. Now she'll know that she's just a piece of trash. I would have liked to take her on, though, just to see how strong she was—just to play with her a bit, but there wasn't time for that. I just wanted to make my point about women like her and what I think of them."

The pictures . . . where were the pictures taken twelve years ago, the pictures that were proof of The Secret?

It couldn't be uncovered. Ever. "I've got to find those pictures. My life will be ruined if I don't. . . ."

Five

MARLO SEARCHED THE MEDICINE CABINET IN ELSIE'S SMALL bathroom. With her hands full of bandages, disinfectant, and antibiotic salve, she turned and found Spence standing close behind her. He closed the door with a firm click.

It was the first time she'd been enclosed with Spence Gerhard, alone and intimate, since years ago.

"Don't panic. I'm not going to jump you. Do you actually think I would? Now?" he demanded with a frown, then shook his head. "Leave that one. We've got to talk. Cherry has to report this."

She could handle this intimacy, Marlo decided. But nerves caused her to lecture him; she had to do something. "You heard her. This decision is hers, not yours. She's protecting herself—and you. After your big blowup with Ted Royston and he's murdered, you were a prime suspect. If you hadn't been in bed with a pretty reputable witness—a flashy New York attorney, no less—you could have been in real trouble. So just let Cherry do her thing—"

"I wasn't in bed with Janie. Or Cherry. I was teaching them how to smoke cigars—something they thought was very chic or funny or something, and would take my mind off old Teddy-boy. Janie thought she might try that in an exclusive men's club sometime, just to test the no-women rules. I warned them, but they both got sick, and I had to play nursemaid." He caught her face and held it up to the light. His fierce expression held anger that bit at her, that caught the light and gleamed in his eyes, stroking the taut ridges of his brows and cheekbones.

Primitive and hard, Spence's big body pressed close to hers. "You want this guy found just as bad as I do. You're all lit up and shaking, like you want to hit something. Imagine that, sweet Marlo actually wanting to use violence."

Marlo fought the fierce reaction of her body to his, the need to meet that wildness within him and conquer it. Or to soothe it.

She moved her head away from his touch. It angered her that Spence was right—she felt helpless and wanted revenge for Cherry. "It might be you, if you don't stop crowding me."

Spence was too close and too volatile. Marlo could feel the waves of his frustration and anger hitting her. She needed balance. She needed distance from Spence. "Let's go—"

Where? Into the kitchen, where she only *sensed* that his mother had been attacked?

The small neat house had its disadvantages. She'd already passed his sister's and his nephew's rooms, and one that had been his mother's. Apparently Spence had slept there periodically, his clothing tossed across a chair, the bed mussed. Each room had its own sense of that person, and all of them bothered Marlo. Spence's loneliness spread into each shadowy room, his aching pain.

And he was too close, watching her with narrowed dark eyes. "What's wrong, Marlo?"

His hands locked to the sink behind her, framing her hips.

His thumbs played with the ruffle of her nightgown. "Well, well, well. You're all flushed and nervous."

Just that quick, without notice, he'd changed and was stalking her, enjoying her reaction. Marlo looked away as he leaned closer. She looked down to the blood spotting the white gauze on his arm.

"Let me look at your arm, Spence. It won't help Cherry if you come down with an infection. She'll blame herself for taking too much of your valuable time. She blames herself for everything . . . it's the *mea culpa* thing. You weren't here when we argued, and she's feeling low enough. Her parents were really into guilt trips, and she's feeling that now—that maybe she caused this whole thing. You and I are not going to do anything to add to what she is already feeling."

He pushed back easily, folded his arms over his chest, and she didn't trust that curve of his lips. "Sure."

Marlo turned to place the medical goods on the vanity. Spence knew how to push her buttons, and she didn't know how to pay him back for that.

She forgave the boy long ago, but the man required a toe-to-toe meeting at some primitive level and besting him. He'd always been able to draw out the competitive instinct in her, one she didn't like. "We're going to have to get along, whether you like it or not—for Cherry's sake. So stop pushing me."

"That haircut really brings out your eyes. Where have you been hiding, Marlo?"

When he pushed, she'd react and lose control, and that wouldn't be good.

She focused on changing the bandage, bending to ease it off and frowned; the puncture wounds were reddened. She set to work and tried to dismiss how closely he studied her. Marlo could feel his tenseness, that hot static alert sense of male attraction. Spence wasn't safe; he knew just how to torment her until she lost control and stepped out of her safe routine, the neat package that she'd constructed of her life. "Get that shot, Spence."

"I like how that little curl comes in front of your ear, how it lies close to your cheek."

While she worked, Spence leaned close to nuzzle her cheek. Marlo eased slightly away. "You're asking for it, you know. I haven't had sleep, I'm worried about Cherry, and—"

"So am I. She's a good friend. I didn't know that about her being raped before when she was just a kid. Now it all fits. Her parents are—she didn't have a good life with them, but she never told me that."

His lips brushed hers, tasted, then lifted away. "Thanks, Marlo. She means a lot to me."

"She isn't Traci. You can't be her brother or the loving father she never had."

"What's this about a séance?"

His voice was low and intimate, and she could imagine it spreading over a woman next to him in bed.

She inhaled slowly for balance and disregarded the imagined bed. Spence was a man to have sex when and where he wanted.

In contrast, she was the kind of woman who turned off the lights, scheduled missionary position lovemaking, then refreshed with a shower before going to sleep. She could deal with him now because of Cherry. Marlo had always been able to deal with what she had to do, and now that was to think of her best friend.

Marlo applied the bandage over his arm. "You know how she is—into New Age stuff. I just agreed to think about it, maybe sometime—"

"Sucker." Spence bent to touch her bottom lip with his tongue.

"Jerk." But she closed her eyes, felt the ground shake beneath her feet as she leaned closer, needing another taste.

That wild urge to capture and defeat rushed through her. Hovering just fractions of an inch from Spence's hard lips, Marlo pushed it back. "I don't want to go on that trip with you, either," she whispered.

"If you think I want to babysit you, you're wrong."

"From what Cherry said, she does the camp cooking and smoothing over the rough spots when you get moody. So it's me who will be babysitting you."

"Think you can?"

"Oh, I can. I just haven't wanted to. And you seem to have enough women wanting to do that already. Who were you with when old Ted was killed? Janie Mills-Franklin, wasn't it? And Cherry, of course."

His eyebrow rose, challenging her. "You already know that. Why bring it up again, unless you've got some private little reason? Did it bother you that I was with them?"

She hadn't intended to express that narrow, cutting edge of jealousy that wasn't what she wanted inside her, twisting every time she saw him—

"So how is that attorney?" she heard herself say. "Calling her much, are you?"

"Seeing Keith pretty regular, aren't you?"

The distance closed between their lips. That raw feline hunger trembled and threatened inside Marlo. She could feel his arrogance, feel the need to take him down. That primitive need to compete with him and win quaked through her, and she didn't like it. "Let me out of here."

"Okay." His answer was easy, but his expression was too taut, and, with a gallant gesture, Spence opened the door and swept out his hand in an after-you motion.

"If you get sick because of that arm, I'm not taking care of you," Marlo warned as she passed him.

"Uh-huh."

Marlo didn't like that sound—as if he were studying the

ruffle over her bottom. As if he were cupping it in his hands, pressing her against him . . .

"Pervert."

Two days later, Marlo's voice shook with anger. It took real effort for Spence to lift his eyes from Marlo's damp T-shirt, from the peaking of her nipples against the cloth. If ever he wanted a woman, it was Marlo. He'd wanted her forever, and the need wouldn't go away. It thumped low in his body, where all the blood from his brain had gone. When he did lift his stare, he didn't bother to hide his desire for her.

It had been gathering since he'd first seen her at dawn, stretching and yawning, when she'd gotten out of her pickup at his cabin. His sexual alert system had gone into overdrive when Marlo walked ahead of him on the narrow, rocky trail. Her hips swayed under those loose bib overalls, her legs long and strong and—

Spence thought about the twin sleeping bags that could easily be zipped together . . . about Marlo naked and close inside with him, tangled around him.

One glance at the high-powered executive with his "secretary," making time in another sleeping bag with assorted pleasured noises, didn't help.

Another couple was doing the same scramble in their sleeping bag on the other side, and it sounded as if they were just getting warmed up for another round.

This bunch hadn't liked the hike, grumbling about the wilderness, even though Spence had rented Spot, Taco Bill's llama, to help pack their sleeping bags and coolers stuffed with party food and champagne. It took just one hour of listening to his customers complain before Spence decided to camp early and shorten the route.

Spence turned to check Spot, who was eyeing him in return. The white llama had black spots, for which he had been named. A male and experienced with high altitudes and narrow trails, Spot's bad moods were legendary—if overloaded, no more than one hundred pounds, he would fold to lie still, and nothing could budge him. But the llama could sense when a cougar or bear was around, a telltale lookout.

And Spot was in love with Marlo, following her lead obediently. Spence almost envied the llama, the way Marlo's capable hands petted him.

Marlo closed her jacket over her chest, dug her hiking boots into the rocks of the campsite, and stared angrily at Spence from beneath her baseball cap. The campfire flames lit her face, catching the slant of her eyes, the set of those soft lips. "Remember . . . I'm doing this for Cherry. If I hadn't agreed to babysit you, she wouldn't have gone away with Billy Bob to recover. You'd better lighten up. You've been bossing me all day."

"I don't know that it was such a good idea, letting her go with Billy Bob."

Marlo lifted one expressive eyebrow. "Like you could stop her. He didn't attack her. She was just bruised—Billy Bob had the strength to break bones, and he's aware of it, that's why he isn't touching her. He's afraid he'll hurt her. It wasn't him. I'm certain of it."

"Sure. Be certain. I'll just feel better when she's back and safe."

Spence cupped his coffee in his hands and thought of Marlo's warm, agile body on a cold fragrant night in the mountain wilderness. Her acquired duties ran to providing suntan lotion for the ladies who forgot it, accompanying them into the bushes and seeing to the proper disposal of toilet paper. She was also the cook helper and chief cleanup captain. Cherry usually acted as a conversation buffer, but with these customers there was no need to cook or integrate conversation and smooth ruffled feelings. The two couples had brought hampers stuffed with high-priced delicacies that no doubt came off some corporate "incidental" accounts.

A distance away, the top-dog executive had just given a muffled shout that could only be the result of good, mind-blowing sex.

Number Two dog was trying his grunting best to compete and gave a muffled groan, still not ready for the finish line.

Spence tried to focus away from the couples, who had been getting worked up during the day.

The short hike had been easy and scenic, just enough so that they could say they were nature buffs and show off a few pictures. Marlo had brought her camera, one like Spence's mother's, and when she paused to take a shot, the customers usually tried to get off a few, too.

From the minute Spence saw their camping gear—obviously new and still wearing big price tags—he knew they were the partiers. No doubt the trip was a "research necessity" for the corporate bunch who wanted to set up camp early. Spence shrugged mentally, because it didn't matter, only the high price he'd set for "special attention," which was finding and stocking an isolated cabin—his own—for two days after the trip.

The damp chilly mountain air smelled of pine and sex, and in the morning he'd either have to ask them to pick up the condoms they were tossing to the bushes, or he'd have to collect them himself—guiding permits came with lots of restrictions on camping, fire use, and cleaning up.

He'd been battling his own needs, had snapped at Marlo more than once. She was doing a good job, better than Cherry, who tended to drift off and talk with the customers, sharing herself too much, feeling too much.

"You're cute when you get all stewed up. I can't help worrying about Cherry, and you know it, Marlo. Do you really think she's all right?"

Cherry's assault was still fresh and ugly, brewing between Spence and Marlo. It was in Marlo's closed expression, the way her eyes would occasionally lock with his. But Spence suspected his anger and frustration went even deeper than hers; he'd added Cherry's attack to his list of loved ones whom he hadn't protected.

Marlo had to know the dangers of letting an attacker go free, but she always had that capacity for hope—and forgiveness and love. And with or without either woman's permission, Spence intended to discover who had attacked Cherry.

"Traveling with Billy Bob for two weeks? Making his route with him, sleeping in that camper cab, then heading off to New Mexico to find a mate for Godiva? I think it's just what Cherry needed, a little escape, before she comes back to face what happened. . . . Spence, you're already planning how you're going to get this guy, aren't you? And because I live alone, you're probably planning to be a real pain checking up on me, aren't you? You'd better not be thinking that, because you are not stepping into my life any closer than you have. I like quiet and peace and routine. You're like a—a storm, lightning and thunder crashing. I won't have it."

Spence had his own ideas about protecting both women. "I want you to work on her, get her to file that report."

"I won't. She's had enough. I'll mention it, and if she doesn't pick it up, I'm not pressing."

His hunting experience in the mountains had taught Spence that a predator's nature doesn't change—and this one would be on the prowl again, looking for a fresh victim, or a repeat on Cherry. "This is only a temporary fix. He's out there somewhere, and no one is hunting him. What if he attacks her again? What if he finishes the job then? What if it happens to you? What if it could have happened to Traci? Do you have any idea if he was a local? Maybe one of the boys in Cherry's stripper bunch? You know, Bjorn and that big

Hawaiian snow surfer made some comments to her that weren't sweet. They are both big enough to do the job."

Spence mulled the size of the Swede and the Hawaiian. They preferred rich women, but any woman would do—they'd even tried Traci after her divorce. Spence had made it his business to see that they left his sister alone.

Marlo studied her sturdy leather hiking boots, used a stick to pick the rocks and dirt from the grooves of the soles, and ignored his question. Spence didn't trust her silence. He took her hand in his. It was cold, and she'd gone inside herself again—for just that fraction of a heartbeat, Spence sensed that she wanted to tell him something. Then she pulled inside herself again. "What's going on, Marlo? Thinking about Cherry?"

The answer came too quick, and she was on her feet, then crouching beside the campfire ring, staring into it. "Yes."

She was brooding, sealing herself away from him. She'd dealt with too much pain, and he'd been a big part of it. Then her ex-husband had used her—Marlo had been too forgiving, keeping a smile on her face over too much devastation.

Now she was brooding about a good friend whose painful past had just leaped back up on her.

With a sigh, Spence lifted one of the fancy picnic thermal baskets the corporate guys had gifted to him. He tucked a tarp that would go beneath the sleeping bags under his arm and walked over to Marlo. He reached down to grab the back of her jacket and haul her up beside him. "Come on. Let's get out of here. They're not going to miss us."

She'd been crying. "It's so awful," Marlo stated shakily, as tears gleamed on her cheeks. "I feel so bad for her."

Spence braced himself against the fresh wave of anger. "Cherry should have reported it."

Marlo frowned and stared blankly up at him. "Who? Oh, yes, Cherry."

"Were you thinking of someone else?"

"Oh, no. I was thinking of Cherry."

But Spence didn't trust that too-quick and innocent answer. Marlo was hiding something, and he knew just how to get it out of her . . . and to momentarily make her forget her troubles—Keith, the boyfriend, the loss of work time, that sort of thing, Spence added, to justify what he planned to do. Besides, it was in Marlo's best interest, he decided righteously. He was only being noble.

Spence picked a nearby spot where a stream rippled and splashed and minimized the sounds of sex. He placed the expensive thermal basket on the gravel, spread the tarp and sat, opening the picnic basket. "Since they didn't want to wait for camp food and they had their own baskets, why don't we see what they gave us—"

"What's wrong with the steaks and the baking potatoes we brought?"

"We can have those for breakfast—if they're up to eating. Ah! Champagne, pâté, good cheese, Italian sausage, caviar, and whoa—smoked oysters." He looked up at her. "Are you going to sit or what?"

Marlo eased onto the tarp and took the plastic champagne glass Spence held out to her. She watched the bubbly fizz into the glass, then took an experimental sip. "I guess this is better than nothing. Do you do this very often?"

Her expressive eyes and distraction said that Marlo was hiding something, and he intended to discover her secret. If she got fuzzy and warm and talkative after a few glasses of champagne, he'd have to listen, of course. It was an old trick, and Spence almost felt guilty. Almost.

"Drink up," he said as he began filling the cutting board with food. "I have a feeling they're not going to be getting around early in the morning. They brought several bottles of champagne on the trip. The rest is at my house."

"Quite the complimentary package—renting your cabin to them."

"It makes for a nice income. The tips aren't bad either. And they've got rich friends, so it could be a profitable summer." Spence refilled her glass, spread pâté on a cracker, topped it with an anchovy, and handed it to her. He'd chosen a very salty cracker.

Marlo sniffed delicately at the snack and lifted the anchovy away. She tasted the pâté. "Turkey and chicken . . . truffles and port."

"Try this one." Spence spread another pâté on a thick cracker, handed it to Marlo, and lifted the champagne bottle to his lips.

"You're not supposed to guzzle champagne as if it was beer," she said.

Spence slapped some dark hard salami and very dry cheese onto a small square of crusty bread and munched on it. He considered Marlo. After a day of looking as if she wished she were anywhere else, but doing the job just the same—smiling when she had to and ignoring the sexual innuendoes of the couples—she was still keeping something to herself, guarding it.

She looked like a young boy in that getup, the worn jacket, the loose bib overalls, and that short, sexy haircut.

Spence inhaled the night and lifted the bottle to her. "Bet you've never guzzled in your life."

A few yards away, a man let out a whoop, and a woman giggled shrilly. Marlo stared glumly out onto the stream and took the bottle he handed her. She lifted it to her lips and drank slightly, wiping her mouth with the back of her hand. "They're scaring the wildlife. I wish they'd finish."

"They're just getting warmed up. They'll be partying tonight and sleeping late. We might as well enjoy the food and relax. I just keep 'em safe. They'll be quiet enough tomorrow.

We'll take them to my house, let them sleep it off, and we'll go back to town."

The bushes sounded and one of the men stumbled through, wearing only his shorts and his boots. Obviously drunk, he leered at Marlo. "Want to join the party?"

"No, thanks. We're having our own," Spence answered, and leaned back, taking Marlo with him. Using his weight, Spence pinned her beneath him. He held her still, lowered his lips to hers, and the other man didn't catch her struggle to be free.

The man smiled knowingly and turned back.

Spence allowed Marlo to push him away, and she sat up, those expressive eyes flashing at him. "You know what they think now, don't you?"

"It's easier this way. No one is offended."

"But I have to look at them tomorrow, and I might see them in town, and—" She lifted the champagne bottle, drinking deeply before she handed it to him. She wiped her mouth with the back of her hand, burped, and blinked at him.

Spence couldn't resist working up a really good burp and releasing it into the night. "Bet you can't do one like that."

"What?"

"A burp. You just let out a pretty good one, but it takes practice. Want me to show you how?"

She looked horrified. "This is awful. Spence, I'm scheduled for more television spots now. What if these people recognize me? What if—?"

"Someone tells good old Keith?" Spence supplied as he sat up and started spreading pâté on crackers, which he lined up on the high-priced cutting board. "In a different setting, doing your wallpaper thing and distressing furniture, they'll never recognize you."

"I am hungry," Marlo said as she took a cracker. "Are you sure, Spence?"

"Never more certain. So what does Cherry want you to tell me that you don't want to let go?"

Marlo licked the pâté off the cracker with her tongue in a gesture that fascinated Spence. She munched on the cracker thoughtfully and followed it with more champagne.

"Whatever secret you're holding must be good," Spence said. He watched, fascinated as Marlo dipped her fingers into the smoked oysters, lifted one, leaned her head back, and let it drop into her mouth.

She peered into the hamper and handed Spence a pickle jar. "Ah, veggies. A well-rounded meal."

He shouldn't have opened the expensive pickles. Moments later, Marlo slowly sucked on one and that sent his body into hard alert. In another minute, he'd embarrass himself. He took the pickle away from her and arced it high into the brush.

"Cherry taught me how to strip. I exercise every night," Marlo said brightly after another swig of the champagne and another burp.

"Thanks for gifting me with that bit of information. Try to keep it to yourself, will you?"

"Your customers would probably enjoy some entertainment. It's quite beautiful. I don't have the pole that Cherry set up in my bedroom, but I could make do. I'm getting pretty good."

Spence knew that his customers would expect to enjoy something more. He took the champagne bottle from her and discovered quite a bit of the bubbly was missing. He turned to see Marlo sliding down on the tarp and turning on her side to watch him. Spence finished the remaining crackers and settled back to contemplate the misery of his life.

The two women customers were apparently competing for the loudest orgasmic noises. The sounds echoed in the back of his brain, and Spence was certain it was because all the blood there had gone south.

He hadn't had sex for over two years, and the woman he wanted most to protect was lying all soft and warm next to him, watching him.

Spence glanced over his shoulder to Spot, who was staring at him, laying on the guilt trip.

"Do you think men really like all that noise?" Marlo asked in a whisper that roared and heated through his blood.

Spence didn't want to talk about what men liked. He knew, and didn't want to discuss it with a woman whose virginity he'd taken and who had been sweet and young, and had gotten pregnant right away. Marlo was one person with whom he did not want to talk intimately. "You should know. You were married."

"Cherry said Ryan was too quick and that I haven't had a real orgasm yet, not one to last on and on. How much longer do you think they can do that?"

Spence tossed a rock into the water and settled into his guilt, the backlash of his plan to get information from Marlo. "Depends. Look, you're feeling the champagne, talking too much, and you'll be embarrassed in the morning. Why don't you go to sleep?"

She lifted slightly and turned her head toward the rousing sexual noises. "But how long can they last, doing that?" she persisted.

"A while. They've had a few 'energy' pills to work off. Go to sleep."

Marlo turned back to him and settled comfortably. "You're wanting to know something I don't want you to know. You've got to forgive yourself, Spence."

He tuned into the change of topic from sex to "something" Marlo didn't want him to know. What was it?

When he turned back to Marlo, she was asleep.

It was a long time before Spence moved, just sitting there,

watching her sleep, wanting to slide inside her, to taste those soft lips, to warm the empty hole inside him with her. . . .

He picked up a stick, broke it as that sex-for-brains boy had torn Marlo's life apart long ago. He tossed the pieces away, listened to the heavy panting noises in the distance, the passionate groans and cries, and heard himself groan lightly with frustration.

And he still wanted Marlo every time he saw her.

And the tidbit that she hadn't had a "real orgasm yet" was enough to drive any man nuts.

He turned to see Spot, legs folded beneath his body, eyeing and blaming Spence, in advance of the deed.

Spence studied Marlo, asleep and without that guarded expression he'd come to expect when he was near. He'd taken her virginity in Lettie's backseat, wounded her terribly when she discovered she was pregnant, and here he was, still wanting to make love to her and give her that orgasm.

But he wouldn't. He was so damned honorable and noble that it really hurt, actually hurt.

Spence looked around, found a sizable rock and decided that he'd lift it for the same reason he lifted Lettie's bumper when he was that teenage boy long ago.

In the privacy of the biker's mountain lair, anger could be freed, and boots tramped back and forth on the old wood floor. "I am very angry. Marlo shouldn't have gone with Spence on that guide trip. She should know better. No lady acts like that. It's all that girl's fault, changing Marlo."

A bitter taste curled in the biker's mouth. *Wrong choices affected others' lives, ruining them.*

Ted Royston had learned that lesson the hard way, and so had Elsie Gerhard.

They'd had to die, and Traci, of course.

Because they had known The Secret.

In the mirror, the biker saw the face of a killer, eyes filled with flashing hatred.

Where were those condemning photographs?

Night had come and the time to hunt. Boots struck pavement, the helmet was on, the visor down. The powerful motor revved beneath the biker, and gravel shot from the tires as the motorcycle sped onto I-90, headed for Godfrey . . .

Six

MARLO HAD HEARD THAT MORNING-AFTER HEADACHES WERE bummers, and the medicine ball that had lodged itself inside her skull confirmed it.

She lay very still and tried to put her world together. It was the second week of June; she was on a mountain, the hovering mist around her scented with campfire smoke. Birds were starting to rouse, twin buzz-saw-type snores came from the direction of the other campers, and she was in a sleeping bag.

She slowly turned her head, waiting for the ball to stop bouncing off the inside of her brain, and saw Spence sleeping soundly next to her. He seemed so relaxed, the tension stripped away, that tough attitude gone.

Marlo didn't want to feel the tenderness that came slipping into her, the ache to hold him—because Spence wasn't a man to hold gently and to soothe. He'd want more, and she wasn't prepared to take him lightly. Whatever ran between them was more than an ache that should have been forgotten long ago—it was a dangerous, simmering fever, waiting to burst upon them. And Spence was pure trouble, not a schedule built into him, set to deprogram every woman in his path. . . .

She had to structure everything—or her world would come apart, and she couldn't trust herself . . .

Marlo eased from her sleeping bag and hurried into her early-morning routine, to the safety of it. She poured warm water from the big bucket left to warm by the evening's banked coals into a small bowl. The snores coming from the tangle of sleeping bags shattered the peaceful early dawn. Away from everyone, Marlo washed her face and, despite the chill, stripped away her jacket, pushed up her sweatshirt sleeves, and briskly washed her arms. In the shadows of the pines, she stretched them high and savored her privacy, the fresh air tingling upon her damp skin.

Behind her, a man's deep, long shuddering groan caused her to turn to him.

Spence, his jaw covered with stubble, his hair standing out on end, was on his feet, scowling at her. His legs were braced apart on the tarp, his sleeping bag tangled with one foot as if he'd just scampered out of it. He kicked the bag away.

In that brief time, the sexual tug between them was impossible to ignore.

Their stares had locked, and before Spence abruptly turned away, Marlo had felt red-hot stake of desire across the yards of mist. That heat had burned her face and body, and she'd never felt the need to walk up to a man, grip his hair, and take the searing kiss she wanted.

Marlo took a deep steadying breath. Spence Gerhard was the only man who could reach right into her and challenge her at a level that was far too dangerous.

She wasn't a fighter, but every time those gold eyes looked at her, that tension flew between them, she wanted to go to battle with him and win.

That evening, Spence followed Marlo's pickup into Godfrey and parked behind hers in the driveway.

When they stood facing each other, she hitched up her backpack and frowned at him. Marlo looked like a teenage boy, wearing a snit, sweatshirt, bib overalls, and her Fresh Takes ball cap pulled low over her eyes. "I've had enough of you."

The cute little strands of hair sticking out above her ears were driving him nuts; he wanted to lean down and kiss the top of her ears and work his way downward. "Likewise. When I get their final check, I'll pay you. Did you get the photos you wanted?"

With his customers using his cabin, Spence didn't want to leave Marlo. Lying close to Marlo last night, and aware now that she hadn't had a "real orgasm," Spence's body jumped into high alert every time she moved—or he saw those overalls tighten over her butt. That nice soft curvy butt running into long and strong legs . . .

Spence walked past her, ignored the sizzle of her temper, and rose up the steps to her back porch. "Let me in."

"You're not staying here. You can stay at your mother's."

"You're done ordering me around."

Spence opened his hand, palm up. "Keys. Because whoever manhandled Cherry might still around. You might think about that. I'll just take a stroll through before you get whatever you need. I'm dropping you off at your mother's."

Fear replaced stubborn pride as she handed the keys to her apartment to him. He opened the door and stepped inside to scan her home. When Marlo hesitated, he reached to grip her hand, tugging her inside. "Come on. You're not staying out here by yourself."

Marlo tugged free, walking to the blinking light on her message machine. Wilma had gone for an afternoon of bingo with the girls; she'd be back late. Then Cherry's cultured voice slid into the room. "Billy Bob turned in his eighteen-wheeler and picked up his restored Cadillac. He says he's taking off work to take care of me. Godiva and I are fine.

Billy Bob is very much the gentleman. He blushes. We're just relaxing by watching old movies and working out. He says I don't look really bad, but no way am I putting some poor cow's beef steak on my eye. I'll call tomorrow. We're in a really nice hotel in Seattle right now; here's the number."

Pearl Henderson's message said that she was rethinking a complete switch from country to contemporary. "Maybe a little something in between? I just can't cook without my little animals around me," Pearl suggested.

In Cherry's next message, she and the trucker had moved into a hotel with a kitchenette, and she was excited. "I've always wanted to learn dirty street fighting tricks, and Billy Bob is teaching me. We're cooking Chinese. He really thinks you should do a séance, Marlo. He knows someone who communicated with her grandmother. What could it hurt?"

Spence shook his head. "She'd better be okay. I didn't think much of her going off with him."

"She's a good judge of character."

He thought of how Cherry had trusted the people around her, how she had gone out into the truck stop's parking lot. "Sometimes she trusts too much. You're not thinking of doing that séance stuff, are you?"

Spence remembered his attack on Marlo, because she'd given his mother hope that Cody was still alive, and softened his words. "Look, just do me a favor and stay out of that mess, will you? Cherry wants that so-called ability so much that she's looking for it in everyone. Even me. Don't cater to her, Marlo."

"Of course I won't," she stated too firmly, just enough to cause Spence to question her with a look. "No," Marlo stated. "Look at me. My hair is cut to nothing, I've taken her place on a hiking trip with a grump—you—but she's not talking me into wooee-oo weird stuff."

"Good." With Marlo close behind, Spence led the way

through the rooms, all neat and clean. He stepped into the bathroom, a miniature feminine room, and caught the scent of her bath powder—everything was small and perfect and delicate, just like Marlo. He pulled away the shower curtain to reveal the bathtub, found a rubber duck and a pink hippo amid the floral bath products, and smiled grimly. "Nice duck."

"I still babysit once in a while, you know."

"No, I didn't. But I know you like it." He opened a walk-in closet door and looked at Marlo, who was standing behind Spence with her arms crossed. Spence scanned the framed photo of his nephew . . . *Cody, where are you?*

A quick cold pain shot through him before he closed the door to find Marlo frowning up at him. "That's quite a collection of cameras and equipment, books on photo developing . . . I didn't know you were that interested in photography and developing your own."

"You probably don't know a lot about me. The cameras are used, but in prime shape. When Mom gets a good one at the thrift shop, she calls me to look it over. I'm a hands-on kind of girl, so I like more than a point-and-shoot automatic. And I haven't tried developing, but I want to learn. I don't have much time, you know. And you just took a big chunk of it. Correction—you are taking it now."

Spence let that one go. The "hands-on kind of girl" remark echoed in his mind. He knew where he wanted his hands—and hers. "I've seen your work in the newspaper and at your mother's. It's good. Let me know if you need to shoot anything in the high country. There are some really pretty lakes up there, fed by melting snow. We'll take another hike."

"No," she stated firmly. "I said I've had enough of you, and I meant it."

"Likewise." Any more of sleeping beside Marlo, and he'd be that hot-hands kid again.

"You could be a lot nicer to people, you know. It's a wonder you have any customers at all. You glower, Spence. They didn't want to pick up the campsite."

"I wasn't doing it for them. I'd had a bad night, and that obligatory cleanup bit was listed in my brochure." Spence wasn't in the mood for a lecture. "You could have pushed Cherry into reporting that assault, but oh no, not you."

Marlo's hand shot out to grip his shirt. She leaned close and frowned up at him. "You are not—repeat not—going to mention that to her again. And you are not going to set off on your own manhunt. And you are not acting like my bodyguard. I know how dangerous this is. I'll be careful."

"She was careful, too—and she could outmatch most men in self-defense. This guy jumps from behind, and he's a stalker, picking his moment . . . I don't like the idea of Cherry not filing a report because she has some weird idea that she's protecting me."

"I don't think you have any say in that. And she regards you as family. Of course she's going to protect you."

Because he wasn't certain of himself now, Spence placed his fingers around Marlo's wrist—it was fragile and the skin soft, and—He removed her hand and moved away, down the hallway. At the back door, he turned to see that Marlo had followed him. "Lock this after me. Do whatever you need to do, and I'll be back to take you to your mother's."

"I lock the door every day and night, Spence," she stated too patiently. "You've got that look, all closed in and dark. . . . Don't go hunting for whoever hurt her. I don't want Cherry to come back and find you're in trouble because of her," she warned again.

"She was half-dead and dirty when he tossed her onto my front lawn. You just want this guy to walk away, after what he's done?"

"You're headed down to the Why Not Bar, aren't you?"

"It's a likely place for local studs, someone bragging about how they hurt a woman. I thought I'd have a beer and relax a bit. Cherry did some dancing there. You wouldn't lower yourself to come with me, would you?"

Marlo studied him; he was certain that she wouldn't step into something she considered to be a male hangout. Her next words wiped the smirk off Spence's lips—"Sure," she said. "Love to."

He straightened, and stared blankly at her. "You mean it?"

Marlo pushed him out of the door, then closed it behind her, locking it. "I want this guy as badly as you do. We might not have Cherry to identify him, but we might get some idea of who he is and do something on our own."

"I like that idea. But you stay out of it—" His suspicions jumped into full gear. "Marlo, you wouldn't set yourself up to catch this guy, would you?"

"Now, would I do that?"

"You saw what he did to Cherry, and you're just—I get it—if Cherry won't report an attack, you will, right?"

"That's logical. Why not?" she invited too easily.

"Because you're soft and sweet and helpless, and—I bet you haven't ever been in that bar."

"Oh, yes, I have. How do you think they got those Greta Garbo and Marlene Dietrich framed photos? And all the rest of them? I hunted for just the right prints, mats, and frames, and hung them. And after two long, exhausting days and one night with you growling at me, and those sex maniacs howling and screaming, I'm not exactly a cream puff. Who would know people would act like that?"

Spence couldn't resist teasing her. "Oh, I sure wouldn't. Would you, cream puff?"

"I have plenty of clues. Come on."

Spence stood still, and Marlo glanced up at him. "Problem?"

"You know people will gossip about us—maybe even say we're having an affair—if we turn up together at the bar." He had her there, Spence thought confidently. Marlo would back down, and he could get down to business. There was always someone who knew some small detail, and Spence was a very good hunter. . . .

"Let them talk," Marlo replied jauntily. "You think they didn't gossip when I was poor little housewife, working so hard to make a living for a man who was using me? I'm on this, Spence. I want this guy. You can come along, or you can stand there and glower at me. I always hate it when you glower. It always makes me want to prove that you have an absolute right to do so."

Marlo was something else, Spence decided. She had that tense, edgy look, and was trying to hide her study of the men at the bar. Marlo didn't know it, but that female-on-the-hunt look was just what men wanted.

Across the table from Spence and seated in the Why Not Bar's beer-scented shadows, Marlo was considering the men—and some were looking back, studying this newly cropped and scruffily dressed Marlo. When the foam from her mug of beer remained on her lip and that tongue slid out to lick it away, the men seemed to hold their collective breath as they leaned forward, wanting a taste of those full, gleaming lips.

Back in the days when they were steaming Lettie's windows and French kissing, Spence had known just how much damage that pink tongue could do.

To distract himself from the memory of how Marlo had enjoyed sucking and licking that pickle on the mountain, Spence thought it was a perfect time to ask, "So what was the trade-off, the reason Cherry talked you into cutting your hair? It must have been good, because you've had that hairdo forever. What didn't you want to tell me at Mom's house?"

She turned to him too quickly, her eyebrows raised, her eyes wide. Spence recognized that expression—like a doe stunned by approaching headlights and unable to move. Whatever she was hiding from him was definitely worth uncovering.

Marlo's expressive face changed, and Spence recognized that suddenly panicked look. "It really must have been good," he added. "Right now, you're trying to come up with something that isn't true. You never could lie, Marlo. Not to me."

Just then, Bjorn Johansen, a ski instructor and hiking guide, shoved off the bar and started toward their corner. Spence decided that the Swede was big enough to control Cherry, but if Bjorn had spoken at all, she would have recognized his accent.

Analu stood at the bar, watching Bjorn saunter toward their table. The big Hawaiian snow surfer, a winter instructor at one of the lodges, had been visiting a friend in the Bronx for two weeks. Or had he actually been in Godfrey? Spence made a mental note to check that out with Analu's live-in, Donna Austin, the local third-grade teacher and cosmetic saleswoman. Donna had worn a few unexplained bruises, and Analu had propositioned Cherry. He was definitely prime meat on Spence's watch-and-discuss-how-to-treat-a-lady list.

Bjorn was headed straight for Marlo, who was smiling at him. If Marlo was having trouble adjusting to the sexual fiesta on the mountains, she'd be really shocked with Bjorn. "Stop that," Spence ordered quietly.

"I never noticed how cute he is. Tall, tanned, and blond."

"Mountain Romeo or Stud Mountain like he calls himself when he's bragging about his women? I hadn't noticed. Good old Keith isn't going to like any of this. You've had a hard day, haven't you? Waking up with a hangover? Maybe it's time you called it a day."

Marlo gave him a shut-up-and-mind-your-own-business look. Then she tilted her head, lifted those fine, arched eyebrows, and challenged, "Are you? Calling it a day?"

He mulled that one over, using the sip of beer to delay his answer. He'd intended to see that Marlo was safe, then he wanted to start looking for the guy who had assaulted Cherry.

But Marlo was primed for an argument. "Oh, I see. This isn't equal opportunity, is it? I'm just a little helpless female."

Spence glared at her. She was definitely pricking his temper.

At their table now, Bjorn nodded to Spence. Spence returned the nod. "Not tonight," he said quietly, warning the big man off. "She's got a boyfriend."

"No, I don't. No one has tagged me like a dead deer. I belong to myself." Anger trembled in Marlo's low, uneven denial, those fascinating eyes narrowed at Spence, and a ripple of uneasiness ran up his nape.

"The lady can speak for herself, Gerhard. Those clothes and that new hairdo make her look perky and ready to party. I heard she took Cherry's place on that overnight hike. And she can speak for herself." The big man's deeply accented voice was rich with invitation, eager to show off his studly powers for a desirable woman.

"I said, she's got a boyfriend."

"Maybe she wants to change that, Gerhard. Step off."

"When I'm ready."

Marlo stared from Spence to Bjorn, and appeared alarmed. "I'll pass," she said quietly.

The big blond man nodded and flipped his business card on the table. "There's my number. You need anything, Marlo, just call."

Bjorn moved away; his look to Spence said there would be

another time, another place, and they would finish a long-standing grudge that had started five years ago. Bjorn hadn't liked his former live-in taking that mountain picnic to pick huckleberries with Spence—and to do other things—enough to get their backsides burned by the high-altitude sun.

"You're not taking your bad mood out on everyone. Let's go," Marlo said as she tucked the card in the front pocket of her bib overalls.

"Don't mess with that guy, Marlo," Spence warned as he reached, sliding the card from her pocket. He regretted the move, because the flesh beneath the denim was soft and pliant. He let the card drop to the floor and placed his hiking boot over it.

Marlo looked down at that boot, then back up at Spence. "I can reach him at any time, you know—if I want. Who do you think you are? My keeper?"

Spence stood, flipped some money onto the table for their bill, and looked down at her. "Look, guys have bar rules. You flirt with some guy, he comes on a little too much, and I'd have to take him on. Either that or I'd have to look him up and pick a fight. Then, when the rumors started about you, I'd have to explain to your mother why I didn't stop you. I like Wilma too much to let her know what a real pain in the butt you can be and that you're not as sweet as people think you are. Think of it, Marlo—two men brawling in the back alley, over a woman—you. Plus, I'm really tired, and it doesn't sound like fun. Bjorn doesn't follow the rules, exactly."

Her eyes widened. "You mean he's a street fighter?"

"He can break a few bones." Spence gave that a moment to sink in, then Marlo stood, sniffed elegantly, and began walking toward the door.

Spence didn't like the way Bjorn's and Analu's eyes followed her backside, as if they was gauging just how much heat was beneath those bib overalls.

Marlo ignored Spence as she walked down the street, into the driveway, and to her apartment's back door. There she shot him a narrow, forbidding look. He smiled blandly and waited, his arms crossed until with a sigh, Marlo unlocked the back door.

He shouldered by her and flipped on the light. The kitchen and living room were just the same. "In," he ordered and tugged Marlo into the apartment, securing the door behind her.

"You've been watching too much television," she muttered, and turned to punch her message machine button. Several new frantic messages from Wilma poured over the line, and before they were done, Marlo called her mother.

"Mom? I was going to call you when I got settled for the night. Are you all right? You said the shop and your house had been robbed?"

Spence moved closer, fearing that Wilma had met Cherry's fate. While she listened, Marlo's gaze locked with his. Then she covered the mouthpiece and whispered, "Someone broke into Mom's house and her thrift shop," she whispered. "She just got home. Whoever broke in just messed up the places so far as she can tell and took some little stuff."

Marlo hadn't protested Spence's arm around her, instead she leaned closer as she spoke, "Spence is here with me. Cherry is still . . . visiting relatives."

A brief hushed argument followed in which Marlo wanted to come to stay with her mother, and Wilma wanted her to stay with Spence. Marlo shoved away from Spence and turned from him. "I'm not going to ask him that."

"I'll stay with her, Wilma," Spence said loud enough to carry over the telephone.

Marlo frowned at him over her shoulder. "No, he's not. What? No, you're not coming over. You stay put."

She continued frowning at Spence while she listened to several worried messages from Keith. She dialed his number. "Hi, Keith. . . . Yes, I know, I just talked with Mom. She's got a houseful of people over there and doesn't need me. No, we just got back off the mountain, and I haven't had time to call you."

Marlo slid a look at Spence. "Um. Yes, we did stop at the Why Not for a beer. Ah . . . no, I'm fine. Don't come over. I'll talk to you in the morning before I go over to Mom's."

Spence settled in to mull Keith's relationship with Marlo; Keith's dislike of Cherry was obvious, and he was keeping track of Marlo. He had the temper to hurt, a sign one male recognized in another—a very possessive man who thought he had "tagged" Marlo. If Cherry was in his way, would Keith make a point of teaching her to stay away from Marlo?

When she replaced the telephone, Marlo explained quickly about the break-in at the thrift shop and at Wilma's house. Nothing expensive was taken so far as Wilma could detect, but she hadn't straightened everything yet. The police were watching the shop and her house. Two Bingo Girls and their adult sons were spending the night with her. Wilma was thriving on the excitement, thrilled to cook and play host, but had been worried about Marlo.

"So you still think Cherry doesn't need to file that report, huh?" Spence demanded as he started moving deeper into Marlo's apartment. "Stay behind me."

Marlo followed him. "Mom has had break-ins at the thrift shop before. It's usually someone down on their luck who takes things that they desperately need. She says if they need it that bad, she doesn't begrudge them. One time, a man just needed a place for his family to sleep in the hard winter. Their car was stalled, and the town asleep. They saw quilts and some food in the shop. They were desperate, and that was enough to break in—just a warm place to sleep."

"I remember. And Wilma took them into her house for a week. She'd better think twice about that now—especially after Cherry's assault. That's another reason, Cherry better file some kind of a report, even now—to warn people what *can* happen."

Spence was moving down the hallway to the shop in front of the building. They made a thorough search before he headed back to the living room. He walked toward the couch, sat to unlace his boots, and said, "I'm not going anywhere tonight. So don't bother trying to evict me, unless you really want to embarrass yourself."

After a long relaxing shower and shampoo, Marlo walked into her closet to deposit her film and return her camera to the shelf with the others. She turned on the overhead light and noted Cody's portrait, tilted just that bit. With a touch, she straightened it and noted a lens cap was off one camera, an older seventies model she'd loved immediately from the moment she saw it in her mother's shop. A photograph had slipped from an album and was lying on the floor.

She picked it up and reached for the shelves filled with her looseleaf archival albums, carefully labeled for each event. The album from which it had come—her collection of fisheye shots of Godfrey's Main Street during the Halloween parade twelve years ago—was missing. So were the negatives that she had labeled and placed within the three-ring archive binder.

The other looseleaf binders, filled with plastic and labeled sheets of her photographs, were rearranged. The ones in which she had taken shots of crowds at different town celebrations had been taken.

The room seemed to shimmer, closing in tightly on Marlo. Then bursts of heat and storm seemed to explode; the small dark room seemed alive with violence and hatred that clawed and lashed at her.

It was the same earthshattering sense of anger that she'd felt in Elsie's kitchen.

Marlo hurriedly stepped outside the closet, slamming the door behind her.

Still caught by the sense of fury, she slowly looked up at Spence.

"Marlo? What's wrong?" Spence opened the door and peered inside.

She fought for breath, her heart beating wildly, as he turned to her. How could *she tell him that whoever had been inside her closet had been the same person who had killed his mother?*

And how could she know that with certainty? All she had was her senses, picking up waves after waves of red-hot fury. . . .

Marlo rubbed her forehead and tried to clear it. Whatever was happening to her wasn't real. . . . It wasn't real. . . .

Then shaking, still caught by the violence and anger she'd felt, Marlo simply moved into his arms.

"Hey," Spence said softly, gathering her against him. "What's wrong? Marlo?"

She couldn't tell him . . .

Spence reached to open the closet door and click off the light. She couldn't move, couldn't speak. He reached down to pick her up and edged through the narrow hallway, carrying her to her bedroom. She clung to his shoulders and pressed her face to the safety of his throat.

He eased her down to sit on the bed and gently pushed her head down between her knees. He sat beside her. "Take it easy, Marlo. Just sit there and breathe deep."

She couldn't breathe, locked in the startling impact of the

rage she had sensed. Marlo focused on his hand, open upon her back, smoothing it. "I'm okay."

"I don't think so." Spence drew her close against him. "You've got to tell someone about what's going on with you, Marlo," he said gently, against her temple.

She couldn't tell him . . . When she eased away and sat quietly, Spence stood. "Okay, have it your way. Just sit there, and I'll be right back in a minute—I'll make tea—"

Yes, that was logical, Marlo thought, fighting for reality. Spence's mother had taught him to make tea at stressful times. He'd made tea for Cherry after the attack. Marlo struggled to pull herself back from the anger she'd felt within the closet. She caught his hand. It was big and safe and warm; she anchored herself to his strength, pulling away from the chill and violence. "Don't . . . don't leave me."

Spence eased onto the bed beside her, clearly concerned. He smoothed her hair. "What just happened? You look like you did in Mom's kitchen."

She shook her head. She couldn't tell him that in her mind, her senses, the link between her closet and his mother's kitchen was palpable violence, enough to kill. . . . "I'm just tired. It's been a long day."

"Marlo, you're not telling me something very important." Violence and anger shimmered around Spence; it was only slightly less than what she had felt inside the darkroom—and at Elsie's.

"No." She didn't want to deal with anything. She wanted to hide from what ran terrifying and unbidden, unfounded in reality, inside her.

Spence cursed again, a raw burst of anger that ricocheted around her bedroom, tearing at her. "Leave me alone, Spence. I can't take any more tonight."

Marlo lay back and curled on her side. The bed depressed, and Spence's hand circled her ankle. "Marlo—"

She kicked lightly, a warning that she wanted to be left alone. His hand remained. Then the bed creaked slightly, and she turned to see him lying next to her. "I'm staying," Spence stated grimly.

Marlo was on her feet instantly. She pointed to the door and found Spence's gaze locked to the gap in her robe. His gaze traveled down to material that parted to reveal her thighs.

An answering jolt of raw hunger shot low and hot in her body and trembled down her legs. Sex with Spence now would be a perfect way to wipe away the anger that had circled her, the fear that she now felt—someone was definitely prowling Godfrey, and Marlo was involved and hated.

She adjusted her robe; she didn't like Spence's satisfied expression—he knew he'd gotten to her. His look at her was meant to distract, and it had been successful. "Out. Just get out. In the morning, I'll tell Mom that I didn't want you here."

"Okay, but it's going to look very strange to anyone passing this place to see me camped out on your back porch."

While she was mulling her choices and weighing the resulting gossip, Spence walked to her, kissed her forehead, and asked, "What's the matter? Wasn't this on your schedule? You get all frustrated and wired when things aren't neatly stacked up to your liking, don't you? The break-in at your mother's house and shop weren't on your daily schedule, were they? You can't arrange everything to your liking, Marlo. And by the way, that's a real foxy look—you all hot and wired as if you'd like to jump me."

Then Spence walked to the bathroom and turned and winked at her.

Marlo was left with nothing to do but hit the door with her fist, "I am not foxy, Gerhard. You are *not* staying the night."

The door jerked open and Spence peered out, clearly using

the door as a shield for the rest of his naked body. "You said something? Did you want me?" he asked with a grin. "Oh, by the way. The couch is fine."

Marlo reached for the doorknob to close it, and Spence's hand reached to close around hers. He brought it to his mouth, kissing it before she could jerk away. His look down at her was grim. "I'm staying, pussycat. Your mother has enough worry, and something is definitely wrong—you were white and shaking when you came out of that closet. If you're going to get sick, you'll need someone—and since I'm here, anyway, what's the big deal?"

He ran a fingertip between her eyebrows and over each one. "Now simmer down. I'll be gone before the town wakes up."

This time he leaned down to kiss her lips. The touch was light and tender, but caught Marlo's lips slightly parted. The contact paused and breathed and waited just on the edge.

In the same movement, Spence brought her hand to his bare chest and moved around to stand in front of her.

"You infuriate me," she whispered, staring up at him.

"You fascinate me," he returned, and smoothed his lips to one corner of her mouth, kissing it. He smoothed his cheek against hers and whispered into her ear, "You're breathing hard, sweetheart. I can feel your heart pound. You want me, don't you? Don't feel bad about that. Most women do."

"Now *that's* confidence."

Her hand was on his chest, open over the hard steady beat. She could almost feel him inside her, wrapped around her, moving and smoothing in rhythm, one breath, one sigh—She should move away, but she couldn't. From her hand, the heat from his body seemed to move up her arm, spreading into her body, flowing as naturally as the tide; it undulated within her, shocking and familiar and necessary, warming all the still, cool corners she wanted to protect.

She caught Spence's quick, questioning frown just before

he deepened the kiss. Her senses leaped, spiked, and smoothed as she moved to meet him on a level that wasn't in the past, or in the future. She let herself flow inside him, blend with him, seeking to find that incredible hunger and match it, tame it.

Spence's arms tugged her close, his body aroused against hers while she fed and tasted and explored and took his hunger into her.

He felt like an explosion of everything dark and wild and necessary and primeval within her, and her fingers dug into his hair, his chest. She flowed deeper, seeking more. Nothing bound her, or controlled her, restraints slipping away.

Spence's heat seemed to throb all around her. She felt inside it, tested it. It was very careful heat, too careful, fearful of her, for her. He was afraid of hurting her, but he cared deeply, leashing what he wanted. In another heartbeat, he'd draw away, keeping her safe from him. . . .

That wouldn't do. Marlo stepped into his fear, wrapped it around her, soothed it by a woman's invitation—Her robe had parted, and Spence's arousal pressed hard and hot, erect against her belly.

"Marlo . . . sweetheart . . ." His voice held just the edge of hunger she wanted, and Marlo prowled around it, listening, waiting as she moved against him, set to take, to tear away what he wanted to protect—

Spence lifted his head, scanned her face, and slowly looked down to where her breast lay exposed and pressed against his chest. His breath came as a low, frustrated groan; and then he bent to taste her.

She had him. Or did he have her? Marlo frowned slightly, her body pounding, heating, flowing.

Pleasure ripped through her, rich and ripe and increasing with each tug of his lips, each seeking kiss upon her breasts.

Her hips moved against him, and she heard incredible sounds—her own, pouring out of her.

Desired by a male counterpart who wanted more, his hands flowing over her, tracing her body, drawing away her robe, Marlo moved into that complete freedom. She flew above logic and won'ts and the structure life had constricted around her.

With a sudden rough sound, Spence picked her up and carried her to the bed, tossing her upon it. He scowled down at her, his lips pressed tight. "Not like this. Not with you."

Marlo drew the bedspread across her shaking body and watched Spence's tall taut body retreat into the bathroom. The sound of the shower began, and Marlo scrambled for her robe, tying it tightly around her.

In just a few more heartbeats, they would have made love.

She'd stepped out of her schedule, out of her control, and she'd almost made love with Spence. Her body still echoed, throbbed with that need. Too much had happened; she had been too susceptible to the couples having sex, and listening to them would stir anyone. Her mother's break-in, her own, and Spence's dark moods were enough to tear away the tight wrap she kept on her emotions.

Marlo hurried to the kitchen, and her hands shook as she made tea. She gripped the cup with both hands, which still felt Spence's hot skin, the way it was tight, almost bursting . . . She'd never felt so strong or so wild as when she was hunting, discovering Spence, seeking to—to what? Conquer him?

She pushed back that thought and it came back again. Her emotions seemed to be jumping everywhere, out of her control, nudged by sensations of rage and sexual need—So much rage, so much primitive, immediate need. . . .

The red light on a patrol car ricocheted off her kitchen window as steady as a human pulse—Always red. Red through glass, red reflected in glass . . . *Why red? Why glass? Why?*

In the closet, Cody's picture had caught her, the glass reflecting the red cloth . . . Cherry's red paisley shirt and her crystal . . . Marlo's own image in the camera lens . . .

Panicked now, she hurried into the shop to seek something that could act as a warning system; whoever had such rage might return to hurt her. . . . She glanced at the familiar shadows and hurried to a box of Christmas decorations—huge sleigh bells, garnished with red plaid ribbons and artificial holly. She slid the attached ribbons over her wrist, and the big bells jingled as she checked the shop's door to find it safely locked. She looped the bell's ribbon around the knob—any movement and the bell would ring. . . . The big brass bells jingled from her wrist as she closed the door between the shop and her apartment, locking it and bracing a chair beneath the doorknob. She attached another bell to the knob, shook it slightly and, satisfied that it would ring, hurried to her apartment door.

The dead bolt was secure, but Marlo hauled a chair to the door, propping it beneath the knob. She quickly hung another bell over the knob.

Marlo rubbed her temple, trying to erase images gripping her. She didn't like this Marlo, or trust her. On her wrist, the remaining two bells jingled, and Marlo stared at the bright red plaid ribbon crossing her flesh—like trails of blood. "Get a grip, Marlo," she whispered unevenly.

The ribbon had twisted, the bells jingling as she worked to free herself, of the cloth, of the images, of the rage she'd felt in Elsie's kitchen. . . .

And it was Spence's fault. He was the only man to break inside what she controlled.

She blinked, recalling what Spence had said, "What did he mean, 'Not this way . . . Not with you'?"

But she knew. Spence knew he had hurt her badly once, and he wouldn't again.

Marlo worked frantically to free herself. She really didn't like Spence calling the shots on what she wanted and didn't want. That was only round one. She intended a second.

Everything had to go back the way it was, when it was safe, when—

The police light returned, cycling a red tint on the window's glass. It lit the room, pooling red all around her, capturing her in the color, and she couldn't move—

"I thought I heard bells . . ." Spence came into the kitchen, a towel wrapped around his hips. Water beaded on his hair and his chest. Toweling fuzz had caught on his jaw's stubble. He turned slowly to see the bells hanging from the doorknobs. Spence shot her a dark look and set to work to free her. "Tell me what's wrong," he said quietly.

Everything was wrong. His mother had been murdered . . . Cody's picture seemed cloaked in red . . . Cherry's attack . . .

The red ribbons bit into her skin, and Marlo worked feverishly to free herself. "Get them off. *Get them off!*"

"You're all tangled. Should I cut them? Marlo, you're shaking. What's the matter? Why the bells on the doorknobs? Why are you so scared?"

"Don't cut them. Just get them off," she whispered desperately. Whatever tangled in her senses, it shouldn't be cut—

Spence freed her hand and tossed the bells and ribbons to the counter. He crossed his arms and looked down at her. "Tell me. Something is really wrong, Marlo. You were terrified just now."

"Lock the door on your way out." The sound of her voice was uneven, unconvincing. She had to say the words to project courage that she didn't actually possess. But she knew he wouldn't leave; Spence would stay to protect her. He was like that—dependable when others were in need—and he knew that she was afraid.

Afraid of ribbon? Again, the color of red, haunting her. Red, the color of rage, the color of blood.

She couldn't explain, not to Spence, not to a man who had lost all of his family, who would hunt until he found his nephew's body.

Marlo left Spence in the kitchen and hurried into her bedroom, closing the door behind her. She slid into bed and listened to the sound of the bells, of Spence moving through her house—the running of water in her kitchen sink. Then the floorboards creaked in her hallway, more tinkling sounds, and Spence filled the doorway. "Are you okay?"

"Sure. Thanks." Her voice sounded too high-pitched, too cheerful.

"You never were a good liar." He crossed the shadows slowly and eased onto the bed, turning to draw her close. "I finished your Christmas decorating," he murmured sleepily. "There is a sleigh bell on the bathroom door, the bedroom door, and your going-to-be darkroom. All we need is a big Clydesdale and a sled."

Somehow that seemed to be the perfect thing she needed to hear. She wanted to say she was glad that he stayed. Instead, she whispered, "Do you think Cherry is okay?"

Things to say, comforting normal things, helped, words flowing in the night . . .

"She'd better be," he answered grimly. "Go to sleep."

Whatever had happened, this was a friend who had come to comfort her, to keep her safe, and Marlo let herself drift into sleep.

She awoke to Spence breathing slowly, heavily at her side. She didn't want to wake him, because then he might leave.

She settled down close to him and admitted that she was very, very frightened. Just for tonight, she needed Spence to stay with her. . . .

The vivid waves of hatred and rage she'd felt in her camera closet were the same as the ones she'd felt in Elsie's kitchen. . . .

Who had come into her home? Exactly what pictures and negatives had they taken? Why?

Seven

MARLO HAD DOZED AND ROUSED SLIGHTLY TO FIND SPENCE spooned against her back, nuzzling her cheek. The sheet had been pulled away, and the only thing between them were a few folds of her cotton nightgown. "Spence," she whispered. "Wake up."

"Um?" The sound was raw and masculine and packed with intimate sensuality. His hand cruised over to her waist, flattened, and slid upward to curve expertly around her breast. His thumb found her nipple beneath the cloth and toyed with it, sending a jolt of pure warm liquid through her. Then it caressed downward, found the hem of her nightgown and slid under it.

She could have moved. Could have pushed his hand away, but the way he was spooning closer, heat vibrating off his skin, the hard nudge that had slid between her thighs, fascinated her. Unscheduled sex, waking up while already making love, fascinated her.

Marlo drifted through her thoughts: No preshower, no clinical sex, just to let herself float and feel, and maybe have her once-in-a-lifetime orgasm.

Spence was breathing slow and hard, his lips busy at her throat while his fingers edged inside her panties, cupping her, caressing her. She gripped his wrist and tried to speak, but that long-awaited orgasm lurked just within her—his fingers slid lower, stroking her intimately, and a hard, hot quiver shot through Marlo as she wondered if it was really true about that little spot—

He began to move, undulate behind her in rhythm to his hand, his breath hot and moist against her ear.

And when she let out the uneven sigh she'd been holding, preparing to wake him, Spence stiffened. He held very still, his fingers still pressed within that slick groove, then in the next instant, he'd released her, flattening to his back, his hand over his face. "Marlo, you should have stopped me," he gritted darkly.

She wouldn't lie; left on the cusp of unfinished pleasure, she wasn't happy. Spence had just ruined another perfectly good plan. She sat up and flopped a pillow over his face. "Do you just automatically wake up in that condition? You know everything, don't you? Just how long does it take a man to learn how to do things like that?"

He crushed the pillow in his fist and brought it downward to cover his jutting erection. He glared up at her. "I'm just a natural. I started with you, remember? If I'd have known a little bit more—"

Her words struck the shadows, echoing around them. *"You were a virgin?"* she asked incredulously.

Spence leaped out of her bed and, still holding the pillow in front of him, stared down at her. He looked rumpled, flushed, and disgusted.

"I've been saving that tidbit for the wrong moment. Or maybe never," he said. Then he turned, leaving her with the image of his taut backside—the pillow still held in front of him—and slammed into the bathroom.

"But I thought that—" she whispered to the empty room.

The sound of the shower running caused her to state grimly, "Well, you sure made up for it, Gerhard."

She snuggled down into her bed, pulled the sheet up primly over her chest, and folded her hands over it. She waited until Spence jerked open the bathroom door and glared at her. "Where do you want me to sleep?" he demanded.

"Preferably your own bed."

"That's occupied. My house is rented, and the beds are probably quite busy now."

"Your mother's place then."

"Wrong. Wilma thinks I'm here to protect you, and I'm not letting her down."

Because she really didn't want to be alone for the few remaining hours until dawn, Marlo said, "The couch is okay. You have a pillow. Sheets are in the living room closet."

After a moment she had to ask the question nagging her. "On the mountain—why did you set out to get me drunk?"

Spence paused on his way out of the bedroom. He didn't turn. "To get what I wanted, little girl."

She knew that while Spence might torment her, he wouldn't cross the line he'd drawn for himself—he'd just proven that truth.

"Spence?" She couldn't tell him about his mother, but— "I'm worried."

"I'll be gone before anyone knows I stayed here."

Marlo looked at the shadows on her ceiling. She had more to worry about than gossip. The rage that had hit her, that she had sensed several times, could kill again. . . .

Or was it all in her mind?

Marlo wasn't the only one to lie awake; Spence lay on the couch, his mind turning. . . .

She was terrified.

Her reaction to his mother's kitchen and to her closet had been the same.

The ribbons had tangled around her wrist, and she'd been frantically tugging at them when he'd entered the kitchen.

The terror on Marlo's face wasn't something he could push away easily.

Lying close to Marlo that first time hadn't helped his need of her—neither had awakening to her snuggling to him, her long soft bare leg crossed over his, her face warm against his throat and her breast—well, her breast lay next to his chest, and only a thin layer of rosebuds on cotton separated their flesh.

At the center of her bedroom, the pole that ran from ceiling to floor had taunted him with erotic images of Marlo moving sensually around it. Spence didn't want to think of what she did in that little cafe-style chair . . . or how she climbed the pole to sunbathe naked on the roof as Cherry had said. The imagine of Marlo's bare bottom going up and through that trapdoor wasn't going away.

He'd been perspiring by the time he untangled himself carefully from her body. But she'd cuddled against him again, and he'd fallen asleep with her in his arms. Then he had awakened a second time, with his hands on her, ready to make love.

Spence tightened his hands behind his head, his body taut with sexual energy. Marlo always had the ability to stir him more than any other woman, and the scent of her, her freshly showered body tucked into that robe, would be enough to set any man off—like Keith.

He inhaled slowly. Good old Keith. He wouldn't be happy, and Keith had some of the same dark edges to him as his father. If he ever hurt Marlo—

She'd been hurt enough by her ex-husband . . .

Spence walked into the kitchen and started making coffee. He was on his second cup when a brisk, commanding knock sounded at the apartment door.

After Wilma's busy night, she wasn't apt to be up at six o'-clock. Cherry was still out of town, and logic said there was only one other person. Spence walked to remove the chair propped against the door. He opened the door to the sound of the sleigh bell, a blast of too-bright sunlight, and a clearly angry man. "Keith."

"Spence." Keith inhaled sharply. His blue eyes quickly scanned Spence's bare chest, boxer shorts, and bare feet.

Spence took in Keith's harried appearance: He hadn't shaved, his usually impeccable brown hair stood out in peaks, his wrinkled dress shirt and slacks looked as though they had been slept in, and his shirt was untucked. In lieu of his usually highly polished dress shoes, he was wearing moccasins.

The next thing Spence noticed was that Keith had beefed up his physique. Keith had always been tall and lean, but there were new bulges under his shirtsleeves, and his neck looked more muscular. His hands had lost that narrow, soft look, the fingers and palms wider, as if they'd been reshaped by hard work. With his shirtsleeves rolled back, the cords on his arms stood out in relief.

In a silent motion, Spence swept his hand in front of him, beckoning Keith to enter. "Marlo is still sleeping."

"I talked to her last night. She—wasn't herself." Keith entered the apartment, standing stiffly as he looked around the apartment. He scanned the apartment. "I heard you two were down at the Why Not Bar. Stay all night after that, did you?"

Keith's tone implied that Spence had plied Marlo with drink and had his evil way. Spence decided that he'd let Marlo explain whatever she wanted. "We had a late night. From the looks of it, you did, too. Coffee?"

"No, thanks."

Spence shrugged, and asked, "You want me to wake up Marlo?"

That brought an angry flush to Keith's unshaven cheeks. "Don't you have enough to keep you busy with that—Cherry—living at your house? Oh, yeah, that's right. Wilma said Cherry was visiting relatives. I guess that explains why you made your move when Marlo was upset about her mother's shop and house being robbed."

Spence decided to let Keith's accusation pass and see just what the other man knew. "What did they take?"

"A few pictures, some albums. They tore everything apart and made a mess. If Marlo was scared to stay alone, she should have called me. We've been dating for a long time. This doesn't change anything—you, I mean. She'll come to her senses. You're not the kind of man she needs."

"And you are?"

"I can offer her stability. What have you got?"

Keith had a point. Spence toasted him with the lift of his coffee cup. "Not much. Hey, Marlo! Wake up!" he called. "We've got a visitor."

"I'll kill him." Marlo dressed hurriedly, splashed water on her face, brushed her teeth, and set off to kill Spence Gerhard. "'*We've* got a visitor . . . *we've*,'" she repeated as she hurried into her living room.

The sight of two men—Spence, dressed only in his undershorts, and Keith, shrouded by a cape of disapproval and anger—stopped her at the doorway. "Oh, good morning, Keith," she managed shakily.

With a look she didn't understand, Spence walked into the kitchen, leaving Keith and her alone. "I—"

"What's he doing here?" Keith interrupted angrily. "Didn't you have enough of him up there on the mountain? I thought we meant something to each other. I thought you'd gotten over him."

Marlo slid an I'll-get-you look at Spence in the kitchen. His expression was too innocent. No telling what he had implied to Keith. She turned back to Keith, who was studying her closely. "You've cut your hair. You knew I liked it the way it was. And you cut it anyway."

His anger and frustration curled around her. But there was something else—something sweet and kind, and she regretted hurting him. "It's more practical this way—"

"If you're going to be hiking and camping in the mountains with Gerhard, I suppose."

"Breakfast is ready," Spence called from the kitchen. "Come and get it."

When Keith scowled and reached for the doorknob, Marlo couldn't let him go away thinking that—She touched his shoulder and stiffened. She could feel anger in him, simmering, unfed . . . Could Keith have anything to do with his father's murder, or with Elsie's death? She had to know. . . . "Keith, please stay, won't you?"

"Is *he* leaving?" Keith demanded darkly.

Marlo looked at Spence, who stared back. By the set of his jaw and the way his eyes narrowed at her, she knew he wouldn't leave. "No," she said. "Not just yet."

Keith was angry now, glaring at Spence, who wasn't making things easier—and Marlo had to probe the sensations she now felt in Keith . . .

In the kitchen, the two men continued staring at each other. Spence leaned back against the counter, then his stare shifted down to Marlo. It was a gauging look, as if he wondered about her relationship with Keith, if they were lovers. Then his lips moved slightly, just enough to taunt her. That hard curve said too much: *If they were lovers, then Keith wasn't very good because she hadn't had that orgasm. . . .*

Regretting her own flash of temper and uncomfortable with the primitive vibrations flowing around her, Marlo moved between them. "Please. Let's all have breakfast together, okay? I'm going over to Mother's later and—"

"And I'll come with you," Keith stated firmly as he pulled out a chair for her to sit. He sat close to her, his arm over the back of her chair. "You both need my support."

"That's big of you, but no thanks," Spence said, as he placed toast and coffee in front of Marlo.

Keith's hard stare at Spence said that "both" didn't include an opponent.

Spence shoved a plate of pancakes in front of Keith and sat, leaning back to study Keith and Marlo, as if he were dissecting their relationship. His legs stretched beneath the table, his bare toes playing with hers. She shifted slightly away, removing the contact. "Ever have breakfast here before, Keith?" Spence asked.

The question was loaded with macho first-come, male-staking-rights possession, and caused Marlo to shove her bare foot against Spence's. He trapped it between both of his and smiled blandly at her, this time with amusement. His toes rubbed her ankles as she struggled to conceal her temper. He didn't stop when she shot him a dark look; Spence had never lost his boyish need to play cat and mouse with her, to upset her schedules and logic. But the adult topics were even more infuriating.

Marlo fought for a normal conversation topic—normal wasn't having two tall, bristling men in her small kitchen.

Keith took a deep breath and spoke specifically to Marlo, dismissing Spence. "I know you two dated in high school and for a time after Spence went to college. So you have a past—and Wilma has always liked you, Spence. But she's been very kind to me in the last few years, since my divorce from Natalie. I can understand Wilma's need to keep her daughter safe in times like these."

He leaned closer, and his voice lowered intimately. "Marlo, I won't say anything about finding Spence here, and I won't be upset about the gossip that is certain to arise about you taking Cherry's place in Spence's outfitting and mountain guide business. I forgive you for that, Marlo. I know that Cherry had to leave immediately to visit her ailing relatives and as her friend, you fell under her childish persistence to have you substitute. I'm certain that everything went well with the trip, did it?"

"Yes, it did. Cherry wouldn't have left without—" One of Spence's big feet had shifted; his toes were smoothing her toe ring, and his amused study of Marlo said that he'd noted Cherry's "wild-side" influence.

Then Spence smiled coolly at Keith. "You look like you're in pretty good shape. Working out much, Keith?"

Marlo glanced at Spence and by the flick of those gold eyes recognized his implication: Keith looked strong enough to control a woman like Cherry. Keith had never liked Cherry, and Spence knew it. Did he actually think that Keith would physically harm Cherry?

She frowned at Spence, who shrugged, then at Keith, who had just taken her wrist. It was a possessive gesture and one that Spence's eyes had noted. A muscle on his throat and running up into his jaw tightened as he met Marlo's stare, locking with it. Shaped around his coffee cup, his fingers had tightened until the knuckles had turned white.

Keith had held her too many times, giving her the opportunity to deepen their relationship. There was no way that Keith would hurt a woman. Was there?

On the pretense of rising and turning off the coffee brewer, Marlo eased her arm away from Keith. When she returned to the table, she served Spence a sideways frown that was meant to keep him civil.

Keith's cool, hard tone broke the static silence. "I manage to work out a few hours a week. My father didn't use his home gym much in the past few years, and I saw no reason to set up a separate one in my home—although Marlo might have used it there. After my divorce, it was a way to spend those empty hours without my sons—and when I wasn't with Marlo," he added carefully. "Do you ever do anything on a consistent basis, Spence? Have a real schedule of any kind?"

"I have a schedule. I get up sometime in the morning, and I sleep sometime before the next morning."

Keith's disapproving expression cleared as he turned to Marlo. "I'll walk you over to your mother's."

"You two kids run along. I'll stay here and clean up," Spence offered, and Keith's frown swung back to him.

Marlo could feel the anger bristling over the table; she placed her hand on Keith's and from the vibration within her, she knew the anger was all his. One look at Spence, and she knew he was deliberately toying with Keith.

"You're not staying here," Marlo stated firmly, and with her free foot added a warning kick beneath the table. Spence was just as irritating as he had ever been, digging in to challenge Keith. She didn't trust that glint in Spence's dark eyes, the way Keith's were narrowing at the other man. In school sports events, Keith could never match Spence; that competitive sense had remained.

Keith took a deep breath, one that Marlo recognized. Like her, Keith liked a peaceful life and sturdy logic. His grim expression said he was working for control. His reply held a primitive growl that surprised Marlo. "Gerhard, I've never said this, but you're a life's dropout. And while Mike Preston and the investigators may have gone easy on you after my father's death, I'm still not certain you weren't involved. Mike

Preston may be your good buddy—because you rescued his son from that snow avalanche, but as Godfrey's police chief, he shouldn't have gone to bat for you during that investigation. I've told him that much."

Spence placed his coffee cup on the table. The gesture was too thoughtful, too slow, like that of a man barely controlling his temper. "Anytime, Royston."

"Marlo doesn't need you pushing her at a time like this."

"Says who?" Spence questioned easily. "By the way, you don't look like you had much sleep. You know where I was for two days and two nights. Where were you last night?"

Marlo was stunned at his blatant question of Keith. "Spence, stop it."

"I understand his need to take what little he can and use it against me, Marlo. We've never been friends. He was jealous of my advantages while growing up. But he only became openly antagonistic toward our family when my father started dating Elsie."

"Was that when it was? Or maybe you just got more sensitive a little earlier," Spence stated softly.

Keith's body tensed, and the angry waves emanating from him startled Marlo—her senses prickled slightly, warningly, as if at any moment the rage she had felt at Elsie's home and in her closet was swirling within Keith. "Keith—"

"Where I was and what I was doing last night is none of your business, Spence . . . but I was going over the store's books at my home." Keith spoke directly to Marlo, and she understood the point he was making: She should have called him, and he didn't like her choice of Spence as a protector.

Spence also spoke directly to Marlo. "I'd like to go to Wilma's with you. Maybe I can help."

"I doubt it." Keith's blue eyes were flashing now, a vein in his temple standing out in relief.

"I know. I have an idea. Let's *all* go to Mom's," Marlo

stated cheerfully. Right then she felt like the bone tugged between two bristling dogs, and she needed to see her mother.

Keith continued to glare at Spence. But Marlo didn't trust Spence's easy smile or his, "Fine with me."

After one look at Wilma's ransacked home and the bustling activity there, Spence had decided that he needed some thinking space and returned to his mother's home.

At nine o'clock in the morning, Wilma and Marlo and friends were busy straightening her house. Later, they'd work at the thrift shop. Keith clearly wasn't leaving the field, taking charge when he could. Marlo was acting jittery, as if she expected the worst from Spence. When they passed, Marlo's expression changed from that slight, distracted frown to one of disdain, punctuated by thoughtful studies of him.

Maybe she was wondering if he had had anything to do with Ted's death.

Spence dropped the unopened mail he was holding onto the kitchen cabinet. He didn't like the way Keith touched Marlo, the way he'd held her wrist—too possessively.

"I see how you're looking at Keith. Don't you dare start anything. He's my friend, and you're acting as if we've got something going. We don't," she'd whispered as she hurried by him in Wilma's hallway.

"Now why would I do that?" he had asked, and knew the reason—a little thing called jealousy said Spence didn't want Marlo waking up to Keith in the mornings.

Wilma's statement to Godfrey's police chief had caused Marlo to flush. "I'm so glad Spence stayed with Marlo last night," Wilma had said. "After this break-in, I just needed to know that she was safe."

"I had that same feeling when my son was caught in the snow avalanche and Spence risked his life to get to him—to stay with him. I really didn't want to bring Spence in for questioning when Ted was murdered, but that argument the day before couldn't be ignored." Mike Preston had continued with his questioning, while Keith had bristled ominously next to Marlo.

Spence had noted the subtle change in Marlo, shifting just that fraction away from Keith when he was angry.

Why? Had he hurt her? Keith had muscled up, and he could easily handle Marlo.

Spence frowned as he collected and went through the mail. He was definitely getting a straight answer from Marlo on that one.

He studied Cody's picture on the kitchen wall. The picture in Marlo's closet was the same one Elsie had on her wall, and Marlo had been very frightened—

What was Marlo hiding? Why had she been so shaken by her closet and Mother's kitchen?

He could understand the kitchen episode, the nervousness one might feel at the site of a death. . . . His mother had died right on this floor—

Deep in thought, Spence rubbed his chest, the ache of love and guilt tangled there, and he glanced at the kitchen floor where his mother had lain. Her photographs had been scattered around her. But she had always worked on her albums, her photos, carefully arranging and dating them. But in the last year, she'd become absorbed in the photographs—when she wasn't dating Royston. It wasn't unusual for her to be working all hours on the kitchen table, or to want better light—if the overhead bulb hadn't worked.

Spence checked his telephone messages—several from customers, and the partiers had decided to rent his house for the entire week, whether they used it or not. At such times, the profit was hefty, and Spence either stayed at his mother's, or he hunted Cody. Cherry's cultured voice purred through the machine: "I'm worried about Marlo. If this can happen to me—keep an eye on her, will you? Billy Bob is going to stay in Godfrey. Is it okay if he stays at our place when we get back? Just until he finds a place?"

"Sure," Spence agreed dryly. "Move Billy Bob into the cabin. The more the merrier."

Cherry's next message slid into the room: "See if you can talk Marlo into that séance, will you, please? Please, Spence? Something is really going on with her, and she won't tell me. Could we do that at your mom's house? Elsie would have liked that, I know."

"Sure. Anything you want, Cherry." Though Spence didn't believe in spirit visitation and voices from the other side, he shared Cherry's concern about Marlo.

What was Marlo hiding?

Why had she frozen, turned pale and shaky after stepping into that closet?

After Cherry had been attacked, Marlo had reacted just that way after entering this same kitchen. Why?

Why not? Returning to the kitchen that held family memories and the image of his mother's lifeless body on the floor hadn't been easy for him. Marlo would have shared Elsie's life, perhaps working on their cameras and photographs on the kitchen table.

Cameras . . . photographs . . . pictures captured moments in time . . . Spence frowned slightly, his mind running quickly now through how Wilma's house had been ransacked and also her shop. Pictures had been scattered in both places—His mother had been tending her albums, her pictures scattered when she fell . . .

They'd been bloodstained and, in his grief, Spence had tossed them away. He hadn't paid attention to the various scrapbook albums she'd been working on, but at such a time, she would have had her camera bag at hand. He held his breath as he remembered that when she'd died, her camera bag hadn't been on the table. Elsie had been very particular about her supply of film and camera—exactly like the one in Marlo's closet.

What had Marlo seen, or felt when she had stepped into that closet? Cody's picture, a reminder of a child she'd loved?

Photographs . . . the break-in at Wilma's home and shop could have been arranged to look as theft, but photographs and albums were missing. The burglar probably needed more time to go through the pictures. Why?

His mother's albums and filed photographs had all been on her table, until Spence replaced them in the closet—

Spence walked to the hallway closet where his mother's camera bag was usually stored.

It was missing.

Eight

AFTER A LONG HARD DAY OF HELPING HER MOTHER straighten up and itemize the missing items in her home and the thrift shop, Marlo badly needed the quiet of her apartment. It hadn't been easy to refuse Keith's offer of dinner, especially when his look had been a blend of concern, jealousy, and hurt. Suspicion was rolled into the mix, a silent accusation that she had made love to Spence.

Marlo left her mother and friends in the thrift shop and walked out onto Main Street. June's summer air was fragrant and cool. The sun now rode the crest of the rugged mountains, and Marlo paused on her walk home to look at the display in Donna's Flowers. Through the window, the huge bloodred roses stunned her. She reached out her open hand on the glass and felt the sun's warmth. She could almost feel a pulse beating there—

A movement at her side caused her to look at Lorraine Ellory, Keith's salesclerk and accountant. "Hi, Lorraine. How are you?"

An attractive petite brunette, Lorraine's reflection in the

glass revealed a bitter, furious expression instead of her usual sultry one. Lorraine was not happy, her blue eyes flashing, her carefully outlined and glossy lips pressed tightly together. "You've just spent the day with Keith when he should have been in the store. He has a business to run, and I spent the day trying to do the work for both of us. How do you think I am? Can't you handle your own life?"

It wasn't the first time Marlo had taken Lorraine's sharp barbs. After the last few days, and worried about her mother's break-ins, Marlo wasn't in the mood to take more. "Let me guess. You're jealous. I am not encouraging Keith, and he isn't your private property."

Lorraine's expression changed to confusion; Marlo didn't usually respond to her barbs. Then Lorraine apparently recovered from her surprise. "I saw the three of you walking to your mother's house this morning. You've been playing Keith for a fool, when all the time, you and Spence—"

Marlo considered Lorraine's overt jealousy. Keith had been firm about his relationship with his employee—"There's nothing between us. I needed someone like her after my wife left, to wait on customers who prefer a woman's opinion, to help with the books. She's an excellent employee. I take her out to dinner or lunch sometimes . . . just as any other employer occasionally takes out help . . . for their birthdays or to cheer them up, things like that. I give her bonuses for good sales and at the holidays. She's cheerful, and customers seem to like her, especially those who prefer a modern decor. She's wonderful at organizing promotional events at the store. But as for seeing her romantically—no."

Marlo's tolerance slipped another notch; she had no reason to explain whys to Lorraine, but she would, in an attempt to pacify her. The other woman's jealousy had dug in too deep, setting off her own dark mood. And Marlo had reached her limit of surprises and disruptions to her schedules. "Keith and Spence both like my mother. It's only natural that they would want to be there to help her."

Lorraine narrowed her eyes, her glossy lips tightened. "Yes, well, that doesn't explain why both of them were at your house so early. Stop playing with Keith. Spence Gerhard and he go way back, especially after Keith's wife had that affair with Spence. If you only knew how Keith suffered—"

Marlo remembered how disheveled Keith had been that morning, as if—"Lorraine, is it possible that you and Keith are involved?" she asked carefully.

Lorraine straightened, her hands smoothing her form-fitting blue dress. She shifted sensually, her smile knowing. "He needs someone. Someday he's going to see that you aren't the sweet and innocent that everyone thinks you are. It's all an act, isn't it? Just to keep him on the string? He recommended you for those decorating jobs and that television spot, and how do you pay him back? By sleeping with Spence. What's the matter, didn't his girl, Cherry, like you around him either? Is that why she took off?"

Marlo had had enough. "I think we're done now, Lorraine."

"Sure. Yeah. Whatever. But Keith deserves better. *Our* store needs some fresh flowers. I'm going to put a big bouquet in the window and take out that ratty patchwork pillow display you arranged with some old books. And by the way, while you were taking Keith's time, the whole town was busy gossiping about how you and Spence got drunk and partied up on the mountain—his customers came down to stock up at the liquor store. They had quite the story—about how you looked cute and sweet, but how Spence warmed you up on that blanket. It was probably only because Spence felt sorry for you. Just wait until Keith gets a load of that one."

"Why don't you just tell him, Lorraine? That's what you're planning to do, isn't it?"

Lorraine sniffed haughtily and looked up and down Marlo's T-shirt and jeans and dirty sneakers. She smoothed her sleek black hair, turned under at her shoulders. "I don't know what Keith sees in you. With that haircut and that outfit you look like a boy. He probably just feels sorry for you. And it's no wonder that Spence ran off from you years ago, or that your ex-husband wanted other women—attractive, feminine women. Ryan told me all about how you would faint if he tried anything other than the missionary position. He said you're so uptight that you have to schedule everything—even sex. Ryan said you get all upset when your schedules are dumped."

Marlo was having a really bad day. She smiled tightly and decided to go all out. "You've been waiting a long time to deliver that one, haven't you?"

"I just think it's time that you know what people think of you. That sweet, innocent, little martyr act didn't fool me. You wanted Keith to feel sorry for you."

Was that the reason Keith wanted to date her? Because he'd felt sorry for her? "Lorraine, I am not going to stand here after a hard day and trade insults with you. I know that you dated Spence, and now I know that you and my ex-husband were probably lovers. And I don't want to know if you and Keith are lovers—"

"He doesn't think it looks good for business to have us date outright." Lorraine's voice was sharp, cutting the summer air between them. "You're just temporary. I've invested time on Keith, and after he gets over the death of old Ted, I intend to marry him. You may have been the only thing available on that mountain camping trip, and Spence may have had too much to drink, but I know that Keith needs a whole lot more than you. So keep away."

"Have you gotten everything you needed out of your system, Lorraine?" Marlo asked quietly, despite the anger inside her. She hadn't shown her anger at Ryan's using her, and she wouldn't now. The emotions she'd bottled for too long came very close to surging out of her.

"For the time being." Lorraine swished into the florist's, leaving Marlo standing and simmering on the sidewalk. She decided to work off her anger by jogging home. She ran past her shop, up the street, around the block. Thoroughly winded, she returned to her apartment.

Somehow, Lettie, parked beside Marlo's pickup, hood lifted as if her engine was being repaired, wasn't a surprise. Neither was Spence, cooking in Marlo's kitchen. He turned a cheese sandwich in the skillet. That and the cream of tomato soup simmering on the stove had been Marlo's favorite childhood dinner. She wished now that her life was back on schedule and peaceful, just as it had been then.

When she could drag enough air into her lungs, she said, "I might have known. Mom gave you a key and sent you, didn't she? Just what I need to top off a perfectly horrid day. By the way, your orgy customers came into the Oasis to stock up and passed around the gossip that you and I were going at it on the mountain. I guess that's why everyone was looking at me funny today."

Spence turned to Marlo. He tossed a little cheese cracker into the air and caught it in his mouth. The little fish-shaped cheese crackers were her favorites, perfect to float in the tomato soup, and she didn't like him eating them. Marlo took the box, shook some little cracker fish into her hand, and sat down to munch on them, to contemplate the darkness of her life, and at the moment, the man ruining it.

Spence reached to riffle her short haircut. "Let me guess. You've had a bad day."

Marlo wanted to settle into her blue funk, to revel in it—alone. She placed the tiny fish in a line, just as she longed for her life—organized, logical. "That's an understatement. I just had a little conference with Lorraine in front of the florist shop. One of the topics was your affair with Natalie, Keith's wife. That's what this morning was all about, wasn't it? You probably fought over Natalie, and now the question is who gets little old me?"

"Ah. That's why you've been running . . . working off temper. You never liked to show your anger, did you? Sometimes it's good to get it out. And no, I never touched Natalie. We were friends."

"Uh-huh. You're 'friends' with a lot of women, Spence."

"What can I say? I'm just plain adorable."

Spence followed Marlo's hand as it gently traveled over the bag she had made; the Southwest chili pepper fabric had been Elsie's favorite. "I had another sizable payment come in, so I put your check for helping me in there. . . . She'd want you to have it. All the Bingo Girls have their own bags, and you made this one especially for her. Her small photo album is missing. She always carried it with her. Do you know where it is?"

Marlo shook her head. Someone had taken her archived photos and the negatives . . . Someone with a rage that could kill . . .

She looked up at Spence, who had just slid the grilled cheese sandwich in front of her. "It's probably in the house somewhere."

"I looked. It's missing," he answered grimly. "So are your

mother's photo albums and boxes of pictures. That's strange, isn't it? Missing pictures? Makes you wonder who wants them and why. Any ideas?"

Whoever it was, they'd kill—may have killed Spence's mother . . . The rage was the same: palpable, hot, biting—

"Marlo, you just went off somewhere. Can I help?"

She couldn't tell Spence what she had sensed in his mother's house. "Like I said, it's been a bad day. Lorraine capped it off by telling me that Ryan was a dog right here, not only while he was in Seattle. Meanwhile, everyone was feeling sorry for me—poor little dumb, trusting me. Did you know that Ryan had been seeing Lorraine? Did everyone know but me?"

Spence shrugged and leaned back against the kitchen counter, his arms crossed.

Marlo noted that when Spence crossed his arms, the muscles jumped and gleamed. When he'd held her on the mountain, his biceps had nudged the outer shape of her breasts. She forced her attention to the cheese sandwich. She was exhausted, upset, and facing her sexless identity. Every plan and schedule in her life had gone awry within a few days. "Well? Did everyone know that Ryan was seeing Lorraine?"

"Probably not everyone. Cherry called here. She's worried about you, and she's coming back early."

"How is Cherry? Is she okay? Did she sound okay?"

"She sounds good. Bubbly, like always. You know, that karma and astrology stuff. Apparently Billy Bob and her signs are in perfect alignment. I'll just feel better when I see her. She's too vulnerable, too much of a child."

The sense that he had transferred his protective big brother to Cherry reminded Marlo that he'd lost a sister—a whole family. "Cherry is perfect, Spence, and you know it. There's a childlike innocence and caring about her that the world really needs. And you have to let her grow up sometime. Billy Bob will protect her."

He shrugged again, and Marlo realized that he was still brooding about the attack on Cherry and how he hadn't protected her—how he hadn't protected his sister or his nephew. "Spence, when Cherry comes back, let her choose what she wants to remember, and if she wants to talk about her attack. Let her lead."

"Whoever did it is still out there. He should be—"

"I know. I don't want to talk about this, Spence. I'm tired and sweaty, and I've just had that informational chat with Lorraine. Do you think she's involved with Keith?"

"I don't think so, because he's set on how things look to the public, and she's got a reputation. She's been around. But she's after him, anyone can see that. Keith keeps a lot inside—like you. It's hard to know what he's thinking, except that he'd like to see his father's murder pinned on me."

"But he was dating me a lot more in the last two years. We have dinner every Wednesday night, and sometimes drive somewhere, or go to a good movie. We've been to furniture sales things. We do other things together. He assured me that there was nothing between them."

"I know what you do together. So what was the final count on what was taken from your mother's house and shop?" The abrupt change of topic signaled that Spence wanted to distract her.

She didn't want to be distracted. She'd worked so hard to put Ryan through college; she'd scrimped—

Marlo was still caught by her conversation with Lorraine, distracted as she answered, "The photographs . . . antique hatpins, a set of hot rollers, all of her antique crystal and cut-glass perfume bottles, some earrings, a few antique hand mirrors, a man's electric razor, small stuff . . . Then the photo albums and some pictures. Mom is having the time of her life playing hostess at her house. She always wanted a big family, and there was only me. They're probably putting in locks and alarms and planning a backyard barbecue over there now. They're going to have a midnight bingo rally. . . . I am having a real bad day. Now, please get out."

Instead, Spence slid two bowls of tomato soup on the table. The red color caught her instantly, but it didn't terrify her as had the florist's red roses, the red tint on Cody's photograph . . .

Maybe it was gone, whatever had gripped her was gone . . . She wanted to go into the closet, to see if she still felt that rage—Marlo stood suddenly, pressing her hands to her head. "I'm tired, Spence. Leave me alone."

Behind her, he took a deep breath. In the next instant, he turned and pushed her back against the refrigerator. His hands braced on either side of her head. "Marlo, you're damned sexy. Lorraine isn't sweet when it comes to competition, and you're definitely that. She was out to hurt you."

"I got that idea. Not one person has said anything like that to me—ever. Not about Ryan. And I don't believe for a minute that she and Keith are having an affair. . . ."

Spence was very close and hard, and she wanted to—

That wouldn't do. There was no reason why her impulses told her to devour him, to rub her skin against his, to tear everything from him, to challenge and overpower him, to be a sexually aggressive woman.

While Marlo was dealing with the shift into her heart-pounding discoveries, she thought it only fair to tell him, "I'm all sweaty."

"I know. You smell really good. Hot. Earthly. Female. Sexy." His eyes darkened as he studied her face, and his hands slid downward to frame her hips, to caress them. Then Spence lowered his face to rub his cheek against hers, slowly, softly. He bent to nuzzle her throat. His voice was husky and low, vibrating against her skin, causing her heart to leap wildly. "You need something to take your mind off today."

"Do I?" she asked unevenly. The air hummed around them, heat from Spence's body sliding into hers.

"You're driving me nuts. You always have," he returned roughly, and, taking her face in his hands, lowered his lips gently, tentatively to hers. His tongue slid across her upper lip, and the jolt shot straight into Marlo's body and headed for points south, landing in a big warm rippling pool. He moved his hips slowly against hers, with just enough pressure to assure her that he was definitely aroused.

"Am I?" His admission had instantly lifted her sexual rating into that of a male-attracting woman.

"You know you are. Now let's see just what you've got."

The challenge and the heat were there, and she wasn't backing down. Marlo slid her hands up Spence's arms, felt the power in them, absorbed it, gathered it, formed it into her own. She slid her fingers into his hair, held him tight, and Spence tensed. In that moment, she knew she'd taken him by surprise and reveled in a score that had simmered in her forever—"Can't you take it?"

Spence's expression hardened; his head tilted. Marlo recognized that look: He wasn't backing down, and if she wanted to play a dangerous game, he'd oblige. "All right. Like I said, let's see what you've got."

His stare held hers as his hands slid down to her bottom, cupped it, and lifted her against him.

"What am I supposed to do now, back off?" she said, and moved closer, upping that dangerous ante.

He looked down to where her breasts rested against him.

She watched, fascinated as the slow color moved up into his cheeks, as his eyes traced her softness. Her nipples peaked, and Spence leaned back to study them. Before he concealed it, Spence's expression was all hunger and desperation. The quiver that ran through him, the anticipation and sexual heat, just could have been hers. Spence was breathing hard and uneven, as if he were fighting an inward battle. That little vein on the side of his jaw appeared, his shoulders broad and strong beneath her open hands.

"You're all breathless and quivery. And hot. You've got all the signals a man needs. If I wanted to, we'd be in that bed right now. Or that table. Or—" Spence held her tight against him, his hands caressing. "I've got nothing against standing right here."

She met that dark gold smoldering stare, and knew by the caress of his hands upon her softness that Spence had no intention of rough, fast sex. She also knew that lovemaking with Spence would consume her. "Don't try to shock me, Spence. You've always tried to zing right in there and throw me off-balance. It won't work this time."

She loved the feel of those shoulders, strong and safe—she dug her fingertips in slightly, testing that sleek power. She edged closer, fluttered her lashes against his cheek, and slid her hands down, using her nails lightly this time. She slid her hands to press against his butt and tug him closer. "You're aroused, Spence. I'm winning this one."

"Boy, you're in a mean mood," he whispered huskily.

"It's been a bad day."

He smiled at that and leaned in for a long sweet kiss. Spence blew the damp hair in front of her ear, his eyes warm and knowing upon her. "Your schedules are messed up and you're off-balance—like that day they canceled your trip to a cheerleaders' conference. You decided to get into that old tractor tire and roll down the hill. . . . When you step out of your box, you're unpredictable. Right now, you've had a bad day, your schedules are shot to hell, and you've decided to go for the gusto and get rid of everything that's been bothering you—like me. Back off."

"Who said you bother me? Your hands are on my butt. Mine are on yours. It's called equal opportunity. I'll let go if you will."

He frowned slightly, and slowly his hands opened, releasing her.

"Thank you," Marlo said very properly. She dropped her hands and eased back.

Instantly, Spence stepped away, glaring at her. "You're welcome."

When she smoothed her shirt, tugged it down and straightened, staring straight back at him, refusing to show any sign that she had been affected, Spence frowned at her. He was trying to get a fix on her mood, wary because she'd met him in an open bout of sensuality.

She could still feel him pressed hard against her, that liquid hot center within her trembling . . . The tension in her small kitchen was hot and ripe and pulsing. In an effort to appear normal when her senses were spiking and hungry, Marlo sat down to eat. She slid the grilled sandwich open and licked the cheese, and when Spence hadn't moved, she looked up at him. "And thanks . . . for dinner."

He looked wary and confused, and she reveled in having him on the run. Spence would think twice about coming after her. She could handle anything he threw at her.

"Do you think they'll catch whoever broke into Mom's?"

"Hard to tell. Mike is working it, putting out feelers, checking with other antique and thrift shops to see if her stuff turns up. The problem is that she's had so many people down on their luck stay with her. She's kept some runaways. She's got to quit that."

"Mom has a really good feel for people. If she thinks they are dangerous, she doesn't invite them. Cherry stayed with her for a while."

Spence was looking at her, studying her with that wary, fascinated expression. After years of doubting her sensual appeal, her low esteem had just risen. To think that she was a woman who could surprise and intrigue this man somehow buoyed her spirits. "So, what did you do today?" she asked lightly.

"Talked to the bikers staying up on the mountain. I thought they might know something about the break-ins. . . . High Cat's woman had another baby. They have to get a new side-car. He's thinking about opening an art shop here. After that, I talked to Old Eddie. He's thinking about giving up prospecting for gold."

"The government closed his mines. If they catch him digging more, he's in for a hefty fine or jail."

"It's his life. He's having a hard time changing."

Spence sat down to eat. He glanced at her meaningfully. "Don't lick any more pickles in front of men, Marlo. It's an image that lasts in a man's mind. They could embarrass themselves. . . . My day wasn't so sweet either. Let's say I woke up on the wrong side of the bed. I had a little problem and Christmas, despite the decorations on the doorknobs, did not come early. . . . I want to know why you were stunned and pale last night when you came out of that closet, and why you wanted me to stay. You must have been shaken pretty bad to ask that."

Marlo stared at the tomato soup and decided it wasn't her favorite anymore. She rose and poured it down the sink, letting the faucet run, taking the red color away from her. "I've got to get back to work. I'm way behind," she said quietly, panic washing over her.

Whenever her schedules were shifted drastically, something always happened. . . .

Only work and schedules would put her back together, allow her to cope with whatever was pushing at her, wanting her to recognize it. "We haven't decided on the stencil for Cecily Thomsen's bedroom—she's only sixteen, and her mother wants lots of ruffles and pink. But Cecily is into goth style, black and gloomy. Her mother isn't going to go for a spiderweb painted on the wall. . . . A television filming coming up, and I have no idea about what I'm going to do. Everything has to be ready, you know."

She had to go over her photographs, to see what actually had been taken—if she could remember the specific shots . . .

"Marlo?" Spence asked quietly.

"I've lost so much work time. I'm worried about Mom. How could anyone do that to Cherry?"

"Marlo?" he asked again, closer this time.

"Mmm?" She had to work on her layouts—maybe a faux window design for her decorator segment . . . four small squares with landscaping in the background, maybe one of the new flower transfers to rub onto blank wallpaper . . .

Spence turned her abruptly, held her by her shoulders, and took a kiss that devastated her, causing her mind to blank and her body to heat.

He grinned when he stepped back and hooked his thumbs into his jeans pockets. "Mission accomplished."

When she could speak, Marlo said unevenly, "Oh, you're good. Really good."

"Hey, don't blame me. All day, I've been thinking about that pickle, the orgasm you've never had, and you pole dancing in your bedroom. To see you bounce in here, all sweaty and fired up, just raised a few things, that's all."

And Marlo knew exactly what. "Maybe you'd better go."

Even as she spoke, Marlo knew that Spence had assigned himself as her protector, and he wasn't going anywhere. "There is enough gossip about us, Spence," she stated firmly. "It's probably all over town now that you stayed all night. I don't know whatever possessed me to ask you."

"I do. Something had just scared the hell out of you. As for gossip, no doubt your run through town has people thinking that you're so steamed up for me that you can't wait—"

"You egotist. Out."

Spence smiled briefly, but he didn't move. Then he leveled a look at Marlo. "Travis is coming over later to help me strip the upholstery from the couch and chair in your shop. If you can get some fabric that Cherry would like, we'll help you with it. I've helped Mom re-cover furniture. I thought it would make a good homecoming present for Cherry."

Spence had the ability to shift the conversation too many times, to distract her—which Marlo suspected was exactly what he wanted to do. "I said I'd do it. Cherry is going to help me."

"More hands work faster, and right now, she's got her hands full with lover-boy," Spence returned logically.

Then he walked to the door and rattled the sleigh bell. "I'll be around, but you need more than this."

With Spence nearby, Marlo's plans and schedules would be shot to smithereens; she wasn't certain about him, or herself. "You can't crash my life, Spence."

He lifted an eyebrow, challenging her. "Don't get too excited. Temporary is fine with me. I'm not the staying kind of guy, remember? It's not in my genes. But I am here until I can get a fix on what's happening with you . . . what's terrifying you."

She couldn't tell him that she suspected his mother had been killed.

She couldn't tell him that she only suspected that Dirk and Traci had been purposely run off that road. . . .

She couldn't tell him that Cody seemed to be calling her, that somehow red and glass connected her to something she did not want. . . .

Nine

TO KEEP HIS MIND OFF MARLO, SPENCE NEEDED THE PHYSI-cal activity of removing the fabric from the old couch. Something had gripped her, frightening her enough to ask him to stay last night.

The driveway running beside Fresh Takes and ending at the old garage was quiet. He hauled the cushions outside to the sweet summer night and sat in a lawn chair. Spence adjusted the outdoor light over the garage-workshop's double-wide door so that he could both work and check on Marlo. Parked beside Marlo's black monster pickup, Lettie gleamed delicately in the light coming from the street.

Just in case whoever had worked over Cherry decided Marlo might be fair game, Lettie stood as a reminder that Spence was nearby.

"Nearby" wasn't in bed with Marlo, however. He was only a few yards away from where she would be sleeping in that feminine bedroom, that pole running from floor to ceiling—a pole that she used for exercise. . . .

His body ached from wanting her. He'd wanted Marlo forever, and no other woman could erase her.

Off-balance now and playing sensually, she could do real damage. The morning she'd returned Cherry's birth control pills, Marlo had probably seen him in the buff, coming down from his loft. He'd been dreaming of holding Marlo, how sweet she felt against him, how ripe and hot, and how—

Marlo could be explosive, unpredictable, and she had just this edge of the savage that lit him up. And he couldn't resist lighting that hidden fuse, testing her.

Right now, his body told him to go to her, to make love to her until he'd soothed that edge—He had no right. He'd torn her life apart. . . .

At his side, eighteen-year-old Travis Preston was in his wheelchair, locked in his thoughts as he worked on another cushion. "I liked this couch the way it was. Why are you changing it?"

"Women. They just can't leave a good thing alone."

"I don't have to worry about that anymore. Women are leaving me way alone."

Girl trouble, Spence thought, recognizing the dark, closed look as the boy stared out into the night. Travis was blond, clean-cut, and extreme workouts had defined his upper body. Mike loved his son, but sometimes he drove him too hard. An excellent skier, Travis had wanted to ski competitively. After his dreams and his back had been broken, he'd become hard and bitter.

They worked in silence, then Travis said, "You're still hunting for Cody's remains, aren't you?"

When Spence nodded, Travis added thoughtfully, "Everyone is talking about you and Marlo. Keith has had her staked out for years, pretty heavy since her divorce. I heard you and she used to date in high school. Then you went away to college, and you guys split up."

"I made a mistake. I hurt her. I've always regretted it."

That quiet ache slid into Spence: He should have—but all the should-haves wouldn't erase what he'd actually done. . . .

But Travis had moved on, digging in the ripper to tear away the old upholstery's seam. His frown said he was deep in thought. Then he said, "The girls came around for a while. Curious, I guess. I could pay someone to—you know—help me out, I guess. Dad would have fits if he ever found out."

Spence understood the ache of a man, the need for a softer hand in his, a body curled close to his in the night. Sleeping close to Marlo had just sharpened that need within himself, a very possessive need.

Marlo was a woman who didn't want to be "tagged," and lately he was in the mood to do just that—to nail her and make certain that every male around knew that Marlo was his. Maybe he wasn't the right one, but that need rode inside him just the same.

In simple terms, Marlo could irritate the hell out of him, drive him nuts, and despite everything in their past, he still wanted to stake a claim. "When the time is right, that will work out."

"Like you'd know." Travis's tone was bitter. "You don't know how it is. You can have any woman you want. That girl who lives with you, Cherry, is pure sweet stuff."

"She's a nice girl, Travis."

"A stripper? She's been around, Spence. That's why you're with her, isn't it? Because she knows that you don't want to be tied down? I saw her the night she left town, after dancing at the fire station for Bud Macy's bachelor party. She's real hot. I went down to the truck stop later and she was still going, but she was moving different, almost like she was in a dream."

"In a dream?"

"Yeah, dazed like. I tried to talk with her, but her words were slurred. She wasn't tracking."

"Cherry doesn't take drugs, Travis. She does the aromatherapy, herbal tea route."

Mike Preston's patrol car pulled into the driveway behind Lettie and Marlo's pickup. He walked to his son and Spence. "They're having a real party over at Wilma's. I just escaped . . . Those break-ins could have been done by anyone passing through. Funny that they would take pictures and albums, and the other things weren't worth much. They took all the old cameras from the shop. Some real cheapies. Wonder why anyone would want an old cheap camera. The rest might be sold for replacement parts for people who have favorite good ones. Some people still like that old rich color, fiddling with adjustments, rather than the auto-points."

Spence's ripper prickled his hand. He decided not to mention his mother's missing camera, or the little album she always carried. It may mean nothing—or everything. And Marlo had omitted the stolen cameras. Why?

"Odd that it was Wilma's house and her shop," Travis murmured.

A big, powerful man, Mike Preston obviously loved his son and ached for him. "It could be someone who came into the shop, and she saw that they needed help, or a free meal—you know how she is. I've advised her that she could have trouble doing that."

Mike pulled up a lawn chair, unbuckled his weapons belt, and lowered his hefty body into the chair. "I hope this thing doesn't collapse. Marlo's light is on in the shop. I can see her from the street. She's working at her sewing machine. I stopped in front, just to check on her and let her know I was around. She's running that sewing machine as if she was in a dead heat on the finish line."

The men watched a black late-model Lincoln pull into the driveway behind the patrol car. A tall, lean man slid out and walked toward the men.

"Royston." Mike's greeting to the newcomer was cool.

The red rose bouquet that Keith held would have cost plenty. Marlo deserved flowers and romance and someone who was steady, like Keith—and that irritated Spence.

Keith's voice was brisk and cool, and he avoided looking at Spence. "Mike . . . Travis . . . Is Marlo around?"

"She's in the store, working late. Looks like she's pretty upset and working it out on a sewing machine," Mike answered. His glance at Spence said he understood Keith's dislike. "We're doing all we can to catch whoever broke into Wilma's, Keith."

"You're not real successful at solving crimes, are you, Mike?" Keith asked quietly, pointedly, a reminder that his father's murderer had never been caught.

"Sometimes there's not much to work with, Royston," Mike stated evenly. "You think of anything that hasn't already been dug through on any case, and I'll head straight for it. As for your father, the investigators checked a whole list of people who had real grudges against him."

Keith bristled outright. "But none like Spence. There were too many witnesses to that argument. . . . Just so you know—if my store has a break-in—I'm not stopping with you."

"Fair enough. But the last time I checked, Godfrey was still in my keeping."

"That just might be changed, if I have any say-so in this town, and I do."

A sleek red classic convertible prowled by the driveway leading to Marlo's shop. It stopped, reversed, and slid into the narrow opening behind Keith's Lincoln. The engine hummed momentarily and died, then Bjorn leaped up and out of the little car. As he walked toward the men, Marlo's door jerked open, and her voice held panic: "Spence?"

She stopped on her back porch, her eyes wide with fear, and Spence was on his feet, striding to her.

Marlo was just taking in the other men who had also come to her porch. She seemed pale and shaking as she had been in his mother's kitchen and after coming out of her closet. "I . . . I . . . What are you all doing here?"

But she'd reached out to take Spence's hand, gripping it so tightly he could feel the icy fear within her, the struggle for a normal appearance in front of the men.

Despite his concern, Spence noted that of the men she could have chosen, she'd called his name and looked straight to him—and that had to amount to something between them.

Keith moved to her and lifted the roses to her. "I thought you might like these. They remind me of you."

Marlo's hand gripped Spence's so tightly, he could feel the fragile bones—"How lovely," she said unevenly, but she didn't take the roses. She stared at them as if they terrified her, then to Bjorn's red car, gleaming beneath the porch light. "Thank you."

But when she lifted her eyes to Spence, he read the fear in her eyes. And the plea for help. . . . "Here, I'll hold those for you," he said as he took the roses.

"They're for her," Keith stated darkly.

"I see you like my car. It is a beauty. I thought you might want to come for a drive," Bjorn stated with a grin. The ski instructor's arrogance said that women usually hurried to leap into his car, or his bed.

"I saw it, passing the store's window, and I—"

Spence was certain of one thing: He didn't want Marlo cuddling up to Bjorn in that tiny car. It was time to move in and cut out the competition. "Lettie hasn't been driven in a while. Marlo and I were just getting ready to do that, take a drive. I was just waiting for her to come out," Spence lied. He didn't like the fear he'd seen in her eyes. What was she hiding?

"Your old car isn't quite in the same class as mine. She might change her mind. I'd let her drive. Women like the feel of a good hard straight stick and a powerful engine."

Spence didn't want to think about Marlo's hands on Bjorn's straight stick. Therefore, he offered the ultimate sacrifice. "She can drive Lettie."

He ignored Mike's snort of surprise and his smothered grin; Keith remained aloof and disdainful, as if he were silently putting Marlo on notice not to accept the other men's offers.

Marlo inhaled, seemed to brace herself, and took the roses from Spence. "Thank you, Keith. They are lovely. Travis? Keith? Would you like to come, too?"

Mike touched his son's shoulder. "I'll take your dispatcher duties while you're gone. You'd better take that ride. Not everyone gets to ride in Lettie, let alone watch Marlo drive."

Spence held his breath; Marlo had that tight, unpredictable look when anything could happen. She seemed to bristle without actually changing her expression or stance.

Marlo said, "Okay, I've had enough. My pickup will hold all of us, and I want to drive. Me. I don't need to drive anyone else's car. There are cars parked all around my shop. I feel like the wagons are circling. Everybody back up and let me out, and Travis, you sit in front with me."

"I was afraid of that. After you, Keith . . . Bjorn." Spence swept his hand in front of him. When Marlo was pressed too close, she was going to react.

When Lettie, Bjorn's sports car, and Keith's Lincoln were parked in front of the store, Marlo reversed her pickup out onto Main Street. Everyone took their places: Travis sat in the passenger seat; Spence, Bjorn, and Keith were seated on the couch cushions in the pickup bed. In a squall of tires, Marlo shot out into the night. Mike's siren whooped once behind them, warning Marlo that she was breaking the town's speed limit.

The paved road outside of town had been abandoned long ago. For years the good straight stretch had served as an unofficial drag strip and a perfect quarter mile to test an engine. Moonlight crept through the tops of the pines as Marlo lined up on the orange starting line crossed by black tire marks. She revved the pickup's motor, and Spence braced himself. Keith was glaring at him. "You got us into this. She's not usually like this. You didn't think I'd come, did you?"

Spence didn't bother to answer. The pickup engine revved one more time, Travis's whoop sounded, and the pickup's tires squealed in the night. It crossed the quarter mile, slowed with a screeching stop, reversed, lined back up, then aimed at the starting line.

"Having fun?" Spence asked a clearly stunned Keith.

"She's never driving my beauty," Bjorn stated adamantly. "But she's everything a man could want . . . looks and acts like a lady and probably a hellcat in—"

"Leave it, Bjorn. Or we will have that little conference right now. And Marlo is a lady."

"She was. You started this, Gerhard," Keith gritted, as the engine revved again. He flexed his hands, easing the cramps from them, and Spence again noted that the width of Keith's palms had changed from the narrow softness of a bookish man to that of a much stronger one. Maybe one strong enough to control Cherry—

Spence's study swung to Bjorn, who had that lit-up, hungry-hunting-male expression. He had made several passes at Cherry, and she'd refused; maybe he finally took his chance—

Then there was Travis, powerfully built and frustrated. But if Cherry had been drugged, Travis wasn't likely to note it—or was he?

Travis whooped again, and the pickup's tires burned rubber before it shot out into the night.

"She needed us for weight, Royston. This bed is too light without it. She would have fishtailed, and probably rolled over." The knot in Spence's gut tightened with the thought that Marlo could be hurt.

"How much longer?" Keith asked wearily after the sixth run.

"Until she gets it out of her system," Spence answered. In a mood, Marlo was unpredictable. The question was: What had set her off? When she had first stepped out into the night, she'd been panicked, calling out to him. Why?

At least it was him she'd wanted, and that soothed the gauche situation of sitting in the back of her pickup with two other men as Marlo drove back into town. She stopped at the police station, and Mike came out, opening the passenger door for his excited son. "It was great, Dad. I've missed that."

Mike grinned widely. "I used to be pretty good on that stretch. We'll try it sometime. And if you feel like driving, it's about time we looked into something for you."

Spence swung over the side to help Travis. The other two men hurried to follow, apparently glad that the ride was over. They had the dazed look of astronauts coming out of a test wind tunnel.

"Thanks, Marlo," Travis said, when he was seated in his wheelchair.

Marlo didn't reply, and Spence looked at her. Her hands were locked onto the steering wheel, and she was staring at the red neon light of the Why Not Bar. When she turned to

Spence, her mouth moved, but no sound came out.

Visibly shaken, she seemed to struggle away from something in her mind, then her smile came weakly. "Anytime."

Spence watched as she refocused and seemed to paste herself together. She slid out of the pickup and faced the men. Spence recognized that cocky tilt of her head, as if she'd just scored. She was cute like that, exhilarated, pleased with herself, and very, very hot.

Marlo studied the men towering over her. That should teach them to congregate on her property. Keith and Bjorn seemed stunned and a little frayed around the edges, their hair standing out from their heads in quite the perfect windblown effect.

Spence was looking at Marlo as if he wanted to strip her naked right there—and a little thrill shot through her. She could almost read his mind—unscheduled sex. Hot. Now. He smiled tightly. "Got it out of your system, Marlo?"

"Maybe." There. The terror that had started when she'd seen Bjorn's car driving by her shop window was gone. It was only a flashy little red convertible, passing beneath the streetlights, but enough to start her senses leaping, chilling.

It was all very silly, Marlo decided, all of it. The roses were red, and they didn't upset her. "So who wants to ride over to my place to pick up their cars?" she asked, pleased that she had put everything back onto a logical shelf.

"I'll walk," all three men said in unison.

"Fine. Then I'm going over to check on Mom. Make sure my driveway is clear when I come back."

"The Secret must be kept . . . The Secret must be kept." Jealousy snapped and popped in the exercise room, the rage building furiously, wildly, in the biker. Pictures had been snapped, proof of a hideous crime that had rippled through families and Godfrey. The sympathy the old woman had given wasn't wanted or needed. Elsie Gerhard shouldn't have started prying; she hadn't expected the crushing blow, not from someone she knew so well. . . .

A body honed and sweaty pressed the heavy weights higher, controlling the flow of breath with each expert repetition. Faster, faster, exhale, inhale, pump iron, get stronger . . .

Rage reached a tempo that threatened to spiral out of control—just as it had when the old man had died. How pathetic and weak he'd been—"He really shouldn't have started that argument."

That girl, Cherry, was a slut, showing off her body, stripping and dancing around that pole. She deserved what she got, just as Traci Forbes had deserved her fate. She'd pried into lives, opened secrets that were meant to protect.

Elsie Gerhard's personal album didn't exist now, the pictures inside it burned. The pictures and negatives in Marlo's closet had met the same fate. Marlo Malone shouldn't be friends with a slut; it damaged her reputation.

Spence Gerhard lived with that girl, and delivering her unconscious to him should have served as a warning.

And now he was after Marlo. He really should leave her alone. Or he would have to pay. . . .

Where were those pictures? The ones taken in Godfrey twelve years ago?

The steroid shot had burned horribly, but now it was worth the pain, pumping more strength into a body already hard. . . .

"Marlo's bedroom looks just as I thought it would—a ruffled bed skirt, framed family pictures on the dresser, even a picture of her at nine, holding up a fish she'd caught, her father at her side."

Darkness came in a storm, and anger, and the barbells lifted more quickly. *Fathers should be nice—but they weren't always, and the scars they created lasted forever. . . .*

It really would be a shame to hurt Marlo, perhaps kill her, but The Secret had to be protected—

Marlo parked her pickup and started to walk toward her porch, then she saw Spence's silhouette outlined in the doorway of her workshop. At one o'clock in the morning, she'd expected him to be there. Spence wasn't the kind of man to walk away from someone he suspected was in danger.

But right now, she needed privacy to restructure her shredded life. Her drag-racing snit had upset her; one look at all the men on her back porch and fresh from another scary jolt, she had needed to hold her own, her independence. It had seemed like a male convention, and it was embarrassing to see all those cars lined in her driveway. Gossip would run rampant—as if it weren't already.

Then after her . . . event, Spence had studied her intently, and the summer air had sizzled between them; she'd almost leaped upon him to top off her walk on the wild side.

She had to retrieve whatever dignity she could. Marlo moved to Spence, held out her hand, and said, "Keys."

In the shadows, Spence's eyes glittered down at her. The light behind him caught on the muscle contracting in his cheek. "So how is Wilma?"

"Fine. Give me my mother's set of keys," she repeated. Spence could set her off too easily, and she was exhausted and on the edge of losing control. "Spence, I'm a big girl now. Whatever happened between us was forgotten long ago. I'm supposed to call my mother when I get in the house, and you need to go home."

"You're forgetting a little detail like Cherry's almost rape, aren't you? And the fact that you wanted me to stay last night, and for some reason, you came outside tonight, calling my name and looking as if you'd been terrified. Why?"

She couldn't tell him about the startling flash of Bjorn's

red car through her shop window, how it had terrified her, how she'd immediately wanted to be held tight against him.

Being held tight against Spence could only lead to one thing—

He dropped a set of shiny new keys into her palm, and his anger simmered around her. "Okay, have it your way. Your old keys won't work. The new locks are European. One of a kind. Mike decided to install them in the front door and on your apartment while we were on your little therapeutic joyride, scaring the hell out of anyone who had any sense. . . ."

The streetlight hit the harsh planes of Spence's face, and his eyes glittered down at her as he ordered, "Don't give out an extra set to anyone, or stash it under the rug on the porch—or that pot of geraniums. Not very inventive, Marlo. Cherry and your mother didn't have the only set of keys. You'd forgotten the ones you'd given to Lou, the plumber, so he could work on your bathroom while you were taking Cherry's place. He happened to mention that fact when I stopped by the Why Not Bar to settle my nerves after that ride. Bill from the hardware store was there, and he said you'd had quite a lot of the same ones made through the years. Maybe you ought to keep a list while you're handing them out like candy."

Marlo didn't like Spence's laying-down-the-law tone. "You don't have one, do you?"

"Does Keith?" The edge to Spence's deep voice said he didn't like that idea.

"So I forgot a few people."

"That's damned dangerous, Marlo." At one o'clock in the morning, she didn't want to hear comments about her intelligence—or admit she'd also given Keith a key two years ago, as a safeguard for when Cherry or her mother misplaced theirs.

She edged by Spence and entered the shop. The couch and chair had been stripped, the old fabric lying neatly folded. "You wanted a project for your show. . . . Here it is," he said. "Mom used to cut the new cover by using the old as a pattern. I'll get the cushions out of your pickup."

"Go home, Spence," she said, when he returned and flopped the cushions on the couch inside the workshop. The quick hard movement said he wasn't happy.

He turned and studied her. "Not just yet. You didn't tell me that cameras had been taken from the thrift shop. Why?"

"Does it matter?" The headache brewing in the back of her brain started moving forward. Whatever wanted her had to do with photographs and the color red. She wouldn't let them have her—

He nodded slowly. "I think it does. Mom's camera, the one like yours, an old eighties model, is missing. Now why would someone want to collect old cameras and photographs? Any idea?"

That edge was there; she'd done something to nettle him.

"Not a clue. That model is a good one though. Some great photographers still prefer their old cameras . . . it's a purist-collector thing. Or maybe Elsie loaned her camera out, or took it somewhere for cleaning. Or wanted the lenses cleaned. You never know."

"Mom would have told me. If you were missing anything, you'd tell me, or Mike, wouldn't you?"

The question was loaded dangerously. She couldn't actually prove that anyone had been in her closet, that she hadn't misplaced the missing albums and archived pictures. It was such a small thing, some old pictures taken with a fish-eye lens at Halloween.

Spence leaned closer and trailed his fingertip down her cheek and lower to her throat. "You've got that panicked look, Marlo, as if you want to lie. What's going on with you?"

Nothing was logical. Pieces of her were falling away—or heating up with an elemental need to back Spence against the wall and—She tried to breathe, struggled for calm as he leaned in close to nuzzle her cheek. "My, my my. You're all worked up and hot. Your pulse just kicked up."

Then he shoved away and studied her again, his head tilted slightly. "I can't tell if it's because you're trying to come up with a good lie about how you get all shook up lately—that stunned, panicked look—or if it's because you want me. All you have to say is, 'I want you, Spence.' Because your motors are humming, sweetheart, and I can feel the vibrations coming off you."

"Not everything is related to sex." But that simmering moment after her drag-strip episode lingered in June's damp, fragrant air. Exhilarated, she'd wanted to top it off by leaping on Spence.

"Correction: It wasn't, but now it is. Whatever jerked you out of a minute-by-minute planning has got you thinking about how much you want me. But you can't have me, and you know it."

It had been a long, hard day, and Marlo couldn't stop her hand from reaching out and grabbing a fistful of Spence's T-shirt. Amused, he looked down at her hand. "You're turning me on, sweetheart."

"Listen, you overgrown—I've got other things to think about than how much you irritate me."

"Really? What are they?"

Spence was always right there, nudging, pushing, challenging her. "You know what? I do not care about anything now but getting some sleep and getting everything back to normal."

But at the moment, she did care about something, and that was wiping the I've-got-you smirk off Spence's face. "So if you haven't had sex since Cherry, that was two years ago, and not very good from the sound of it—you must be dying for it, Gerhard. Think of it—me, all hot and sweaty and dancing around that pole in my bedroom. Think of what you're missing. And you're right, basic upholstery technique for a home project would make an excellent show. Now go home."

She turned and took a step before Spence's arms circled her from behind, tugging her back to him. "Not so fast."

His hands opened, flattened on her belly and just below her breasts. The sound of his harsh breathing hissed by her ear, his jaw, rough with stubble rubbing up and down her throat. The edge of his teeth bit gently, and the vibrating heat within her spiked, causing her to shiver, to lean back against him, to arch her throat for his lips, his tongue.

His taste of her skin was slow, luxurious, and something she had to return, to match. She turned suddenly, caught the flare of those eyes, and knew she'd surprised him. Arching up on tiptoe, Marlo whispered against his lips. "It's been a long day, Gerhard, and you're pushing."

"Push back," he invited huskily. "You're not ready to call it a day yet, and neither am I. You're still all charged up from your drag-strip snit."

"I wasn't in a snit."

"Sure you were, and you were out to prove—whatever it was. You've got quite the little temper when you get going."

"That makes me sound—illogical, emotional."

"Makes you sound like a woman."

"I am, you idiot."

"Oh, I know."

He smiled just that knowing bit as she pushed against him, and Spence took a step backward into the workshop. Lovely, exciting, wildly fascinating game, she decided, pushing him back one more step and another. "I've got to call my mother. . . . I should go upstairs and try to organize the mess of my life. I should try to rest because tomorrow—rather it's today already—is going to go on forever, and I just might lose my temper with my clients."

She tasted his lips with her tongue, felt the static electricity between them zip through her. "I'll bet every inch of you is taut and waiting now, isn't it? But you won't cross that line, will you? Because you're still brooding about what happened years ago between a girl and a boy who don't exist anymore. I can't deal with that, Spence. I've got enough problems of my own—how do you think I feel when my life is traveling at warp speed, out of my control? Every schedule I have has been shredded, and you want to be noble, do you?"

Spence had that narrowed, honed, grim look that said he was fighting, and she wouldn't let him withdraw into safety now. She had him on the line and determined to maintain control. Why should he have control when she'd lost hers?

"You'd better back off, little girl," he warned in a low uneven tone.

"I'm just getting warmed up. In the morning, everyone is going to be talking about me driving around with a truckload of men. There's enough gossip about you and me on that mountain. Do you know exactly how hard it is to maintain professionalism and arbitrate between two couples who are battling on how they want their homes decorated? The word 'divorce' popped up. . . . I could lose a lot of invested time and energy if both couples decide to divorce, Spence. Money, Spence. Time is money, you know . . ."

She shook him slightly. "Do you know how hard it is to sparkle—try to look like I know what I'm doing when the show is being taped? Do you?"

She leaned in to taste that hard chin, to nibble on it. "I'm too wired to sleep now, to make any sense of my life. I've probably lost some really good jobs, by canceling out for that guide trip with you. Word gets around, you know. So why shouldn't I just go for the gusto?"

"You should get some rest, Marlo," Spence agreed unevenly. "You're scaring me."

"I intend to. How's that arm? The one the bear nibbled on?"

"Fine—"

"Then I won't have to worry about hurting you. Here's the deal—you're used to making deals, aren't you? A long time ago, you wanted something from me, and I gave it. You think you owe me, don't you? Maybe you do. Yes, you do. You owe me for tormenting, for pushing, for upsetting every bit of logic and the last few days of schedules—that I may never fix. And I will have to work my butt off to explain and complete some projects. I've got a filming this afternoon, and I'm not prepared. I have to lay things out, make notes, and, on top of that, try to look nice. And on top of that, my best friend isn't here to do whatever she does to settle me down. So you're going to have to do, because I know how truly evil you can be."

Spence scowled down at her. "Sure, I owe you. I wrecked your life—"

"You can't brood about that forever, Spence. Or any of the other things you like to heap upon yourself. I made that choice, but since you feel the need to erase that debt, I'm going to let you help me out of a situation."

"And that is?"

"I think you know what it is." She pushed him just enough to send them toppling to the couch, Spence beneath her body. He was hard and hot and shaking, his hands open beneath her shirt, stroking, caressing.

"Watch it, Marlo," he murmured unevenly—just before she dived into him.

"Too late, Gerhard," she whispered. "I'm on a roll."

"Then I guess I'd better come along." Spence eased off her shirt; the hunger in his eyes, the way he looked at his hands slowly caressing her shoulders, said that he'd be very careful with her, that she could trust him, even though at the moment, she'd tossed away all caution. . . .

"Do you think I would be forward to ask for that orgasm now, Spence?" she inquired after a long, erotic kiss that shimmered and gathered into a heated knot low in her body. "That would erase any debt you feel toward me. . . . Right now. Now," she amended as his warm rough face moved downward to nuzzle her breasts, to nibble on them through her bra.

His hands shook as he removed her bra, cupping her softness, caressing it. Then his lips fitted over her nipple, suckled gently, and the jolt shot straight to every nerve in her body.

"Marlo . . ." he whispered achingly against her skin as she struggled with his shirt, tugging it away. He turned her to lie facing him, moving against him. Skin slid against skin, the different textures exciting even more, then Spence's hands were at her jeans, loosening, fingers sliding inside to the waiting dampness there, stroking—

The first ripple caught her, held her, and Marlo stiffened, capturing it, breathing hard, straining for the next, which drove her higher. She moved against him, wanting, needing more, and then everything stopped, pivoted up high on that peak and burst into pieces.

Marlo floated softly down, aware of Spence holding her so tightly that she seemed a part of him. She tightened her arm around his very taut, powerful body that would hold her safely, and snuggled her face into the cove of his shoulder. She wrapped herself in the rapid beat of his heart, in the heat and scent of him. Marlo smoothed her open hand over his chest, the bunched muscles beneath the hot damp skin, his nipples etching her palm.

He shivered against her, his body jerking just that once, as her hand moved lower, resting over that long, hard mound. "Having fun?" he asked rawly.

"Uh-huh, I really am. But I'm really, really, sleepy now," she whispered against his throat, as exhaustion set in and she felt herself slide into sleep. . . .

Spence shifted slightly, tensed, and Marlo felt a warm flannel length slide over her back, as she sank more heavily into sleep.

Spence forced himself to breathe slowly, while every molecule in his body told him to make love to Marlo—her hand still resting over his erection wasn't helping. With a silent groan, he nuzzled her hair, taking in the sweet fragrance, and tried to calm the fire within him. Marlo was definitely dangerous. Long and sleek and silky and curved, she fitted against him, the snap of her jeans opened, the sweet scent of her wrapping around him.

This won't do at all, Gerhard, the voice within him cautioned. He'd almost slid into her, needed to feel everything soft and tight as a part of him, the good part. But he'd taken her once in a situation no better than this couch without its coverings, and Marlo deserved far more than he could give her. . . . *Not with her.*

Whatever was nudging Marlo, frightening her, was enough to send her over dangerous edges.

He rubbed his cheek against her soft hair and smiled. She'd always fascinated him, stirred him into teasing her, just to see her light up. He gathered Marlo closer, accepting painfully the slender leg that slid between his, the warm brand of her femininity resting against his thigh.

The hours until dawn and when Marlo awoke were going to be sleepless ones. . . . Why had she come running from her house, her eyes wide and frightened as she called his name?

Why hadn't she told him about the stolen cameras?

All the answers came up to one: Marlo didn't trust him and she had good reason. . . .

* * *

"Marlo really needs a lesson in how to behave like a lady. No lady would take a pickupload of men down that drag strip. And she's taken Spence to her bed. I don't like this. I don't like this at all. They shouldn't be together. They're dangerous together. I've seen how he can make her step over the edge, do things she would never do otherwise. She's not so perfect. And he brings out all the bad things in her. Bad things. Bad girl."

The biker was furious, boots hitting the floor, the hard tramp echoing off the walls. An electronic chime sounded; the black leather boots stopped and turned toward the computer where a message screen blinked. The incoming, carefully worded message was for the black-market sale of old Royston's coins. The transaction would be handled as usual, the money necessary to the biker's very private hobbies.

Pressure built again and curled out in a steady stream of curses, words spiking, hitting the ceiling, bouncing back again.

Marlo was dangerous when she changed into that other woman.

She just knew things, felt them.

Marlo was a hunter, the same as Spence, and together they were very bad news. The warnings had to get stronger. . . .

Ten

"MARLO?" IN THE DISTANCE, HER MOTHER'S CALL SOUNDED frantic; the rapping noise cutting the soft sounds of the mourning dove. Marlo surfaced slowly, aware of the heat wrapped around her, the man holding her, watching her intently. She tensed, fully aware that she had slept yet another night with Spence.

When she started to scramble away, his arms tightened around her, and Spence warned quietly, "Careful. We could fall off this thing."

"That's *my mother*! I didn't call her last night." Marlo shoved away to stand on her feet, frantically searching for her shirt and bra. She zipped her jeans, snapped them, and looked to where Spence was swinging her bra by one finger. She grabbed it and quickly put it on. Sprawled on the uncovered cushions, one arm resting behind his head, Spence studied her grimly. His gaze flickered over her. "So my debt to you is paid, right?" he asked tightly. "I'm not supposed to feel guilty, now. Is that it? Everything is back to nice and neat. That's the picture you want, right?"

"Oh! You can be so dense when you want to be. I'm not

getting into this now. That's my mother out there!" she whispered desperately while she tugged on her shirt.

Spence stood to smooth it over her, fitting his hands possessively over her breasts for just that heartbeat, and she didn't trust his amused expression. "You won't go out there. . . . You won't let her see you, will you, Spence?"

"What will you give me if I don't?"

Spence tilted his head and studied her hair. He ran his fingers through the short length, smoothing it. He was back to the tormenting boy again, disarming her, inviting her. Marlo didn't have time to think, she just reached for his head, tugged him down, and kissed him hard. "There. Be quiet and don't come out until we're in the house."

He reached to pat her bottom. "Okay, honey. Don't forget the keys. See you later."

"No, I—I have to go." Her heart stopped, and her blood warmed, as Spence continued looking at her, the sensual electricity zipping around them once more. "Thanks," she said unevenly, because he'd been very careful with her, despite his own needs.

"Anytime. It's nice to know you trust me."

Marlo frowned at his grim expression, but she didn't have time to deal with him. She hurried out of the workshop, closed the door, and walked toward her mother. On the apartment's porch, Wilma considered her daughter. "You're all flushed and wrinkled. What have you been up to?"

"I couldn't sleep and just thought I'd put in some time this morning—"

Wilma tilted her head and narrowed her eyes in *that* way, just the way that could cause Marlo to feel guilty even if she wasn't, which she was. She shouldn't be afraid to admit that she'd been *rolling on an uncovered couch with Spence.*

That he was very, very good in lovemaking.

That she'd . . . that. . . . She was an adult woman, after all. She shouldn't have to feel guilty for having a bad day and almost-sex with Spence and the need for the real deal.

Then she glanced at the workshop and prayed Spence would not emerge. Her mother could spot guilt a mile away.

"But you didn't call last night. That's not like you. I know you get up early, and you looked so tired, and you apparently took every single male in town for a ride in your truck last night—and I would think that you could at least *call your mother.* I was so worried, and my keys won't work. Why won't they work?"

After spending an hour settling her mother's riffled mood, Marlo closed the apartment door behind Wilma. She closed her eyes, shook her head, and walked slowly to her bedroom, where she sprawled onto the bed, face-first. The telephone rang, and Marlo let the message machine do its thing. She couldn't handle Pearl Henderson waffling about her kitchen, the Petersons' ongoing arguments, or anyone else.

Somehow, she'd justify the past few days, place them into perspective, and logically deal with schedules again, her very safe schedules. . . . "I was doing just fine without all this—one foot in front of the other, just trying to keep all the pieces in line," she heard herself say sleepily. . . .

"Oh, Marlo . . ." a deep voice singsonged in the distance.

She was dreaming, and Spence was tormenting her, just as he had when they were teenagers. "Go away. Life is bad enough without you making it worse, Spence."

"Oh, really?" That deep voice held amusement now.

Marlo snuggled her face against her pillow and settled in to sleep deeply.

A sharp tug on the blanket she'd wrapped around herself and Marlo was flipped to her back. She stared up at Spence's wide grin and blinked. "What are you doing here?"

"Waking you up. I thought you said you had a filming this afternoon. It's eleven o'clock now. What time does it start?"

Dazed, trying to leap from sleep into reality, Marlo pushed herself from the bed. Off-balance, she staggered and Spence's hands grabbed her upper arms, supporting her. He chuckled and said, "Time to wake up, morning glory."

"Spence, I have a contract with the television station. I have to get something going and quick. It's at one, and I need a finished project to show and things laid out, and—"

"So, I'll help. Tell me what to do."

She slumped to sit on the bed. "My life is in the toilet, Spence. There's just too much happening at once. I can usually handle a few interruptions, but everything—my life is a disaster, and every time I see—"

She stopped, because she couldn't tell Spence too much. "The workshop is a mess—that's where we film."

"Okay, I'll straighten that up. What's the project?"

She rubbed her temples. "Stop talking. You're putting more pressure on me. I have to think."

Spence was staring at the pole in her bedroom. The air seemed to crackle and heat around him, then he looked down at her. "If you don't want me on that bed with you, then I suggest you get up."

Marlo stood and smoothed her clothing. Spence's dark look followed her hands as if he wanted to replace them with his. He stared at her nipples, nudging the cloth, and the open hunger in his expression startled her. "How did you get in here?" she asked unevenly.

"You didn't lock the door after your mother left. Penny Nichols caught me on the street out front. She said she just wanted to browse and you hadn't opened Fresh Takes at your regular time. There was no usual note on the door that you were working elsewhere and when you'd be back."

Marlo shook her head. "Penny wanted gossip. She wanted to know why you and every other man in Godfrey were riding in the back of my truck last night. What did you say?"

"Honey, you can always trust me—" There was that dark, taunting edge again that she didn't understand.

Spence looked too innocent as he continued, "You didn't answer my knock, or my telephone call, and from the looks of your message machine, you didn't answer anyone else's. The Petersons filed separation papers this morning. Seems they couldn't agree on the decorator's ideas, and they've decided to split the house into two distinct parts and separate their lives as well. Jack Peterson blames you for messing up his life."

"Aah! She wants French provincial and he wants a hunter's lodge theme. The both of them are pack rats and there is too much everywhere to work with, and they want it all displayed. They fight all the time, and there is no way to pacify them."

Marlo threw up her hands, and when they came down, Spence took each one and kissed her palms. His voice was low and intimate and inviting. "Tell me what to do, honey. I've been helping women all my life."

She retrieved her hands and, with them, the startling need to toss Spence upon the bed and forget everything else. "Okay, go clean up the workshop, try to make a space around the worktable to give me room to demonstrate—whatever I can find to work on."

"What about my couch?"

She didn't want to work on something that held memories of her first orgasm. She fought the blush rising in her cheeks; Spence's fascination with it was causing her body to react—warming—with that quivering need to lay him out and have him.

She was off-balance, that was all, and her emotions had been tangled with disasters that never seemed to stop. "I don't think so. Needs to be something simpler. Get out."

Spence leaned down to kiss her lightly and, in the process, patted her bottom. "That's my girl."

He did know how to take care of a woman, Marlo decided later, as she spread out her index cards on the shop's cutting table. The filming had gone well, despite the time crunch.

Marlo studied her notes and rearranged the time-scheduling cards to manage more time with the Petersons. She just couldn't be the cause of a divorce. There had to be a solution.

Spence had straightened a filming area, carried her sewing machine from the store to the workshop, and watched as she demonstrated how to make inexpensive valances and swags. He'd charmed the young cameraman, offering him a free hike into the mountains. Spence had been pleasant, and had brought her a cup of tea later and a hefty slice of double chocolate cake that her mother usually sent when she knew Marlo was having an upsetting day. He'd even taken messages from a filled message machine, clearing it for more.

And now she owed Spence.

And he knew it, she decided as she hurried to the closet that night and itemized her photo and negative archives.

Someone had taken the archives from twelve years ago—that would have been some of her first attempts with a starter camera. The town's Halloween kiddie parade had crowded Main Street, and attractions for children had been everywhere. The only thing unusual about the pictures was that event when Marlo and Elsie had experimented with black-and-white film, checking the contrast in the shots, catching the children and the crowd . . .

Who would want them? Why?

The new locks would prevent anyone from coming back . . . wouldn't they?

It was best that no one knew about the missing pictures. Everyone, including Marlo, had enough on their minds these days. . . .

And she was safe behind the new locks, she repeated. But what was happening inside her mind, her senses screaming danger, terrified her—

The picture of Cody caught her, and she studied it. "Go to sleep, Cody. Rest. Please rest," she whispered desperately.

What was happening to her?

The biker's heavy boot tramped the stolen cameras into the gravel, crushing them into pieces. The photographs and negatives taken from Marlo's closet had captured the evidence that could expose The Secret . . . nothing could reveal that darkness . . . it had to be erased.

The biker tossed the camera pieces over the side of the road and listened to them tinkle softly in the night. Ted Royston had been erased, and Elsie removed. Marlo's pictures and negatives were already burned, a small glow of coals barely showing in the night.

The biker's slap against leather pants echoed in the cool night. Had Elsie been telling the truth that she'd lost that roll of film? Or had she developed it and stashed those incriminating pictures somewhere else?

An old woman, shocked by truths, and a blow or two, might not have honestly remembered. But then, she was already too close, prodding carefully hidden bits and pieces, not very skillfully, laying plans to reveal, to tear apart lives . . .

Night concealed the biker. Lights of the traffic snaking down the mountain could easily be seen, but no one would drive up the gravel intended to slow runaway trucks. The lights of Godfrey created a soft glow in the distance, and, during the day, the biker could use binoculars to trace cars leaving and entering the town, passing the truck stop. The house in Godfrey provided a better view, but wasn't always available, and that reminder set off a fresh blast of anger.

A path led from the runway to the old house hidden deep in the woods, which had been forgotten by its owners.

In the style of a Swiss chalet, decorated with gingerbread trim, it had once been elegant. Despite the exterior's ruin, it was really quite nice inside, made comfortable by ultramodern camping conveniences.

And now, the spiders were gone. The biker shivered at the memory of so many spiders, crawling everywhere, the one lifelong terror that never ceased, causing a fearful panic that could not be allowed. . . .

In his cabin a week later, Spence placed his boots on the table and settled down to brood about Marlo. Outside, the third week of June was a full blast of birdcalls and the woodpecker rapping away at his cabin.

The rattan chair he was sitting in creaked, protesting his weight. He lifted a pair of designer thong panties from the cushion and tossed them to the heap of his customers' abandoned clothing on the floor.

Marlo's panties were nice and sweet and white and fragrant, just like her bra, and he'd awakened every morning, painfully erect and groaning—

It had been a full week since he'd seen Marlo, and she'd quivered in his arms on that couch. He'd had a couple of hiking trips, a young couple excited about nature, and a woman's group of birdwatchers, both paying well and easy to manage.

Spence had watched Marlo's videos, appreciated her dedication to quality, and decided to give her thinking room. Whatever she was holding was big and bad, and it grated that she wouldn't let him help. It nettled that she might be seeing Keith, talking with him. There were just certain things a man expected when he'd just given a woman her first orgasm.

Some kind of commitment—but then he wasn't the kind of guy who did those, was he?

He'd passed her on the highway; she had that high-nose, tight, prim look, one that he just wanted to dive into and peel away.

So they had a deal, did they? Did she honestly think that little sexual jolt she'd had was payback for years ago? For the guilt he carried?

She still wasn't sharing whatever set her off, terrified her, and that fact said one thing—she didn't trust him.

Fresh air fluttered the curtains at the open windows, washing the stale smells of liquor and sex out the front door. The cabin had been demolished by the two couples, but then the fat check on the table more than covered any damages, and they'd left a nice stock of high-class alcohol, some first-class frozen steaks, and jars of caviar and various brands of cheese that no doubt were high-priced, but stank to high heaven.

On the beds, blankets were rumpled, needing washing, and so did the sheets—and trash was on every possible surface.

Spence had already thrown a jar of pickles away. He didn't want to remember Marlo licking them; a pickle would never appeal to him again. He slapped an anchovy onto a fancy cracker, added a blob of stinky cheese, shoved it in his mouth, and chewed on why Marlo was so frightened.

Marlo had been desperately terrified of something, and she wasn't talking. Why?

Spence poured French champagne into a chipped cup, took a swig, and gargled with it before swallowing. He focused on the deer coming to graze just past his front window and listened to the sound of a chipmunk racing across the roof. The big buck swished his tail to dislodge the mountain flies that had moved in to score. A woodpecker was pounding his house outside, probably on that spot near the back, where Spence had nailed a tin-can lid to keep him away.

And somebody had shot the hell out of his storage building.

Spence rocked on the back legs of his chair. She hadn't told him about the seventies cameras, the ones like his mother's, and hers was missing, too. Marlo was definitely keeping a lot of secrets she didn't want him to know. . . .

Someone had taken the small photograph album from his mother's bingo bag, and from Wilma's house and shop.

Why?

Spence came to his feet with the next thought. The new bullet holes in his shed weren't from a pistol. He doubted that the partiers were carrying; they knew he'd take care of them. Spence was suddenly on his feet, slamming out of the house, striding down the porch and walking to the shed. He turned and gauged the angle of the shots with where they had been initiated. A straight straw, inserted into the bullet holes, supported his guess. The shots would have come from the road and, from the size, probably from a high-powered rifle. Spence entered the building, shot his flashlight beam into the clutter, and found what he'd been seeking—he used his knife point to dig out the slugs. They rolled in his hand. "Definitely high-powered hunting rifle, probably using magnums."

A deer hunter sighting his weapon for fall tracking could have shot wild—or someone had just served Spence a big, deadly hint.

Spence Gerhard couldn't have Marlo. It just wasn't right. He needed to be shown that they weren't a match; he needed to be warned to keep his place. He'd had his chances, and he'd failed; he was nothing but a mountain bum now, and he could have had everything once—

Inside the old chalet, the heavy barbells pumped faster, the burn causing heavily defined arms to gleam with sweat. *Where were the pictures? Where was the damning evidence?*

The Secret couldn't be discovered; it had to be protected. . . .

Marlo shouldn't have disgraced herself by taking her pickup out and driving those men through town, showing off to everyone that Keith Royston was just one of the men after her.

Marlo had always been desired, wanted by men—

Rage bloomed and hurt; it was the same fury that had killed Ted Royston. Old Ted. Dirty old man, drinking and swearing, belittling everyone—Ted, who long ago had forged the cause of The Secret, the shame.

His wife was no better, helping him, and dying too easily—a heart attack one day, and Margaret Royston had never paid for all the pain she'd caused. . . .

Traci had chosen to run, and to die. That was her choice. It was her fault that she died, that she caused the death of others, including her mother. . . .

Wild erratic laughter erupted in the old house. Did Spence actually think he would find the body of his nephew? He wouldn't. Ever.

The shots fired into his storage building were meant to warn, and Spence had better take the hint. If he didn't, what happened was his fault.

Fierce hatred and drugs drove the athlete on, the power to kill, the need to kill. . . .

Where were those photographs, the ones that held The Secret? Where? Where was that roll of film?

Soon it would be time to go back, to conceal the rage, to play the role.

Then up on the ceiling, a tiny shadow moved, and the old fear shot higher to lock heavily defined muscles, to chill the sweat on the biker's face—Spider!

Hurrying quickly, the biker took an insecticide can from those lined on a shelf and sprayed the spider. It hung, suspended from its web, then dropped to the floor, to be stomped savagely by the biker's heavy boots. "I hate you! I hate you!"

Winded, the biker pushed down the fear and slid into a cold, purposeful mode.

There was a secret to be kept, a very naughty secret . . .

Eleven

"IT'S GOOD TO BE GETTING BACK TO NORMAL."

In the fourth week of June, Marlo had worked hard to place her perspectives in order: Speeding through town two weeks ago with a truckload of men wasn't her usual event, nor was lying, getting overheated on the couch with Spence. Neither would happen again.

She studied the index cards she had placed in neat rows on Fresh Takes's cutting table. Since four o'clock that morning, she had been using her project notebooks and day planner to organize the index cards into exact, very neat fourteen-day columns. She had color-coded the cards, the blue shade blocking off one-half to time spent working in her store, the pink for one-quarter working on-site in the afternoon, and one-quarter of yellow working at night, back at the store or the workshop.

The Klikamuk project was her biggest opportunity yet. She had a rough number of design ideas already, but would get the owner's approval before investing blocks of time in development.

By eleven o'clock in the morning, the usual gossip hunters

were already revolving around her store, chatting and browsing. It would take a long time for her guide trip with Spence, followed by cruising through town with the men to leave the gossip mill. Two weeks had passed, and Godfrey was still keenly interested.

Cecily Thomsen's mother, still fighting the goth decor but easing up a bit, had slid in a sly question about Spence.

Spence wanted answers Marlo didn't want to give. She'd decided to avoid him until she could mount a firm defense. That wasn't easy, especially when his voice came across the telephone lines, and her body started humming, remembering how they'd shared that couch. He appeared to be in a male snit of some kind, and when she was ready, she'd deal with that.

Personal mortification took time to deal with, Marlo decided, and her pickup episode would last a long time. When life settled more firmly, she would deal with Spence. The chilling sense of rage, the red color holding her, the pulsing she'd felt on glass hadn't appeared since that pickup ride.

"Maybe Cody has finally gone to sleep. I hope so."

Bjorn wasn't giving up and had stopped by Fresh Takes, but she'd applied the too-busy-to-talk routine. He'd called a few times, but after hours, she'd let her message machine answer. Bjorn would move on.

But Spence wanted answers, and he'd be coming after them. Marlo recognized the tactic—give the lady some space, then start hunting again. . . . She would not tell him that she even suspicioned that his mother had been murdered.

All that was gone now. Her life had settled down.

It never happened, she told herself repeatedly, hoping to believe it.

Keith hadn't been happy when she'd refused his invitation for dinner, his anger simmering over the telephone lines. "You're trying to do too much, Marlo. And you really didn't need to take Cherry's place with Spence. People are gossiping about how you used to date in high school, and that you just married Ryan because Spence decided that he wasn't coming back here to live, that he wanted to work in Seattle. Now look at him, a mountain bum, barely making a living, looking like a tramp half the time, and on some ghost hunt for his nephew's body. Get your priorities straight, Marlo. And I also don't know how you ever came to be friends with that girl, but she is no good for you."

"I choose my own friends," she'd said very carefully, warning him off Cherry, a dear friend.

But Keith had pushed: "Just how long are you going to play games with me, trying to make me jealous? Don't you know that you've made me the laughingstock of Godfrey? Everyone knows that I want to marry you, that we had an understanding—"

"I didn't know."

"I thought I made myself clear," he'd stated sharply. "Think of what I've done for you."

That remark had nettled. Marlo had worked night and day to build her business. But Keith had helped, referring customers to her, letting her decorate his showroom, and letting her have first look at any trade-in furniture. He hadn't implied previously that he expected repayment. Now that an underlying demand came up, Marlo hadn't liked it. "Exactly what?"

A vibrating, harsh silence had been his answer. "I've had enough of Spence Gerhard," Keith had said tightly. "You'll come to your senses and see that he and that Cherry-person are no good for you. You've been acting strangely, and you're under their influence."

His statement had sounded oddly like his father, and Marlo had ended the conversation on a crisp "Good-bye, Keith. Have a good day."

His reminder that he had helped her and expected to be able to choose her friends irritated.

Marlo shoved that aside; she had work to do, and while she appreciated Keith's help and the orders for his store, she could survive without owing a debt to him. . . .

She reached for a stick of strawberry licorice, her best think-food, and forced herself back to the work at hand. The Klikamuk project would take immense focus and dedication, but she already had previous obligations that required time, too. The pads and backing for the Lamberts' rustic chairs should be easy; using her serger, Marlo could embroider "Ls" and a design at the upper back pad and the filling was only foam, easily cut. The material was a beautiful creamy linen.

Marlo ran her fingers over the large swatch she had placed nearby, enjoying the cool, sturdy texture. The shade would harmonize perfectly with the dark, slightly battered-looking chairs.

Her fist crushed the material when Keith's underlying you-owe-me popped back up again, irritating her. What was it about men, that they felt everything had to be kept on a pay-as-you-go basis?

Which took Marlo back to Spence, and the burden he had carried for years, and the way she had chosen to let him off a nonexistent hook. That heavy warm tingle shot through her, her body in instant replay, reacting to his careful caress, the way he held her—very gently.

Marlo groaned as the need in her body spiked. She tried to focus on the work before her—stacking overdue projects and upcoming ones, and facing the fact that she had probably caused the Petersons' separation—or at least served as the catalyst when she'd arrived all fresh with ideas and notebooks, ready to get started. She'd already had a walk-through with Felicity Peterson, who had been insistent that French provincial was perfect.

But then Jack Peterson had reacted instantly, adamantly, to Marlo's notebook of fabrics and window coverings. "Real men don't sit on sissy chairs," he'd said, adding that the fleur-de-lis pattern reminded him of tiny pitchforks, which reminded him of hell, and that was exactly what his marriage to Felicity was—pure hell. Jack had demanded that Marlo return any down payment his wife had already made. Now, apparently, the house was to be split into different decors, suiting each one's preferences

Marlo sighed, and made a note to balance her checkbook. She remembered the check that Spence had placed in Elsie's bingo bag. It was still on the kitchen table. She would need to deposit that.

"Hello, Lorraine," she greeted the woman entering the shop. Lorraine smiled tightly and browsed through the decorating books on display. Then she turned to Marlo. "I don't know why anyone would want a houseful of recycled junk. . . . So you've finally ticked Keith off. Did you actually think that he would enjoy being made the laughingstock of Godfrey? What were you thinking—two weeks ago—driving around with all those men in the back of a pickup? Everyone in town knows that big fancy pickup is a symbol for something you envy. But of course, as a woman, you don't. Most women drive something less masculine."

The late-morning sun slid through the windows and framed Lorraine's pretty but furious face. After the past few days, Marlo wasn't up to catty remarks. "My pickup was chosen because I needed it for my work. And thank you for waiting this long to bring up that incident. I'm certain that was difficult for you. Is there anything I can help you with, Lorraine?"

"I don't think Keith will want to throw any more business your way, television star or not. You've hurt him deeply."

"Did you say you were just leaving?" Marlo asked tightly.

She had had enough interruptions from the gossip seekers, who included every Bingo Girl. Each one had something to say in favor of Spence, who, after all, was Elsie's son, and therefore part of an extended family—sort of.

Marlo looked at the man who had just entered the store. Tall and lean, in a long-sleeve summer shirt tucked into nice-fitting jeans and rolled back at the cuffs, Spence caused Marlo to stop breathing. He was all angles and dark masculine planes, those gold eyes watching her, studying her. She wished she could forget how he had felt without a shirt, pressed close and hot against her, how those lips felt against her own, against her skin, her breasts. Part of her had gone all warm and liquid inside, and that just wasn't safe, not around Spence, a man who knew women.

He looked at her, then at Lorraine, and Marlo didn't like whatever passed between them. "Spence," Lorraine said huskily, invitingly, "I was just leaving. See you around?"

He nodded slowly and slid a look at Marlo, who had leaned back against her cutting table and had crossed her arms. Spence looked like trouble; in fact, he was trouble. But this morning, Marlo promised herself, she would remain cool and in control—and he wasn't setting her off.

Lorraine swished out of the store, her short skirt flipping around her thighs, and Spence closed the door. "So?" he asked, warily. "What did I do wrong now?"

"You probably had an affair with her, too." At the sight of them together for just that instant, Marlo could easily imagine Lorraine lying in Spence's arms.

The lift of his eyebrows admitted nothing. "You don't have to be jealous, honey. I'm all yours."

He was walking too slowly and purposefully toward her, and Marlo refused to move. Spence placed his hands on either side of her hips and leaned closer to look over her shoulder, studying the neat columns of index cards. "Doing any good?"

He turned his head slightly and his lips brushed her ear; Marlo resented that shiver that revealed how he affected her. He smelled like clear mountain air, pines, soap, and man, his jaw slightly rough against her cheek. "This is a nice little orifice," he murmured against her ear. "Cute, sweet, tastable."

"Stop playing around." Marlo eased back farther against the cutting table; Spence leaned over her, his hands braced on the table. It was difficult in that position to be adamant and in control, so she tried a bluff. "You mess up hours of work, and I'll charge you for my time."

"Did you think that two weeks were going to make any difference? Ah. You did, didn't you? You thought you'd just wait this out, and everything would settle back the way you like it, nice and neat." Spence's gaze roamed over her lips as if he were tasting them. "What's the matter? Having a bad morning?"

He was right, of course, and that irritated. She had thought that everything would settle down, and it had—until Spence had walked in. Now everything was vibrating again, warming. A tiny prickling sensation ran through her as she remembered how they'd made out on that couch. "I'm trying to recover some losses. No, it hasn't been a particularly great morning. Why are you here? The couch isn't done, if that's what you came for. I'm going to need some time to catch up."

"Nice try. I came to see you." He glanced at her work, the columns of color-coded index cards. "You're too neat. You make me want to shake you up, watch you get all panicked and rattled."

He'd jumped off course, an honest admission that she hadn't expected, and that sent her emotions into overdrive. "And Lorraine? And Cherry? And your lady lawyer? And how many others do you torment on a regular basis? You haven't had that many guide trips. What do you do with all your spare time?"

"Things. I enjoy women, but you're the most unpredictable. I can't figure out what makes you tick—one minute you're all in command, and the next—well, who knows about the next. But right now, I'm concentrating on you, sweetheart. You smell good."

He moved slightly, brushed his lips across hers and started smoothing her ear, breathing unevenly. "People are gossiping about us. I came to see how you're coping."

"I'm doing just fine—"

"Are you?" The low, sexy drawl said he'd come after her, for more. She should have moved away, but she couldn't. Spence eased his work boot between her feet and nudged her legs apart with his thigh. In another minute she'd be grabbing him. Off-balance, bent back, Marlo reached for Spence's arms. He was against her, hard and big, his legs between hers. He looked down at her body, then at her, and she knew that he meant to have her.

But then, maybe she wasn't finished with him either. His lips cruised the corner of hers and back to the other side, and she stopped thinking. His tongue flicked her lips, teasing her. "Strawberry licorice, Marlo?"

"Mmm, my favorite. It helps me think. Basic brain food."

Spence leaned back slightly, and she came after him, wanting more. He straightened, and, with her hands still on his arms, Marlo stood upright. With a grim, satisfied smile, Spence stepped back just that bit, freeing himself. "A girl like you should have better sense than to get all hot and bothered around someone like me."

"Tell me you're not 'all hot and bothered,' " she managed to return and purposely looked down his body to where his jeans were stretched tight across a heavy bulge. She refused to let him intimidate her, or warn her off; she would choose what she wanted.

In a flash, Spence's hand reached out for her nape, circled

it, and he moved in to kiss her. It wasn't a sweet claiming, rather pure heat and possession, a dominant male demanding and careless.

She could match him at any time, Marlo thought, opening her mouth to his, grasping his hair with her hands, holding him. She stepped into a feverish kiss, matching his passion.

In the next heartbeat, he was stepping back, his eyes narrowed dangerously. His voice was low and uneven, a dark flush riding his cheeks. "You want to play games? I'm ready, anytime. Just call it."

Just like that—no sweet talk, no little flower bouquet or just-for-you presents, nothing but the steamy reality of sex.

That hard curve of his mouth, his narrowed eyes and grimly tense jaw said that Spence was warning her off. He wanted to show her how unsuited they were, that she'd given herself to him once, and the consequences of that had shattered her. He was trying to take her back to a time where she wouldn't go, the sweet, timid, yes-girl, not the woman she had become.

More than that, Spence was wading through very uncertain emotional ground, certain that she would get a taste and run.

"Are you trying to play the Big Bad Wolf, Spence?" she asked, deflecting anything that might expose the pain that Spence held so deeply. "You think I'm not up to handling you?"

The only surprise Spence revealed was that flickering of his eyes, a deepening of the lines between his brows. She traced a coarse, thick eyebrow with her fingertip. "You'd better back off, Gerhard," she whispered in what she hoped was a sexy tone.

He jerked back from her, tilted his head, and stared warily at her. Clearly, he hadn't expected her to give as good as she got.

But Marlo had tossed away caution from the moment

Spence had entered the shop. Her life was a mess and so were her teeter-tottering, raw emotions: It was the second time within two weeks that a man had tried to tell her what was best for her, and that wouldn't do at all. Marlo's hunger turned to a fine, simmering anger. If he wanted her to deny what she felt, she wouldn't. He'd started it, and she'd finish it. "This is how I see it. You're drooling, bub. You've been thinking about sharing that beat-up couch with me, and you're so worked up that you couldn't stay away. You want me, and you don't know what to do about it. And somewhere in your mind, you've decided what's best for me—and it isn't you. You came in here to prove just that—that you're bad medicine. You thought I'd go all wilty and scared. Well, I'm not, and I'm not letting you make *my* decisions."

Spence's hard, short curse hit the shop and ricocheted around her. "Don't call me on this. You think you see something in me that's not there. I know what I am. You're a dreamer, Marlo. You always were."

After Spence left the store, taking his dark mood with him, Marlo's legs gave way, and she slumped into her sewing chair. Spence could stir her on a level that was risky, and fascinating, and she had to play—she couldn't not play, and let him win. . . . "Every time he throws something at me, I just have to match him. He just sets me off. I should know better by now."

She was still sitting there, fifteen minutes later, trying to stuff herself back into the efficient business mode she'd been in before Spence arrived, when an eighteen-wheeler truck with a sleeper cab and orange flames painted on the front slid to a stop in the middle of Main Street. When the big engine revved, the colored glass ornaments on the shop's window danced on the ends of their transparent fishing lines.

Cherry burst from the truck's door, hopped to the ground, and ran crying into the shop.

Marlo stood to hold her and glanced at the big truck slowly moving past the window. "Cherry, what's wrong?"

"It's awful. Billy Bob has changed." Cherry was holding Marlo tightly, sobbing deeply. Then she flopped dramatically onto the cutting table, leaning back on it, and covering her eyes with her hands. She rolled over amid the index cards, and grabbed a piece of creamy linen fabric for the chair cushions, dabbing her eyes.

The fabric swept across the index cards, dragging them along and some fluttered to the floor, but Marlo was only concerned for her friend. A path of index cards followed Cherry to the display bed, where she wrapped up in the butterfly quilt and sat, tears dripping from her cheeks. Marlo spared only a minute, glancing at hours of work lying everywhere. At the moment, Cherry was more important, and she sat on the bed with Cherry. "But your messages and phone calls . . . you seemed so happy."

"I was . . . I truly was, but . . . but Billy Bob is a changed man—for the worse. He says I can't dance in the nude anymore, and *he wants to get married!*" she cried out desperately. "He wants the little house and kids and the whole thing, and I can't do that, I just can't. A big church wedding, and all that stuff—I'll just die, just shrivel up and die. . . . I'm not made to fit into molds, and that's what he wants from me. It's that or nothing he says, and—and I just can't. . . . I grew up in a box, and I will not be put back into one, playing something I don't feel like doing—I won't."

Cherry flopped the cream linen square over her head and sat, legs crossed. Marlo placed her arm around her and leaned back against the ornate antique metal bed. She rubbed her friend's back. "Cherry, this is going to be all right. Billy Bob really seems to care for you."

Cherry's anguished howl erupted suddenly. "Of course, he loves me. I know he does. But kids, Marlo . . . little people . . . babies. You have to be very careful with them, you know. There's all that stuff . . . I have no idea. I'd be an awful child-raiser. I didn't know he'd want all that."

Spence stalked into the shop and stopped abruptly. He stared at the two women seated on the bed. He frowned as he studied the cloth over Cherry's head. Then he walked to the bed and opened the package of strawberry licorice, handing a stick to Marlo. He stuck another stick in his mouth, and around it, he asked softly, gently, "What's up, Cherry?"

"I want to die, that's all." She lay down, careful to keep the linen cloth over her face.

Marlo was quick to interpret Spence's fierce, dark, protector look. "She's fine. Billy Bob wants to get married—"

"A church wedding and me in a long white dress. He wants kids, Spence. *Babies*." Clearly terrified, Cherry shuddered.

Spence nodded; his "Ah" said he understood perfectly. He lifted the cloth covering her face and stuck a licorice stick in the vicinity of her mouth. "*Merci*," Cherry murmured.

He sat on the opposite side of the bed and propped his boots on low table nearby. He surveyed the index cards scattered on the table, floor, and bed. Spence collected those within easy reach, then straightened and handed them to Marlo. The look he gave her was meaningful. He understood her time crunch and her need to comfort Cherry.

Lying on her back between Marlo and Spence, her face covered with the linen, Cherry groaned loudly, painfully. "I can't do it. I just can't. My life is over. He's leaving me, the only guy who really loved Godiva. He's got custody now. She loves him more than me."

"Cherry, he'll be back." Marlo tried to soothe, then looked at the paper cigar band that was on Cherry's third finger, left hand.

Her friend's loud groan echoed in the shop, followed by muffled sobs. "I'll never see him or Godiva again. I didn't think he was serious. Men just don't see me like the mother of their children—I'm a free soul! I'd never be good at women's committee meetings! I've done welding and hard-hat construction work, because I can't stand all that chatty teatime stuff. And I will not cook grits like his mother did. I took cooking lessons from world-class chefs in France, for gosh sakes," she ended in a defiant note.

A male caught in a situation that obviously caused him to be uneasy, Spence murmured warily, "She's just getting started. You handle this. Maybe it's just her time—you know, her regular time."

Marlo stared at him. He looked as if he wanted to escape and leave her with the Billy Bob problem. "That 'time' isn't the cause of all problems, Gerhard. And you're not going anywhere."

Cherry's loud wail erupted, and Spence shivered slightly. "Do something, Marlo."

She glanced at the crowd gathering outside her shop window. Her life was in the toilet; she had become the center of the local soap opera. "Your call. I'm fresh out."

While Cherry sniffed beneath the linen, Spence chewed on the end of his licorice stick. The look he gave Marlo was one that raised the hair on her nape. "I know," he said cheerfully. "Let's have that séance you wanted, Cherry."

Cherry tore off the linen, used it to dry her eyes, and blinked at Spence, then at Marlo. "You mean it?" she asked, like a child instantly diverted from the pain of a scraped knee.

"I could kill you," Marlo murmured darkly to Spence.

"You will, Marlo? You'll do the séance?" Cherry asked excitedly.

Doom rolled over Marlo like a big, dark, heavy cloud. She was far behind, facing hours of work time and unhappy clients, and a looming mortgage payment. "Sure. I already told you I would—sometime. Just sometime when it's convenient for everyone. I'm trying really hard to meet my contracts, you know. Sometime," she underlined darkly, and hoped that gave her time to squirm out of the dreaded séance. "But I'm not promising anything but a big fat failure."

Marlo's fear spiked and chilled her, despite the grumbling to Spence and Cherry. She didn't understand her senses leaping at the sight of red, or how she had seen Cody's face in her shop window that day. If she really opened herself during the séance, what could happen? Would that awful rage she'd felt in the Royston house, in Elsie's kitchen, and in her own apartment appear again?

The thought that Cody might be trying to reach her from his grave was too terrifying. . . .

"That's my girl. Always cheerful." Spence stood, reached for Cherry's hand, and grinned. "Let's get out of here, Cherry, and let Marlo get some work done. You've got work to do, setting up for the séance at my house. We're staying there for a while."

"I'll need time to set it up. I have studying to do. The spirit world has to be contacted just right. I didn't actually think I could talk Marlo into it," Cherry was saying, as Spence guided her out of the shop.

Before he closed the shop door, Spence shot Marlo a narrowed, warning look. If she played games with him, she would lose; Spence had always been very good at games. "How much time do you need?" he asked.

Forever. Never. "Everything I can get. A few days maybe, but if she needs me, I'm here. And Spence, don't try that bad guy routine again, okay? If you'll remember, we're even."

"Not quite," he returned tightly, grimly. "Not even close."

Spence studied the stock market report scrolling on his computer screen. Keeping Cherry busy for the three days since her return—when she wasn't working at the cafe—was fattening his portfolio; she was asleep now on his mother's couch, surrounded by a stack of books and her notes on spirit-world contact.

He had decided that Godfrey was safer than his isolated cabin; her attacker hadn't been caught, and he could be anyone, anywhere. The high-powered rifle slugs in his storage building could have been an accident, a hunter sighting his gun and overshooting the mark—or they could have been a warning. . . .

From whom? Bjorn? The big Swede had wanted Marlo, and because Cherry had turned him down, preferring Spence, the grudge ran deep.

Or Keith? Because of his father's demands, Keith was an excellent marksman, participating in community events. He'd beefed up, but the smooth muscles hadn't come from hard physical work; they came from carefully noting his anatomy and exercising for specific development.

Cherry moved restlessly, cuddling Cody's teddy bear, and Spence's thoughts turned to Marlo and his hunger for her.

He'd gone into the shop to demonstrate just how wrong he was for her—for any woman who deserved better.

In a harried mood, she'd been all cute and off-balance and sweet, and exotic. Her body had quivered, that feminine little telltale sign that had set him off. And then she'd turned on him, flipped over his noble attempt, and served it back at him. Women were tricky, Spence decided.

Spence studied Cherry. She was exhausted after another telephone session with Billy Bob trying to convince her that life on the wife-side wasn't that bad. These intense sessions led to crying jags, then to mounds of cooking, à la her French culinary training.

Spence profited from these dishes, because courtesy of Cherry, he delivered them to Marlo. This allowed him to check on her. She was focused and tired, but not terrified, and that was good. Those absentminded little thank-you kisses on his cheek were just fine—momentarily.

His body hummed with unfulfilled and sometimes painful reminders that Marlo and he hadn't actually made love. She was able to trust him enough for making out on that couch, but not with whatever had terrified her so.

He'd give her just so much time, then he was moving in to straighten out their complex relationship; men needed simplicity, and women knew how to complicate life. If he pushed too hard—because he was wanting to take possession of a very independent woman—he'd set her off again.

That would be bad. Marlo had a real thing about the arrangement he wanted now, exclusive rights. He had to be cautious, advance slowly, carefully, and take possession of the woman in his sights. Locked in his thoughts of Marlo and the humming need of her, he sat in the armchair she had reupholstered, and stared at the static on his television set.

"Spence?" Cherry asked sleepily.

"Mmm?"

"I don't know if we should have the séance here or at Ted Royston's place."

Puzzled, he turned to her. "Why Ted's?"

"Marlo freaks out at the thought of going there. You can just see the goose bumps on her. Maybe Ted is trying to communicate with her. What do you think? Here with your mom, or at Ted's? Who do you think wants to speak with her?"

Marlo freaks out at the thought of going there. And she had been pale and shaken in his mother's kitchen. . . . "What makes you think that Mom or Ted would want to do that?"

"I've studied this for years, looking for some talent in myself. I don't have it. Marlo does. She doesn't want to be intuitive—she's fighting its development, and it has her anyway. You know how structured she likes her life, how all her ducks have to be in a row. This ability doesn't do what she wants, and she's scared. That's why your mother asked her about Cody, if he was alive. Elsie believed in Marlo's intuition, too."

Cherry slid into sleep again, leaving Spence with more questions: Ted's death had been violent, Marlo had been shaken by just stepping into the kitchen where his mother had died, and after leaving her closet—What was she hiding?

He listened to the rumble of a well-tuned motorcycle on the street. It slowed in front of his house, then sped away. If that was Billy Bob, set on courting Cherry, he'd have to wait.

Spence turned back to the television's black-and-white static and his thoughts about Marlo.

One thing Marlo wasn't hiding was her sensuality; it was there in her every look, in the awareness, that humming feeling he got when he came close—Spence could still feel her body in his arms, the heated softness, pressing against him.

Spence pushed himself out of his chair and headed for a cold shower. . . .

Twelve

AFTER AN EXHAUSTING DAY IN WHICH SHE CONTINUED TO field friendly gossip-probe questions as pleasantly as possible, Marlo sat at her kitchen table.

She looked at the usually neat and clean countertops, at the sinkful of dishes; it would take her forever to put her life back together. She closed her checkbook, turned off her calculator, and groaned. Cherry's emotional dilemma, Keith's rigid anger, Lorraine's attack, and Spence—Spence had come on to her full force, an attempt to make her see how wrong he was for her.

He still hadn't put away his anger, and he didn't want her forgiveness, resenting it. He wanted to protect her from himself—And who was he, anyway, to make the decisions about who she wanted, who she wanted to hold her right now?

She groaned again and watched the faucet drip onto the dishes heaped in the sink. The time invested in the Peterson project was gone, so was the time she'd spent guiding with Spence. Spence had only provided a temporary reprieve, and Cherry was busy at work, setting up a potential psychic link with Elsie.

Marlo studied the bingo bag that Spence had placed on the table three weeks ago and drew it to her. She'd been so busy trying to catch up that she'd forgotten the check in it.

Elsie had wanted desperately to believe that her grandson was alive, and maybe Spence was right—Marlo had fed that hope, by honestly stating that she didn't think the boy was dead.

Elsie. Eyes alight, the older woman had had a determined look, then she'd started dating Ted Royston, a well-known letch. He died savagely, and Elsie had had that accident—Accident? If so, why did Marlo sense such rage coming from the kitchen—and from the old Royston house?

The sensations were prowling around her, wanting her, and Marlo pushed them back. She scrubbed her face with her hands, willing herself to work just a little more on the Klikamuk project, trying to wedge more time into a heavy schedule. She listened to the rumbling sound of a loud engine that had pulled into her driveway, and rose to her window, looking out into the night. The streetlight silhouetted a motorcycle and a rider, back-walking the machine onto the street. Her driveway was often used for that purpose, and Marlo rubbed her aching shoulders, returning to sit at the table.

With a sigh, she stroked the bingo bag's cheerful chili pepper fabric, thought fondly of a woman she had loved, then opened the bag to find Spence's check. His handwriting reflected the man—harsh, brief, strong. . . .

Spence had to believe in himself. . . .

She placed the check aside, and, still thinking of how Spence could both soothe and irritate her, Marlo began taking out the felt-tip bingo markers. Big and stubby, each color had its own pocket on the outside of the bag.

Methodically, Marlo tested the markers, intending to give the good ones to the Bingo Girls. Then from inside the bag, she began to remove Elsie's usual pack of gum, hand cream, her extra pair of glasses, and a pad and pencil. When she had played, Elsie's good luck charms, a little green hairy gnome and a laminated picture of her family years ago, had always been placed at the ready.

Marlo traced the photograph of nine-year-old Spence standing beside his father; it had been taken just before Wes Gerhard stepped into that RV with a woman, and Spence had been horribly wounded when his father had deserted.

Wes had loved his family, and yet he'd left; he'd never contacted his family and couldn't be found. . . . .

Marlo retrieved Elsie's covered travel mug, BINGO BABE written on it.

Something rattled inside the mug and Marlo tugged off the top.

A sound just outside her apartment brought her to her feet. Someone had been in her closet, had taken photographs, and Ted Royston had been killed violently, Cherry had been hurt, and Elsie—Marlo could only *feel* what had happened to Elsie. . . . What if someone . . . ? Marlo grabbed a potato masher and held it as she peered out her window.

A shape moved in the night and Waldo, a big buck who liked to browse on tender grass lawns and tender new trees, peered back at her. "Shoo, Waldo . . . shoo!"

Marlo breathed deeply, trying to steady herself. She wouldn't be terrified by every simple noise, but escalating the simplest everyday things into potential danger . . .

She returned to the table and braced herself to look into the mug. Inside was a roll of undeveloped black-and-white film with a brochure of Rosewood Village Care Center rolled around it. Elsie had circled the visiting hours and written, "Paula."

The brochure was dated the previous summer, just before

Elsie had started to date Ted Royston. It had been about that time that she'd asked Marlo to close her eyes and to feel, to sense Cody—"Is my grandson dead?" she'd asked anxiously.

Marlo frowned and studied the brochure. Inside was a list of visiting hours for the new year, and Elsie had circled the times, underlining them. Parking passes tumbled onto the table, one dated just before Elsie's accident in April and one dated nearly three years ago.

Marlo studied the roll of undeveloped film. What did it hold, and why had Elsie hidden it inside a plastic travel mug?

She turned the roll slowly to find Elsie's handwriting—"Margaret."

On impulse, Marlo dialed Spence. He sounded distracted, and in the background the clicking sounded like he was working on his computer. His "Whoever this is, it's one o'-clock in the morning" didn't sound friendly.

"It's Marlo. How's Cherry?"

The typing stopped. A chair creaked, and a computer chirped as if it were dying. Spence took his time in answering, "Sleeping. Why are you calling?"

She decided not to upset him by referring to his mother. "Just checking on Cherry."

"She's mooning over Billy Bob. Since she won't commit to a wedding, he's gone off to heal his broken heart by getting a motorcycle. She's worried he'll find someone else to ride it with him. I'm up to here with Billy Bob. . . . Why are you calling, Marlo?" he drawled in a low husky tone. "Did you miss me?"

She fought the shimmering warm glow inside her that understood it would be only a short time until she had to nab Spencer Gerhard. "I want you to talk her out of this séance stuff. I don't like it."

"Uh-huh. I haven't been able to talk her into reporting that assault. What makes you think I can talk her into anything else? But tell me why you get all spooked now and then and I just might try."

Marlo couldn't bear to step into Elsie's kitchen, to see Cody's photograph, to feel the unknown sucking at her, terrifying her. "You're determined to make my life miserable, aren't you?"

"Sure," he agreed cheerfully. "Been doing any pole dancing lately?"

If Spence was making her life unbearable, the least she could do was to torment him, just that bit. "Uh-huh. I'm all hot and sweaty and wrapped around it now. How did you guess?"

She smiled at the sound of his uneven breath, at the pause that said she'd nailed him once more. "Thanks for helping with Cherry. I love her, but I am really in a time crunch, and this is between them. I was thinking today about how nice it would have been for Paula to know her. Cherry is such a loving person. And Elsie always thought that Paula just needed love and attention. Remember how Paula used to be so shy around you? Have you seen her lately?"

The silence at the other end of the line said Spence was thinking very hard, circling her reason for calling. "Not in years."

"Oh. Good night. Please tell Cherry I called, and if you can, try to talk her out of that weird séance idea."

"Does the old Royston house make you as jittery as Mom's kitchen?"

His abrupt question stopped Marlo. Spence was prowling, digging at something, and he was very smart, catching her unprepared.

"I'm fine with either," she managed.

"You just paused, you're breathless, and I don't believe you, sweetheart."

"Good night. Tell Cherry I love her. Bye." Marlo put down the receiver. Spence was definitely suspicious—and dangerous. If his mother had been murdered, and he glimpsed any wrongdoing, he wouldn't let go until the killer was caught.

Marlo rubbed her aching temples. She could be wrong. . . . She could just be overtired, and maybe she had misplaced the archived photos and they weren't missing at all. . . .

Maybe . . . maybe . . . Then why did Cody's photograph disturb her so much? Why did the color red seem to snake out and grip her with icy fingers? Cherry had said that the sensations were supposed to come in groups, and it had been weeks since the Why Not Bar's red light had captured her. "Captured me, that's what it does. The sensations capture me, hold me."

She studied the roll of film. Why had Elsie placed this special roll into her travel mug with the Rosewood brochure and visiting hours? Had Elsie visited Paula during those times? Why?

What was on that film?

Marlo studied the spice rack on her wall, all the little ceramic boxes neatly within a wooden frame. The blue Dutch designs were all in a row, except one, which had been inserted to expose the back.

She stood and turned the paprika box so that its design matched the others and wished that the rest of her life was that easy to organize.

Everything was tilting, slipping, sliding out of her control and she was a part of something that had taken over her life and wouldn't let go. . . . While she denied it to others, Marlo knew that something in Godfrey was very, very wrong and waited for her. . . . .

Marlo hurried to the closet where she kept her cameras and photos and took a deep breath before she opened the door. The waves of anger were gone, only the picture of Cody, a tiny little boy who even in death would not let her go, remained—

Testing her reaction to the red cloth, reflecting upon the frame's glass, Marlo lifted the cloth and a sudden chill gripped her, as if Cody was trying to reach out to her.

It was starting again, churning inside her.

Marlo dropped the cloth and hurried to step outside, closing the door. "Cody, please, please go to sleep . . ."

At noon the next day, Rosewood Village Care Center quietly reflected its wealthy inhabitants. Lush greenery, sculptured around homey-type offices, and the individual "guest" cottages made the upscale care center resemble a small peaceful town.

After a two-hour drive from Godfrey, Marlo slid her pickup into a visitor's parking place. A friend with a home-developing lab and who specialized in black-and-white pictures was working on the film; Marlo would collect it on her return trip.

Earlier, at ten o'clock that morning, she'd given up any pretense of concentrating on work and had called her mother. Her excuse was reasonable: She was shopping for new upholstery material and supplies for upcoming jobs; she would visit several used furniture stores. Since she often did the same, Wilma easily accepted this with a "That will be good for you, honey. And by the way, don't worry too much about the pickup ride with all those boys, and that scene in your shop window—with all of you on the display bed. With Cherry and Spence around, such things are going to happen."

Anything could happen with Spence nearby, Marlo decided uneasily as she pushed aside the quiver deep inside her and the heat that sprang within when she thought of him touching her, kissing her. . . .

On the other hand, watching him respond was an excitement in itself and a challenge she couldn't seem to pass up. Marlo had never been a game player, but there was something about Spence that demanded she hold her own and up the ante just that bit. . . .

In late June's sunlight, Rosewood Village was quiet. Marlo walked across the carefully manicured grounds, spotted with large creamy rhododendron blooms, to the main office. A brick-and-wooden-shingle affair, it was only a bit larger than the other cottages, linked by curving stone walkways; a smooth wheelchair access route was shielded by more rhododendron.

Inside, a tranquillity fountain's water flowed upon the smooth, multicolored stones, and an aquarium gurgled, softly lit to reveal the tropical fish swimming within the waving, artificial grass and coral. Relaxing music floated over the muted shades of beige and light jade green, the textures and patterns blending harmoniously. A picture with profuse flowers tumbling in a patio scene echoed the landscape outside.

Marlo flicked the switch that was labeled, PLEASE USE AND WE WILL BE WITH YOU SOON.

A pleasant, grandmotherly type came into the waiting room. Mrs. Henry introduced herself and exchanged the usual pleasantries. "Paula Royston? Yes, of course. You'll need to sign in and get a parking pass. Just write your license plate number on it and place it on your windshield when you visit. Let me get her special guest book . . . we keep them for each person."

She hurried to a cabinet and withdrew a book, handing it to Marlo. "Strange—for years, only her brother and a few family friends visited, then about a year ago an older woman—my age—came every once in a while. Then about six months ago, only her brother visited, and not that often. Paula is doing very well. She could really go home, but I suppose after all these years, Rosewood Village really is her home."

"Oh, my. I think I hear something coming from the back. Do I?" Marlo asked; she needed time to view the book in private, to see if the "older woman" was Elsie. As the woman hurried out, Marlo flipped through the book. Elsie Gerhard's signature was the only one other than Keith's in the last six months. Elsie Gerhard's visits had become more frequent just before her death. There were only two tickets, yet she had come more often than that, at least four times. Why?

Marlo inhaled slowly, calming her unsteady senses. Logic told her that it would be in Elsie's nature to want to soothe Paula, a girl whose father had been brutally murdered.

Marlo just had time to turn back a few more pages in the "guest book." With few visitors, only Keith's monthly visits, and a spattering of Elsie's from last summer until her visits increased in January—

Instinct told Marlo to go back even more, to three years ago, six months before Traci and Cody were killed. Marlo ran her finger down the signatures and times—Keith had been consistent in his monthly visits, a few other people, and then . . . Then Traci Forbes's name had popped up twice, just six months before the wreck, and the dates matched the one on the parking pass in Elsie's bingo bag. *Traci Forbes . . . Traci Forbes . . .*

Mrs. Henry came back, and Marlo forced herself to smile. She handed the guest book to the other woman. "All checked in."

"Have a nice visit, dear," Mrs. Henry returned.

On the curved stone path to Paula's cottage, Marlo's mind flew over the discovery that Traci had visited—Traci was three years younger than she and hadn't been friends with Paula. *Why would she visit?*

Elsie had always liked Paula—perhaps Traci was delivering something for her mother?

Apparently prepared by Mrs. Henry's intercom call, Paula opened the door to Marlo. "Marlo! How nice to see you. It's been forever, hasn't it? My, how the years have passed so quickly. You understand, don't you, why I needed to be feeling better when we saw each other again? Of course, you do. You're always so understanding. I've got tea steeping in the pot. I remember how your mother used to love to chat over tea."

She took in Marlo's long-sleeve gray summer sweater, black jeans, brown penny loafers, and practical backpack. "You look marvelous. Keith told me about your new look. It really emphasizes your eyes—he wasn't exactly happy, you know. Men have a thing about long hair. Do come in and have that tea with me."

"I'd love that. Thank you. I'm shopping for upholstery goods and browsing in some Seattle shops and thought I'd stop by," Marlo lied.

Paula drew Marlo into the cozy cottage and hugged her briefly. "Come in," she invited warmly. At six feet tall, Paula was a feminine version of Keith, with the same angular facial features. Careful cosmetics emphasized her vivid blue eyes; her shoulder-length hair waved to soften her jaw. She'd gained weight since high school, but she stood straighter and moved more gracefully. Paula wore a loose, long-sleeve hostess gown of sky blue with embroidered butterflies. She seemed poised and calm.

On a side table, a laptop was in screen-saver mode. Periodically, images of butterflies fluttered their wings across the screen, and a melodic rippling sounded.

Marlo sat as Paula indicated and studied the living room and kitchen. Butterflies decorated the walls, the fabrics, and were placed on every possible display. "This is very nice. Many of my clients like butterflies for a decorating theme," she said, as Paula sat to serve tea from a pot gaily decorated with butterflies.

The tiny silver butterflies on Paula's charm bracelet tinkled merrily as she poured tea. "I do. But I love moths, too. I have a lovely little garden in the back, and they fly in to visit. Tell me, how is everyone in Godfrey? I'm on constant e-mail with Keith, but I'm certain that you know far more interesting things than my brother can relay to me. I was sorry to hear about Spence's mother. He's had such an awful time."

Paula settled gracefully upon the sofa beside Marlo, her face averted as she poured tea into cups that matched the teapot. A tiny tranquillity fountain gurgled from one corner of her home. A shadow crossed her face, and instantly Marlo felt sympathetic to a woman who had been hurt by her parents, ridiculed if her grades weren't high enough, if her manners weren't perfect, and whose tall, angular frame had been the object of her mother's disgust. A shy girl, she'd been dressed in expensive, but unsuitable clothing for her age and never permitted the usual teenage fads in hair or jewelry. Television and movies had been disallowed, and Paula could not enter the other teens' lively excitement about the shows. Excluded and alone, she'd retreated into her own world.

Marlo noted the entertainment center, a large television screen, and an expensive sound system. Feeling so much for the girl long ago, for the woman who preferred to hide from life, Marlo placed her hand over Paula's. "I'd love for you to come see me, Paula. To stay a while in Godfrey."

Paula withdrew her hand, and Marlo ached once more for the girl who had had little parental affection. Keith was not one to display affection either; both were products of a cold childhood.

"I have everything I need here. I watch movies for hours, and listen to music and watch television at all hours. There's a lovely garden, and I watch the butterflies. One of the women here has a son who visits. Fred is wonderful, really terrific. He's—" Paula's look at Marlo was shy, taking her back to years ago when the stiff exterior cracked and the girl needing love peeped out to share a secret. "He's wonderful," she whispered softly. "He's been taking me for rides, and I—"

She seemed to glow, a woman excited about the attention of a man, and Marlo was happy for her. "I'm glad, Paula. You can bring him, too, you know."

Paula's blue eyes widened, and the shadows were back again. "To Godfrey? No, I don't think so. Everything is perfect the way it is. I don't want anything to ruin it now. I'm very careful to maintain everything, to keep calm and quiet. I don't like medication."

Aware that she had upset the other woman, Marlo moved into a gentle conversation about butterflies and that she had the perfect quilt in her display room for a butterfly lover.

"I'd love it," Paula exclaimed. "And a discount? Tell Keith, will you? He'll bring it when he comes. You know, Mother would never let me have anything so—she called it, 'frivolous.' But now, I can do what I want, dress how I want. Here, I can eat all the junk food I want without anyone stopping me."

She sounded so fierce and so much like a rebellious child that Marlo once again tried to distract her. "I don't understand the difference between moths and butterflies. What is it?"

Marlo stood to face the framed display of butterflies.

Paula's mood immediately changed, and she brightened, answering that moths basically had the stouter bodies, but she preferred the butterflies because of how they emerged into beauty. She stood to stand beside Marlo, giving names to them, "The Blue Morpho, a Nero, a Southeast Asian Moth—oh, and the Postman, very interesting species and poisonous to predators. Each has their own defenses . . . sometimes camouflage, their antennae picking up scents—"

She studied Marlo and smiled warmly. "You're like the Cinnabar Moth—brilliant, almost scarlet . . . beautiful."

The moth's color seemed magnified by the glass cover, and a sudden chill went through Marlo. She hurried to change the subject, to turn away from the display.

On the way home, Marlo thought of how Paula had seemed confused when asked if Elsie had visited. "No, no, I don't think so. Did she?"

She appeared confused and rubbed her forehead. "Sometimes they give me medication to relax, and I forget. Keith tells me that I've got to forget everything but getting well, but things keep coming back to me. He tells me that I'm confused, that they never happened, and sometimes I don't really know if they did . . . I guess Elsie did visit. Yes, she did. I remember now."

Paula seemed so upset that Marlo moved the conversation away from Elsie and, before leaving, had promised to visit Paula again.

On the way home, Marlo stopped at her friend's to collect the developed pictures. Seated in her pickup, she opened the envelope and studied the black-and-white pictures. They were simple snapshots taken of a children's Halloween parade: decorated bicycles, little witches and cowboys and fairies passing along Main Street. Several shots were of the crowd standing in front of store windows, people watching the children and talking to each other—nothing at all unusual, except that the parade would have been the same one that Marlo had photographed, those pictures stolen from her closet. On that day, Elsie had shot the same scenes, using several rolls of film and advising Marlo about depth and contrast and how to adjust her camera's focus. . . .

And now Elsie's small album was missing . . . and cameras and photographs had been stolen from Wilma's home and store and several albums . . .

Marlo focused closely on the pictures. Twelve years ago, she'd been twenty and trying to paste her life together; before she'd started dating Ryan, she'd had time to play with hobbies, to try to fill her life.

The children were in costumes, and Old Eddie, gnarled and weathered, a cigarette dangling from his lips, led his llama. Two children sat on the llama's makeshift saddle. The Godfrey High School beauty queen waved at the camera, seated high on the mayor's convertible.

Margaret Royston leaned next to a young tough, and seemed to be in earnest conversation with him. She appeared in two other pictures: in conversation with a young mother holding a baby and with a heavily pregnant woman.

Mrs. Royston had been a traveling nurse, working in other towns and clinics; she often substituted for nurses who wanted vacations. It was logical that she would be interested in the baby, smiling at the mother.

Margaret. . . . Elsie had written "Margaret." Why?

Late June's afternoon sunlight slid across Godfrey's Main Street as Marlo drove into town. She noted Keith talking to Travis, seated in his wheelchair. Both men stared at her, a reminder that they'd seen her at her worst, driving like the proverbial bat out of hell on that old drag strip, not once but several times.

Keith waved her to one side of the street, where she parked and removed her sunglasses. He slid into the passenger seat. "Hi, Marlo. Thanks for visiting Paula. She really appreciated it, and I'm supposed to pick up that butterfly quilt for her. Are you going back to the shop now? You look like you've had a trying day. Would you like that, to come over to relax, have dinner, a glass of wine, and a good movie?"

He seemed to have forgotten his temper and his curt orders, and Marlo shook her head. "I'm tired and headed for home. Maybe some other time?"

"We could go out to eat, if you like."

"I think I'd better call it a day."

Instantly, Keith frowned, and his grim expression reminded her of his other mood. For just a heartbeat, a hot terrifying tingle ran up her nape as his anger vibrated in the small cab. "I see," he said stiffly, and slid from the pickup. The door clicked shut between them and through the open window, his words were harsh, "Call me when you change your mind."

Marlo watched him in her rearview mirror. The set of his shoulders and his brisk stride said he was angry. Was it possible that Keith was capable of enough rage to harm her? Or to kill someone?

Just to test her previous reactions, Marlo drove by the old Royston house. It looked as unloved and untended as ever. But the chill was there, that terrifying spine-tingling chill, her senses spiking at the red stop sign—

"Is Cherry here? I went by your place, and no one was home . . ." Marlo asked anxiously when Spence opened his cabin's door. In the evening shadows, her face was pale, her eyes dark and wide upon him. Spence sucked in his breath at the jolt of seeing her, at the scent so close—But then he wasn't happy with her, and he didn't care if she knew it.

He placed his hand on the doorframe and soaked up the sight of her. Marlo was wearing a Fresh Takes ball cap, sweater, and jeans, and she looked so sexy that his body had gone into hard alert, despite his frustration with her. "She's out riding on Billy Bob's motorcycle. They're having a date. He wants to do the courtship thing—he even asked my permission to see her."

Billy Bob had been almost comical in his romantic pursuit of Cherry: The seven-foot burly trucker wore an ill-fitting suit and well-polished, but worn biker boots; he carried a big bouquet of flowers in one hand and a helmet painted with Cherry's name in the other. "I'm going to make an honest woman of her, if she'll have me, and I'd like your permission, sir, to court her. And I'd like to speak about that with you, if you've got time," he'd said, and his eyes had never left Cherry who stood shyly eyeing him.

She'd come to take Godiva's small traveling terrarium from where it was tucked under his arm. While Cherry had sat primly on one end of the couch, Billy Bob had earnestly addressed his intentions to Spence. "I'll get a good job here—because I know Cherry likes this town. Right now, I don't have much, but I will, sir. I'll make a good husband for her—if she'll have me."

"I will not cook grits," Cherry had interrupted adamantly.

But set on his purpose, Billy Bob had continued, "We started out like chili peppers ablaze, and that was wrong, sir. I know that now. But it isn't Cherry's fault. I'm pretty irresistible when I turn on the charm. I know that I'm potent where women are concerned and should have been more careful with such a sensitive female. She just couldn't help herself."

While Spence had tried to keep a serious expression, Cherry seemed frustrated. She had handed Godiva to Spence and hurried into her room. She emerged quickly, wearing a short, flowery dress. Billy Bob had looked stunned; he stood slowly and gulped. Cherry had tugged the helmet from Billy Bob's hand and jammed it on. She had taken the bouquet, and said, "Let's go."

Billy Bob had stood and nodded to Spence. "Good evening, sir. I'll have her back before ten."

"Don't count on it," Cherry had said firmly. "Take care of Godiva."

Now, Marlo shifted uneasily on the cabin's porch and looked away from Spence. "Uh, tell Cherry to call me, okay?"

"Sure. Care to tell me where you've been all day? And don't hand me that baloney about shopping for used furniture or upholstery material. There's still a murderer and a possible rapist out there, plus someone in love with photo albums and cameras, maybe all in the same person, and you're driving all over kingdom come without checking in with your mother—or anyone?" he demanded furiously, then realized he did sound like a worried, outraged father.

But then, that was in keeping with his last words to Billy Bob and Cherry, "Have fun, kids. Be safe. Call me if you have trouble."

Spence was still dealing with his newly recognized father figure image when Marlo's prim "I've been busy" set him off again.

She had that too-innocent look, her eyes wide upon him. He tugged her into the cabin, slamming the door behind her. "What's with you, Marlo?"

His next question actually did sound like a worried father, "You should have checked in with someone."

"I was taking care of business," she stated tightly, and studied Godiva, who was sitting inside her aquarium's tin can, looking out. "Hi, Godiva. What are you doing here, Spence?"

He'd been checking on his property. Whoever had dumped Cherry on his mother's yard wasn't friendly, and the bullet holes in his building might not have been an accident.

"Cleaning. Don't change the subject. The spider is fine. I'm babysitting. Where were you?"

Marlo eased by him to study the rattan chair's broken leg, which he'd been trying to repair. "You'll feel better when you have your own furniture back. I'm sorry it's taking so long, but Cherry seems engrossed in other things, and I'm still way too busy to do it by myself."

"I'll manage. We're staying at Mom's house anyway. You know, Keith's been looking for you—"

"He found me," she said, and her grim tone lightened Spence's mood. Good old Keith didn't seem to be in such good standing for some reason.

"Have you had dinner?" Spence withheld the small burst of anger inside him. Marlo had avoided his question about her day away on her own. Wilma might accept Marlo's reasons, but Spence didn't. She had the tense, wary look of a hunter, and Cherry wasn't the only thing she was seeking.

"No. I told you, I was busy."

Busy doing what? he wanted to ask. But Marlo wasn't a woman to push too soon. He intended to get her very relaxed, even more so than their episode on the couch, then, when she trusted him fully, he'd have the answers he needed.

"Hungry?" Spence reached out and removed her ball cap, smoothing the strand of hair that stood up in a cute little peak. "Want me to feed you?"

He stroked her cheek with his thumb, enjoying the soft, warm texture of her skin. He wanted to do more than that, to make love with her, assuring himself that she was safe and— and there was that other little thing: Call it primitive caveman technique, but he wanted to make certain Marlo knew he was making his move, his claim. Maybe with full-blown love-making, she would trust him all the way. . . .

"You want to make love with me, don't you?" she asked

softly, as she searched his expression. "You're desperate for me. Right now. Right here."

She'd anticipated his smooth moves and boiled them right down to the nitty-gritty. He didn't want to admit the bald truth to her. And that Marlo could read him so easily was frustrating. "I thought we might eat first, then we could take it from there—"

Her eyebrows lifted, a delicate winged line questioning him. In the past, he'd mocked her need of planning, and now she served it back to him. "Schedules, Gerhard?"

Marlo walked toward his kitchenette area, and Spence was left to study that sway of her hips, the softness he ached to cup, the long legs he wanted wrapped around him. She had that taut, explosive look, the one that he'd experienced before she did something unpredictable. Spence tried a second gentle approach: "What's up, Marlo? You disappear for a whole day, then you turn up here. Why?"

"I wanted to see if Cherry is okay."

Her answer was evasive; too light and easy, and that raised Spence's suspicions even more. She opened the refrigerator door and leaned down to study the contents. Then she asked, "Did your mother ever say that she had visited Paula Royston at Rosewood Village?"

Marlo's tone was just enough to tell Spence that her interest wasn't casual. He intended to discover why.

"You don't want any of that." Spence walked to Marlo and closed the refrigerator door.

"Why not? There's all kinds of food here. Some kind of butter . . . mmm, says flavored—mmm, body? Body what?"

"They're left over from the bunch that stayed here last, and you don't know where they've been. I haven't cleaned the refrigerator yet." Spence popped open a fresh jar of peanut butter and one of raspberry jam, and made a sandwich, handing it to her. "Eat. And Mom did visit Paula, more often after old Royston died. She was worried about Paula. What about it?"

Marlo shrugged too carelessly, and Spence knew she was anything but casual about the question. "Just wondering. She's fine, by the way—Paula, I mean. Mmm. Do you know when Cherry might turn up?"

"Both Wilma and Cherry are supposed to call me if they know you're in town. You've been gone all day, you know. *Somewhere*," he added for emphasis.

He looked at Marlo, caught that flicker of her eyes, and knew that she wanted to keep her day private, probably for good reason. He decided to continue a normal conversation on his way to get her into bed. "If I'm not at my mother's house, then Cherry is supposed to go to Wilma's and stay there. I doubt they'll be back very soon. After their motorcycle ride, Billy Bob apparently reserved a table at Pascal's Italian Restaurant. He's going all out for a romantic evening, and Cherry told me that she is going to nail him and make him forget about all the romantic courtship stuff."

Spence poured a glass of milk, handed it to her, and leaned back against the counter. That bit of raspberry jam at the corner of her lips was causing—He leaned forward to place his hands on the refrigerator, framing her with his body, then scooped the jam away with his tongue. "Okay, Marlo. Give. Tell me."

Her eyes were too wide, too innocent with a who-me expression. "Tell you what?"

He tugged her against him, wrapped his arms around her. The quiver that ran instantly through Marlo wasn't fear and Spence had held enough women to know. "I could make you."

Her "Mmm" was skeptical. She pushed him back slightly and reached for the milk, drinking it slowly while she watched him. "I think it's time for me to go home now. I know what all this is about, you know. You're about to lose your chick, and you're looking for another one to protect. Don't pick me. I've been taking care of myself for years."

"Tough girl." Spence leaned down to nuzzle her throat, to feel that exciting ripple of her body next to his. "You can go if you want to, but you'd be missing me."

The kiss he placed at the corner of her mouth was meant to tease, but Marlo turned slightly accepting the slant of his lips upon hers. "You're all worked up, Gerhard. Admit it," she whispered.

"That's pretty hard to deny right now," he admitted, moving closer to her, testing her. He eased his knee between her legs and gently nudged the heat there.

He'd never been more fascinated by any woman, more pleasured by just one look of those earth green eyes, the softness of her mouth. She moved her lower body against his. "Yes, it is. You don't exactly know what to do with me, do you?"

"No, I don't—" Spence stared at Marlo, who had just stood on tiptoe to lick on his chin. He was having trouble keeping his hands in respectable places and was losing his perspective. That wasn't good when he wanted answers. Then he gave up and let his hands roam over soft curves. "But if you don't stop that, I think I'm going to do something with you."

Marlo's lips were soft and prowling along his jaw. "You're predictable, Gerhard. I like that."

"Like this," he said roughly as he moved in to take her. "Yes or no," he demanded later when she was panting softly, her hips meeting against his, and her breasts were bare and soft.

"What do you think?" Marlo stood away and started backing away as she unsnapped her jeans.

The zipper slid down slowly, and she turned, swaying as she walked toward the stairs leading to his loft. At the banister, she stopped and slid the jeans from her, placing them over it. "Lock the door, Spence."

She waited until he had done as she asked and walked to where she stood, her body pale within the shadows. She backed up one step when he came to study her. Aroused now, he knew that pacing lovemaking with Marlo wasn't going to be easy. "You're tan. Been using the tanning beds, Marlo?"

"Nope, sunbathing. My rooftop, with Cherry. Much better than being spotted in the woods by some jerk's binoculars. Or getting tasted by every possible crawling, biting insect."

Spence was thinking of places that he'd like to nibble on himself. He ran a fingertip around her white briefs and tugged slightly downward. "Tan all over?"

She backed up one more step. "That's for you to find out."

"Maybe I just will." Spence's deep voice was uneven and husky, his eyes taking in her body, giving her back the womanly pride another man had taken away.

He slid both hands downward, over her hips and thighs, taking away her briefs. When she stepped out of them, Spence bent to nuzzle her stomach and lower, sending riveting jolts through her, an anticipation that grew and warmed and heated. When he stood again, he removed his shirt and tossed it away.

Marlo ran her hands over his shoulders, the textures and the cords, the strength that quivered at her touch. Then Spence was in motion, wrapping his arms around her, lifting her to nuzzle her breasts, and all the while easing her back and up the stairs.

In the loft, he fell with her onto the bed, pinning her. "I guess we've got time to kill before Cherry checks in."

"I guess we do," she answered breathlessly.

Spence pushed back his need, and instead rested his weight over her, needing her to understand that at any time, the choice was hers, every step was hers . . .

Meanwhile, he decided to enjoy that fascinating moist soft mouth, the way her breath came in smothered bursts against his cheek, the way her throat tasted, the pulse leaping there.

Her fingernails dug into his shoulders, and that revved him even more, pushing back his urgent need to claim her. Because once Marlo was his, the rules were changing, and he decided to keep that fact to himself—for the moment.

Spence bent to lick the skin between her breasts, then nuzzled each one, enjoying those sweet, short, gasping breaths, the way her hips rose to answer the movement of his.

He had just worked free of his jeans and shorts with Marlo's help, had just slid on a condom with shaking fingers, when she whispered against his ear, "So you were a virgin, huh?"

Thirteen

SPENCE FROZE, HIS TAUT BODY RESTING WITHIN THE CRADLE of her thighs, his arousal just there—

"Uh-huh," he admitted darkly, and eased to his back, his hands behind his head. He slanted a look at her as she turned on her side and smoothed his chest, toying with the hair there. "Did you have to bring that up now?"

"Can't you take it?"

"Men don't talk about this stuff—not now, and not with the woman who took it—"

"It? Your virginity?"

"Well, how would you say it?" he asked darkly.

"So I 'denoued' you?" She toyed with his hair, the damp strands curling around her fingers.

"Sure. Yeah. Whatever."

Her breasts moved softly against his side. "You're cute like this, big guy."

"You've just killed the moment."

She moved her hand downward, over the six-pack muscles on his stomach to his lower belly, and smoothed lower, finding him. "I don't think it's quite dead."

Spence sucked in his breath and watched her warily. "I never know what's coming from you."

She wanted the past stripped away from this time, this moment, which she knew would be different from any sex she'd had. . . . Because Spence had always been very careful with her, and he wasn't Ryan. . . . "Understand this, Spence: We're different people, not kids anymore, and I make my own decisions. Are you agreed?"

His answer was slow and deliberate. "You ask a lot."

"I want a lot. I need to be myself, to hold true to what is important to me. And it's important to me to have this cleared—now, with you. I can't bear how you look at me sometimes. We can't go back, and we can't change it. Is it a deal?"

"You would ask me that now. . . ."

"It matters even more now."

"I can only try, Marlo."

He lay beside her, perfect for the taking. Marlo eased slowly over him, watching him just as closely, positioning him exactly where she wanted. The role of a sexual aggressor was new and thrilling, and Marlo needed to experiment, to see just how far she could push Spence to make him break—

His body jerked slightly as she found him, closed gently upon the blunt tip, invited him warmly, moistly. "Having fun?" he asked roughly.

She intended the role of Spence's vanquisher to last a long time, but her body was streaking out of control, needing more. "Do I have to do this all by myself?" she demanded against his jaw, nipping him a little, because whatever ran on inside her was savage and hot and urgent. . . .

With a rough growl, Spence's arms came down to hold her, his hands and mouth busy, raising the fever pitch higher until he was lodged deep within, their bodies struggling in a primitive heat, meeting, separating, deeper . . .

Staked out on that white-hot plane, locked to Spence,

Marlo let herself fly, her body taut, catching every ripple deep within.

When she came down, lying upon him, breathing unevenly, trembling against him, Spence soothed her with tender kisses, his hands caressing her.

She could feel him thinking, the silence wrapping around them, shaking her. "I'm okay."

"I was just going to ask that. Are you sure? Because if you aren't, we should stop now."

"Ah. You still have a delivery to make, right?"

"You could call it that, pussycat," he whispered, as his hands smoothed her hips and began moving her against him. . . .

An hour later, Marlo roused against Spence, her body feeling heavy and relaxed and complete. A mountain wind stirred the pine trees, and the swishing sound slid gently around the house. Beneath her head, his heartbeat had just slowed from a third lovemaking; his hands slowly caressed her, tucking her close to him beneath the sheet he'd pulled over them.

He wasn't sleeping, and Marlo sensed again that he was deep in thought. She thumped his chest with her finger. "If you're thinking about that first time, I'll kill you."

Spence nuzzled her forehead, kissing it. "You've kept me so busy, you've wiped out anything else. And stop smirking. I can feel you doing it."

She raised up, braced an elbow on his chest, and looked down at him. "What's going on?"

"More than all the stuff that has happened lately? Maybe I'd better tell you—"

But Marlo wanted to wallow in her change from the woman without an orgasm to one who had had several—all quite delicious. "Why did you call me 'pussycat'?"

"Feline. Cute. Arousing. Soft. Sweet. Desperate for me, stalking me . . . Hey—"

She licked the male nipple she had just bitten lightly. "Tell me what else is going on."

"Sex temptress," he finished with a grin that faded away as he smoothed back her hair from her ear. "I love these—little and sweet and tempting . . ."

"Tell me."

Spence lay quietly watching her. "Okay," he said slowly as his arms closed firmly around her, holding her tight and immobile. "Maybe we'd better tell each other a few things . . . since we're officially lovers now and in a relationship, so to speak. I'll go first, then if there is anything you want to tell me, I'll listen."

"I don't know if I like the sound of this. And why are you holding me so I can't move?"

Spence needed to hold her until they settled what ran between them, and cleared away any issues of trust. "Like I said, I'll start. You follow . . . You're not going to like this, but when I found out that Ryan had been playing around—"

She started to struggle against him. "It would be so like you to go after him. Tell me you didn't."

"Ah . . . I did."

"And what gave you that right? To interfere with my business, my life?"

"Honey—"

The sound of a motorcycle revving outside the cabin stopped Marlo's struggles. The sound slid away into the night, and Spence said, "It wasn't Cherry. Billy Bob's big road hog has a different sound to it. Probably just someone who got lost and needed to turn around. They do that sometimes."

When she started to struggle again, Spence moved over her, pinning her wrists. "Stop that, Marlo. You'll hurt yourself."

"I manage my own life. Got that?"

"Now I do." He tilted his head and listened to an approaching motorcycle. "That's them, Cherry and her boy toy."

"Get off me."

Just then, the door burst open, and Cherry rushed in. She looked rosy and windblown and Billy Bob's bulk moved silently inside. "Hey, what's the door locked for? I see Marlo's rig outside and she's been looking for me, and—"

Cherry looked up to the loft, to the bed where Marlo was pinned beneath Spence. "Um, should we wait outside? Or just go away for the night?" Cherry asked with a grin.

Then, because she was impetuous and happy, she rushed up the steps to the loft. She plopped down at the edge of the bed. "But this is great."

"Uh-huh," Spence said grimly. "Things couldn't be better, right?"

Marlo stared up at him, because somehow in the struggle, he was aroused and poised for lovemaking. She'd seen enough of that primitive expression, the flaring of his nostrils, that grim set of his lips and jaw to know that he—

"We'll be down in a minute, Cherry," Marlo said quietly.

"Oh! Oh! I'll just go show Billy Bob around." Cherry scampered down the stairs and danced around Billy Bob.

Whatever she whispered caused the big man to look embarrassed. "We're going outside," Billy Bob rumbled loudly.

"Oh, no, you're not," Marlo called back. "Stay right where you are."

Spence gave her a dark, grim look and eased away. He slid into his jeans while he stared at her. "We're not finished. The rules have just changed," he stated ominously.

"Mine or yours?"

"Both." He studied her lying on the bed, then moved quickly to wrap the sheet, cocooning her so that she couldn't move.

Marlo scowled up at him, caught his grin, and gasped as he reached down for her. "Don't you dare—"

Spence handled her easily, placing her over his shoulder,

before he turned to go down the stairs, his hand on her bottom. He sat with her on his lap and wrapped tightly in the sheet, Marlo couldn't move her body. She lifted her head away from his light kiss.

"She's cute when she gets that snooty look, isn't she?" Spence asked, then he looked at Cherry, who was standing and smiling at them as if her dream had come true. "So, Cherry. Marlo has been hunting you. Why? What's up?"

Marlo stared at him. "Did you take me to bed to get answers?"

Her voice rose despite her attempt at control. "You'd use sex to get what you want?"

"It seemed reasonable. We were just getting to the lovers telling each other secrets part."

"That is horrible."

"I wanted you, Marlo," Spence stated grimly. "I thought we could work together on whatever is worrying you, but dammit, that doesn't change the fact that we wanted each other."

"Let me go."

Spence's lips tightened, and the vein in his forehead throbbed, but he took a deep breath and released her. Marlo made her escape as soon as she could draw the sheet firmly around her and waddle to Cherry's first-floor bedroom. "Clothes!" she yelled, and in another minute Spence's big hand thrust them through the door.

In a flurry of anger, Marlo dressed quickly, opened the door, and strode out of the cabin without looking at Spence. "Talk with you later, Cherry. Call me," she said to her friend.

In her pickup cab, her hands were shaking as she inserted the key and reversed, pulling out onto the mountain road. But her body was still wrapped in a hungry ache; she should have had enough orgasms to last at least a month—and with every dark look, Spence told her that he knew it as well.

What rules?

She was halfway down the mountain road when his Jeep Wrangler came up behind her pickup. His headlights followed her down Main Street and at only nine o'clock in the evening, there were enough people to notice.

She pulled into her driveway and parked, and his Jeep slid in beside hers. They looked at each other across the distance of metal and glass. Then Spence opened his door, slammed it with just enough power to echo in her shaking body, and rounded the Jeep to tug open her pickup door. "Out. I'm seeing that you're safely tucked in. It looks like Cherry and Billy Bob are set to have a romantic evening at the cabin, so she won't be stopping by to check on you."

"I don't need anyone to check on me," she said firmly.

His "Too bad" was harsh.

Spence made the rounds of her house as he had before. In the bedroom, Spence stopped beside her bed and groaned. He looked at her pole, then at her. "Are you inviting me to stay?"

Then the telephone rang, and the message machine picked up Keith's voice: "Marlo? Are you there?"

"Better answer that. He doesn't sound happy, and he saw us pull into town."

She couldn't deal with Spence, apparently angry, herself, and Keith, all at the same time. "Good night, Spence."

He nodded curtly. "Okay. But while you're trying to put everything in neat order, think about this—"

By the time his hot demanding kiss had finished, Marlo's knees were weak. Spence's grimly satisfied look said that he'd made his point, and when she leaned weakly against him, he picked her up and dumped her in the bed. "Sleep tight. And don't forget to give good old Keith a call."

Marlo was still lying on her bed when the door slammed behind Spence. She placed her hand over her eyes and shook her head. "Just wait, Spencer, dear. You're no sweetheart, and you will definitely get yours."

But her body told her that he already had.

It had taken exactly three days to get Marlo where she wanted to go, the vacant Royston house. Three days and three nights of deciding that while Spence might have had an ulterior motive to get her into bed, she'd been with him all the way. Her body was now at a steady hum, and she'd just gotten snippy with her mother.

Spence had all the smooth moves of a man involved in a possessive takeover. He'd been very clear about his lover status and their "relationship." He wanted *rules*, and she wanted to break into the Royston house with Cherry. She owed him one—something.

"You look great in all black, Marlo. Especially with the makeup emphasizing those eyes. You do look like a cat burglar, or a pussycat. That's what Spence calls you, isn't it? Isn't it wonderful when a man slips those little endearing terms into lovemaking? Do you think we're overdressed?" Cherry asked, as Marlo and she stood in the night shadows.

"How would I know? It's my first time to break into a house. Black sweater and jeans should be perfect. I'm told that a black outfit goes with anything. But these gold hoops you made me wear feel funny."

"The two things my mother taught me that I agree with is that accessories make the outfit, and you can never go wrong with basic black."

But Marlo was thinking about Spence and his grim note that the rules had changed. *Rules? What rules?* That statement had bothered her since she'd made love with him.

As irritating as always, Spence wasn't calling. He seemed to be more visible in town, but then Cherry and

Billy Bob were playing house in his cabin. Marlo had passed Spence on the street and in stores. There was always that intense hot look, quickly shielded, as if he'd wanted her on the spot.

On the spot. Hard fast sex with Spence. Wide-open, pulsating, wild sex.

Or the soft, sweet gentle kind that said he cared how she felt and that she should be pleasured and complete before he released himself to her. Of course, his restraint had only challenged her to break it.

And he knew it. He knew exactly what he was doing and she didn't, and the rules, whatever they were, weren't hers. She decided to change the "rules" and make them hers.

"You're thinking about Spence again, aren't you?" Cherry asked. "You always get that intense, grim look as if you're out for revenge, and since Spence is the only one who can put that expression on your face, I know it's him. Don't have to be an intuitive like you to know that you're determined to waylay him. Besides, you look really sexy in that outfit."

"Hush. I only let you put on all this makeup to kill time until the town settled down. I'd think everyone would be asleep by one o'clock."

"I'm glad we're doing this. I just know that you have talent, and if Elsie were killed, and you get those flashes, maybe there's something here. You know that the flashes come in groups, don't you? Maybe in threes?"

"Oh, is that what your books tell you? How are we going to get into this place?"

Cherry moved past her and up onto the back porch stairs. She withdrew a small folded packet from her jeans pocket. A slender flash of silver appeared before she inserted it into the old lock. "Don't ask how I learned this. I've led a busy life," she said.

"I don't want to know. It's bad enough that we're doing this."

The door swung open to an interior that was dark and forbidding. Cherry gripped Marlo's hand and tugged her inside.

"This is just wrong. If I wanted to get inside, I could have asked Keith to see something—"

"Don't you get it? He could be a part of all this. He's got a temper, you know. And we already know that you are susceptible to areas where rage has burned enough to kill—"

"We don't *know* that at all, Cherry. I can't prove anything. Neither can you."

They moved down the narrow hallways, past an elaborate exercise room. "Maybe not," Cherry whispered. "But it sure wasn't friendly vibes that killed that old goat."

Cherry glanced at Marlo. "Are you feeling anything? You'll tell me when you do, won't you?"

But Marlo was concentrating on what she felt. The thin beam of Billy Bob's borrowed flashlight cut into the shadows. In the ornate, cluttered living room, the scent of Ted Royston's cigar and pipe tobacco filled the stuffy room, his humidor standing by the old worn chair and footstool.

Flashes of a heat storm buffeted Marlo, the violence taking away her breath. She gripped Cherry's hand. "I . . . it's so awful . . . the anger that's here."

"Close your eyes, Marlo. I'm right here with you. Do you see anything? Hear anything?"

Rage surrounded her, beating at her like big hard wings, pressing her air from her lungs, clenching her heart, chilling her body. . . . "I want to go—"

A door closed, the floor creaked and in the shadows of the room, Keith stood, legs braced apart. In sweat-stained T-shirt and jogging shorts and shoes, he looked powerful and savage. His body was rigid, his voice uneven as he spoke, "What are you doing here, Marlo?"

She held the miniflashlight behind her and clicked it off. "Mmm. . . . I was just—"

He reached to flip on a Tiffany lamp, and his stare pinned Cherry. "You. I might have known that you'd be at the bottom of this."

Keith's anger shook the room and when he moved menacingly toward Cherry, Marlo stepped in front of him. "It was my idea. You'd said you might be wanting to sell some of these antiques. I wanted to look them over and asked Cherry's help. Sometimes when things are of sentimental value, it's best to appraise them without the owner's presence," she added.

Marlo understood the weakness of her excuse, but it was the best she could dredge up.

Keith's narrowed eyes blazed down at her, his lips tight and forbidding. His hand shot out to grip her upper arm, and he hauled her closer. "Look at you. She's done this to you—the haircut makes you look like a boy, and that junk on your face makes you look like a whore. You're running all over the country at odd hours, and you've apparently taken Spence Gerhard into your bed. The least you could do, the most sensitive thing, since we have dated for six years, is to try to put a decent face on it."

"Let me go." Marlo barely recognized her voice, it echoed the dark anger in her.

"Let her go," Cherry said furiously, and moved to stand beside Marlo.

Keith's dangerous stare slid to Cherry, and he released Marlo. "You," he said as if the word were a curse. "You were trouble from the moment you came to Godfrey."

Cherry leaned forward. "Yeah. And what of it?"

Marlo had to ease a little to the side, this time to stop Cherry, who looked as though she would attack Keith.

"You are a very, very bad girl."

Keith's low voice shook with barely leashed anger, and Marlo knew that she had to act quickly. She took Cherry's hand and tugged her friend as she walked toward the front door. "We're going now, Keith. Do whatever you want. Think whatever you want."

Her fingers shook as she tried to open the series of dead bolts and locks. Keith's arm reached past her to open the locks, and his whisper was close to her face. "For now. Call me. We can work this out."

"He means sex. He wants to trade sex for—" Cherry stopped talking when Marlo tugged her out onto the front porch.

The door closed firmly behind them, and Marlo hurried her friend down the steps and out across the lawn onto the street.

Beneath the streetlight, Travis sat in his wheelchair. "Glad you came out. I was worried how I would make it up those steps."

Marlo hurried to push him away from the Royston house. "So what brings you out tonight, Travis?" she asked as casually as she could.

"Dad. He didn't want to get involved until he had to. He saw you and Cherry all decked out in black and moving through the bushes. I came around the back just in time to see you pick the lock—record time, by the way, Cherry. . . . Just a few minutes later, Keith jogged across the street and went into the back. Dad figured it was bad news for you to get caught inside. I'm supposed to come up with some story for the reason you were in there . . . like I asked you to go in and check on a gas leak or something."

"Heroes come in good-looking packages, Travis, and you're mine," Cherry said smoothly, and leaned down to kiss his cheek.

"So what's up?" Travis asked excitedly. "What happened? You're pushing me fast enough for a race, Marlo."

She was still bound by the brutal sensations in the room, by the encounter with Keith. He'd been threatening, and without Cherry's explanation, Marlo had known exactly what "trade" he was suggesting. Only a bully would move into a situation and push—then she thought of Travis and how many times she'd seen him wheeling down the street.

His upper body development was very strong, and he was skilled at manipulating his body into different positions, using whatever he needed at the time to brace himself. If he had a woman down, as Cherry had been in that trucking lot, he—

But Cherry had been tossed onto Spence's lawn, and that would take some doing.

Marlo felt guilty that she had even thought of Travis as an attacker. Stressed by her intuition that Elsie had been killed, by the different sensations in the Royston house and in her own, the thought that someone stalked Godfrey with a vengeance, wanting photographs, had her suspecting the most innocent. "Thanks for watching out for us, Travis," she said.

"Sure. But where are we going?"

"To Spence's house," both women answered firmly.

Fourteen

"WHAT DO YOU THINK THE GIRLS ARE UP TO, SPENCE?" BILLY Bob asked as he picked up his cards with one hand. With his other, he reached for another of Spence's freshly baked double-chocolate brownies.

Spence glanced at the clock. At two o'clock in the morning, he would have preferred Marlo's company to Billy Bob's. On the other hand, playing poker with the big trucker was better than roaming his mother's empty house and wishing for the woman he'd made love to three nights ago. What was he waiting for? A romantic invitation to dinner at her place?

The mental image of Marlo, dancing sensually around her pole, had cost him too much sleep.

Spence placed the deck of cards on his mother's coffee table. In her small "visiting" aquarium, Godiva came partially out of her can to study him. Her furry legs swept out to capture a cricket that had hopped too close. She retreated to enjoy her meal and, out of habit, Spence picked up the misting bottle and applied it inside the aquarium.

He was irritated with Marlo—and with himself. Rather, he

was uncertain of himself—Marlo needed the best, and with his father's genes, he wasn't first-class romance material. Godiva's furry gray legs came partially out of the can, and she watched him. Marlo's legs were smooth, sleek and long. "The girls are doing whatever women do. Waxing their legs, maybe."

"Mmm. I had my back waxed once for a woman who couldn't stand hair there." The big trucker grimaced. "Never again."

Spence picked up his bottle of beer and clicked on the television. He'd watched Marlo's taped shows repeatedly, and now her filmed segment about valances sprang onto the screen. "Here's a simple idea—use a heavier paisley material, mark into regular segments, hem and on the top, sew enough width to allow your window—whatever you're using—"

On screen, Marlo eased a long thin wooden pole into the material, working it through to the end. "Now hang this on the supports."

Spence's body tightened as Marlo stepped up onto the ladder, lifting the pole and fabric until it hung over the window in her workshop. The camera angles caught the lift of her breasts and the curve of her butt and those long, jeaned legs.

"That's interesting," Billy Bob murmured. But Spence was thinking about how Marlo had felt against him, how those legs had wrapped around his, how she'd tasted, how her breasts were rubbing against him, the shades of her body, pale and tanned—tanned all over.

He was hard even now, locked on the sight of her image as on-screen she continued working. "Then, taking these long ties—notice how the checks in the fabric match the maroon in the paisley design? Matching the connecting color is important when you're working with different designs. It's a case of match-unmatch and planning your color palate. Just place the ties intermittently, like this—knot gently at the bottom, allowing the ends to overlap. Then if you want to conceal the ends, place a tie there. See?" she asked brightly.

Three nights of fighting the feel of her in his arms, in his bed—of hearing her breathe against his skin, of her lips on him, had taken more than a few cold showers to ease.

Spence wasn't certain that he was the best man for her, but he wasn't getting her warmed up for Keith, either.

Keith's hard looks at Spence—which Spence had returned, of course—weren't friendly, but then they never had been.

Billy Bob leaned forward, taking in the valance segment. "Now that is really interesting. Why did you say the girls are out so late?"

"Cherry said it was a girls' night out. She said you've been keeping her so busy that maybe she was ignoring the best friend she'd ever had. She just wanted to spend some time with Marlo." Spence arranged his cards automatically, but his mind was on Marlo, on how she'd felt moving into him, inside him, as they'd made love. It was as if she were feeling around inside him, touching the dark and bruised areas, smoothing them. "It can make a man damned uncomfortable," he said aloud.

Whatever was going on with Marlo, she was too nervous, as if all of her were on edge.

She was definitely sexually aroused. Spence settled in to savor the thought that he'd had a part in that. He could feel her going into hot, moist alert each time he came near, as if her antennae were prickling.

But she was holding something inside, something that terrified her, and she wasn't letting him in that door—why had she reacted in his mother's kitchen? And what had she experienced in her closet? And why hadn't she told him about the cameras stolen from her mother's shop? Why was his mother's camera bag missing?

His first attempt at getting her to trust him in pillow talk had been foiled. She'd been gone all day, and she wouldn't tell him where she'd been. "That doesn't sound like trust to me."

"Huh?" Billy Bob asked, as Marlo began to end the segment. "What did you say?"

On the television, Marlo smiled at the camera. "And to all our new Chicago viewers, we love having you join us here at the Club Renew. I especially want to say hi to Timmy, who is five years old and saw my first show last February. Nice to see you on Club Renew. His grandma says he loves to watch us, and he sent me a drawing of myself. I framed it, Timmy. See?"

On-screen, Marlo held up the framed crayon drawing of herself and smiled. "Thank you. The other hosts and I love to answer your e-mail. And don't forget, you can order the segments you like. Until next time, I'm Marlo Malone."

Spence clicked off the taped segment. Restless with his thoughts of Marlo, and wondering why Cherry had been so secretive about "the girls' night out," Spence stood and stretched. "Want another beer?"

Billy Bob laid down his cards, and the chair creaked as he put his hands behind his head. "You got to get romantic, boy. You're all stewed up, and you're holed up, too. By the way, thanks for working with me on my investments. I appreciate that. I need a nest egg with our big wedding coming up—when I can talk Cherry into setting a date. I've probably got enough now, but I'm taking some time off work to corral her for sure."

Spence knew exactly how the other man felt about tying up a woman; Marlo was his woman, and he wanted more than an affair. Most of the time, though, he felt as though he were skidding on uncertain ground with her, and after a few "intersections" with women, he knew that no other woman would do. He just had to make her see it that way, too.

One look at Billy Bob, all stretched out and relaxed, and Spence knew that the big trucker was not suffering from lack of exhausting, good sex.

But Spence had already played one game wrong with Marlo; he didn't want to ruin this one. The element of male pride was there, too; he felt delicate, vulnerable to her, and that wasn't a feeling Spence enjoyed. He went to his computer setup in the corner of the living room and quickly surveyed his own investments, tapped a few keys, then shut down the machine. Investing was a game he enjoyed, and during his stay in Godfrey, his portfolio had grown. That information wasn't something to hide, just a fact that he didn't care to share.

His mind swung back to Marlo, whose taped show was still playing. What was bothering her? Why was she on edge, and why had—?

He walked into his mother's kitchen and stood still, trying to see what Marlo had seen, what had shaken her so. Cody's picture was on the wall. Spence had changed the linoleum immediately; in his grief, he'd needed something to pit himself against, and he couldn't bear the thought of his mother's blood on the flooring.

Spence studied the neat countertops, the kitchen window that overlooked his mother's backyard and flower garden. He saw nothing out of place. Nothing to cause Marlo's reaction. Still. Marlo had been pale and shaking, and she hadn't wanted to return to the kitchen. Why?

He heard Cherry's yell and the stamp of feet up the steps on the front porch. He was halfway across the living room when she burst into the house. Breathless and flushed with excitement, she stared at Spence, blinked, looked at Billy Bob, and blinked again.

"Gee, I guess the kids are home," Spence said as he moved past Cherry to see Marlo standing beside Travis's wheelchair at the bottom of the steps.

One look at Marlo, and Spence knew she was terrified. Marlo seemed rooted helplessly to the spot, her eyes wide upon him, her face pale in the night. Travis was beaming and excited, looking as if he'd burst; Cherry was already sitting on Billy Bob's lap, cuddling close to him and starting to go to sleep.

Anytime Cherry went to sleep that fast, she was momentarily escaping something dark and bad.

"Coming in, dear?" he asked, even as he moved down the steps to help Travis and Marlo inside.

Spence managed to play host for another half hour, quietly surveying the tension in Marlo, the looks shared by the threesome. Cherry was eating her way through the cookies and brownies that he'd baked earlier, and Cherry only overate sweets when she was really upset.

Travis took a load of cookies home, wheeling off into the night, and as Spence watched him go, he wondered again about that upper body strength and what it could do to a woman—to Cherry. Her childlike innocence, mixed with a woman's body and love of it, could arouse any man, much less a frustrated, uncertain Travis, who thought no woman would have any use for him.

Marlo seemed shell-shocked, making distracted conversation only when needed. She took a brownie and stared at it, before placing it back in the plastic container.

Evidence, Spence decided. Big clues as to Marlo's actions. That clue was small, but a gem. Marlo had always loved his mother's recipe for nutty brownies with chocolate bits. And Cherry had apparently had her way with Marlo tonight—the big gold hoops, the frisky, spiky lift of her hair, the careful makeup to exaggerate those eyes.

The next clue came when she didn't object to Spence sitting beside her, taking her cold hand, and lacing his fingers through hers. She gripped his hand tightly, and in that brief glance he read fear—and relief. A shudder ran through her body, as though she could now relax slightly.

One way or the other, he was getting to the bottom of the secrets the two women withheld. It was just a matter of time.

No one seemed tired, and the women weren't talking. Spence clicked on the rerun of Marlo's valance creation, and they watched television until he clicked it off. "Congratulations on getting that Chicago station, Marlo."

"Thanks." She glanced uneasily at the kitchen, and Cherry stiffened, leaning forward expectantly and watching Marlo.

Spence decided to uncover whatever they were hiding. "I've called the Bingo Girls for that séance. If Cherry is ready, all we need is a time, and we can have it right here."

He was testing Marlo, and when she didn't protest, he knew: She was still locked in whatever had happened before coming to his house.

He hadn't called the women, but Marlo and Cherry didn't know that; he'd call them first thing in the morning. In a simple one-two plan, they'd be excited, they'd pressure Marlo, and he could see what sifted out.

Meanwhile, he wasn't letting Marlo out of his sight; she looked as if she'd just been through a shredder. "The next thing I want to know is where are we sleeping tonight?"

Cherry scrubbed her face. "I can't stand it anymore. We went to the old Royston house, broke in, and Keith found us there. He was really, really mad—"

"Cherry!" Marlo cautioned, suddenly breaking out of her distraction. "Don't say another word."

Spence stood and tugged Marlo to her feet. He was making it his business to find out everything Marlo guarded so closely. From the look of her now, though, she'd crumple if he pushed too hard. "Like I said before, where are we sleeping tonight?"

He waited just that heartbeat for an adamant refusal and when it didn't come, he knew that Marlo was terrified. That she still didn't trust him grated. Yet, just as she had that night on the porch, she'd come to him for safety, and he was giving it to her.

In return, he hoped for answers. He stuffed some brownies in a plastic sack. You just never knew when you could use a good brownie on a reluctant female.

When they walked to her apartment, the streets were quiet. Spence still hadn't pushed for answers when they entered her bedroom. He silently undressed her and stepped naked into the shower with her, soaping her down gently. "Turn," he said quietly, and rinsed her with light sweeps of his hands.

A moment later, the steam beat down upon them, and Spence's hard face seemed softer, concerned. "It's going to be all right, Marlo. You're just having a rough patch."

She wanted to tell him everything. Everything? Including that she suspected his mother had been murdered?

"You're naked, Spence," she said, stating the obvious as he bent to study her earlobes.

He concentrated on removing the hoop earrings, and the grim set of his lips told her of his frustration. "Damn things. Yeah, well, you're naked, too. So we're even in that, at least."

No matter how frustrated he was, Spence worked very gently. She wanted to paste herself to him, to feel his safety, but she stood while he worked shampoo into her hair and stuck her beneath the shower to rinse.

"You look like you're in pieces, so everything is going to wait until—I guess it's tomorrow already, but we're not getting into anything until you're up to it. . . . Just don't try to take advantage of me, will you? I've had a hard day."

His grim humor reflected her own tension, and Marlo relaxed slightly. Spence handed her out of the shower, stepped out and dried her briskly, then himself. He reached for the nightshirt she'd hung on her bathroom door and pulled it over her head. He scanned her vanity and dabbed some eye makeup remover onto a cotton ball; he tilted her head to wipe away the remaining traces of Cherry's artistry. He ran a washcloth over her face and tossed it away.

"Jeez, I'll be glad when you grow up and can do this stuff for yourself," he muttered. "By the way, you're dynamite when you go for the sexy look."

Her sharp crack of laughter echoed off the bathroom walls, and she realized that it was an explosive release of her tension, held too tightly.

Spence looked at her sharply and tugged on his boxer shorts. "You need something to take the edge off. Get into bed."

"You're really mad, aren't you?" But Spence's anger was different from Keith's; Spence's ran to frustration and concern.

"I'd back off if I were you . . . unless you want to answer my questions," he warned, and walked out of the room. She heard cabinets open and close, then Spence returned with a bottle of her favorite wine, a glass, and a plate of brownies; he placed them beside her. He looked down her body, covered by the sheet, and he seemed grimly satisfied.

Spence circled the bed, lifted the sheet, and slid in beside her. "I'm going to sleep. I'm tired," he said, and turned his back to her.

But Spence lay wide-awake while Marlo slowly drank her glass of wine and ate brownies. By her second glass, he knew the dawning day wasn't going to be a good one. When she snuggled to his back, her arm around him, Spence resisted turning to her. He would not question Marlo now; she needed her rest.

"Spence?"

"Hmm?"

"Don't be difficult. I know you're awake, and you're angry. But do you suppose you could hold me just the same?"

"If I have to," he said casually, when he ached to hold her close. "But I've got a headache, so don't try anything."

She didn't answer, but moved into his arms when he turned. Spence held her as she slept and braced himself for whatever lurked inside Marlo, terrifying and driving her.

Marlo awoke to bright sunlight, to the brownie crumbs in her bed, and the empty wineglass beside her clock. Spence's deep voice rumbled indistinctly in her kitchen; she sniffed lightly and caught the mouthwatering aroma of cinnamon and something baking.

She turned over to her stomach, and spread out her arms and legs. She wanted to let sleep erase the brewing trouble; she wanted to wake up to a day when everything was scheduled and predictable and safe.

Spence wasn't safe. He wanted answers and he was definitely angry. Marlo turned to her back and lay listening to the two men talking in her kitchen, one of them Spence. The clock read one o'clock. . . . She'd slept past her appointments and hurried to dress quickly. Her life was in more crumbs than the brownie residue in her bed, and somehow the séance that she didn't want was scheduled.

She hurried to the kitchen, already making notes on how to waylay the Bingo Girls and fight her way back into the land of schedules and safety—but first she had to make certain that Spence understood he was going to find a way to back out of the séance situation. Marlo had no intention of following through and it was his problem to get her out of it gracefully.

In the kitchen, Jack Peterson and Spence were cooking something spicy with sausage and onions. The two six-foot-plus males filled her kitchen, moving around each other easily. Decorating magazines were spread all over her table—they weren't in her usual specific order, placed so that she could easily refer to the exact how-tos and style ideas she wanted.

Spence glanced at her, then continued expertly chopping vegetables. Marlo sat down and picked up a freshly baked sugar cookie and munched on it as she tried to decide how to approach the men. Spence had to go—somewhere else, and Jack probably was there to tell her about the divorce she'd caused.

The telephone rang, and Spence reached for it, cradling the receiver on his shoulder as he spoke. He stirred a skillet of kielbasa medallions at the same time, browning them. "That's right, Nadine. Next week. The first week of July ought to be a great time for reaching out to the spirits. Cherry is working on the details. I haven't ever been to a séance before either. But if Mom is trying to reach me, I want to try it. Pretty exciting, huh?"

He turned and showed his teeth to Marlo; she was frowning at him and shaking her head. "Uh-huh. She's really excited, too. No, just you ladies, Marlo, and me. That's all the room there is in Mom's kitchen."

His smile slid into a dark, determined expression that Marlo didn't trust. The hair on her nape lifted. She began hurriedly shuffling through the stack of messages written in Spence's bold scrawl: They all referred to phone calls she hadn't returned and appointments that she'd missed. Her business was sliding down the toilet—

Spence's unrelenting stare caused her to start sorting the magazines into an order she could use. Several of the ones with contemporary stainless kitchens had been flagged with sticky notes. Beneath one of the magazines was her open workbook, turned to the page where she had stuck Traci's, Elsie's and her own Rosewood Village parking stubs. Spence wouldn't have missed the progressive trail of dates, and now she understood his dark, grim look.

He knew where she had gone that missing day; she was following that trail, and she owed him answers.

She closed her workbook and returned his stare with a bland one of her own. She couldn't let him find out the knowledge that churned inside her—what nudged and pushed and wanted to be freed . . . *that Elsie had died violently at the hands of a killer.*

But Jack had just noticed her and paused to talk. "Sorry about what I said about your interfering with my marriage, Marlo. I came over here to give you hell, but Spence and I've been talking. Maybe Felicity and I could go for an eclectic mix as you had suggested. I see in your magazines there things can be mixed up okay. But I'd really like you to think about keeping the kitchen plain—at least the cooking area. My wife can garbage up the rest of it, the breakfast nook, but I'd like one of those big stainless-steel gas ranges, and maybe two or three ovens."

The kitchen hadn't been on the Petersons' list, and the supermodern makeover, designed for a male, would definitely add to her offerings list, and to her checking account.

The other male in her small feminine kitchen leaned back against the counter and crossed his arms. Spence studied her, and said quietly, "Jack was just leaving. And so are we."

When Jack had gone, Spence flipped open her workbook to the parking tickets. He reached onto a shelf and retrieved the black-and-white pictures she'd had developed and tossed them onto the table. "Just a guess, but I'd say that those pictures were from Mom's camera, and it's missing. A lot of cameras are missing, as well as photographs. Must be some collector wanting parts, huh? Or someone who wants certain pictures. Want to tell me about this now? Or while we're on our way to see Paula?"

"I can't go. I've got too much work—"

Spence's smile was tight. "Then I'll go alone. But you

won't know what Paula and I talked about, will you? You won't be able to feel around in those little vibes, will you?"

"You'll tell me, won't you?"

"Nope."

"What 'vibes'?"

"Hey. I'm just repeating what Cherry says, that you tune in to people, feel what's going on with them. After all, I'm just the man who's taking up your bed space once in a while, aren't I? What the hell would I know about what goes on with you?"

"It's not like that—"

"Isn't it? What, then, is it?"

"I have work, you know. And I don't like you pushing me around." Marlo glanced at Spence, who drove his Jeep in grim silence.

In the shadows of the raised soft top, his face was all harsh angles. "Honey, I'm pushing until I know what's up with you. You came in last night all wired and scared, painted up, and dressed for breaking into that Royston house. Cherry has been wanting to 'do-you-up' for a long time. You must have been distracted, or you wouldn't have let her. That's not sweet, little, scheduled, professional Marlo Kingsley, all her ducks in a row—"

"Malone," she corrected. "I got married, remember?"

Spence's wry "Who could forget" wasn't a question.

Marlo thought of how Ryan had come to her after their divorce six years ago. Before entering her shop, he'd looked back as if to see if anyone was there. "You made Ryan apologize, didn't you, Spence?"

"We had that chat I told you about at the cabin, ready to share pillow talk, remember? Because we'd just made love and usually lovers have those moments of sharing, right? Of course, I got my part out, and yours is still holed up somewhere. I agreed with Ryan that an apology to you was a good idea. How did you get Traci's parking stub? That's her license plate number."

"As I remember, you were deliberately using sex to find out where I'd been that day. That was not cricket, Spencer."

"I hate being called 'Spencer,' and you know it. I wanted answers. I thought I'd just make it easier on you. Now stick to the question, what about Traci's parking stub?"

"Easier on me, hm?" Marlo opted for the truth, minus the roll of film she'd found, Elsie's black-and-white pictures of the town's Halloween parade. "Those tickets were in your mother's bingo bag. And I'm not up for a séance, Spence."

"Too bad. The 'girls' are already planning on what to wear. Cherry is at my house, downloading everything she can from the Net on proper etiquette to communicate with the other world. She's going to break my checkbook on telephone calls to Ireland and France—she's fluent in Gaelic and French, by the way, and a few other languages. She's working full out to get ready for next week. Now, if you want to break her heart and ruin the 'girls' fun, that's up to you. I'm only the host, providing a humble abode for your use. It's all up to you, pussycat."

"Great. Put the blame on me. . . . I can't go into the kitchen again, Spence," Marlo stated unevenly.

"Why not?" His demand shot across the cab's shadows.

Marlo hunched down in her seat and watched the narrow waterfall tumble down the mountain's rocks. It flowed into a stream at the side of the highway, disappeared into a deep gorge, and disappeared into a thick forest of pines. Whether she liked it or not, she was exactly like that water, carried along on a fast, hard journey.

"That's it—sull up," Spence said. "That will settle everything. It's not as if I've got any particular right to whatever you're holding, is it? It's not as if we're in a relationship, is it? Gee whiz, I'd hate to think that I'm interfering with your privacy."

"Lay off."

"Sorry," he said curtly, without a wisp of apology in his tone. But his hand reached across to hold hers, to draw it to his thigh. "Why did you go to see Paula? She's refused to see you in the past."

Marlo looked down at his hand over hers, his thumb slowly caressing her skin. "We were friends in school. I wanted to see her."

"For old time's sake." It wasn't a question; Spence's tone said he didn't believe her. "The way I remember it was that you were kind to her. She used you when she could, just to be with you made her feel popular."

"I felt sorry for her. Her parents were so demanding and strict. And Paula worshiped you. You could have visited her. I'm sure that Elsie felt sorry for her, and probably Traci, too."

"Uh-huh. Sure. Try again. Traci was a year younger than you and Paula. She didn't like Paula or Keith. By the way, Keith called this morning. He didn't sound happy. But don't worry. I'll bail you out of jail."

"Jail?" Marlo's eyebrows lifted, her eyes wide. She blinked once and again. "Really?"

"You broke into his house, remember? That must have been some scene. Ever think about asking me to help you?" Spence's frustration was in his voice as they slowed at the entrance of the Rosewood Village parking lot. He removed his hand to use the floor shift, and Marlo's hand remained on his thigh, comforted by the powerful muscles there. He parked and turned to her. "Just one more thing—"

He leaned over to kiss her, to rub his lips against hers. "Take it easy, Marlo. I could help, you know."

"I don't think so." How could anyone understand the chilling sensations, the premonitions of disasters before they occurred, and the residue of rage that she could experience in a room. The Royston house had been filled with it; so had Keith's house.

He'd held her in his arms, kissed her, and she'd trusted him. Last night, in his father's house, Keith had menaced and threatened. "I really don't want to go to jail, Spence."

"Uh-huh. I wouldn't recommend that trading-sex-for-silence deal. Besides that, we're in a relationship, remember? One of us is, anyway. And if you want to know why Natalie came to me—with her boys—it was because she was afraid of him. He hadn't hurt her or the boys, but she was afraid he might. She asked me to help her. I never liked bullies, so I did. We had an exchange, old Keith and I, and it wasn't pleasant."

"But I dated him, Spence. I—I trusted him."

"If you remember, things have changed between us, sweetheart. There's no erasing that you gave yourself to me, all the way. In fact, it was more than making love, you were in me, feeling around somehow. Or maybe I was just too far gone to make sense of anything but how you felt, how you tasted. But Keith isn't on your calendar now, got it? We're playing one-on-one, you and I. So maybe we'd just better leave that one alone, okay?" The dark edge to his tone reminded her that they'd made love and enjoyed each other for hours at his cabin.

She decided that at the moment, she couldn't disagree that they'd made love and that Spence was the only man on her calendar. She also decided prudently that silence was her best option; Spence wasn't happy about the trust issue, or what he thought was her lack of it, concerning him.

Inside the waiting room, Mrs. Henry hurried to bring the guest book. "I understand my mother was here. I'd like to check, please?" Spence asked with a winning smile. He flipped through the pages, finding his mother's signature, then he flipped back to the date of Traci's ticket to find her signature.

Marlo caught his dark glance at her and on their way to Paula's cottage, Spence gripped her hand. "The day is warm and you're ice-cold. Want to tell me why?"

She shook her head; Spence wasn't letting go. He was searching for answers, and she feared what he would find. . . .

Paula's smile was brilliant, but her eyes flashed furiously as she greeted them. "How nice of you to come, Spence. Nice seeing you again, Marlo. You look lovely in that sweater and slacks set. Come in, please."

In her cottage, Paula again played the hostess; she served tea and chatted about how much she loved her home, her butterflies and moths, and the little idiosyncracies of the care center's residents.

A tall rugged male, Spence overpowered the small cottage's living area. He felt like an oversize predator. Paula had changed from the shy, gangling girl he'd known, but her disturbing, erratic conversation, leaping from one topic to another, told him that she wasn't as comfortable as she appeared.

Why had Traci visited her? Traci's differing age and interests had been far away from Paula's. Why was Marlo subdued and watchful, her body tense on the sofa beside him?

He noted Paula's computer screen. "You have a message."

"That's Keith. You know we e-mail each other constantly. He's upset now. He said that you and Marlo are having an affair after he had dated her for six years. He's invested six years in getting her into shape for marriage, and suddenly Marlo dumps him and crawls in bed with you. Don't you two have any sensibilities? Everyone in Godfrey is talking about it. He said that girl, Cherry, and Marlo broke into Father's house."

Paula's intense blue eyes pinned Marlo. "Don't deny it,

Marlo. Keith was there. He saw you. You've just got to pick better friends than that . . . that prostitute."

He'd expected that first jab; Paula was prowling, prodding, seeking confirmation to send back to Keith.

"Cherry is my friend, Paula," Marlo stated quietly, but her temper was simmering; her dark green eyes narrowed.

Fine. Spence had two women at odds with each other, tension brewing in the small cottage, and no answers. "Cherry is my friend, too, Paula. She's—"

Paula rose to her feet, her anger ricocheting around the room. "I don't know what she could have gotten in financial repayment from you—you're like my brother said, a life's dropout. You had potential to become someone. Now look at you—a mountain bum, no better than your father."

At least he had deflected her attack on Marlo, Spence decided grimly, and tried for another avenue to reach Paula. "Paula, my mother died accidentally in April—"

Apparently surprised, Paula sat quickly. She seemed to pull herself together, and her grimace might have served as sympathy. "Yes, of course, I know that. I liked Elsie. Keith keeps me well aware of what is happening in Godfrey. I'm so sorry for your loss. Tell me, how are the other Bingo Girls?"

Beside him, Marlo was too tense. "They're fine. We need to go, Spence."

"Not yet. Paula, what did you and my mother talk about—when she visited?"

Paula's hand fluttered, the butterfly charms tinkling at her wrist. Her blue eyes darkened before she looked at the framed butterfly collection. "Things women talk about. She was trying to help me deal with my father's death. . . . Marlo, you said you have a perfect quilt for me. I told Keith. Has he picked it up yet? Why didn't you bring it?"

Spence studied Marlo, who was reacting, to a lesser degree, the same way as she had in his mother's kitchen and her walk-in closet. She stood and moved toward the door. "Keith knows. He spoke to me about it, but he hasn't come to collect it, and I'm sorry that I didn't think to bring it. We need to go, Spence."

He stood slowly and nodded. "Paula, why did my sister come to visit you three years ago? I didn't know that you and she were friends."

Something flickered in those blue eyes. "Oh, we were. Great friends."

Somehow, Spence didn't believe her. "Since I know now that you like butterflies, I'll keep an eye out for something else for you, Paula."

Eager as a child, Paula was instantly pacified. She smiled warmly at him. "I'd love that. Come back to see me, Spence."

She turned to Marlo, and the smile slid away. "Stay out of my father's home. You'll be lucky if we don't file charges. You have hurt my brother. He wanted to marry you. You'll have to beg him now."

"I won't be doing that."

"She's still in love with you, and she's furious that we're together," Marlo said, as they got into his Jeep.

"I got that impression. She's out of luck. I'm taken."

Marlo was pale, her voice uneven. "I wish you'd stop pushing me. You were watching me for a reaction. I know what you're doing."

"Too bad. I want answers, and I'm getting them."

On the way back, Spence pulled over to a roadside scenic parking area. He let the windshield wipers work on the condensing mist, then turned them off. Rain pattered gently on the Jeep's raised soft top for a moment before he said, "Cody and Traci died at that curve."

When they'd stopped for gas, Spence had gotten her a single rose from the cashier. "Here," he'd said, and gave her a kiss to go with it. "I'm taking Billy Bob's advice and being romantic. The great sex comes later."

"Now that *is* romantic." Marlo could have cried, but had leaned against him, wishing the nightmare would end. The visit with Paula had been tense, and she'd been furious with Marlo.

Paula's anger equaled Keith's quieter version, and Marlo had edged against Spence's body. He'd placed his arm around her and guided her to the Jeep, driving silently away from the care center and Paula's fury.

Now, Spence looked out into the night, switched on the engine enough to use the windshield wipers a few times, and turned it off. "Mrs. Royston was a cold witch, and old Ted had a temper. No wonder Paula is like that."

Marlo stepped out into the cold, refreshing rain, turning her face up to receive it. She'd passed the roadside parking area many times in the two and a half years since the Forbes family had gone over the side, tearing away the guardrail. But she'd been afraid to stop, to let herself feel anything to do with Cody—

Cody. Go to sleep, Cody. . . .

"Cody, where are you?" Spence asked quietly. He turned to Marlo and smiled slightly. "That's what I ask when I'm down there, digging in the rocks, or hunting in the mountains. 'Cody, where are you?' "

Marlo looked down into the steep canyon, concealed by the rainy night, and she saw Cody. . . . Cody, only three years old, looking up at her and smiling shyly, showing off his new creation, built of blocks and complete with a parking garage.

Cody, lying on his floor mat, clutching his toy truck as he fell asleep.

Cody, with his cap of dark waving hair, and licking on a spoon, his mouth coated with a ring of chocolate frosting.

Marlo watched an approaching car as it passed them. Slowing for a curve, the driver applied the brakes, and veiled by rain, red taillights flashed.

Night enveloped the car, and in that moment, Marlo realized that she'd spoken quietly, "Cody isn't here."

Spence stared down into the black abyss. "I doubt it. His—body could be anywhere."

But Marlo's senses caused her to shiver.

When she tossed the rose into the night, it was for Traci and Dirk, who had died.

She wasn't certain about Cody's fate. He was calling her somehow, needing her . . .

Spence's arm circled her, drawing her closer, and Marlo leaned into his comfort and strenth. But her mind was on a little boy who kept calling to her.

Cody, go to sleep . . . rest . . .

Fifteen

SPENCE PULLED INTO MARLO'S DRIVEWAY AND PARKED. IN the night, she was huddled into her seat and too quiet. "I want this to go away," she whispered unevenly.

"I don't. I want answers."

"Then we've got a problem. You didn't tell me before that your mother's camera bag had been taken." That nettled; he'd been asking for honest answers from Marlo and yet had withheld that tidbit from her.

She had a point. "I would have gotten around to telling you. I had planned to do just that at the cabin—before we were interrupted, and before you got all steamed up about my little chat with Ryan."

Paula's rage had upset Marlo, but not to the degree that he'd seen before, in her walk-in closet and after the Royston house break-in. Someone was prowling Godfrey, stealing cameras and photographs, and Cherry had been attacked.

With the ease of a man who spent time in the mountains, alert and wary of potential danger, Spence noted a shadow in the large bushes beside Marlo's workshop at the end of the driveway. That placement provided a good view of her apartment's back door. The distinctive silhouette of a man in a wheelchair said that Travis Preston was sitting there. Travis, restless and familiar with Godfrey's back alleys, often turned up unexpectedly. Spence suspected that the lonely teenager needed to feel useful and was acting as his father's unofficial representative, patrolling at night. "Hey, Travis. What are you doing here?"

Travis wheeled toward them; in the dappled shadows created by the streetlights coming through trees and bushes, he looked wary. "Just thought I'd keep an eye on Marlo's place. Keith seemed pretty mad last night. Are you going to be hanging around?"

"Maybe." Spence got out of the Jeep; he intended to do more than "hang around." He glanced at the old iron fire escape ladder, now covered with ivy, which led up to Fresh Takes's rooftop. The trapdoor cut into Marlo's ceiling led to the adjacent pole in her bedroom. The pole was bolted into the floor and probably into a support out of sight—Cherry had once worked in construction; she knew the value of bolts set into sturdy wood and metal. As an experienced welder, she had probably set that pole well enough to hold a man's weight.

"Good night, Spence . . . Travis." Marlo had just stepped out into the night, circling the Jeep and hurrying up her steps. Her keys jingled in the quiet night.

She was running from him and the answers he wanted. "Marlo, flip the light switch in your bedroom when it's okay," he ordered quietly. She paused, used the keys, and slid inside.

Spence waited until he heard the series of dead bolts and locks click shut, then held his breath until her bedroom light flipped on and off. "Maybe you'd better leave now, Travis."

"Maybe I'd better stay." Travis's return was that of a male protecting his territory against another male.

"Checked on Cherry yet?" Spence asked, testing Travis. The boy was definitely keeping tabs on the town.

The boy's big strong hands tightened on his wheelchair's tires. "Yes. She's with that trucker at your cabin."

"How would you know that?"

"I know what goes on in Godfrey. I make it my business," Travis stated harshly, and rapidly wheeled down the driveway and out onto the street.

"So do I. Now."

Marlo listened to the heavy footsteps crossing her roof and turned off her exercise music. Someone had been in her walk-in closet; they'd taken photographs, and now they were coming back—

She picked up the telephone to dial the police and the trapdoor on her ceiling jerked open. Spence peered down at her, noted the telephone in her hand, and said, "Good girl."

She slammed the receiver down. "I ought to hit you with this."

He eased through the opening, caught the pole, and slid down to the floor. "Like I said, where are we sleeping tonight? And here's something else I'd like to know—someone has been using that old fire escape ladder to get up to your roof. The wind didn't rip those vines away. Someone jerked them free, probably for a better grasp. Would you know who?"

That's how the burglar got into her apartment, into her bedroom, and into her closet! Marlo shook her head, overwhelmed that she could have been sleeping in her bed and—

"That's what I expected. Just keep hoarding those secrets, honey. I wouldn't know what to do with all your trust."

Spence was already stripping, removing his shirt and tossing it aside on his way to the bathroom.

Then he stopped, turned, tilted his head, and crossed his arms. Those dark eyes flowed over her body as Spence began to walk toward her. "Nice. A lacy rose bra and matching thong panties. Who would have known? And stiletto heels? My, my."

Her body had already recognized his and the sensual tension brewing between them. Marlo could almost feel those muscles and cords and heat move against her, and her heartbeat kicked up, her stomach tightened. Excitement raced through her, prickling and heating her skin.

Marlo had known Spence would come to her tonight, seeking answers she didn't have and didn't want.

And she'd known that he would want her. To feed upon her just as she would him, to take possession of her, just as she would claim him. In this, they were equal, truthful, demanding the ultimate from each other.

The snap of his jeans was undone, and the sexual tension in her bedroom had just spiked. Retreat from herself and her needs wasn't that easy. . . .

"At least you're not fighting this. You've got that still, waiting, drowsy, steamy look, like you're already damp and hot inside and you're ready to take what you want. It's nice to know I'm useful in some ways." His finger prowled beneath the bra strap and slid it from her shoulder.

It was important that Spence understand her feelings about him. "You know I'd never give myself to you unless I felt something for you."

"Uh-huh, I do know that."

Marlo thought of the other women Spence had known and those still chasing him. If he had rules, so did she, an equal opportunity sort of thing. "I'd appreciate it, if during our—relationship—you were . . . ah—"

"Monogamous? I'm that kind of guy, if that's the question. And you're what I want. You can consider me 'tagged.' "

She relaxed a bit, a little surprised at her territorial instincts. "That's nice."

"All tidy and neat."

She wanted to nail him, to pit herself against him and win. Marlo met that dark, sultry look evenly and knew they wanted the same thing, and Spence wasn't going to make it easy. Fine. She was up to challenging him; in fact, he *needed* someone to chip that devastating confidence.

And then, of course, there was her own sensual need, alert now to that tall, hard body—because now she recognized the power of her own, the pleasure Spence could bring her and take as his due. If it was more than that, she didn't want to know—not right now. She needed to live in perfect crystalline moments, keeping all else away.

Her other strap slid down, and Spence's fingertip prowled across the lace on her breasts.

His shoulders gleamed in the dim light, his skin taut and warm and smooth as her hands skimmed over it. She dug her fingertips into the rippling power, felt the heady jolt of her own power as he tensed. Fight her, would he? Choosing his time? Then she'd make the running difficult for him, she decided, and choose her own time to have him.

Rich with sensuality, his deep voice curled around her with just that raw edge that said he couldn't wait long—nor could she. "You were just getting ready to exercise, weren't you? Work off a little of today's tension?" he asked.

"If I don't, I won't be able to sleep." She pushed away, turned, and hooked one leg around the pole, slowly sliding up and down as she met his eyes. She could feel his heat, the desire riding him, as she repeated the movement. She turned her back to him and looked at him over her shoulder, using the slow, sensuous, tantalizing technique Cherry had taught her.

But Spence wasn't in the mood to play; he tugged her back against him and cradled her breasts in his hands. His head lowered against her throat, his teeth nibbling on her ear. "You know what I want," he stated unevenly, and his urgency ignited her own.

The game was soaring out of control; she should have known that Spence would take the lead from her . . . already her body flowed back against his, softened into his hands, her throat arched for his open lips. A tiny bite set her quivering back against him. His hands pressed lower, thumbs caressing the skin over her hipbones, his fingers low and intimate, trailing over the dampness between her legs. Pressed tightly against her bottom, his body was hard and bulging within his jeans.

"If this takes very much longer, I won't be able to get up and jog in the morning, or do anything else . . ." she whispered, as his lips moved across her shoulder and her bra came away. "This is all so easy for you, isn't it?"

"No," he answered firmly, and turned her quickly. His arm circled her, easing her tight against him, those dark eyes looking down at her breasts. "No, nothing with you is easy."

"You're not going to talk about today, are you?" she asked quietly, as he found the elastic of her thong and eased it downward. His eyes glittered as he watched her step out of the lace and her shoes, and Marlo smiled as she ran her fingertip across his chest and the muscles there leaped to her touch. Delighted, she licked her fingertip and circled his nipple, watching, fascinated as it peaked.

"I've got other things on my mind right now, and I sure like those heels." His voice was low and husky as he gripped her hips and brought her tight against him, his body thrusting against hers.

"Do you? So do I," she admitted as she back-walked him to her bed and pushed him down on it. The hunger for Spence overpowered everything else, and Marlo followed him, lying over his body. "The question is: Who has who?"

"That's a good question. How long are you going to take before you take what you want?" he asked unevenly. His hand moved between them and when that hard, blunt tip pressed intimately within her thighs, Marlo knew that he couldn't wait long.

"Hotshot. You're so desirable, are you?"

"Right now," he admitted unsteadily, "I hope so. With you, the whole ball game is different. You're too unpredictable for one thing."

"I can live with that." She basked in the confidence soaring through her, a desirable woman, reformed. Good-bye to blah. Hello, woman in charge. Sexy woman in charge, Marlo corrected. The ripple that shot through Spence's hard body said he leashed his need, waiting for her to think through exactly how and what she needed.

And she needed him.

Marital sex had taken something from her; Spence was giving it back very carefully, pacing himself when another man had disregarded her sexual needs. She smoothed Spence's hair back from his rugged face, his weathered skin, loving the feel of Spence under her hands—big, powerful, sexy. His were open and warm and caressing her back, her hips, and cupping her bottom, rhythmically bringing her against him.

He was so prepared and controlled, was he? And letting her set the tempo? Well, then, she had everything to gain—and the game was hers. She couldn't wait, diving into him, taking his lips, his mouth, and easing down upon him, accepting him.

Spence's body tensed, then he was devouring her, his mouth open on her skin, his breath hot against her throat, her breasts. His hands slid over her, just lightly testing that quivering, waiting, sensitive nub, finding her slick and waiting and aching . . . It was enough to send her body convulsing against him.

He turned her suddenly and eased slightly away, but Marlo held him, watched the dark passion burn in his eyes. Spence wanted to control the fire, and she couldn't have that. She opened her lips on his shoulders and lower, biting gently on his nipple.

He arched against her, going so deep, the friction rising, tightening deep inside her, into a knot that clenched and shot pleasure through her. Spence's muffled shout, the hard taut length of his body, his pounding pulse said he was with her, with her . . .

"Spence . . ."

Marlo fell asleep almost instantly, but Spence was left to think about the day—and that he was lying with his jeans and shorts down to his knees.

"I needed my sleep, Spence . . . not running before dawn. And I didn't appreciate the slap on my butt to wake me up." Marlo ran beside Spence before dawn, coursing down the quiet residential street, and she wasn't happy. Her ball cap was pulled down, her T-shirt was damp at the throat and arms; her legs gleamed with sweat, muscles surging with each stride.

Spence had kept his eyes away from the bounce of her breasts, ones that he'd held and caressed, and tasted. This morning, his need of her had grown, and to stave off his own passion, he'd awakened her to run. Then there was something else, which put a label on Spence that read "blatantly primitive male": Keith had shown a dangerous temper, and Spence wanted Keith to know that he was out of the Marlo ball game, and she had a protector.

If Keith touched Marlo, he'd pay.

Spence glanced at her. "You usually start your day by running, don't you, sweetheart? Just think about all the schedules you're messing up."

Her dark look at him said she didn't appreciate teasing, and Spence just couldn't resist. "Boy, you're sexy this morning. I had a choice of either slapping that pretty little rump, or doing other things."

"Bite me," she muttered darkly.

"I think I did, didn't I? Just a little when you were making those quiet little yells. Maybe that's why you were biting my shoulder—to keep quiet? Honey, you don't need to worry about that." Marlo's feminine snits fascinated him; he had to tease her, to watch the temper flash in her earth green eyes.

"I do not yell."

"Oh, no? Correction, it's more like a muffled shriek."

"Give me a break."

"Okay." Spence glanced at Danny Ferris's Healthy Breads truck, parked along the sidewalk. It stood in front of Rick Ferris's home, who was Danny's brother; Rick must have taken the bread route yesterday.

Spence bent and lifted a surprised Marlo over his shoulder. "Spence, this is no time to play caveman. Put me down."

He controlled her easily by placing one hand on her wriggling body and the other on that soft bottom. "Can't. And the more you wiggle, the harder I get. I can barely walk now."

"Sure. This is idiotic."

"No more than last night when you were seducing me. This is man-woman stuff, Marlo. Get used to it."

"Just wait. If you do not put me down, I am going to give you a wedgie."

"I'm not wearing any shorts, so that might be difficult."

"You're not wearing underpants?" she asked in a shocked tone. "Everyone wears underpants."

Spence carried her to the truck. The back door was usually unlocked, and when it opened, Spence lowered her into the truck and closed the door behind them.

In the tight dark fragrant space, with racks of bread and

packaged donuts on either side of them, he tugged Marlo against him. "What did you say on the street, some little munch-on-me phrase?"

She struggled against him, and Spence secured her hands behind her back, arching her against him. In the slight melee, loaves of bread and boxes of donuts had tumbled to the floor of the truck.

"I said, 'bite me' and after that 'give me a break.' I won't even mention *that I do not yell or shriek.* What do you think you're doing? Mmm—"

A man had to have some pride, Spence thought as he eased Marlo down to the floor and tugged up her shirt to lick the sweat from her stomach and lower. She was giggling and squirming, and he felt young and happy. "You're all sweaty," she whispered breathlessly. "We have to get out of here. What if—?"

Spence did what a man has to do when a woman is sweaty and sweet and hungry, and in a fragrant bread wagon—he quickly applied protection. "This is for last night. That smirk on your face was there all night. I just want you to know I can hold my own with you."

"Oh, my," Marlo whispered unevenly while her body was still quivering in the orgasmic aftershocks, and Spence was easing away to lie flat beside her. He held her hand, pushed a crushed loaf of bread aside, and opened a box of donuts with his free hand. He handed her one and lay back to enjoy his own.

"Idiot," Marlo stated darkly around a mouthful of donut.

He rose to grin and lick the powdered sugar from her lips. She frowned up at him. Marlo was adorable, all rosy and shaken and nettled. He kissed her and grinned. "You just did that muffled shrieking thing, honey. Point won."

"I refuse to debate this any longer." With feminine dignity, Marlo eased unsteadily to her feet and tugged up her shorts.

Spence stood carefully, and when he opened the door, a crushed loaf of bread tumbled onto the street.

"What if someone sees us?" Marlo asked, as he stepped onto the pavement and lifted a hand to help her down. She hesitated and looked warily each way on the street, before Spence reached to grip her waist and lift her down.

Dawn was just beginning to lighten the streets, a cool mist hovering on the ground, the pale rhododendrons spotting the shadowy bushes. Azaleas provided borders and colors. Rick Ferris's American flag was hanging from his porch, and a cat ran across the street and down an alley.

"Then I guess I'll be buying a lot of bread." He bent to retie her running shoes and his own, which had been retrieved from his Jeep.

He lifted her hand and licked the sugar from her fingers, one by one, sucking them slightly and enjoyed her dark intense steamy look. Marlo needed to make up her own mind about their relationship; he needed her to come after him. He was feeling a little delicate and uncertain, especially about Marlo. She apparently needed space to place their relationship firmly in her mind. And he needed to know that she trusted him; whatever Marlo knew, she wasn't sharing—not even with a lover. "Marlo? If Keith wants to trade sex to keep quiet on your little break-in, I'd rather you didn't."

"You think I would?"

"Any man can see that you're well warmed, honey. Right now, you're all flushed and quivery."

"And you're proud of that, are you? That I'm 'well warmed'?"

Spence didn't trust her brewing temper. "Just watch it with Keith."

Marlo tossed the box of donuts to him. She looked at him from the shadows of her ball cap's brim. He turned the cap around, the better to see those fabulous, revealing eyes. They were narrowed and furious. Something within Spence quivered just that bit, because when upset, Marlo was unpredictable. "Does that mean that you're telling me what to do?" she challenged.

If Keith hurt her—"Wouldn't think of it. But as for myself, I'm committed," he finished, just to lay that necessary guilt trip on her.

He tossed the box back to her, and donuts spilled onto the pavement, a reminder of the hot, fast sex they'd shared on the floor of the bread wagon. Marlo looked down at the scattered pastries, and quickly hopped on them several times until they flattened and turned into crumbs. "And that is exactly what I think about your inference that I would ever, ever work several men into my calendar," she said, glaring at him.

"That isn't what I meant—" Too late. Spence watched her sail out of sight, her long legs gleaming—legs that had minutes ago cradled him tightly. That bounce to her bottom caused him to harden again.

He took a deep breath, scratched the stubble on his chin, and decided to wait out Marlo's temper—just after he safely secured that trapdoor in her ceiling.

They were lovers, attuned to each other's bodies, but Marlo wasn't sharing her secrets with him.

When he'd noted that someone had torn away the vines on the old fire escape, she'd had a definite reaction. Those expressive eyes had flickered with fear before Marlo had shielded it.

If someone had actually entered that trapdoor, Marlo would tell him, wouldn't she?

What was she hiding?

Marlo returned from the Klikamuk Ski Lodge after a morning of measuring for fabric and going through her fabric swatches with the owners. The owners were impressed with her Club Renew television segment on valances, asking for that print-and-check look for their windows and a matching fabric on the quilts. They wanted an exclusive quilt design for use in their guest rooms, and planned to market the quilts, along with other unique items, in their lodge's gift shop and in a catalog.

That required a modification to the contract, offset by a longer completion date. She was to have the rooms completed by spring. With her prior obligations to other people, that meant she'd have to hire at least five seamstresses and work like the proverbial dog. That was fine—a really good challenge with a major payoff.

To give the lodge a homey cottage look, she'd need to set up an appointment with Keith to see if his new furniture discount still held good. If it did, and stock was readily available, the stripped pine collection would be gorgeous.

She wasn't certain about doing business with Keith now. If he proved antagonistic, she'd have to look elsewhere for the lodge's furniture. She'd bartered for two of the lodge's old sofa and chair sets; she had a signed agreement to complete by spring, and had a hefty down payment check in her backpack.

Marlo opened the door to her apartment and found her mother washing dishes. She went to Wilma and hugged her. "I've just gotten the most fantastic opportunity. It's my first really big chance to move into a larger-scale business, and—you don't have a key. How did you get in?"

"Cherry. She and Spence were working on the roof when I came over, and she came down to let me in. Apparently there's no lock on that ceiling door and anyone can climb up the ladder outside. Spence thought it best with the break-ins to keep you safe. He's so thoughtful."

"Oh, he thought so, did he?" Spence seemed to have taken

over her life and her decisions. She was still stunned by the nabbing in the bread truck. "Mom, has anything new turned up about the break-ins at the house and the thrift shop?"

Wilma shook her head. "Nothing. Whoever did it is probably long gone. Travis has been working at both places, installing alarms. I can't remember how to use all that fancy modern stuff. He's always been good with gizmos. He comes over to the house a lot and to the shop. He's restless, and be careful with him, Marlo. I think he's in love with you. Now tell me everything about this big opportunity."

Marlo explained briefly as Wilma placed three plates on the table. She dipped food from a huge pottery bowl onto the plates. "That's wonderful. If you get into a pinch, the Bingo Girls and I can help you get by. If this pans out, you'll have to take on employees. . . . Spence asked me to finish the rice and browned kielbasa sausage dish he'd started yesterday, when you slept in. This is Elsie's recipe. Chicken broth and Dijon mustard really set it off. The trick is in choosing the right rice. I miss Elsie. Sit down. We'll catch up. *Cherry! Time to eat!*" she called.

In her usual running dialogue, Wilma covered many topics all at once. "I closed the shop this morning. I had a coffee for the girls at my house. We're all so excited about the séance. I didn't know you and Cherry sunbathed in the nude on the rooftop."

"Daughters don't tell their mothers everything, you know."

Wilma fixed a knowing mother's stare at Marlo, the kind that said she hadn't had anything really noteworthy until lately. Marlo decided to skip a debate on that one and divert her mother from the séance *that Spence was promoting*. She'd have to get out of that somehow. There was no telling what could happen, if she opened herself, her mind, to whatever was pursuing her. . . . "Mom, this resort job is really big.

The profit margin is high. Klikamuk wants signature quilts. I'll design them."

"This is everything you've worked so hard for, dear. You're already a television celebrity, but it's time that you paid more attention to your private life. It's unusual for you to sleep in, Marlo. But then you've been so busy. I do appreciate you calling to check in periodically, though. I saw Spence and you running this morning. . . . I thought you might be sleeping in again after visiting Paula. He seemed really interested in anything I might know about why Elsie would visit Paula. And the strangest thing—he asked about Margaret Royston. Goodness, she's been dead for ten years."

Marlo caught heavy emphasis on "sleeping in again" and on Spence. She didn't bother to correct her mother's impression. Instead, she placed glasses of water on the table. Why would Spence ask about Margaret Royston?

That roll of film had been marked, MARGARET. "Did he say anything else?"

"Only that if you're missing something from your backpack, he has it. And he left a package for you. He'll see you later. I can't tell you how excited the girls and I are over this séance thing at his house. What if Elsie does want to communicate? How do you think she'll sound?"

"I don't have a clue, Mom. This is all Cherry's deal—and Spence's. Not mine." Marlo sorted through her backpack and found the black-and-white pictures missing. Spence was definitely into her business, and as a hunter, he was very good.

If he thought for a moment that Elsie's death wasn't an accident—Marlo wasn't certain how long she could hold out against Spence's revealing-secrets, pillow-talking technique. In the bread truck this morning, she'd discovered that he'd been right about her little, muffled shrieks as she hit bingo in their lovemaking.

Cherry walked into the kitchen, took off her tool belt, and slid into a chair. She dug into the rice dish, carefully separating the chunks of sausage to one side of her plate. "I'd like to see anyone get in now," she said. "It would take two gorillas and a jackhammer to open that sucker without the key. Spence is frosted by the way. Dunno why. Billy Bob has had a few local job snags, and Keith doesn't like me taking messages for you. Bjorn was at the hardware store when I was getting some bolts. He asked about you and said he'd be around. Don't mess with him, Marlo. All his brains are in his pants."

So much for Marlo getting back on track with her work, focusing on paying jobs and big breaks. Spence had the pictures that Elsie had taken, and he was after answers.

He might not like what he found.

Like the man who had killed Ted Royston and Spence's mother just may have been the one to attack Cherry; it would take a strong man to control her. "How are you, Cherry?"

"Just fine." Then Cherry's expression flickered momentarily, darkened just that bit, a reflection of her attack. "You really did need a lock on that trapdoor, Marlo. I'm glad Spence thought of it."

Spence was thinking of too many things, including that morning hop into the bread truck. Despite Marlo's enthusiasm for the Klikamuk project, her body had been simmering all day—and that might be exactly what Spence had intended.

"Cherry, I could use some help on a project for Cecily Thomsen's bedroom. Her mother has just agreed to go with the goth look, and Cecily wants a big fake spiderweb on the wall over her bed. I can't find any of the size she wants, so you might have to paint it. I can draw the outline."

"Sure. I'll take Godiva along for inspiration. It'll be good for her. But I don't like taking much time away from setting up the séance next week."

So much for distracting Cherry from the séance that Marlo did not want to do. Marlo took the large padded envelope marked "Marlo" from her mother. She opened it to find Spence's note. "Read these. See you tonight."

"Oh, he will, will he?"

Inside was a neat bundle of Dirk Forbes's letters to Traci.

Spence pulled his Jeep into the woods, geared down to bounce along the deep ruts, and stopped. Following an almost invisible trail on foot, he hiked up the mountain to Old Eddie's summer camp.

In a forest clearing, the old miner's small cooking fire was illegal, of course, but tended by a skilled camper who treasured the mountains, his home. It had been years since Old Eddie had found "color," and the mines were closed now; he survived by Godfrey's generosity, wintering in town and in return, provided local color and stories of the "good old times."

The aged miner sat on a log, sharpening his pick. He noted Spence's backpack and the large garbage bag he carried.

"How's it going, Eddie?"

"Not bad, not bad. Sit down and talk a spell. Damn laws. They condemned my best mines." Old Eddie's mines had been more like small tunnels into the mountain's rock face, just large enough at the opening for a man to crouch and enter. The cave-ins had created avalanches and blocked roads, and now those mines were legally sealed.

Spence placed the garbage sack on the ground, then slung his backpack to the log. He sat and surveyed the tent, observing the miner's necessary etiquette. Rushing Old Eddie wasn't wise; the miner could get mulish and not reveal what he knew. Spence handed Old Eddie the contents of his backpack—basic necessities—and waited for the old man to examine them. The protocol wasn't a hardship. Spence had often brought supplies to the old miner and enjoyed watching the old man's delight.

He handed Eddie the large garbage sack filled with squashed loaves of bread and battered donut boxes. "Nice camp."

"Passable. Why are these loaves of bread all squashed?"

"Day old." It was an easier explanation than what had actually happened to the bread. And Old Eddie was used to getting food that couldn't be sold as prime.

Eddie frowned at Spence. "You're looking at that bread like you're swooning over some female, boy."

Spence smiled; maybe he was. But Marlo and he had made love, and he knew the difference between a woman giving herself because of softness and emotion, and one who needed a quick fix. This "female" in question didn't trust him, hiding her secrets, and from their past, she had good reason. She'd rather he didn't push for answers, and he had to—the parking stubs led from Traci to his mother to Marlo, a direct trail. Marlo's reaction to Paula's anger had been only a fraction of the other times, but she'd turned cold and pale. Then there was the matter of the trapdoor and that flicker of fear from Marlo, as if she suspected that someone had already entered her home.

That grated; a woman half in love—or that's what Marlo's body and kisses told Spence—usually told the lover she trusted if she was in danger. But then, they had a history, didn't they? And his father wasn't exactly a staying kind of guy, either. Maybe she was right not to trust him fully.

"I thought maybe you'd like to look at some old pictures with me."

Old Eddie remembered the youth who had talked with Margaret Royston, and "the kid's" silver-tipped Western boots. "There I was, five years ago, in a condemned mine, having broken the law to get into it, when I found this skeleton under some rocks. Now did I report it to the law and get hauled into prison, or didn't I report it? I chewed on that for a while before I hightailed it down to the law and told them about the bones."

The old miner looked across the tops of the mountains to the blue-gray in the distance. The nearby stream gurgled over the rocks as moments went by, but Spence knew better than to push the old man.

Old Eddie stared at one high peak known as Red Mountain, because of the color, and said, "I knew it was that boy in the picture from the minute I saw those silver tips on those boots in the mine. No one knew anything about him . . . just some tough passing through town who had bit off more than he could chew. No one asked me if I knew him, though, so I didn't see any reason to tell the law that it was the same kid. It was the law that said I couldn't mine anymore and I didn't see how I owed them one."

He beamed at the roll of toilet paper. "Gotta love that soft two-ply."

Then amid the weathered wrinkles on old Eddie's face, his eyes turned cold. "That Margaret Royston, she was a cold old bitch."

The mountain's five o'clock shadows were crossing the narrow mountain road when Spence headed back to Godfrey. His mind was on the pictures and the dead tough who had talked with Mrs. Royston. Why did Marlo just have the pictures developed? Where had the film been for all those years, and why that special roll?

Spence reached for the floor shift and geared down for a sharp curve on the winding old logging road. Years of erosion had cut deep ruts into the narrow, unused dirt road and the deep canyon on one side.

He had to have answers, and Marlo didn't trust him. . . . She had been terrified, and she wouldn't trust him enough to—

A sharp crack of a rifle echoed off the mountains and his Jeep went out of control. . . .

Spence and Marlo were lovers. It was there in how he touched her, looked at her, how she eased slightly against him when disturbed. . . .

They'd spent the night together . . . again. . . .

Hadn't Marlo learned anything?

Hadn't she learned that Spence wasn't for her?

The biker eased the motorcycle down the same path it had gone many times before and carefully hid it behind a thicket. Clad in black riding leather, the biker hurried up the steps of the old Swiss-motif chalet, tossed the high-powered hunting rifle and scope aside, and started to pace the bare wood floors. Above the tramp of boots, the biker's voice came out in a hiss of hatred; it ricocheted off the peeling wallpaper, growing into a litany of shouts and angry curses. . . .

"Marlo was the cause of everything . . . She is after The Secret. It has to be kept. That girl, Cherry, wasn't taking the hint that her kind wasn't wanted in Godfrey. She brought her punishment on herself, bad, bad girl." Needing to calm the furious unrelenting bitterness that ran inside, the biker quickly hurried to swallow a handful of pills and followed them with a whiskey neat. Pills smoothed the fury, allowing the biker to appear normal and return to regular life.

"They are after The Secret, all of them, and they have to be stopped."

Others had already been stopped—Traci Forbes, old Teddy, and Elsie Gerhard.

Traci had known everything, fearing for her child, Spence's nephew. She'd tried to run, and she had died. . . . "Tattletale, tattletale . . . no one would have believed you, Traci."

The biker picked up a can of insect spray and began the relentless routine that kept spiders away. "I hate spiders. . . . Poor Spence, hunting for the boy's body . . . The boy's remains will never be found. . . . What a fool he is—what a fool he was. There is no way he could have survived that wreck, going over the edge of that canyon. He never should have gotten involved with Marlo—not again. She has made me very angry, that bad, bad girl. They are lovers, and she's made her choice. Like Romeo and Juliet, if one lover dies, so should the other. It's all a balance that needs tending. . . ."

A spider hurried across the bare flooring and, fearful of it, the biker sprayed furiously. "Die! Die! Just like Marlo and Spence. She's meddled, and now she needs to be punished. And Marlo should never have made love to Spence . . . she's the reason he's dead. It's not my fault. It's that bad, bad girl's fault."

Sixteen

MARLO STOPPED PUNCHING HER CALCULATOR'S KEYS, LEFT the thick stack of notes and costs, and looked out of Fresh Takes window. At seven o'clock in the evening, the shadows had begun to close, and she'd had an exhausting day.

Concentrating on business and the plum Klikamuk Ski Lodge job wasn't easy. Lovemaking in the back of a bread truck had left her pleasured, simmering for more, and anxious for her next chance to one-up Spence. She'd showered, pasted herself into one piece, and prepared quickly for another consultation at the lodge. She studied her rough drawing of the Klikamuk proposed quilt design, using a blackberry theme from which the lodge had taken its Native American Chinook name. Given the time that she'd spent helping her mother straighten after the break-ins—then visiting Paula both times and the two sleepless nights with Spence—the first draft wasn't her best, but a basic design that could be tightened . . . if the lodge owners approved the theme.

Spence. He wanted answers, and he wouldn't stop hunting, just as he wouldn't stop looking for Cody.

How could she make love to him and yet hold so much apart that he needed to know?

One brief read of Dirk's letters to Traci and anyone could see how much he loved her and his son. Dirk Forbes would not have hurt his wife or Cody. Tenderness and lonely ache for a loved one had spread across the pages; the passages that mentioned Traci's responses reflected two people who genuinely loved each other, trying desperately to relate and change.

In the last letters, Dirk had said he would come when she wanted, when she needed him—in the instant she called. When had she called? Had Traci unexpectedly left with Cody because of a romantic tryst? Why just that night, and without notice to her mother?

Elsie had been in favor of a reconciliation; Spence hadn't been.

Marlo spread her fingers over the deep purple fabric swatch she'd been pricing for the lodge. She could *feel* the love between Traci and Dirk, just by holding the packet of letters; it pulsed warmly, softly into her hands. The red ribbon holding the letters had flowed around her hands gently, not hurting as those on the Christmas bells.

Maybe it was true; maybe she had better deal with the reality that she was intuitive—she had to be to feel so much, especially the rage pounding viciously at her when only air surrounded her, a space where someone had once stood, furious enough to kill. . . .

A flash of motion drew her to the shop's front window. Keith, dressed in an upscale top and shorts, jogged past slowly, glancing in to find her at her desk. In a few minutes he appeared at her shop's door and rapped on the glass. From his grim look, the visit promised to be unpleasant.

Marlo decided that she might as well deal with him now, for business reasons—and for personal ones. She opened the door, and Keith placed his hands on his hips. Busy with pricing and availability calls for the fabric, lining up experienced quilt makers, and calculating yardage and costs had left no time to change from her professional, but casual outfit. Keith looked down and up her dark gold sweater and slacks set. "Coming? On a run with me? Then you'd better change." The snapped invitation was a direct order.

Maybe she'd deserved that; for six years and especially the last two, Keith had made his intentions clear—he wanted to marry her. Her new and committed "relationship" with Spence must have hit Keith hard. "I'm working, but come in. I want to talk with you."

He entered and walked slowly around the shop, stopping at the butterfly quilt on the display bed. "My sister wants this. How much?" The harsh demand didn't surprise her, but that it sounded so much like his father's harshness.

Marlo named a price, discounted, and just enough to cover costs of the quilter; she folded and handed it to him. "You don't have to pay right now."

Keith took the quilt, holding it against him. "It's not as if you owe me anything, is it?" he asked in a tone Marlo didn't appreciate, indicating that she owed her success to him.

She'd worked too hard for anyone to diminish what she'd built. "What exactly do you mean?"

He moved toward her meaningfully, and Marlo braced her hand against the quilt between them, staying him. "Don't."

Keith's hand wrapped tightly around her wrist; he'd handled her so carefully before that the painful grip surprised her. "Let go of me, Keith. I realize that you're upset, but you don't want to do this."

"I thought I'd make you my wife . . . I waited until you'd crawled out of that damned marriage, got yourself on your feet with some confidence, enough to appear in a television show. And you do this to me? Bed Spence Gerhard in front of the whole town?"

Tremors of rage bounced off the walls of her shop, emanating from a man much larger and stronger than she. She was alone, and Keith's unexpected brutal streak frightened her. "I will not discuss that with you."

"Why did you and Spence visit Paula? The real reason? She said you were after something. She's sick, and when she's upset, she's hard to control."

"We didn't intend to upset Paula, Keith. We were just visiting an old friend."

His smile was only a tightening of his lips; his blue eyes glittered like sharp, cutting ice. "You're not going to tell me what you and Gerhard have cooked up, are you? Then discuss why you were in my father's house. I could have reported you and that—that girl. But I didn't. That amounts to a big debt, Marlo."

"Just what are you going to do with that house?" she asked, trying to sidetrack Keith the same as Spence had done with her. "The house and the contents—that's why I was there, to see if I could help you through the emotions tied to taking apart a family home. That's what you'd said you wanted to do, didn't you? Get rid of everything, minimize expenditures and upkeep?"

He tossed the quilt back to the display bed, grabbed Marlo's upper arms, and tugged her to him. "Let's go to bed right now and resolve this. I'm tired of being put off and made the town fool. Get Gerhard out of the picture and make it public. We'll go back to where we were. I'll forgive you. I won't remind you that you were leftovers when we marry—"

"*Leftovers?*"

The word came as a verbal slap. Keith intended to have her, to dominate her, to force her . . . "Leftovers because you're still competing with Spence, just like in high school?" she asked carefully. "Then I guess our business is terminated. I've just got a deal with Klikamuk Ski Lodge. I'll be placing a hefty order for furniture elsewhere."

Keith's fingers tightened painfully on her arms. "You do, and I'll—"

She wasn't letting him intimidate her, diminish her hard-won confidence. Keith's pride, his need to succeed, was also his weakness, and she went for it. "It's just business, Keith. You keep me happy, I deal with you. What would it look like if I took a big order out of town? That you couldn't handle a bigger deal?"

He flinched; her unexpected assertive-woman mode had scored. "You do, and you'll be sorry," he said.

She didn't like that snarling threat. "Find someone else to handle whatever you don't want in that house, Keith. I want no part of it."

Emotions slid across his face like a viewing screen. First surprise, then anxiety, followed by apprehension and distress. His hands loosened and smoothed her arms, caressing her. His tone coaxed softly, "Marlo . . . I need you, Marlo. Come back to me. It's been six years, honey. Don't toss that away—all the time we spent together, enjoyed each other, the things we have in common."

He leaned to give her a soft kiss and Marlo stood rigidly, waiting for him to finish. When Keith straightened to study her cool reaction, his eyes pleaded with her. "You don't know what I'm going through, Marlo . . . It's difficult . . ."

His whisper was uneven, his tone contrite. "I'm asking that you think very carefully about an affair with Spence. Just look at what his father did—deserting a good woman and two young children. He's shown signs of the same trait—a known womanizer, who never stays long enough for an attachment. Spence won't give you the children you should have—have a right to have. I know you want them . . . I've seen you care for them, that wistful look . . . I can give you all that. Please . . . don't throw what we have on a momentary weakness for a man who knows exactly how to use women."

Keith seemed more logical now, his anger tucked away. Handling him would be very delicate, but she had to get him out of the shop before something triggered that anger back into life.

Marlo walked to the bed and picked up the quilt, handing it to him. "I think Paula will really like this. It will be perfect in her cottage."

Keith's expression stilled. "Yes, Paula likes butterflies."

She forced an apologetic smile. "I really do need to work tonight, Keith."

"Some other time then? I've made up my mind to sell the old house, and those things will have to be handled. As you say, I am emotionally attached, so I will need someone who understands to help me. I'd like that someone to be you. I'm available anytime for a walk-through. I'd give Wilma a break for the lesser items."

It was always there, Marlo thought, the subtle emotional inclusion of her mother and beneficial income to her. In the past, that technique had been effective and appreciated, but no longer. "That would be nice. But I really don't think I have the expertise for handling the antiques."

"But I'd appreciate your input. I'll see that you get a key, and you can come and go as you like then. I don't have to be with you."

He was backing away, easing down, placating . . . and Marlo wanted to keep her options open; she might want a return visit to the Royston house, a closer look, and one untempered by Keith's furious presence. "That would be nice. But I can't guarantee that I'll take the job."

His smile was warm and tender, his hand gentle upon her cheek. "It's enough that you consider it. I'd like to start our dinners again—dating again—get back into a routine, and forget this unpleasantness."

Unpleasantness? Spence had said that Natalie Royston had come to him for protection. Now, Marlo understood why Natalie would go to Spence. He would take care of her as best he could and had arranged a deal to get her most precious possession, her children, away from the Royston temper.

"That would be nice . . . but I'm overloaded right now."

For an instant, Marlo feared she had misjudged her careful handling of Keith—his blue eyes flashed with anger that vibrated around her before he leashed and forced it back inside him. "Overloaded" would have meant that she was seeing Spence and had no room for any other man—including Keith. "I've just got to get this Klikamuk job done well, Keith," she quickly amended. "It's my first big job, and with my Club Renew television spot taking so much time, I—"

"I understand." But Keith's eyes glittered with anger that belied his soft tone. "I can wait. You might decide to change your priorities."

After he had gone, Marlo locked the door with shaking fingers. *Had Keith actually hurt Natalie?*

There was one way to find out: In the safety of her apartment, with the number she'd found for Natalie, Marlo carefully dialed Keith's ex-wife. The women exchanged pleasantries and when Marlo cautiously asked about Keith's temper, Natalie's answer was wary. "We have an . . . arrangement. I have the boys and Keith isn't challenging my full custody. I don't think he will, unless he can get a woman really upstanding and unimpeachable to marry and back him. I feel sorry for that woman, and Marlo, don't . . . do not—"

Natalie stopped and paused for a few heartbeats, then she said, "That's all I can say."

"Then about Spence. We're . . . involved now. How do you feel about him?"

"Spence Gerhard just may be the best friend I've ever had. I will always be in his debt. I know that I can call him, if I have more . . . more trouble. That's it. But as I said, Keith and I have an arrangement, and it is private and between us—and Spence. If he told you, then he must trust you implicitly—your integrity, and so do I."

Natalie hestitated for a moment, and then she said, "I'm glad you're together. He's a fine man. I knew that I could trust him in every way. Maybe it's because of his father, the way he left his family, but Spence understood a woman battling life. Whatever the reason he stepped in as he did, I'll always be grateful to him. We see him now and then, and Spence gives my sons something their father never did—respect for themselves. Respect is very important to a woman, too," Natalie stated unevenly. "I had it once. I'm working on getting it back."

When the conversation ended, Marlo returned to the darkened shop and sat on the display bed. Without seeing them, she stared at the evening's joggers and walkers and vehicles pass by her window; her mind was on Natalie's cautious answers that implied more than the words. *She kept quiet about their marriage details, assumed the label of wayward wife, and kept full custody of her sons. She was protecting her children, and, perhaps, herself. . . .*

Spence hadn't been Natalie's lover, only her protector . . . And Keith Royston had chosen Marlo to be his next wife, to set up a home to reclaim his sons. For the second time, a man had used her . . .

Flashes of her marriage to Ryan, the blithe innocent she'd been—the stupid supporting wife she'd been—passed through her, mixed with Keith's ongoing subtle mentions of marriage . . .

Marlo realized that she'd been sitting for two hours, staring at the street that no longer held joggers and walkers. Cars and trucks were parking beside the Red Hog Tavern, and the loud jukebox music throbbed into her shop.

She released the breath she'd been holding and stared at the blinking neon light inside the Red Hog Tavern. It wouldn't release her; she couldn't tear free, her throat drying, her shaking hands gripped the mattress.

Something hated her, wanted to hurt her, vicious stabs pulsated at her in sync with the sign. . . .

To free herself, Marlo pushed herself from the bed, hurried back to her apartment and out onto the back porch. She breathed deeply, hauling the night air into her lungs, pushing away the panic caused by the red light. The sensations were coming again, the residue of Keith's anger clinging to her. She wrapped her arms around herself and stood in her driveway, looking up at the stars in the clear night sky.

A motorcycle sounded and thinking it might be Cherry and Billy Bob, Marlo turned to look at the street.

Lorraine had omitted her helmet; her long sleek hair, red tank top and tight, high-cut shorts identified the woman driving the motorcycle.

The man seated behind her was Spence Gerhard.

After his shower, Spence ran a towel over his hair, slung it around his shoulders, and dialed Mac's Tow Truck service. He quickly arranged for his Jeep to be collected in the morning, and he would ride with Mac for a second look.

Spence tugged on clean jeans, and thought back to his accident. An experienced hunter, he had recognized the crack of a high-powered rifle; with a mountain of rock on one side of him and a steep canyon on the other, he'd fought the Jeep with all of his strength. Out of control, it had skidded, tilted, and gone into the canyon side. Just over the edge of the road, the front end of his Jeep had struck and lodged against a big Douglas fir tree. Stunned and hurt, Spence had crawled out slowly and eased up onto the dirt road. When he had walked a good mile or so down the dirt road, Lorraine had come by on her motorcycle, and he taken her offer of a ride into Godfrey.

Lorraine apparently had gone riding after work, but she had the hot, tousled look and scent of a woman who had just been thoroughly rolled on a mountain blanket.

When the ride had ended at his house, Spence hadn't taken the blatant offer of her body.

That high-powered rifle crack echoed again in his head. From what Spence could see from the road, pieces of that front right tire were strewn across the mountain.

Whoever had served him notice by shooting his storage building had now decided to make the game real—

Spence's hand was just over the receiver, ready to dial Marlo, when the telephone rang. It was Lorraine, apparently sitting in a bubble bath and still steaming. Spence wondered briefly just who had been on that mountain blanket with her. Had that unidentified man fired that expert shot?

Spence had seen Lorraine's shooting ability at the local shooting contests and dismissed her; her ability ran to posing, showing off her body, rather than hitting a bull's-eye.

Next question: Did someone miss the target—Spence—and hit the tire instead?

"Marlo is busy, you know," Lorraine was saying huskily. "Keith's making a play for her. I called him tonight, just on some excuse. No offense, Spence, but Keith is quite the catch. My chances just went up. He was in Fresh Takes today, got this fabulous butterfly quilt from Marlo apparently, a gift for his sister. Marlo would be a fool to turn him down, lover. I can always tell when he's steamed . . . he's pretty easy to read."

Spence realized he was gripping the telephone hard; if

Keith hurt Marlo . . . "Was that what you were doing earlier on the mountain, Lorraine? Were you reading Keith?"

Her laughter was low and sexy. "Wouldn't you like to know?" she teased. "Are you coming over? Or do I come over there? We might as well enjoy each other—no strings, right? That's your style . . . women usually run after you. If that makes it easier for you, I'm fine with that. But I could really use some relaxation tonight—"

"Thanks, but I'll pass. Rough day on the mountain, you know. You wouldn't have happened to hear any shooting up there?"

"Just the blowout. Sounded bad. You've never let anything stop you with other women—or you didn't, before Cherry moved in with you. Maybe some other time?" she asked softly.

"Maybe." He decided not to close the door on Lorraine's offer; she might have information that he needed—like where Keith was target practicing. Before the call ended, he said, "I'd rather not let Marlo or Keith know we had this little conversation, Lorraine."

Would Marlo tell him about Keith's visit today? Spence would soon find out.

She laughed knowingly. "Gotcha. Get what you can get while the getting is good, right? And to be truthful, it wouldn't do me any good if Keith knew you were interested in me."

He let her have that little ego trip, then called Marlo. He explained briefly that he'd had a tire blow out on the logging road and that he wasn't hurt.

Spence was about to give her a subtle opening to tell him about Keith's visit. He wasn't expecting her frosty comeback: "I'm glad you're not hurt, but no, I do not need company tonight."

Company. Just like that . . . an un-invitation. "Bad day?" he asked cautiously.

"Several of them. I'm busy working, Spence—"

Fear shot through him; if someone was there, hurting her . . . "I'm coming over."

"No, you're not. I've had enough of men pushing me around today."

That tone sounded more normal. "You're still mad about this morning?"

He shouldn't have nabbed her that way. But there she was, all ripe and sweaty, and—Just thinking about her lying beneath him, tearing at his clothes, hot and tight and eager for him, caused Spence's body to go into full hard alert.

"In the back of a bread truck, Spence. That is just awful. Just think of how I acted. And you—you weren't any better. What if someone had opened that door and found us—busy in there?"

" 'Busy?' " Spence smiled slightly. Marlo wouldn't be recalling their hot, fast lovemaking if anyone were in the vicinity and listening. "Is that what we were? Busy?"

"You know what I mean. People just don't behave like that."

"Prude."

"I am not." The answer came back like a shot. "Are you really okay, Spence?"

"Really. Care to come over and kiss my bruises and make me feel all better?"

The silence at the other end of the line told him Marlo was trying desperately to think of a suitable comeback. When the silence grew, Spence said, "You said 'men' as in plural. What other man is pushing you?"

Marlo's hesitation told him she was avoiding his question—probably for a reason. "You know how it is. Clients change their minds and don't understand that they aren't the priority of the day."

But Spence recognized the evasive answer that led to

Keith. Keith had openly squired Marlo for six years, more intensely in the last two, and he wasn't happy with the gossip circling her and Spence. The Roystons didn't like being crossed, and Spence remembered how violent Keith had been when Natalie had left him.

Protecting her, Spence had negotiated the stand-off, and the keep-quiet deal that said Natalie had full custody of the boys and a hefty maintenance sum in return for her silence. Natalie had worn a few bruises when she'd come to Spence, fearing for her children. They'd had a passing friendship for years, and she'd claimed it was the first time Keith had abused her. Natalie wanted it to be the last—smart woman. Most of all, Natalie didn't want her sons to be involved in a lengthy and painful custody hearing.

"Marlo, I'd like to know one thing—are you all right?" he asked carefully.

"Yes. Of course. My life is in shreds, I'm up to here with work, there's not a schedule left intact anywhere, someone could have seen us in that bread truck, and hey, everything is just fine. . . . I don't want to talk anymore."

Spence couldn't resist: "About those loaves of squashed bread. It seemed only right to buy them. I just happened to be running by when Danny opened his truck this morning. He thought Rick's kids had gotten into the truck again and was worrying about how he was going to deliver the day-old stuff to the rest home. He'll donate money instead."

"Oh, my—How did you explain that? I mean, why did you say you wanted so much bread?" She sounded horrified.

"That I was taking it up to Old Eddie. Are you going to exercise on that pole tonight?" Spence closed his eyes, and visions of that lacy bra and Marlo's thong against her pale skin, those stiletto heels, danced behind his lids. . . .

Or maybe he just wanted to hold her, to comfort himself,

because he was sliding into full-body pain from wrenched muscles and a hell of a bruise on his ribs. . . .

"Something is wrong. You just groaned as if you're in pain. I thought you—You usually want to sleep—I want to see you, Spence," Marlo said quietly, as though she sensed his pain. "To know that you are all right. You could have a concussion."

He didn't want her to see him at his most vulnerable. "I'm fine. See you tomorrow."

"Now I know that something is wrong."

"See you tomorrow, sweetheart." Spence took pain pills and settled into his armchair to watch Marlo's taped wall-stamping video. She reached for the different-shaped stamps, demonstrated what they could do, and he reached for the package of black-and-white pictures. He studied them intently as Marlo explained how to create painted picket fences, decorating them with flowers made by the stamps.

Old Eddie had identified the youth as the body found in a condemned gold mine; the youth had been talking to Margaret Royston . . . Spence scanned the other photos and could see nothing unusual.

Mrs. Royston, who as a nurse, often did on-the-spot and unofficial consultations just to show how intelligent she was, a woman neglected by her playboy husband. The youth could have asked a simple medical question and received the whole verbal book on his ailment. In glossy black and white, Mrs. Royston also spoke to other people, including a young mother, cradling her baby, and a heavily pregnant woman. That wasn't unusual; mothers and expectant women often asked the experienced nurse questions.

Next, Mrs. Royston was leaning into an argument with her husband in front of the store; in those days that had been a usual sight.

There was a photo of Marlo, her camera in hand, the case dangling from the strap around her neck, but she hadn't taken the pictures. The photos were twelve years old, according to Old Eddie's account of the unlucky youth who had worn the silver-tipped fancy boots. Spence rose stiffly to turn on his computer; he rummaged through the electronic archives of several area newspapers until he found what he wanted. The headline read: *Miner Discovers John Doe Skeleton.*

The youth had been in his early twenties, no identifying dental work or information on his body. Old Eddie hadn't given the information about the silver-tipped boots to the criminalists, about how he'd seen the youth in Godfrey. But then, anyone dismissing Old Eddie's protocol, heading for direct information and pushing, wasn't going to get far.

Spence leaned back and closed his eyes, letting the pain pills do their work; he let himself slide into sleep with the memory of Marlo curled softly around him.

A soft drift of hair caught on his skin, and Spence smiled in his sleep and nuzzled against that warm hair, scented of flowers. "Marlo . . ."

His cheek rubbed against stubble, and Billy Bob growled in his ear, "If you kiss me, Gerhard, you're dead."

Spence pushed his heavy lids open to see Marlo and Cherry hovering nearby as the trucker's arms slid carefully beneath him. "I know, *chèrie*," Billy Bob murmured. "Be careful with the big baby."

"Put me down, you oversize ape," Spence ordered, when Billy Bob lifted him effortlessly.

"Can't. There's two women here, one of them mine, who think you need help. You don't have a concussion—"

"How the hell would you know?" Spence grimaced as pain shot through his ribs and two tons of brick had lodged itself inside his brain, shifting with each movement.

"Lifted your eyelid. Looked at your pupil. You're bruised pretty good, a few scratches, but you're okay."

"All I need after today is some trucker feeling me up . . . I can walk—get the hell out of my house, all of you." He didn't want Marlo to see him weak and bruised; he felt too exposed, too vulnerable.

"Now don't be nasty, hon," Cherry was saying, as Billy Bob carried Spence into his bedroom.

"Dammit, I can help myself."

"Shut up, Spencer," Marlo ordered, in a tone that reminded him of his mother. His poor mother . . .

"Okay," he agreed meekly.

"Now I know he's hurt," Marlo stated wryly.

Spence was carefully eased onto nice cool sheets. He studied Marlo as she bent to adjust his pillow. She had a tight, grim look and he decided to test her mood. "I thought you didn't want to see me tonight."

"It's almost morning, and I was worried about you. It's just like you to get all banged up when I was planning on getting some peace in my life. You're a real pain in the butt, Spencer Gerhard."

That crisp statement would have to do for a loverlike comment. He managed to lift a hand to caress her bottom. "In your specific butt? Worrying about me, are you?"

She caught his hand and held it. "Stop that. Someone has to take care of you. That's what you do, isn't it? Take care of everyone else and not yourself. Big, strong, he-man Spencer Gerhard, tough guy, doesn't need help from anyone, right? You ought to know when people are trying to help."

"Will you shut up? Ouch!"

Marlo ignored his protest and continued to dab disinfectant on his scratches. "You didn't even see a doctor, did you?"

"Listen, you can just chew on someone else and stop torturing me."

"Too bad. I've picked you."

"Isn't that cute, *mon cher*?" Cherry asked dreamily. "They're making love-talk."

Billy Bob didn't think so. "He's about as cute as the backside of a—"

Spence felt someone open the snap of his jeans. He placed his hand over Marlo's to stop her. "I can manage. What is all this *cherie* and *mon cher* stuff? Her name is Cherry, dammit."

"I believe Mr. Gerhard has a headache and is not feeling well," Marlo stated very coolly. "You two should get some rest. But thank you. . . . Lock the door and turn off the television set. I feel like I'm in living stereo."

That startled Spence; he had a whole collection of Marlo's television spots, and now she knew he'd been—"Mom taped those," he lied. "Cherry mucks up electronics. Don't let her even close to—"

"She's my fiancée," Billy Bob said gruffly. "I'll handle it, you big baby, and some of those were made too recently to pull that one off. You might as well tell the lady you've been mooning over her. I've got enough handling my own love life without having to coach you, boy."

"Oh. And he's been mooning over me, has he? Just me? As in one woman?" Marlo asked as she dabbed slightly faster—and harder.

Spence was getting the idea—Marlo was definitely in a snit for some reason.

"I am not your fiancée, Billy Bob," Cherry began hotly.

"We'll talk about it in bed, honey-bun," Billy Bob drawled softly. "You know how you get, all—"

Spence groaned loudly for effect; he was on what felt like his deathbed, and Billy Bob's crooning was really making him sick. "Make them go away. Please, Marlo."

After they had gone, Marlo sat on the bed. She kicked off her shoes, adjusted the sheet over him, and lay down beside him. She looked across the pillow to him, all soft dark eyes filling with him. "You either should have come straight to me, or you should have told me to come right over. I'd hit you, but you have enough bruises."

"You could kiss them . . . What time is it?"

She ignored his invitation and skipped right to the time. "About two. What difference does it make? You're not in shape to go anywhere—even to your girlfriend's."

Since Marlo was his girlfriend-lover that didn't make sense at all. He turned to kiss the hand she'd placed on his cheek and closed his eyes. "I've got to ride out with Mac at seven and tow in my Jeep. Are you going to stay the night?"

"What's left of it."

He'd missed her forever, hunted her in every woman . . .

"I'm self-elected to see that you don't end up dead in the morning . . . unless you want Billy Bob sleeping next to you. He's not going to let Cherry stay with you. She's already asked. But then, I guess Lorraine would come trotting over, if you asked."

Spence wasn't certain why Marlo would bring up Lorraine, and he didn't feel like querying her. There was just one place he wanted to be, with one woman. With noble effort, Spence eased himself closer to Marlo. She moved slightly, and his head rested on Marlo's soft breasts. With a sigh, he nuzzled her, let her scent wrap around him, and listened to her steady, soothing heartbeat.

"Comfortable, Spence? Lorraine is bigger-busted than I am. And she's definitely more experienced, too."

Her tone had an uncharacteristic bite that didn't register until moments later—Marlo must have seen him with Lorraine. He needed to explain that nothing had happened, that Marlo was all he needed, all he wanted, that sex with any other woman just might have been impossible.

Her arms came gently around him, her hands smoothing

his hair and stroking his back lightly. She kissed his forehead and softly murmured the endearment every injured man holding his sweetheart wants to hear, "You big jerk. Just wait . . . when you feel better, I am going to make you so sorry . . ."

Spence smiled drowsily; Marlo was cuddling him, whispering sweet nothings. Words didn't come, but lying next to Marlo, holding her, sleep did, and Spence gave himself to it. . . .

"It's a long walk home, son. You want me to send up one of the boys to collect you after a bit?" Mac asked as he looked down from the tow truck at Spence. Hoisted to roll on its back tires behind the truck, the Jeep's front end had been smashed. It reminded Spence of how he could have died.

"Thanks, that would be good. Do you have a garbage bag? I want to clean up the mountain a bit."

"Yeah, sure. That tire is in pieces, but your rig is going to cost plenty to repair."

Spence listened to Mac shift gears, preparing to haul the Jeep down the rough old logging road. Then he carefully retraced the path back to where he'd thought he'd heard that shot echo in the mountains—and it was definitely the crack of a high-powered rifle.

But echoes could play strange tricks in the mountains, and it just could be that the shot came from someone target shooting elsewhere.

Spence had already inspected the Jeep. There were no telling holes in it, so if a slug had hit his rig, it would have hit a tire.

The Jeep's bent wheel rim had dug deeply into the dirt, crossing several deep ruts, before it went over the deadly edge of the canyon. Spence had been driving slowly, careful of those same ruts, caused by natural erosion. He'd crossed them at a diagonal angle, rather than the sharp impact of a direct route. He was just crossing—

He crouched and studied the deep rut that he had been easing across when the shot had echoed and the tire had blown.

Suitable for rough mountain terrain and maintained properly, the tire had suddenly blown . . .

Spence picked up a pinecone and cast it aside. Just there, the rim had cut deeply into the rut; that meant the rim could have cut the tread. He followed the rim's mark to another deep rut, and this time, no rubber had buffered the metal as it sank into the dirt.

He had struggled with all of his strength to control the vehicle as it had hit two additional lesser ruts.

Spence came to stand at the edge of the deep canyon. Pieces of the tire lay strewn across rocks and brush on that short, deadly path to the tree, its bark scarred by the impact. The tall Douglas fir tree had saved his life.

He edged down the rocks and brush and began collecting pieces of the tire.

Then he found what he wanted—a perfect slug hole. The slug was probably heavy-duty. He stuck the tip of his finger through the hole. It matched the ones in his storage building.

A dangerous trail was stacking up: First Cherry, then the break-ins, then this. If they were all related, then someone really wasn't happy. Add old Royston's murder and the kid's body up in the old mine, and someone was mad enough to kill.

Spence hauled the filled sack up to the road and crouched again, surveying the soaring mountains.

A high-powered rifle with a scope and a good shooter could hit a tire from almost anywhere. But from down in the canyon, shooting upward, only a top marksman could hit a tire like that, at just the right moment in that series of deep ruts.

Unless that shot had been meant for him—but then it wouldn't look like an accidental death, would it?

Someone knew the mountain, the road, and Spence's Jeep. "Someone with a big, bad personal grudge," he said aloud to the mountain wind whistling around him. "So let's just keep it personal, because if he's the one who worked over Cherry, I'd like to get to him first. It's just a matter of connecting the dots, and Marlo just may be keeping a few of them to herself. First Traci visits Paula, then Mom, then Marlo. It's all too neat, and Marlo, sweetheart, we're going to have a little chat . . . Question: Just how did you get those pictures? And what else do you know?"

The wind's whispers held too many questions—and no answers. . . .

Seventeen

"YUCK. I WILL NOT HAVE BILLY BOB'S STUFFED, DEAD animals hanging anywhere near me," Cherry finished emphatically. Her long telephone dialogue about reasons she was not marrying the trucker had taken a good half hour. Marlo's busy morning in the shop had had other interruptions—like her mother calling with the daily inquiry on how well she'd slept. Wilma's calls came like clockwork—every time gossip noted Marlo and Spence's nights together.

Cherry switched topics as easily as she switched her moods. "Did you check on Spence this morning? I mean later this morning, after he left his house. Mac came into the cafe around ten, and he said Spence laid one on you on his front porch at seven this morning. Mac said Spence was moving pretty stiffly, and he figured that Spence had just—um . . . had a busy night. Boy, I'm glad I never married and got a rep for being a hot-to-trot divorcée. Oops, just kidding, Marlo."

Her last remarks had caused Marlo to stop punching her calculator keys and push away the swatch of fabric she'd been matching to others. She'd been ordering unique fabric for the quilters and called the Petersons for an appointment to discuss their eclectic mix of French, outdoors male, and renovated kitchen needs. Meanwhile, Spence's long, knee-weakening kiss had simmered deep within her. "Oh, Mac did, did he?"

"Mac said Spence isn't going to take it up with the manufacturer for that blowout. Gotta go. It's the eleven o'clock lunch crowd coming in. Bye."

"Bye." Marlo thought of how Spence had grimaced when he had stepped up into the wrecker, of how he'd been even earlier, groaning slightly as he moved. When the alarm had rung, he'd forced himself slowly, painfully out of bed.

She'd been sitting in a chair by the window, watching him. She had wondered how she could possibly be so involved with Spence that she ached just to look at him. The bruise on his side had spread even farther, but it was the way he moved that dried her throat. Then he'd turned, found her in the shadowy room, and smiled just that lopsided, wry bit. "Hi," he'd said.

That soft, unguarded "Hi" set her heart flip-flopping.

"Thanks for coming over last night." Aware that she'd removed his jeans sometime during the night, Spence had lowered one hand to cover himself.

The very vulnerability of his pose, leaning to one side, favoring that side yet concerned for her sensibilities, had caused her to ache. She'd forced herself to remain sitting; otherwise, she'd have risen and kissed him, and he would have seen the tears in her eyes. Spence's pride wouldn't tolerate sympathy. And if she had walked those few intimate feet, she just might have admitted that she loved him, and that wouldn't do. Not when a woman wanted a life of independence from upsetting males. "You're welcome. You might want to apologize to Billy Bob. You weren't sweet."

He'd stood, one arm braced against the doorframe, his face in shadow. "Did you sleep?"

The conversation had flowed between them, soft and gentle, then Marlo had moved past him into the living room. She'd sat, waiting while he dressed, and fought going into the kitchen—it was there, whatever *It* was, calling her . . . and she wouldn't come to its beckoning. . . .

In her shop, Marlo yawned and scanned her calendar. With luck, she'd have the quilts designed and instructions written before the majority of the fabric bolts arrived. Because time was short, she'd ordered more material than she'd actually guesstimated; she could always use extra yardage.

The check that Keith had personally delivered for Paula's quilt lay on her checkbook, ready to be deposited. Keith had been brisk, and Marlo had felt the waves of his anger emanating throughout her shop; she had been relieved when he left quickly. "You're tossing away everything, Marlo, for a few cheap nights with that go-nowhere . . . just like his father. I'd advise you to reconsider, and I just may accept your apology."

"I appreciate the advice, Keith, but I think our business is ended," she'd said.

His blue eyes had flashed dangerously, and, for just that moment, Marlo had been afraid he'd finish what he'd started yesterday. "You'll come around. You and I are the same. We like the same tidy lifestyles, a logical order to our days and years. Gerhard doesn't understand people like us. I'd think that after him and your ex-husband, you'd learn what was best for you. But then, some women never learn, do they? They just don't know what's best for them."

He'd turned coldly and walked from her shop to his furniture store. He'd stood in front of it briefly, staring at her.

Marlo placed the check inside her backpack and the black-and-white pictures she'd retrieved from Spence last night slid onto her desk. To get a better look, she pulled out a magnifying glass, and, in so doing, the paisley swatch slid across the picture's envelope. Through the glass, the paisley pattern's spots leaped out at her—only tiny red spots, like an intricate trail of blood droplets, they gripped and chilled her. She found herself tracing the curved designs, leading first one way, and then the other, pulling her . . . *Cody? Cody?*

Determined to fight whatever called to her, to ignore it, Marlo took a deep breath and spread the glossy black-and-white pictures across her desk. The roll of film had been labeled with one specific woman's name. "Margaret," she whispered, "Margaret, where are you?"

Marlo found the pictures containing Mrs. Royston and isolated them from the others. There were four pictures. "Margaret, come out wherever you are. . . ."

In one picture, Mrs. Royston was talking earnestly to a tough-looking youth. In another, she was smiling at a newborn baby, cradled against a young mother. In the third, she was talking to a heavily pregnant woman. In the fourth, her expression was fiercely angry as she spoke to Ted in front of Royston Furniture.

The store had changed quite a bit in the last twelve years; while in college and majoring in business, Keith had come home to work every spare moment in the store. By that time, Paula had been in therapy at Rosewood Village. To his credit, and his industrious mother, who had recommended the store at every chance, the store and the elegant Royston house had survived.

Marlo shivered slightly; the Royston house and the money to go with it originally had been inherited by Margaret Davis Royston. A second huge inheritance to Mrs. Royston had salvaged the crumbling finances of the family. That second burst of wealth had infused the furniture store with enough capital to renovate, buy better-quality stock, and begin a huge ad campaign, all managed by her and Keith . . .

Elsie Gerhard had saved this undeveloped roll of film, labeling it "Margaret," for a reason. Why?

Or was it just a quirk of fate, a roll of film misplaced in the bingo bag?

Marlo studied the pictures again. There was something familiar about one woman—

The slam of a car door outside the shop caused the window's glass ornaments to jingle and dance. Marlo looked up to see Spence pushing open the shop door; Lettie stood gleaming in the background. . . . Lettie, on whose backseat teenage Marlo had given herself to young Spencer Gerhard.

Spence moved just the same, like a stalking graceful hunter as he came into the shop. Nothing remained of this morning's painful movements, almost as if he'd never been hurt. And he could have been killed—

But it was this Spence who had made her angry; the man who had made earthshaking love to her . . . and then rode into Godfrey on the backseat of Lorraine's blue motorcycle.

"Feeling better?" Spence asked coolly. "You looked a little tired this morning."

Beneath the scratches and bruises, Spence had a look that said he was hunting, and he was focused on her. *She couldn't tell him what she had sensed about his mother. . . .* "Depends. Having a good day?"

"Not too bad. My Jeep is out of commission for a while. The front end has to be rebuilt. You know, my sister and her ex-husband and Cody died, going over a canyon wall as steep as that."

The way he braced his legs apart, the set of his shoulders told Marlo that he'd come for answers. "You know what I want, pussycat," he said quietly, gold eyes locking on her.

"Lorraine?" Marlo asked too sweetly, and met his hard stare.

Spence frowned and looked puzzled. "What do you mean?"

Marlo closed her calendar workbook with a snap. She'd

been made a fool by one man, and she wasn't letting Spence do it again. "You rode on the back of Lorraine's motorcycle—right down Main Street. I saw you."

She truly resented that dip into jealousy, that raw need to call him out for explanations. She wasn't backing down or accepting an innocent act. Marlo stood up and faced him. "I saw you," she repeated.

Spence's frowned deepened. "She came down the road just after I'd hauled myself out of that wreck."

"You should have let her stay and patch you up. Or did she?"

Those gold eyes narrowed. "She offered. I turned her down."

"No man turns Lorraine down. If you're okay, go away. I have work to do." She didn't trust Spence's satisfied expression, or the way he moved purposefully toward her. Her body was already tense, quivering, alert to his . . . Marlo looked away.

Spence's hand drew her face back to his. "You want me. Say it: You want me."

"That is just ridiculous. Now, Spence, I'm way behind on work, and you're keeping me from it. Pull up your shirt."

"Why?" He seemed puzzled, then he grinned knowingly.

"Not that. I want to see your ribs."

"I'd let you see more of me," he offered pleasantly.

"Up." Marlo gently tugged his shirt from his jeans, lifting it to inspect his sides. They were badly bruised. "Ohh!"

"I don't like this," he grumped, frowning at her. "I feel like a kid."

"Too bad, and sometimes you are a big kid . . . like last night when you should have called me to come over right away—or had *Lorraine* drop you off here." She ran her hand experimentally, lightly over the large bruises, and looked up into Spence's amused expression. She stood on tiptoe to kiss the ones on his face briefly. "I was so worried, Spence."

She caught that flicker of satisfaction and didn't like it. "You should have come here. Right away," she repeated.

"Am I being scolded? So you're committed to our relationship, then? It sounds like it. I'd like to know."

"I just don't want anything happening to you," she returned unevenly.

"Because . . . ?"

Spence was asking for a verbal contract, exclusive rights, and though they were already in his hands—she was in his hands, so to speak—Marlo chose not to reveal that he was probably the only man she would ever love. Spence would take that one inch and walk the proverbial mile with it. She had to maintain her borders, her independence, and there was a big fat secret she wasn't ready to give him—

He stood too close and Marlo backed up just those inches until her back met the cutting table. Then Spence moved even closer, studying her as his finger reached out to trace her ear. "Do you think we could call this an argument, and that would justify reconciliation sex? And by the way, your breasts are just perfect, and they're like little berries when I—"

Marlo was having difficulty breathing, the sensual tension between them now was enough to melt her insides. But she wouldn't be played again. "Lorraine wears a 36D bra, Spence. Don't tell me that you haven't noticed."

Spence lowered his eyes to her breasts, studying them. "Noticed maybe. Any man would. And you did. But I haven't touched or wanted to, and that's the difference between you and Lorraine."

His hand caressed her breast, cupping it. "I like this game. Indignant woman plays all snitty and proper, and I get to—well, I'm hoping to get to. Thanks for helping me last night, by the way. I'm feeling a lot better today. A lot better," he added meaningfully.

"You just can't—" Marlo fought quivering and reaching

for him as Spence eased to stand between her legs; the heavy pressure between her legs told her that he wanted her. "I will not allow couplehood overflow to another woman."

Spence chuckled, and said, "I love it when you get all snitty and proper. That means I'm getting to you. You smell so good . . . are you wearing some of that lacy stuff under this? Or maybe just those pretty little virginal white panties? They may be even more of a turn-on."

"Which kind was Lorraine wearing?" So she was in a snit, so what? Yesterday, she'd made passionate love with Spence in the back of a bread truck. That amounted to a whole lot of monogamy obligation.

"You're serious, aren't you? Do you really think I can think about anyone other than you?" He leaned forward, brushed her lips with his, and asked quietly, "I've never touched Lorraine. How can you forgive what happened years ago so easily, then get all hot and bothered over me riding behind Lorraine?"

"What was she doing there, just when you needed her?" She couldn't help running her hands over his shoulders, satisfying herself that he was alive.

"This is no joke, is it? You're really upset. . . . Lorraine looked like she'd just had sex higher up the mountain . . . probably with someone who didn't want to be known. It wouldn't be the first time she's had a married man. I don't think she's the one who shot out my tire, though. She can't hit the broad side of a mountain, let alone a moving vehicle. And she would have heard a shot. All she heard was the blowout. She's easy to read. She was telling the truth."

Terrified for him, Marlo gripped Spence's shoulders. She shook him lightly; he had spoken so casually, when he could have been killed! "Do you mean that wreck wasn't an accident? On the mountain? You could have been killed!"

Spence's open hands caressed and rotated her hips, working her body closer to his. He watched as he rhythmically nudged her, a pale simulation of the lovemaking he really wanted. "That probably was the idea. I found a couple of holes in what was left of the tire . . . one that was probably the entrance and one where the slug came out. Hell of a shot. Hit just right, at the perfect time. I'd say it was the same rifle that marked up my storage building. . . . Are you wearing those thong panties?"

"Why?" Marlo gripped his shirtfront, and he grimaced slightly.

"Don't women usually wear panties?"

She gripped tighter. "Don't irritate me now, Spencer Gerhard. Why do you think anyone would shoot at you?"

"Ouch! Marlo, there are just places not to grab a man, and those hairs are attached . . ." Spence rubbed his chest and continued, "I'd say that someone thinks I'm messing in their business and decided to give me a few warnings. Cherry could have been one of them, tossed on my mother's front yard like that . . . and that is why I want to keep this very personal. . . . Speaking of getting personal, I'd really like some of that now with you. Are you going to switch the sign to CLOSED?"

Marlo didn't want any interruptions; she wanted to know everything that Spence had to say about any connection to the attack on her friend and possibly her lover.

That's what he was, like it or not, she decided grimly, and both her friend and her lover could be in danger. . . . She hurried to flip the sign to CLOSED. She turned back to find Spence leaning his head to one side as if he'd been studying her bottom. "I'm hot for you, babe. You look like you mean business. Bring it on," he drawled, teasing her.

"Stop that. I want to know exactly why you think someone would have reason to shoot your tire and your building. Your building could be anything, someone target practicing—you know how they do up there—or it could be that woodpecker."

Spence tilted his head; his wry expression was that of man who had lived among hunters all of his life; he knew the difference between slug holes and those created by a woodpecker. "It might have meant nothing. Probably shot just for fun. For kicks."

"Don't hand me that. Spence, if they would have missed, they could have shot you! Your rig, your place. It's too—"

"Coincidental? Very personal?" Spence was leaning down to look at the four black-and-white pictures she'd spread on her desk. He picked up the magnifying glass and slowly studied each one.

Marlo used the opportunity to slide her hand inside his shirt and lightly smooth his side. "Maybe you'd better tell Mike Preston."

"No. Like I said, this might be personal. Or that's how I'm taking it. I've just canceled all my trips for the next month. I don't want anyone getting hurt while we're hiking and away from help. Or while they're in my keeping. That includes you."

The hair on Marlo's nape lifted. Spence didn't just happen to be in the mood for sex; he'd come for answers. Maybe he had the right to know everything—well, some of it. She slid her hand from beneath his shirt and smoothed his hair. *He was safe, right here, with her, warm and alive—breathing. . . .* "The pictures were in your mother's bingo bag. I just had them developed."

"I thought as much. The parking passes were in there, too." He tapped the pictures. "Why did you pick these special ones to study?"

Marlo took a deep breath; she'd been right. Spence had come after answers.

"Because a name had been written on the roll—'Margaret.'" Marlo carefully omitted that his mother had written it.

"Margaret Royston?"

Marlo smoothed her hair in a nervous gesture, and Spence frowned quickly, his hand wrapping around her wrist. He turned it slowly, inspecting the pale inner surface and the distinct finger-shaped bruises left by Keith's hard grip.

"What's this?" he asked far too softly. "Keith?"

"I'm handling it, Spence. He did not hurt me. He was just upset because there is so much gossip about you and me. Don't you dare interfere."

But Spence was already in movement, headed toward her shop door on his way to Keith. Marlo hurried in front of him, blocking his way out the door with her body. "You're not going over there, Spence."

He showed his teeth, and the smile didn't reach those cold narrowed eyes. "I'm not?"

Marlo had to think fast to create a distraction, that much she'd learned from handling Cherry. "I know. Take me for a ride in Lettie."

His hand was on the door knob. "What? Now?"

"I've always wanted to really make love in that backseat when both of us knew what we were doing," she lied. "If you're up to it, of course."

Spence appeared stunned, and he blinked twice. "Huh?"

Then he smiled slowly. "Oh, I'm up to it. And then when you're all soft and wilty and doing that purring thing, you're going to tell me why you freaked out in my mother's kitchen and in your closet and after coming from the Royston house."

"Didn't anyone ever tell you that you're not supposed to use sex to get information? That's awful."

"Let's just take these," he said as he gathered up the photographs and stuffed them into her backpack. He carried it as he opened the door and guided her out into the sunshine. His hand slid to caress her bottom. "Let's see if I can do better this time. But I'm a little old and sore now for backseats."

Marlo was instantly concerned. "Spence, maybe we shouldn't. You were hurt—"

He bent to kiss her, to flick his tongue across her lips. "There's just some things a man has to do, and that is to make love to his . . . relationship-woman after a near-death escape."

Marlo wanted that affirmation, too, to hold Spence tight and close and know that he was alive. But she noted his underlining of "relationship" and decided that it was time to give Spence the answers he'd been seeking—some of them, anyway.

Forty-five minutes later, Lettie pulled into the dirt road leading to Spence's cabin.

He turned to Marlo. "You're awfully quiet. Change your mind?"

"No, I haven't." She had to tell him. But how? How could she tell him that she only sensed his mother had died violently? Next question: Should she tell him anything about Elsie's death?

Spence decided to let Marlo take the lead; she'd been silently chewing on something while Lettie slowly worked her way up the mountain road. But Marlo didn't go into the cabin; she went instead to his storage building. Her fingertip touched the holes lightly, and when she turned to him, her expression was that of torment. "I don't know how to begin. This is awful, Spence. You really think someone is trying to kill you?"

"Those were slug holes in my tire, honey. Yes, I do think someone would like to see me dead and make it look like an accident. Few people would examine a blown tire on that road, it happens too frequently."

She hurried to him and forced herself not to hold him too tightly. Within his arms, Marlo was shaking, and Spence murmured softly, "I lived, you know, but this is really nice, being cuddled by you."

Marlo snuggled closer, then pushed back, looking up at him. "We've got to talk. I've got something to tell you."

Inside the cabin, Spence leaned back into the shadows and watched Marlo. She was sorting through something very difficult, and he could only wait. "I'll make tea, if it will help you."

"Yes, that would be nice. Thank you. . . ." Then those hazel eyes met his. "Spence, Dirk loved Traci. I could feel it in the letters you gave me. I could feel the love between them. They were just trying to sort things out, and Dirk had matured since their divorce. He was honestly trying to change, and he'd come to collect her—because she'd called him."

Marlo sank onto the couch and put her hands over her face. Her voice was muffled and unsteady as she said, "She called him because she was terrified, for her and her son, and because she loved Dirk. She didn't call you, because she knew that if you saw her so terrified, you would blame Dirk. From there, things would get complicated. She was panicked, fearing for her child, and she needed to get out of town—fast—to protect her child and possibly Elsie. Traci just took the simplest route and called Dirk. She would have eventually called you with whatever evidence she'd found—but she never got the chance."

"You don't know that, Marlo. The guy ruined her life."

Marlo raised her face; it was strained and pale. "She, and Cody, changed his. They were working things out, Spence. He didn't kidnap her and Cody. She wanted to go with him, and quickly. Otherwise, she would have packed better and told your mother. There had to be good reason to leave as she did."

"There was. He was threatening her. He caught her at night at the supermarket, and he threatened her. She had to go with that bastard to keep Cody safe."

"You're wrong, Spence. They loved each other. Dirk loved his son. More than that, he treasured him. He wanted more children with Traci, and he had turned his life around. Traci was proud of him. She loved him, Spence."

Spence turned his back to her and walked out into the clean fresh July afternoon. His mother had decided the same thing, and in turn, Spence had argued with her. Marlo came to stand behind him, her hand on his back. "I know this is hard to take, Spence."

"Tell me how you know all this—what you *think* you know."

She turned him gently to face her, framed his rugged face with her hands, and ached for him. But she had to continue. "I know how it feels to be a woman in love. I've always loved you, Spence. I was destroyed when you didn't want to get married."

He closed his eyes, pain shooting through him. "I'll never forgive myself for that."

"I have, and you're going to—or you'll destroy us. But then, what I'm going to tell you might do that anyway," she whispered sadly. "And you're not going to like it. I'm going to need that cup of tea. Please?"

Spence feared for what they had just found. "You just said you love me, Marlo. Let's leave it at that."

"It's because I love you that I can't."

"Damn, I was afraid of that."

Minutes later, Marlo was sitting on the porch. She took the cup of tea from him, and Spence leaned back against the building. He knew for certain that he wouldn't like what she was going to say; Marlo was working too hard to phrase her words carefully. The woods filled with familiar sounds, the woodpecker working on his cabin, and he was staked to the next few moments. He waited for Marlo to speak, his throat drying.

Marlo looked at the chipmunks racing up the tall trees, the birds swooping through the dappled sunlight, then she turned to Spence. She rose to her feet, placed the cup aside, and faced him in the shadows of the porch. "I feel things, Spence. Don't ask me how, but it started sometime after I lost the baby. Waves of impulses just seem to come at me, and I feel things, somehow. I know things. These . . . sensations are getting really strong now—as if they have a purpose, and they won't leave me alone. I've tried to bury them, to push them away, yet they come back."

He held very still. When they'd made love, he'd felt Marlo come inside him, soothe the rough, bleeding edges. Or he'd thought he'd felt that—"You felt Dirk and Traci's love?" he asked roughly, needing confirmation that he'd heard her right earlier.

"Yes, but more than that. My small impulses—I've underdeveloped skills, according to Cherry. Anyway, they made Ryan uneasy. I was able to hide them from everyone, until Elsie noticed, then Cherry. Cherry has been pushing hard. I knew somehow when things would happen, but I didn't want to know. Not all things, but just once in a while, I'd be standing in front of the shop window and something would hit me. Remember when Ed Miller broke his leg, falling off that ladder and couldn't work for months? Somehow I sensed that. I couldn't tell whoever was going to be hurt, because how would I justify that? How could I logically justify anything I only *feel*?" she asked unevenly.

"This is a lot to handle. . . . Let's get one thing out of the way. You said you love me. Are you just 'feeling,' sensing that, too?"

"I *know* that," Marlo stated firmly. "I said it. I meant it. But that doesn't change the rest of it."

Marlo loved him; she'd admitted it into the first of July air. Spence allowed himself to bask in a warm heady glow and sought to justify the rest. He walked down the steps and turned to face her, placing his boot on the first one. He leaned in close to kiss her. But Marlo wasn't responding, and he asked gently, "Well, then, as a woman in love, you might be swayed by romantic letters, right? You might be misled?"

She smiled sadly. "Nice try, Spence."

"Can we make love now? That seems to be the right thing to do at a time like this." He had the feeling that he wouldn't like what else Marlo had to say. He wanted to take the best offering of the day and leave the rest alone.

Marlo shook her head, held her breath, then released a fact she'd held too long into the fresh, clean day. "I knew Ted Royston was going to die. I saw him pushing his weight around in front of my shop, angry because someone had taken a parking place he wanted. I knew that. I knew that your mother was going to die. And I don't think that Cody is dead. I won't back up on that, Spence. Elsie knew that I— that I sensed things, and that is why she asked me about Cody. I really don't think he's dead. I feel like he's alive."

"Jesus, Marlo!"

Her statement slammed into him. Spence took a moment to recover, then he said roughly, "Okay. Let's have all of it. The facts, I mean. Why did you go to Paula's? Why were you in such a state after getting back from the old Royston house? Why did you almost come to pieces in Mom's kitchen? And why were you terrified after coming out of your walk-in closet?"

He watched the impact of his attack, the widening of her eyes, the way she shivered just that bit, and he regretted lacking control. Marlo sat on the step and placed her arms around her knees, her forehead on them, and hunched into herself. "You were right about that trapdoor in my ceiling," she admitted quietly. "Someone did break into my apartment. They took some photographs and the archived negatives."

She'd been in even more danger than he'd suspected, and she hadn't told him. Spence fought his frustration. How could a woman love a man and not trust him? "You should have told me."

"It was what I felt inside that closet that terrified me, Spence—such terrible rage."

He struggled to understand. "When your mother's shop and home had been broken into and someone burglarized your apartment, that didn't scare you? But what you felt inside you did?"

"I knew it was the same person who had been in the old Royston house. That's why I went back with Cherry to verify what I felt after Ted Royston died. It was still there—the rage, furious, hot, killing rage. It had waited all that time, just for me, because it's angry with me, too. It's focused on me, hating me. . . ."

"Jesus, Marlo! And I pushed for that séance with the Bingo Girls? I just thought I could get you to open up a bit about what was going on with you—I didn't know it was this bad with you. So much for my brilliant ideas. . . . I can't think of one person who hates you, Marlo. And it doesn't take psychic ability to know that Royston had gotten quite a few people mad, including me. Anyone could see that from the way he'd been hit, from the way the house had been torn up."

"I never saw all that. This was what I felt, Spence. Sheer, undiluted rage. Horrible sensations, as if they were spilling all around me, gripping me . . ."

Spence took her hand. It was cold and trembling. "Like the Christmas ribbons that tangled around your wrist? Everyone has fears, honey. Maybe you just heard about Royston, and it was so gruesome that it caught on you somehow."

"You're trying to justify this, aren't you? Trying to come up with reasons you can understand? Well, I don't understand it, Spence. I just know that it is." She turned to him, and tears shimmered in her eyes. "I think it comes in groups . . .

sometimes through glass, or red reflected on glass. It's really strong now, Spence, red on glass, through glass. That's the way that I know Cody is alive—like what I feel from that picture in your mother's kitchen and in my closet. I knew that Cherry was going to be attacked, and I could have . . . I could have stopped it."

"Wait a minute. You just said that you felt rage in that closet, the same as you'd felt at Ted's house. You looked terrified and shaking in Mom's kitchen. It was more than Cody's picture, wasn't it? Marlo, do you think my mother was killed?"

"I—" Her helpless expression told him too much.

Spence was frustrated and worried. His mother was one thing—and he had to deal with that separately. If she had been murdered, he'd tear apart the countryside, hunting her killer. Her accident had seemed so likely, a woman with a bad hip, climbing a step stool, getting off-balance and falling to hit her head on the edge of the counter—

He remembered her blood staining that sharp surface and pushed away the earthshaking notion that his mother could have been killed. Marlo had to be wrong about that; the entire town loved Elsie. His mother had no enemies.

Spence struggled through another deadly scene, a pickup crushed at the bottom of a steep canyon. There could be no way that Cody could have lived. Marlo had known a little boy, loved him, and she'd held that grief deep within her—just like she'd held her emotions from miscarriage, his defection, and the humiliation of her husband's betrayal. A loving woman, Marlo would feel heartbreak deeply, and hadn't dealt with Cody's death inwardly.

Marlo had been hiding even more than he suspected; he had to help her. He'd start with the facts and work his way down to logical answers: "Okay, tell me how. Tell me how you could have stopped whoever worked over Cherry."

Her answer sailed through the dappled sunlight, through the clear crisp mountain air. "Because I saw Cherry that day she was wearing that red paisley sweater and her crystal necklace. I was looking through the shop's window to you two out on the street, and then I knew. I should have warned her . . . she would have believed me."

Marlo rubbed her hands on her arms as if the warm day had chilled her and continued, "When I saw the taillights up on the highway, when we stopped overlooking the canyon—where your sister and Dirk died—when I was in my truck and saw the stop sign outside the Royston house . . . all those times, I just knew, Spence. While I might feel terrible rage, there is something about red and glass that connects me to Cody. As if he's on the other side of it, trying to tell me something. Maybe it's his spirit, but I don't think so. I really think—feel—that he's alive. Maybe Cherry is right about reaching him somehow."

"Honey . . ." Spence reeled from what Marlo had said, trying to find a justification for it, wanting to help her. She'd been searching the pictures when he'd come in; perhaps he could find something, anything, to help Marlo, something he'd missed.

Spence retrieved her backpack, sat beside her on the porch, and opened the envelope containing the pictures.

"I don't know what good that is going to do. I still feel what I feel," she whispered unevenly.

"So what about Paula? When we visited her, you were a little shaken. Honey, it's because you care so deeply, and want everything to be good for those you care about. You knew her history and why she is in Rosewood. You felt bad for her. That's it, you feel too much for those around you, and it—"

Marlo shook her head. "No, I just felt that same anger in Paula that I sensed in Keith—"

Spence decided darkly that the bruises on her wrist required a reckoning with Keith Royston. But for the moment, he wanted to keep on track with Marlo—to sort out all the things she'd been holding deep inside her. Maybe if she had shared those things earlier, she wouldn't have been so troubled. "Okay, let's look at these pictures together. You were pretty into them at the shop—"

He placed her four pictures on the porch between them. "Your four. That youth is the same one that Old Eddie found in the gold mine five years ago. He didn't tell the investigators that he'd seen those silver-tipped boots. The investigators must have set him off wrong—you know how he is, you have to come at him in the right way—his way. If they didn't take the time to do it, he would have sulled up."

Marlo scrubbed her face with her hands and her cheeks glistened damply in the shadows. "Spence, there's something you should know about that roll of film," she said quietly.

He stared at her. "Oh, boy. There's more?"

"It was your mother who wrote 'Margaret' on the roll."

"Damn, I was afraid of that. You had the bingo bag, you had the parking tickets, and the roll of film. So much for logic." He took the rest of the photographs out and studied them closely. "Maybe there's something we've missed. Here's a shot of some old broken-down chalet up in the mountains . . . recognize it?"

Marlo didn't, and Spence continued, "This picture of old Teddy-boy is shot at an odd angle. It's out of focus."

"Spence?" Marlo was studying the picture. "He's wearing a camera strap. That's one of those hard leather cases for a model the same as your mother's and mine. He took—"

"A self-timer. Old Teddy-boy used a self-timer to shoot himself. He shot this whole roll of film. The next question is why? And the question after that is why was the film in my mother's bingo bag?"

"I don't know why, but I do know that woman." Marlo pointed to the picture of the pregnant woman talking to Margaret Royston. She handed it to Spence. "I had set up a booth at the craft fair and was selling baby blankets that I'd made. I remember how beautiful she was, Spence, just glowing and beautiful. She gave me her card. She was a potter."

Spence leaned back against the porch support and stared into the sunshine and shadows. "You know what I think this is? Some kind of blackmail that Royston held. Maybe he'd been threatened before he died. Just maybe he gave it to the woman he trusted more than his little flings. Maybe he gave it to my mother as some kind of insurance."

He breathed slowly, hit by the implications of what he'd just said. Marlo stared at him and smiled weakly. "You know what, Spence? Now I think you just may have psychic ability."

He slanted a wry glance at her. "Let's not get carried away, honey. There's always a logical reason for everything. We just don't know the answers yet. What about this one? Whoever is hunting cameras and film was looking for these pictures, but he took anything approximately close to what just might be evidence. . . . Of what? There's some link here. We just have to find out what it is. Do you still have that pregnant woman's card?"

In Chicago, a five-and-a-half-year-old boy lay on his stomach, staring at the television, his crayons and book open on the floor beside him.

Ilene Jacobs came into the cheaply furnished tiny apartment's living room and carefully placed her one luxury of the day—a cup of tea—on an old table heaped with bills. She sat tiredly in her favorite chair, eased off her shoes, and rubbed her aching feet. After a day of working in the clothing factory, she was glad to be home. Every day was a struggle, trying to keep her grandson with her, and she worried that one day Timmy would be taken from her.

The boy showed none of his father's ugly street traits, and he was a joy to love. How could her son have gotten a woman pregnant who didn't want her own child?

The question flipped and came back painfully in another: How could Ilene's own son just dump his three-year-old boy on her doorstep, stay a few minutes to take what cash she had, then run off to die in New Mexico?

But then, it was Joey Jacobs's nature to move fast and stay in trouble, and she'd expected that one day he'd die early. She'd been right; a shootout in a liquor store had ended his sad life.

Ilene reached to waggle her grandson's worn tennis shoe, an easy show of affection; she just had to do a better job than she'd done with her son, Joey. But what chance did Timmy have, growing up with a widow-woman who had aged beyond her years?

Next year he'd be a first grader and going to school all day, and that would help with babysitting fees. Ilene looked tiredly down at the basket of hand-patching that brought in a few extra dollars; she pushed away the thought of working at her part-time job at the corner grocery store on Saturday and gave herself to the moment with her grandson.

With an expert eye, she tested the distance between the boy's toe and the end of the shoe. He was already pushing it, needing a bigger size, and the medicine for his last bout with the flu had taken the last of the cookie jar money.

Timmy was watching his favorite tape—not a cartoon, like most children his age—but that of a lady decorator who had thanked him for his crayon drawing. He loved the "nice lady" and Ilene knew that he dreamed of having a mother like Marlo Malone, not an old lady, worn by a troublesome son and a no-good husband.

Odd, Ilene thought as she sipped her tea, that the boy would be so fascinated by a television decorator. But from the moment Timmy had seen her segment on Club Renew, he'd repeatedly watched her presentations.

"I love her, Grandma," he said softly. "But I love you most of anybody," he quickly amended, because his heart was good and kind.

"And I love you," Ilene returned, worrying for what would become of him.

Then Timmy turned and grinned at her.

He was missing a front tooth, the next one only half-grown in, and his eyes were the oddest shade of light brown, almost gold.

Eighteen

"VIRGINIA ANDREWS KNEW MARGARET ROYSTON. THAT'S why she was talking to Margaret in that old picture. Margaret had been substituting as a nurse at the hospital where Virginia's baby was born, just fifty miles from Godfrey," Spence said quietly as he sat in the passenger side of Marlo's pickup.

While Spence and Marlo had talked quietly with Virginia Andrews at her home, her five- and three-year-old girls had played with a dollhouse their father had built. Virginia's husband had been working overtime in his mechanic's shop on a rush job. Marlo had used the excuse of shopping for unique pottery for her decorating jobs. Virginia had been thrilled. "Oh, I've been intending to come see your shop. My husband and I stopped in Godfrey a couple times to eat dinner, but you were closed—and these two keep me pretty busy."

Marlo had examined Virginia's work and somehow introduced into the conversation that Margaret Royston had favored the pebbled stoneware texture. Virginia had recognized the name as a nurse who had cared for her when she'd had her son.

Spence and Marlo did not comment when Virginia sadly noted that her son had been kidnapped from their home.

On the drive back to Godfrey, Marlo wasn't talking, focused on the curving mountain road, the knuckles of her hands showing white as she gripped her steering wheel. Spence reached to massage her neck and found it taut. "I remember that kidnapping. The parents were asleep. Her newborn baby was stolen right out of his crib while his parents were sleeping."

"Margaret would have known everything—medical records, everything—about that baby. She was Virginia's attending nurse. She would have known how to care for a newborn and where the Andrewses lived."

"About that time, Royston Furniture wasn't doing too well. The Roystons were in danger of losing their home."

"That house was in Margaret's family for years. As the only living Davis child, she inherited it." In the light of the dashboard, Marlo's face was pale. "I can't remember the other woman with a baby in the picture. If her baby was stolen, too— Oh, Spence, this is awful."

"Margaret worked all over the region, staying away from home at times. But then, home wasn't a pleasant place to be with Ted and the responsibilities that a mother would normally have."

Marlo gripped his hand tightly. "Spence, she came to see the babies after they were home. She would have known the layout of the house."

"She would have known a lot of things, including how to get that tough with the silver-tipped boots to do her dirty work. That's probably why he died. Just a guess, but he looked like an addict, and she had access to fatal doses," Spence stated grimly. "About that same time, maybe six months or so later, there was a baby taken right out of a Seattle hospital."

"Oh, Spence! I can't believe all this. It's too much," Marlo cried out painfully. "Babies taken away from mothers . . ."

"Honey, you're too upset. Pull over. Let me drive."

When they pulled into the parking place beside Marlo's apartment, Spence went inside with her. He stood and held her. "You're exhausted. I want to use the computer at the house—it's faster than yours—and I want to see what else I can find."

Marlo snuggled close, holding him tight. "Mrs. Royston was supposed to have come into some money about that time."

"She would have had an expensive commodity to sell. I'll be back. Lock up."

Inside his mother's home, Spence stood at the kitchen door and surveyed the room. Marlo had been terrified in this room. There was Cody's framed picture . . . Spence's mother had lain on the floor . . .

He walked to the center of the room and tried to comprehend whatever had terrified Marlo. She'd said that she'd known Elsie was going to die—

What Marlo had not said—that his mother might have died by a killer's hand—was enough to turn him cold.

Ted Royston had taken those pictures. That could have meant he used that roll of film as his life insurance policy—because Margaret Royston would have known how to make his death look like an accident. But after she'd died, he'd still kept the film, then he'd given it to someone he trusted to protect it—Elsie Gerhard.

Elsie might have deliberately cultivated that trust—because she believed that Cody might still be alive. . . .

Maybe he was grasping at no more than smoke and mirrors, but Spence didn't like how the pieces of the puzzle were fitting together as he sat down to his computer and began pulling up newspaper archives. . . .

* * *

"Spence?" Marlo asked as she opened her apartment door.

"So you're alone then. Sorry to disappoint you, but this just makes it easier for me." Paula Royston stood in the sweet July night. Tall and dressed in a black leather jacket and jeans, her hair was tethered back from her face on one side by an abalone barrette, handmade in the shape of a butterfly with intricate metal antennae. Marlo recognized it immediately as a gift from teenage Spence. It had been in Marlo's old room at her mother's, and it had been stolen the night of the break-in.

The automatic pistol in Paula's hand lifted. "Let's go. Bring your backpack. I don't want it to seem as if you were forced out of your home."

Marlo skipped the usual "Where to" question. She didn't have to ask—Paula was taking her to die. . . .

"You killed Elsie, didn't you, Paula?" Marlo said quietly forty-five minutes later. Her pickup had been concealed on a rough all-terrain riding path; her hands were tied behind her back. She sat on a rickety wooden chair in a Swiss gingerbread-style chalet. Located off the truck runaway ramp and down a path into the woods, the house was in disrepair, with only a few necessary camping items in the main room. Several sets of barbells stood in a neat row on the floor. Cans of insect spray were lined up on a high shelf.

"It's hot for a July, don't you think?" Paula said as she removed her leather jacket to reveal well-toned arms. At six feet and wearing a sleeveless black sweater, tight jeans, and biker boots, she appeared very strong—strong enough to hurt Cherry. The flowing gowns Paula had worn at Rosewood Village had concealed a bodybuilder's physique.

"Very warm. Why did you do all this?" Marlo asked simply. She fought the waves of fury that pounded at her, then she knew that this was where Paula came to spend her rage—keeping her home serene and apart from the life that had harmed her and the deaths she had caused.

Marlo also understood the cause of Paula's fascination with butterflies: She simply aligned her life to theirs—They emerged from their chrysalis stage into beautiful creatures . . . ready to fly into the world and hold their own. . . .

Paula's stare at Marlo flashed with anger. "You're here because you've interfered in my life enough. You were always the best—sweet little Marlo Kingsley. One of the in-girls, who made my live miserable. 'Why can't you be like her?' Mother used to say. Dear sweet Mom. Always there, supporting her children, loving them," she replied sarcastically.

She'd gotten that tight, introspective expression as if she were slipping back into the past. Marlo had to know everything and tried to keep Paula focused. "It was Spence, wasn't it?"

Paula's eyes flashed with anger again. She kicked an airtight plastic box with her boot. "Yes. You and Spence. I worshiped him, waited for just one look from him—but he was looking at you. All that time in high school, Spence was looking at you. Keith wanted you . . . he was the better choice for you, but oh, no, you had to take Spence from me."

Marlo fought for control. "Does Keith know this?"

"Of course he does. My brother is not stupid, except where you're concerned. He e-mails about his broken heart to me several times a day. He wanted to marry you. And that would have left Spence to me."

Paula came to slap Marlo's face hard, enough to snap her head back. "You should have married Keith, then none of this mess would have happened, you bad, bad girl. He wouldn't have married Natalie and—she just may have to pay for hurting him, for leaving him. My brother has pride—

all Roystons do—and she had to have that affair with Spence."

Her words came out in a low venomous hiss that reminded Marlo of what Cherry had said about her attacker's voice. Marlo struggled to be calm. "How did you manage to travel from Rosewood?"

"You twit. I wasn't under lock and key. I drove, of course. I was a perfect resident of Rosewood Village and they never suspected anything. I learned how to drive years ago. I can teach myself anything. I've been traveling back and forth for years. It wasn't difficult to store a motorcycle in the shed behind my cottage. If I needed to be gone during the day, I simply informed the caretakers that I was watching movies all day and resting. They like the residents to rest a lot. The distance from my backyard to a small service road isn't much. Anyone hearing the motorcycle would have thought it was one of the many laborers working at Rosewood."

"You attacked Cherry, Paula. Why?"

Paula nodded grimly. "She needed a lesson. She was interfering with what was supposed to be. Keith was taking his time with you, trying not to push you. Six years, Marlo. He invested six years in you and she was ruining it, Spence's little house pet. She was a bad influence. But she was fit, I could see that, and I needed an advantage."

Marlo pushed down her furious response. "A little something in her orange juice to drug her? A little something you learned from your mother?"

Paula smiled coldly. "Right on, from years of taking sedatives. Experience pays. You're so stupid, Marlo. I don't know how my brother—or Spence—ever saw anything in you, other than you're so dumb and believe anything you're told."

"Why steal the cameras and the pictures?"

Paula's smile was brilliant. She picked up the ten-pound

barbells and began a series of expert lifts. "Because The Secret has to be kept. Because you have been very, very bad. Did you actually think I was so stupid that I didn't know what was happening? If I could understand why Traci had come to visit, then Elsie, then you, and finally you and Spence—did you really think that I wouldn't have an idea that you had found something that might let our family's naughty little secret out?"

She picked up Marlo's backpack and began riffling through it. She found the envelope of pictures and quickly rummaged through them. "Dear old Dad. So they actually exist, just as he said—his little blackmail roll of film. You have them after all. I thought they might be in your closet, but here they are. These were his protection while Mother was alive those two years, and then later against me—when I became strong. He was afraid of me, you know. I liked that. And Father knew I wouldn't like evidence of our little secret."

"That your mother was into stealing and selling babies?" If Marlo was going to die, she wanted answers. She pushed a little harder when she saw Paula pause. "Your mother worked in a fertility clinic at one time, a temp position. She would have had access to who could pay for babies they desperately wanted. And as a temporary nurse in hospitals, she could check out the health of a suitable baby and the parents, right?"

"You guessed it. Dear old Mom didn't want her beloved family home going on the auction block. She would have done anything, including selling her own children—if we would have been little and sweet. But that's not a Royston trait—sweet. And I definitely wasn't cute—she told me how ugly I was often enough." Paula spread out a padded mat and began a series of push-ups. Then she turned over and with her hands behind her head, started doing sit-ups. "You're going to die, both you and Spence. I'll keep you alive until I can get to him—he'll fall for some sob story to meet him someplace to talk about you visiting me yet again. He'll follow your trail, or rather the one I lead him into, until you die together."

Marlo's body went icy cold, but her shiver wasn't from being chilled, it was from true, deep, burning anger and the need for revenge. The emotions curled out of her, and she stared at the cracked mirror, pushing them down, looking to the glass for answers. "You forced Traci and Dirk Forbes off that road and into the canyon, didn't you?"

The other woman got to her feet and began jogging in place. "Of course—I just borrowed the store's furniture truck. When Traci came to see me, she was too nervous. About that time, Keith had needed an extra bookkeeper, and she'd worked part-time in the evenings at the store. My brother wanted her to go over past tax receipts to see if Father had kept track of the expenses in the remodeling of the store. She must have hit Mother's old tax records, too. Mother had a really bad habit of keeping newspaper clippings that interested her and stuffing them everywhere. Somehow, Traci must have put two and two together, because I could see it in her face—that she knew our little family secret. I gave her fair warning a couple of times, but anyone looking at her could see she was ready to come apart. I couldn't trust her."

"Did Keith know anything about all this?"

Paula picked up a jump rope and began skipping it with practiced, intricate moves. "Rosewood Village has a very good gym. And so does my father's house. Father didn't use it. It was to keep me busy and pacified when I visited—I get edgy without hard exercise. In the past few years, I had begun to challenge him, and he was uneasy about me. When I'd come into Godfrey, I'd use it—that was the only thing that my brother knew—that I didn't like people knowing when I came home. And Father didn't like people knowing it either. He was ashamed of me. My brother still thinks that extra money to rebuild the store and pay off the house's mortgage came from Mother's inheritance. No, Father and I were the only ones to know."

She tossed the rope aside and stared at her powerful arms. She flexed her muscles and clearly admired her physique. "Father never should have told me that I was insane. Never. I knew he'd been dating Elsie Gerhard, then Elsie came to see me with that same expression of Traci's—"

"And you thought that Elsie might have that roll of film."

"And I thought that Traci might have told her something. I'm not stupid, you know." Paula stopped, stared at a tiny insect crawling along the floor, and hurried for the insect spray. When the spider was dead, she shuddered and tromped on it furiously with her boot. "I hate spiders. Father knew that, and he teased me with them—I hate them! You have no idea how hard it was to get all the spiders out of here!"

"Leave the spider in the truck, Cherry." Spence prayed that his hunch was right, that somehow the old Davis chalet, which was now owned by the Roystons, was where he would find Marlo—alive.

"I told you. Godiva has to have my body warmth. It's too cool up here in the mountains for her." Cherry hugged Godiva's traveling yogurt carton close to her body and ducked a pine branch as she followed Spence through the night.

In sight of the old dilapidated chalet, Spence turned to her and whispered harshly. "Be quiet. That's Marlo's rig, parked back in the bushes. If anyone is in there with her, we don't want to let them know we're coming."

"Oops."

Cherry had called him from Marlo's apartment where she was to stay until Billy Bob picked her up. Instead, Spence was moving the moment he knew that Marlo was gone; he'd borrowed a pickup and collected Cherry.

Marlo could have gone anywhere, and she could have left a note. Either it was an emergency—or that special someone had finally decided to make his move.

Once more Spence hadn't been near to protect his loved one.

When he stood close to the building, listening beneath a window, Spence didn't like what he was hearing. Paula was screaming. "You had everything—the good father, the loving mother, the boyfriend I wanted."

He recognized the next sound, that of an open hand delivering a hard slap. Spence fought hurrying into the chalet; any noise, and Paula might kill the woman he loved.

Then Paula's voice hissed in a string of curses, and Cherry's fingers dug into his arm. "That's the voice I heard when I was attacked. Spence?"

"Figures. Be quiet. And stay put until I need you, then move fast."

Marlo was talking quietly now, steadily, but he couldn't make out the words. Spence gauged the steps leading up to the chalet and the door's strength. He waited until Paula's ranting, furious yells began, then eased up the steps and opened the door.

"Bad, bad girl!" Surprised, Paula's hand was raised, poised for another slap. Instead she reached for the automatic pistol on the table. She motioned him inside. Spence was careful to leave the door open as he moved into the single room, lit by an upscale battery lamp.

"Why, Spence. How nice to see you. How nice of you to make my job easier. I knew you were driving Lettie, and that you wanted me to come out and play with you. Lettie—remember that deep scratch down the length of that old car after your high school graduation? My treat. You loved that junker more than me . . . How did you know that we were here, waiting for you?" Paula crooned.

"Hello, ladies." Spence nodded to Marlo, whose cheek bore the reddened imprint of Paula's hand. Her eyes were wide and filled with fear, her body straining forward.

"Spence—"

"It's okay, kiddo. Looks like you're all tied up." He tried to sound casual while his heart pumped with fear. If Paula knew how much he loved Marlo, she might shoot her immediately and that wouldn't give him time. . . . He pushed down the need to rush to her, free her—but then that could get him shot, and Marlo would die. For her sake, he had to take his time and distract Paula. If he could maneuver her back to the door, Cherry could cause enough of a diversion so he could move in . . .

His own safety didn't matter, but he couldn't help Marlo—or Cherry—if he were dead. The best thing was to wait and play Paula's cat-and-mouse game. . . .

Spence moved to the opposite side of the room, drawing Paula's attention from the door. He pointed at the pictures she'd dropped to the small table. "Old Eddie. He said someone had been parking their motorcycle back here."

"You should have died, you know," Paula stated quietly. "And don't move, I'm an excellent shot. I had to sell Father's coins and most of his guns for my little goodies—my secret life outside Rosewood, you know. But I kept the best ones."

"That was a good shot on the mountain."

Paula preened a little. "Why, thank you, Spence. I was angry at first, because you didn't die, but then I started to think how much fun I could have with you. You know, like this little game."

"You're welcome. How are you, Marlo? Having fun yet?"

"Having a ball." Her face burned with Paula's open-handed slaps, her wrists were chafed raw from trying to free her hands, and she had never been so angry . . . or filled with the need for revenge. It wasn't a pleasant feeling.

Spence seemed at ease, looking around the one room

Paula had cleaned. But the powerful lines of his body seemed ready, almost like a cat waiting to move at the right moment. A very big lethal mountain lion, ready to pounce . . . Only that slight flicker in his gold eyes and that telltale muscle in his throat said that he was tense and angry.

And afraid.

Terribly afraid for her, not himself.

Spence was going to go for Paula, try to wrestle that deadly automatic from her.

He tilted his head and leisurely studied Paula's muscle-builder physique. "Looking good, Paula."

"I work out. Steroids help."

"Do I smell insect spray?"

She shuddered visibly; her eyes darted momentarily around the corners of the bare room, then up to the ceiling. "There are spiders everywhere. Disgusting things."

"I remember that you used to be afraid of them, even when you were young." His voice had risen slightly, and he repeated, "Really, really afraid of them. It's called arachnophobia, I think."

"So the shrinks say, and you don't have to talk so loud." She moved closer to Spence, a sensuous move of a woman after a man. His hands were in his pockets, and he had that hipshot arrogance that said he was interested. "Too bad that you and Marlo are going to have that little accident."

"Like my sister."

"Shh. Everyone knows that lovers wrapped up in each other don't pay attention to the road. That's going to be your story, too. There you were, probably kissing and not paying attention to the road and—well, you know the rest of the story. That deadly little drop into the canyon just happened to be there. Or I could do you right now, both of you, and make it look like a homicide-suicide. Everyone's been worried about you, Spence, those endless trips to hunt for your nephew's body—your sister and mother dead. You will have had all you could take of this life, and decided to take your lover with you."

Terrified for Spence, Marlo said quietly, "You can have him, Paula. Just don't hurt him."

"What am I? A surplus commodity? You're giving me away?" Spence asked wryly.

"Don't interfere in this, Spence. This is between Paula and me. I want you to live—"

"How noble of you, Marlo. But I could have him anyway, without your permission." Paula tilted her head and studied Spence. The deadly automatic prowled up his chest to caress his jaw. "How about it, Spence? Think I should keep you a little while and entertain you? Not here, but someplace with a bed and a lot nicer. You'd get to live a little longer. You might even get to like aphrodisiac drugs."

"You know, that's something I've never tried," he said as if the idea appealed. "Nice barrette."

"Thanks. Different woman, different tricks."

"So you're afraid of spiders," he repeated overloud.

"Spence!" Marlo could have killed him—but not quite. He was in enough danger right now, standing and flirting with Paula as if he enjoyed it.

"Shut up for once, Marlo," he said quietly, without looking away from Paula, whose free hand was stroking his body. He seemed to enjoy her touch, even moving slightly into it.

"What?" Marlo demanded. "What did you say?" She'd never been so angry, she could feel it boil inside her. Tied behind her body, her hands itched to grab Paula and fling her away from Spence.

"I said that if you'd keep your mouth shut, Paula and I could get down to business."

"Mm. That could be interesting," Paula purred. "You'd have to be tied. I don't trust you, Spence."

"You'd do the whip thing, of course."

"Of course."

Godiva came walking into the room on her big furry gray legs. She seemed to be sizing up the room, looking for a nice big juicy cricket. At the doorway, Cherry's hand was doing the fluttery shoo-shoo thing to urge the spider deeper into the room.

Spence looked around Paula toward the door, and his eyes followed Godiva. Paula smiled knowingly. "That won't work, Spence, there's no one out there."

"Nothing but that big spider."

When Paula turned, Spence grabbed for her gun hand, and Marlo cried out, trying to scoot her chair closer to help him. The shot made an earsplitting sound, and wood flew from the hole in the ceiling.

"Sorry about this, Paula," Spence muttered, before his fist tapped her jaw.

When she was on the floor unconscious, he emptied the clip from the revolver, tossed it away, and said, "You're no lady, so I guess that rule doesn't apply."

Cherry was already in the room, hurrying to untie Marlo. When she shook free of the ropes, Marlo stood shakily, only to be tugged into Spence's arms. He held her face up, those gold eyes searching her abused cheek. From his expression, she knew that he was blaming himself for not protecting her. "Marlo—?"

"I'm fine, Spence." Marlo held him tightly, her body shaking. "It's all over now."

Cherry's arms quickly surrounded them, and she pasted a flurry of kisses on Marlo's cheek.

The three of them stood together, breathing hard, filled with emotion and relief.

With a shriek of terror, Paula dusted Godiva from her stomach and leaped to her feet.

She almost made it to the door when Cherry caught her. In a series of exotic kicks and slashes of her hand, too fast to follow, Cherry maneuvered Paula away from freedom. The flurry ended with Paula being flipped and landing on the floor with a thud. She lay there, winded.

"Oops," Cherry said cheerfully.

"Paula isn't talking to anyone," Spence said curtly as he followed Marlo into her apartment. "We may never know the whole story, but the authorities have enough information to hold her. Tomorrow is going to be rough on everybody involved. They're doing to tear apart the Royston house and the furniture store. From what we told the authorities, they aren't holding Keith—but he'll be investigated, just the same. Paula used him to keep track of everything in Godfrey, even her own father."

At three o'clock in the morning, neither Marlo nor Spence was tired. Spence had been grimly silent on the way back to her apartment. The click of the door behind them held just a little too much force. He walked straight into her bathroom and started running a bath for her.

He stayed in the bathroom until he turned off the water; Marlo knew Spence was giving himself thinking room. "Show me those wrists again," he said when he returned.

Marlo tossed her backpack to her kitchen table and extended her hands; Spence looked closely at them. "Rubbed raw, dammit. You shouldn't have struggled so hard."

"I don't feel like a reprimand right now, sweetheart," Marlo stated. "They had to give Paula a shot to calm her down. She was raving. I feel so sorry for her."

"You think that I don't?" he returned too quickly, with just that edge of temper she knew had been brewing. "Just what do you think of me, Marlo?"

She turned to Spence and folded her arms. She stared at

him. "Okay, let's have it. You're mad at me. There's just a little something about how you snap at me that's a big clue."

Spence tossed the keys from the pickup truck he'd borrowed onto the table. "If I were you, I'd leave it alone—for tonight. But yes, I'm damn mad."

"I was the one tied to the chair getting slapped."

He glared at her. "You don't have to tell me that. You could have told me everything a hell of a lot sooner and avoided this whole mess. Those pictures told the whole story, and if you hadn't been—"

"If I 'hadn't been' what? Trying to make sense of something that only I felt? How do you think that would have gone over?"

Spence slapped his open hand on the table, jarring the condiments there. "Dammit, Marlo. You didn't trust me. We're lovers, and you didn't trust me. That doesn't say much for a relationship, does it? Or it doesn't in my book."

Marlo tapped her foot. "You know, I got very angry up there in that cabin when you were flirting with Paula. You were enjoying it just a little too much, and you didn't seem very interested in how I felt."

He groaned slowly, impatiently. "You . . . I had to provide a distraction. Any idiot would know that."

Her hands went to her waist. "Are you calling me an idiot, Spencer Gerhard?"

"I hate that name, and you know it," His tone was a quiet roar.

They were face-to-face now, Spence leaning down to Marlo to make his point. "I'm angry, you know," Marlo stated tightly. "I've never really been so angry at anyone in my whole lifetime."

"Yeah, so? Am I supposed to be terrified?"

"Idiot. Jerk."

"Well, let's have it all. You think I'm an idiot, do you?"

"Sometimes." She wasn't giving in to the simmering need to kiss him. She wouldn't—"

Spence reached to grip her shirt and tugged her close against him. "You're not so sweet, dear heart."

"Neither are you."

His lips fused to hers, slanted, and his hand lowered to cover her breast. "You drive me nuts."

"Likewise. You've ruined all my schedules, and—"

"Schedule this—" he returned roughly. But Marlo was already moving into the kiss, her hands beneath his shirt, fingers digging in to hold him. Then in a flurry, heat and fire, they stripped away each other's clothing, and Spence was lifting her astride him.

She could have devoured him, going wide open into love-making, holding his hair, his shoulders, meeting his lips, his tongue with hers. In a storm of uniting, becoming one, Spence filling her, Marlo cried out when his mouth found her breasts, his skin rough against hers, his breath uneven and hot upon her skin.

In the hallway to her bedroom, he paused to lift her higher, to bring her down more completely, and Marlo braced her hand against the wall, pushing back, tightening upon him.

They tumbled into bed and caught in the breathless storm, straining against each other, against themselves, skin on skin, hands caressing, digging in, lips burning— As his hands cupped her bottom, bringing him home, Marlo felt the world begin to shake, or was it her? Or was it Spence?

She held on with all her strength through the wild ride, capturing him with arms and legs, and she cried out, straining for the ultimate, her heart beating wildly.

Then suddenly the world stopped spinning and Spence went taut as the rings of pleasure shot deep within her and constricted. The explosion on that high plane where her very being seemed riveted, focused, and throbbed and breathed, burst and continued on and on, gradually lessening.

When Marlo floated softly down to earth, Spence was breathing unevenly, dragging air into his lungs. His heartbeat slowed against her own, his body heavy and lax over hers. She gathered him closely, smoothed his taut back with a sense of gentle homecoming. His lips moved against her damp cheek. "You bit me, honey-bun," he singsonged drowsily.

"Sorry, lover."

She could feel his lips curve into a smile. "No, you aren't."

Marlo floated for a while in the aftermath of their fiery lovemaking. Spence was safe and in her arms and in other places and she loved him. It was a good place to be. Then she asked, "Don't you think this is a bit unusual? This immediacy, tossing everything else away?"

He smoothed her hair, her throat, and his hand wandered over her possessively. "No. I intend a lot more of it with you. You really let go, so it's a little hard not to—embarrass myself."

Marlo understood that their fiery lovemaking was the aftermath of the terrifying fear they'd both experienced and the dark discoveries they'd just learned. On the cusp of death, they'd needed to celebrate life—together. "We should do it more often, then, just so you won't embarrass yourself. Damage control, so to speak."

"Good idea." Spence moved heavily from her and lay prone at her side. With all her remaining strength, Marlo flopped her hand to his chest. Spence laced his fingers with hers and slowly, luxuriously rubbed her hand up and down his chest.

She could feel him mentally prowling, thinking about the day's events, trying to sort through the deaths of his family and Dirk. Spence folded her against him and kissed her forehead, and she knew that he was easing away from the tension of their escape from death.

Everything could wait until tomorrow. . . . Marlo was just where she wanted to be, with Spence, she decided as she slid off into sleep. Tomorrow, she had to tell him . . . tomorrow. . . .

During those few restless hours, Spence eased from her side and returned to sit, gently rubbing antibiotic salve on her wrists, then wrapping gauze lightly around them.

"I love you, Spence," she whispered.

"I don't ever want to go through anything like that again," he stated unevenly, and lay down beside her, holding her close. He turned her face up to his and kissed her lightly. "Nothing can happen to you. You are to stay beside me at all times. You turn, and I'll be there."

But Spence didn't know yet what she would ask of him. . . . Or what she must tell him in the morning. . . .

Cody, where are you? Please answer me . . . Cody?

Nineteen

"DON'T TELL ME THAT KEITH ISN'T INVOLVED IN THIS SOME-how, Marlo. Was that what this early-morning chat is about? So you could protect Keith? Worse—to ask me to protect him? After what has happened to my family? You'd ask that?" Spence demanded as dawn became morning; it slid brightly through the tall Douglas firs surrounding the small glade off the jogging path.

With his hands on his hips, strong legs braced against the argument that Marlo knew was certain to come, Spence was furious. "Okay, you wanted a run out of town this morning, Marlo. I understood that, and how you've gone inside yourself—people do that when they're sorting out what matters and what doesn't. I understand running off the tension you've been under—almost getting killed takes some unwinding. So you've got me out here in the woods for this 'private, undisturbed conversation,' as you say, and you want me to be careful about what I say to the authorities about Keith. And you've got something else on your mind. Let's have it. Now."

Marlo hugged herself. Birds swooped through the tall, shadowy trees; wildflowers reached into a patch of sunlight.

She looked at the strip of morning sunshine crossing her jogging shoes; as she had during the restless night, lying in Spence's arms, she searched for a way to serve him what Paula had told her, and it could shatter him. . . .

"Paula told me that she used Keith to get what she wanted."

"Aiding and abetting, I think it's called. He should have known she was up to something. She knew everything that was going on in Godfrey—because he kept her up to date. She saw everything, through his eyes."

"You saw Keith last night, how shaken he was. He couldn't believe Paula could do anything like those things—that she could kill their father."

Spence stared grimly at her. "Keith had to know. I was just going to bring that up when you needed attention—oh, yeah, that's right. About the time I started for him last night at the police station, your wrists started hurting really badly, and we needed to go home. You were protecting him. Dammit, Marlo. The guy is up to his ears in this whole thing, and you're protecting a man who had to know something about my sister's death—and my mother's? Let alone his own father's?"

Marlo prayed that their love would survive. She braced herself against Spence's anger, understood the righteousness of it, but there were facts he needed to know—

"Okay, let's have it. But I'm not going to agree to anything that has to do with Keith, not yet," Spence stated roughly as he jammed his hand through his hair, and those gold eyes narrowed dangerously at her.

Marlo lifted her hand to stroke his cheek, and the vibrations of his anger tangled around her. She drew the warm sunshine into her, gifting it and her love to him. "You're doing it again," Spence said warily. "Moving inside me, trying to comfort. This must be real bad news. What else did Paula tell you—other than that Keith was innocent of everything? She'd protect her brother, you know. He's her guardian. He's financially responsible for her. If he goes down, so does she. But then, Keith was the only one in her family who tried to help her. Maybe deep down, she actually loves him. On the other hand, with her rages, she might go off at anything, any minute, and decide to murder him, too. Keith has always been protective of her. He would have had her in his will, providing for her in the event of his death. It just wasn't his time to die yet, I guess."

Marlo placed both hands on Spence's stubble-covered cheeks and drew his forehead down to hers. She willed every bit of her love into that contact. If she had any powers at all, she desperately needed them now. "I'm asking you to forgive . . . because—because Cody doesn't need an uncle, or a father now, filled with hatred."

Spence pushed away from her. His hand slashed out, a gesture meant to silence her. "Dammit, Marlo. Don't start on me. Don't try to make me believe that Cody is trying to reach beyond the grave."

"I'm not. I've always felt that he was alive. I told you that." Marlo felt so helpless against the battery of truths that she must reveal. She took a deep breath, listened to the dew drop quietly from the lush blades of grass in the clearing, and whispered into the clean mountain sunshine, "Paula had a lot to say while I was tied up in that chair. Cody escaped that wreck. Somehow Dirk didn't have the car seat fastened properly . . . he was probably excited and hurrying, and he'd just gotten that pickup, still unfamiliar with the features when Traci needed him. They must have been only a little off the road when the cab's back door popped open, and Cody was ejected. That heavy-duty car seat, their thick winter coats, and a pillow protected him."

Spence's fierce frown wasn't encouraging, but Marlo forced herself to continue, "Paula went to check on her dirty work, and because Cody reminded her of you—she decided to let him live. But it was snowing heavily then, and she was afraid he'd die, so she rescued him. She was going to keep him somehow, set up a separate life somewhere, to keep him as her child by you. She quickly realized that wouldn't work, and she hired someone to take him elsewhere—somewhere away from here. Whoever he was never came back for the final payoff—and it would have been very final."

Marlo forced herself away from Spence's stunned and concerned expression. "Honey—" he began moving toward her. "This has been too much for you. Last night you almost died—you were slapped, hard. You've been pushing and trying to deal with too much . . ."

Marlo shook her head and braced herself to argue with him. He had to believe her, in her. "It's true, Spence. I feel that Cody is alive. I've always felt that."

"Honey." Spence shook his head. "Paula—"

"She was telling the truth—I could feel it."

"No. . . . You were reeling from those open-handed slaps, from seeing how cruel she could be. You're exhausted, Marlo, wrung out emotionally. Don't do this to yourself. Let's just . . . just make a life for ourselves . . . and—I know that look. You're not going to give this up, are you?" he asked warily.

"I'm getting stronger, Spence. I'm feeling more. The connection is too real. I can feel his heartbeat. Cody's favorite color was—"

"Red. He was wearing his favorite red coat when they wrecked—when Royston Furniture's truck muscled them over that canyon."

"That's the link. Cherry says that psychic guides deceive—mislead—sometimes. But Cody is out there somewhere, alive. I know it."

Spence looked up into the blue sky, framed by the tall fir trees. He shook his head. "You've—we've been through a lot . . ."

"There's more. Much more." She reached out to hold his rugged face between her hands, drew him back to her, and struggled with what she must tell him next. . . . "It's so quiet here, Spence. Feel how gentle it is here. Soft enough for a man to sleep a long time, a very long time."

His concern for her quivered, ran through her fingers, blended with the love they shared. "You're doing it again," Spence stated unsteadily.

"Yes. I want you to open yourself and feel, just feel. Feel me, feel how much I love you."

He nodded, but the wariness was there, the concern for her. He smiled slightly. "What are you getting back from me?"

"Truth. Fear for me, for the unknown. Hope. Denial," Marlo answered simply. "But most of all love."

"There are other ways to show it," he drawled, but she understood his need to divert her, his uncertainty about her intuitive ability.

"This is important to me now, Spence. Please?"

His essence settled slowly, softly into her hands, and she treasured his trust and understood his uneasiness. "Okay, I'm feeling a whole lot of love."

"Hold that thought. Keep in mind that I truly do think Cody is alive and that someday we'll find him."

His smile was wistful. "Maybe."

"We will. You have to believe that, Spence. I'm asking a lot, but—"

"You said there was more? What is it? Marlo?"

She eased away from him and walked slowly to the edge of the clearing. Long ago, someone had cut initials into the tree there. Bears would come to fatten on late summer's berry bushes. Birds would raise their young in the trees. Joggers and hikers would pass nearby, chatting with each other.

Marlo traced the scarred tree trunk, then knelt. She worked away the weeds from a small pile of stones. They were smooth, flat river stones, not from this area. Spence crouched near, watching her worriedly. "Marlo—"

"It's a nice place here, Spence. Look at the ground. See the length of the slight mound. This is what else Paula told me . . . what she planned to use to torment you. This is what she and Ted Royston were arguing about when she killed him—that she was like her mother. He was drunk, tossing away his usual caution. He told Paula that she was ugly, dumb, and crazy just like Margaret, and those words were his death sentence . . ."

Marlo held his hand, willing her love into him. "Margaret Royston killed what she couldn't have, just like Paula would have murdered you. Spence, I'm so sorry . . . the last person to see your father was Margaret . . . she was the one who said she'd seen him getting into that woman's RV. She lied. Paula heard Margaret talking in her sleep, about Wes. Her mother took walks down this path, and one day Paula followed her. She heard her mother talking to Wes, who is buried right here, beneath the initials she had carved for him. For twenty-five years, Margaret Royston kept your father for herself. . . ."

Spence's rugged face had paled. He stared at the length of the mound and hurriedly tore away the grass to expose more river rocks, framing Wes Gerhard's grave. He opened his hands, and they hovered above the length of the mound, struggling to accept the possibility—"No . . ."

The immensity of something so unbelievable, so horrible had clearly stunned him. He shook his head, wading through years of memories, of the way his mother had fought to survive, never believing that Wes Gerhard had deserted her.

Spence cleared his throat. "I hated him all this time—"

Marlo wrapped her arms around Spence and leaned her head on his shoulder. "He never would have left Elsie, or you and Traci. He loved you all so much. He was a good man, Spence. A very good man, just like you."

She ached for him as he tried to comprehend the ugliness, the lie that had ruined so many lives, and tears shimmered in those gold eyes.

It was a long time before Spence moved to stand. When he did, it was to tug her into his arms and hold her tight. "All this time, he was right here. . . ."

The decision to reveal what had happened to his father was Spence's alone. Grim and silent, he answered the authorities' questions, but said nothing about Wes Gerhard—a man who had not deserted his family, who had loved them deeply.

In the next few days of interviews and legalities, Spence stayed protectively close to Marlo. But when the authorities were finally done and Paula had been taken away, Spence was suddenly missing. Marlo knew that he'd gone to the clearing to be with his father, to mourn a man he'd hated for years. It was a very private healing, spanning twenty-five years of pain. Spence wasn't ready to share his father just yet, but Marlo knew that soon Wes Gerhard would be brought home to lie beside his wife and Traci and Dirk.

At night, Spence lay awake in Marlo's arms, struggling to deal with the past.

She couldn't give him back those years, but she could give him comfort, patience and understanding.

And she could try fiercely to give him Cody. . . .

Where are you, Cody? Come to me . . . come to me . . . Cody?"

Spence stood in the shadows of Marlo's workshop. Spotlights had been set up and in mid-July, the room was heating rapidly with the intense light. Tension ran through the several members of the filming crew, and today, a newscaster had come to introduce Marlo. Jerry Hughes's well-groomed head was leaning close to Marlo's, and together they were going over the notes on the clipboard.

Spence knew every detail on that clipboard; he watched Marlo move around the various filming lights and crew members to come toward him.

Her face was pale with tension, those earth green eyes huge and concerned.

"You don't have to do this," Spence said as he drew her into his arms. After two weeks of living together, he'd known that nothing could deter Marlo. Every time she looked at Cody's framed picture, her reaction was too startling to miss.

Spence believed the woman he loved. After years of hunting the mountains for Cody's remains, he had the shaky confidence that Marlo knew what she was doing, hunting in another way—through a connection of glass, of camera lenses.

Marlo looked up at Spence and smoothed his cheek. "You've been through so much. It's only something to try, Spence. The authorities are cross-checking Margaret Royston's work places against those areas of the missing children. But there's no information on Cody. He's been missing too long—all they can do is put out information that may lead to him, hoping that someone will call."

"I don't like to see you straining and exhausted, going through this."

She had moved inside Spence now, soothing those raw fearful edges and letting him know that she had to follow whatever led her. . . .

"The television cameras are a medium that connects us somehow—Cherry says that's possible. What if he's out there, watching my show, Spence? We can't just let that chance go by without trying, can we?"

Spence swallowed tightly. Marlo had been right about so many things—but he was still afraid to hope. "Honey—"

"I feel it, Spence," Marlo's tone was strong and fierce. "I feel him trying to contact me. He just might remember me."

Spence ached for her, for the disappointment that would surely come. "Do it then."

"I'm sorry this hurts you. I love you so much, Spence."

He nodded, and said, "Then let's do what we have to do, play it all out, and see where it takes us. Don't stop until you're satisfied, Marlo. I'm with you all the way."

Marlo smiled softly. "Even though you don't fully believe that I'm intuitive."

That term still startled and caused him to be uneasy. "I know you're something. I know that every time you put your hand on Cody's picture, on that glass, you're feeling something—but Marlo, that could only be love for a child that you'll never see again. There's been no closure—"

The director came toward them. "Marlo. We're ready. We want to get this on the news tonight, and we'll start running it for the next week. After this segment, we'll do a little introduction for Club Renew and use it in that spot, too."

Marlo stood on tiptoe to kiss Spence. "I have to do this, Spence. You know that I do."

She moved toward the blue background that had been set up. Behind her, a picture of the mountains surrounding Godfrey appeared. Several shots of the town changed; this was an effort to remind Cody—if he was still alive—of where he'd once lived.

Marlo found her spot, took a deep breath, and waited. Across the distance of the lights and cameras, she found Spence and silently told him of her love. He nodded slowly, as if he understood.

He looked so grim, so concerned in the shadows. No one but her felt how deeply he ached, how desperately he hoped, despite what he'd said.

He worried for her, too, trying to understand the ability that she had finally acknowledged. *Spence, I love you. . . .*

Spence nodded again, as though he understood, as though he'd sensed her thoughts. He was becoming very good at reading her.

"Go." Jerry's curt word drew Marlo's attention back to the job she had to do—to find Cody.

After the newscaster gave the announcement of a missing little boy, he compared it to a computerized projection of what he might look like now. He described what Cody was wearing when he was last seen, his height and weight, and then Marlo was introduced.

She focused on the camera and began speaking. "This is a special program to find a special boy. His name is Cody Forbes, and he once lived in this house—"

Marlo indicated different shots of the Gerhard house. "This was his room and his toy box—a great big turtle, and Cody loved to sit on it. This is his favorite teddy bear. This is his grandmother's kitchen. This is his grandmother."

A picture of Elsie appeared, then Traci. Marlo sucked in her breath, the impact of Spence's ache and love for his family had just slammed into her. She braced herself against it and continued, "This is Cody's mommy. She loved him very much, and this is his daddy, and his uncle, Spence."

Marlo turned full to the camera. "I'm Marlo, and I used to babysit for Cody. Cody is a very special boy with dark hair and light brown eyes. At three years old, he had a bow-shaped birthmark on his upper right thigh. His mother said that when he was born, he'd already been wrapped as the best present she'd ever had."

Marlo smiled at the television's lens and willed herself to fly through the wires to a little boy, to connect with him. She prayed that whoever cared for him would see the telecast, and that someday the telephone would ring—"Cody would be five and a half years old now, and we're hoping that someone out there will call us. We love him very much, and we want to hear from you at the following 800 number. Please write it down, and if you know of a boy matching Cody's description, please call immediately. Just one more thing—"

She focused every bit of her mind and soul on the next words. "Hi, Cody. I love you. Come play with me."

When Jerry ended the segment, and the camera crew swung into action, packing away the equipment, Spence hurriedly made his way to Marlo.

She was pale and drained, and seemed to be barely hanging by a thread. She'd put everything into that filming, straining to bring Cody home. Spence knew that at the last, she had pitted herself against the camera, trying to connect with Cody. "Come on. That's enough," he said quietly, and placed his arm around her.

Marlo was already crying quietly against his shoulder as Spence nodded to Jerry and the concerned crew.

"Honey," he said, when she was seated on the couch in her apartment, her face held in her hands. "This is all you can do. Let the authorities do the rest, filter the crank calls. All we can do is wait—"

"Spence, this has just got to work. Cody has to be out there somewhere. I know he is."

"Sure." Spence sat beside her and drew her into his arms, rocking her. Was it really possible that Marlo could draw the boy to her, that Cody was out there, somewhere, calling to her?

Did Spence dare to hope that he would ever see Cody again?

In Chicago, Ilene Jacobs sat very still, watching the evening news. She couldn't move—her grandson had such a birthmark, and he'd been three when Joey had brought him to her.

Timmy had been wearing a red jacket that matched the newscaster's description.

Timmy's birthmark was on his upper right thigh—and it was bow-shaped. . . . Could he be Cody Forbes?

Ilene's work-worn hands gripped her chair's padded arms. Timmy had always been drawn to the "nice lady," and now Ilene knew why—because he'd known her. . . .

She swallowed the fear tightening her throat. They'd take her precious little boy away from her. . . . She loved him so much. . . .

Then she looked down at Timmy, who was playing with his blocks. Her precious little dark-haired boy, the boy with light brown, almost gold eyes . . .

He turned to her and smiled. "Don't be sad, Grandma. They'll find that little boy, and everything will be all right again."

"I know. Everything will be all right," she said as she prepared to do the most difficult thing in her lifetime—to make one simple call.

Spence stood beside Marlo as they waited for an answer to their knock on the apartment door. All through the night and the plane trip to Chicago, he'd feared for Marlo, and prayed that the little boy was Cody.

"She's expecting us at this time," Marlo said quietly, and held Spence's hand.

He was too still, those gold eyes staring at that door as if he could see through it to the boy inside. . . .

Ilene Jacobs opened the door and invited them inside the cheaply furnished but clean apartment. A shy little boy stood at her side, gripping her hand. His gold eyes stared up at Marlo, and those eyes were a perfect color match to Spence's.

"Hi . . . Timmy," Spence said softly, as he crouched down to the boy's level. "Brought a present for you."

Spence felt a soft loving glow surround him, and he glanced up at Marlo, who stood closely at his side, those eloquent eyes shimmering with tears. She was sharing his emotions, lending her strength and comfort to him.

Cody held traces of Spence's sister and his mother, and Marlo placed her hand on his shoulder, transferring a gentle comfort to that grief. Spence held out Cody's favorite teddy bear, and the boy hesitated before taking it.

"I don't have anything to give you back," Cody said shyly.

"It's yours to keep. Do you like it?"

"I'm a little old for this stuff, but it feels good," Timmy said as he held it against him, and something moved inside his heart, like little happy tugs. "My grandma said you might know me. My dad died, you know. He's not coming back. Did some other little kid have this before me?"

"He sure did, and he loved it very much. That's why you might like it better than a new one—because it's stuffed with love." Spence ached to take Cody into his arms, but he wouldn't move too soon, letting the boy become accustomed to him. A warm soft quiver enfolded him, and he knew Marlo's abilities were at work, soothing him.

Cody looked straight up at her. "Marlo," he whispered slowly. "I remember you. Not from television, but from before—sometime, before."

Then he looked back at Spence, studied his features. "You've got eyes like mine. I think . . . I think I know you, too—from before. Do I, Grandma?"

"Let's sit down and talk a while," Ilene said gently as her heart was breaking. She loved him so, and now he'd go away—it was the best for him. Spence Gerhard had already talked with her about Cody, and she knew Spence to be a true, good man.

Her "grandson" needed every advantage possible, and she could barely pay their rent. . . .

Today, Timmy-Cody sat in her chair, close to her, almost protectively, in the way that children do when they sense uneasiness. "I love my grandma," he said suddenly while he watched the adults.

The big man had tears in his eyes, and the nice lady did, too. Marlo moved to sit on the arm of his grandmother's chair; she took Ilene's hand in both of hers. The older woman frowned slightly, then looked up at Marlo, who nodded and smiled gently. They seemed to be sharing something that Timmy did not understand, and his grandma seemed so sad.

"I love my grandma," Timmy said more loudly to make certain that they understood. Nothing could happen to his grandmother. He eased close against her, the woman who had always been there for him.

Timmy relaxed a little while the adults talked about the weather and traffic, about the flight to Chicago from some place called Washington state. After a while, he felt that his grandma was okay, and he moved to sit by Marlo, the television lady. She smiled down at him. "Hi . . . Timmy."

"I sent you a drawing, and you showed it to the whole wide world. It was in a picture frame."

For a moment, the nice lady seemed startled, then she remembered with a smile, "You did, didn't you?"

"I watch you more than cartoons. My grandma taped your shows, so I can watch them whenever I want."

The big man was looking at Marlo and Timmy, and he seemed so alone and sad, that Timmy went to sit by him. "Hi," he said. "I've got airplanes. Want to see them?"

"I'd like that . . . Timmy. You know, I was wondering if you and your grandma might want to come visit us—we live in the mountains far, far away. You could ride on a real airplane and come see us."

Ilene gasped and placed her hand over her heart. "I can't afford anything like that."

Spence looked directly at her. "Now you can. I'd like you to come live in Godfrey. If you do, there's a house waiting for you. It was my mother's. It needs a woman like you in it. And Timmy already has a room. Godfrey has a really active bunch of ladies—the Bingo Girls. You'd like them."

"Oh, I couldn't—"

Marlo took Ilene's hand in both of hers. "We need you, Ilene. Please?"

"Even after my son—?"

"You took good care of . . . Timmy, and we're grateful," Spence said quietly. "Marlo is right. We do need you. But it's up to you. If not, we'll work out something else so we can all be together—if you want."

"Oh, I want," Ilene stated adamantly. "I want Timmy to have the best. He needs clean air and a bicycle and—"

"I've got an idea you are the best," Marlo said softly, and leaned to kiss Ilene's cheek.

Timmy was studying Spence closely, his little hands drifting over the man's harsh planes and weathered skin. "You're like me. You're big as a mountain, but you're like me, somehow."

"Yes, I am." Spence cleared his throat, a sign of his deep emotion. "Very much like you."

Epilogue

"GERHARD." KEITH ROYSTON'S GREETING WAS UNCERTAIN as he stood on Marlo's back porch, his appearance that of a man who had been through hell. He'd visibly aged in a short time, his hair gray at the temples, lines etched deeply into his face.

In early September, the night air was chilly and stirred by the wind; leaves rustled across the driveway like secrets of the past.

"Keith." Spence gripped the doorknob tightly while momentary bitterness and the need for revenge churned within him.

"I—I hear that you and Marlo are married now. . . . Congratulations. I really mean that. I know that she's going to be well cared for, and somehow that makes this easier. Can I come in?"

Spence took a steadying breath. This man's family had hurt his so deeply. "What's this about?"

"I need to see you—and Marlo. Please?"

For a fleeting moment, Spence thought of Paula, who had

come to this same door to collect Marlo, to kill her. Then Marlo stood beside Spence and took his hand in both of hers. "Come in, Keith."

Spence moved aside to let the other man inside. He glanced out at the used pickup Keith had parked beside the apartment, then shut the door. The Royston Furniture store had closed immediately, and once legalities had been cleared, it had been sold to new owners. Keith had stood by his sister, to the point of endangering himself, and he'd spent enormous amounts on medical care and legal fees. Because of her brother's endeavor, Paula would spend the rest of her life as an inmate in a better class of medical prison.

"I don't know where to start—"

"How about turning around and—?" Spence's anger and his need for revenge flared.

"Let him talk, Spence," Marlo said softly. "We were friends once. He gave me so much."

"I loved you, Marlo," Keith said quietly, his eyes pleading with her.

"I know you did."

"Isn't that nice," Spence stated roughly.

Without malice or offense, Keith met Spence's scowl. His expression was that of a man who had carried many burdens for too long, trying to find reason that wasn't there. "I'm sorry for what my family did to yours, Spence. I can't undo it. And I never would have believed it possible. I never had any hand in it. That is hard to believe, but it's true."

He seemed to shrink into an old man, who'd lost everything. "I had to say that. I'll be going now. I'm not coming back to Godfrey again."

Marlo inhaled sharply, then she looked at Spence. "This is up to you, not me. It's your decision."

A woman who had forgiven young Spence for that devastating trauma in her life was asking him to consider the other man's pain . . . because Spence knew what it was to lose everything, even those he loved.

After years of antagonism, Keith had just humbled himself; his apology rang true. Spence remembered a shy, bookish, awkward boy berated and humiliated by parents who demanded too much, who tried to care for a sister damaged beyond recovery.

Keith had never known the gentleness of a mother's love; Spence had. Nine short years with Wes Gerhard as a father was more than Keith had ever had in an entire lifetime with Ted Royston.

Spence took his time in sorting his emotions. The woman he loved, his wife, stood by his side, those hazel eyes filling with him. They had a future, an entire lifetime waiting for them with Cody, who was safe and healthy. Spence took a deep breath, and said quietly, "I can't say it is all right. But I understand. Good luck to you, Keith. I wish you could have had a better life. Let Marlo know where you are and that you're all right."

Visibly touched, Keith blinked back tears. "I don't know what to say."

"Just take care of yourself. Marlo would want that . . . me, too, I guess." Spence turned his back and cleared his throat. "Do that thing you do, Marlo. The guy needs some help. Give it to him."

He walked into the living room and into Fresh Takes's darkened shop. He stared out at Godfrey's quiet Main Street, the fall leaves tumbling down the sidewalks, the Why Not Bar's blinking red neon light, and took a deep breath. They'd all come such a long way; there was no reason to cause Keith more pain or humiliation than he had already suffered. . . .

In a few moments, Marlo put her arms around him.

Against his back, she murmured softly, "Tough guy. You really gave it to him, didn't you? Really told him off and made him sorry."

"Lay off."

"It takes a forgiving man to do what you just did, Spencer Gerhard. You gave him something he desperately needed, that he had to have to go on. You're wonderful and you know it and that's why I love you."

"Yeah, I am wonderful and that's why you love me." He smiled and moved back against Marlo, letting himself wallow a bit in the softness of her body—okay, maybe he was feeling good and generous and kind. "Keith needed a break. You did that feely soft thing, didn't you? Got inside him and smoothed the rough, hurting edges? Did it help him?"

She kissed his shoulder. "I think so."

"You're not going to set up business in doing that, are you?"

Her hands were moving downward, stroking him. "I think it's leaving. I think it was here because I needed it, but now I've got you."

"Keep doing that, and you'll really have me."

"I thought I might exercise first. Give me a minute to get set up—you know the thong thing, the heels, and the cafe chair." She laughed softly and moved back into the apartment.

"Payoff," Spence murmured as he grinned.

Because he felt good and clean and new.

Marlo came to stand beside Spence in Fresh Takes's driveway. They watched Cody ride his bike in circles. "Keep watching, Uncle Spence. I'm good, aren't I, Marlo?"

"Really good." Spence reached to ease Marlo close to him; he'd never get tired of cuddling his wife. "He gets any better, and we're going to have to start practicing on our bikes."

She leaned her head on his shoulder, and peace settled over Spence; everything he'd wanted was in his arms and riding that bike.

In mid-September, Cody was excited about his new school and friends, and Ilene was starting to get a life of her own: She was busy sewing on projects for Marlo, watching the shop at times, and playing bingo. Ilene was a different, happy woman, who had started cleaning Elsie's untended garden. Cody moved easily between Ilene's new home and Marlo's apartment. On weekends, Spence, Marlo, and Cody stayed at the cabin and hiked in the mountains, enjoying each moment together.

"Look at this." Cody skidded to a stop in front of them and giggled, then he tore off again, riding in circles.

"Cherry is pregnant," Marlo said quietly.

Spence stared blankly at Marlo. "Huh? Cherry? Our Cherry?"

"I guess it was one of those 'Oops' things. Billy Bob can't wait to tell everyone . . . he's picking out invitations and wedding dresses and planning the reception. She wants to wait a while. Cherry has decided that if Billy Bob will play Mr. Mom and help her, life with babies might not be so bad."

"Maybe that's just what she needs, what she's been looking for all this time. My little Cherry, all grown up." Spence watched Cody proudly ride his bike. "He's getting good."

"Very good. I'm glad that Ilene is so happy here, and Cody, too. It's working out, don't you think?"

"I do. I'm grateful to Ilene."

The past three and a half months had been frantically filled with discoveries, good and bad. Cody was moving easily into his new life, loving the name-change game. Adoption plans were already under way, and Ilene would definitely remain a part of their lives.

While the stripper pole in Marlo's bedroom held some fascinating memories, the apartment was far too small for the family they wanted. Spence and Marlo were studying house plans that included an office for his financial management business, a large area for Marlo's worktables and desk, and a stripper's pole in the master bedroom.

Getting Cody settled and happy had been a priority, but now it was time for Spence to make his move and get that necessary time alone with his wife—a minihoneymoon that they had missed. "You're going to be so busy with the Klikamuk contract that you won't have time to take that hike in the mountains with me. It's pretty rough terrain, too. I thought I'd spend a week backpacking and staying out of your way."

She turned to Spence and smoothed his hair, winding it around her finger. "I asked for an extension. Klikamuk agreed. The lodge owners liked my work so far, enough to give me extra time, at discount, of course. I'd have time to go with you."

Marlo was already nibbling at his challenge.

"It's a big hike, not an easy trail. You have to be in really good shape to make it. There's a little snow lake up there, icy cold, good drinking water. I'll bring you back a bottle of it."

Marlo frowned, and he could sense her moving in to accept his subtle challenge. He upped the ante. "You wouldn't like it, Marlo. We didn't get along the last time we camped together."

"Are you saying, Spencer Gerhard, that I can't match you?"

He toyed with that cute little ear. "Honey-bun, I'm only saying that this hike is really tough—a man could make it, but a woman . . . it would be too much for you. It might even snow up there. You'd get cold. You better just stay here and take care of business."

"Don't you pull that 'little woman stays at home' stuff on me. You're not going without me," Marlo stated firmly.

"You wouldn't like it. You'll have to talk me into it—"

"I'll do better than that later. Cody is staying the night with Ilene," she whispered. "I'm going to convince you so much you won't even think of hiking off without me. And if you did, I'd find you. I'd track you down and—"

Spence ran his hand down the curves he loved; he patted her bottom. Just one careful step at a time, and he'd have her alone and cuddling next to him in that double sleeping bag—or in a remote cabin, where they could lie naked in front of a fire and make love and he could enjoy teasing Marlo. Now, that idea sounded even better. All he had to do was to get Marlo and their supplies into his Jeep. He'd have the cabin stocked, the fireplace laid, and Marlo well warmed by the time they got there. Spence really liked that last part.

He just had to play her a little bit more, and they'd be making love in front of Rocky Morales's fireplace. "You'd convince me? I don't think so, sweetheart. I mean, it's not likely you can do that. Not this time. I'm not giving in, no matter what you do to me. Uh-uh, no way . . ."

He patted her bottom again and called to Cody. "Come on, Cody. Let's go show Grandma how good you are."

Then with Cody riding beside him, Spence walked down the driveway and out onto Main Street.

He started to smile as he heard Marlo call, "Hey, you. Spencer Gerhard! You are absolutely not going hiking and camping without me. I know what you're doing . . . I do."

Spence's smile widened. So did he.